Italian
BACHELORS

BROODING
BILLIONAIRES

D1586043

ITALIAN BACHELORS
COLLECTION

July 2017

August 2017

September 2017

October 2017

November 2017

December 2017

Italian BACHELORS

LYNNE GRAHAM
CATHY WILLIAMS
LEANNE BANKS

Published in Great Britain 2017
By Mills & Boon, an imprint of HarperCollins*Publishers*
1 London Bridge Street, London, SE1 9GF

ITALIAN BACHELORS: BROODING BILLIONAIRES © 2017
Harlequin Books S.A.

Ravelli's Defiant Bride © 2014 Lynne Graham
Enthralled by Moretti © 2014 Cathy Williams
The Playboy's Proposition © 2010 Leanne Banks

ISBN: 978-0-263-93131-0
09-0717

RAVELLI'S DEFIANT BRIDE

LYNNE GRAHAM

For Michael and thirty-five happy years.

Lynne Graham was born in Northern Ireland and has been a keen romance reader since her teens. She is very happily married, with an understanding husband who has learned to cook since she started to write! Her five children keep her on her toes. She has a very large dog, which knocks everything over, a very small terrier, which barks a lot, and two cats. When time allows, Lynne is a keen gardener.

CHAPTER ONE

CRISTO RAVELLI SURVEYED the family lawyer in disbelief. 'Is this an April fool joke falling out of season?' he enquired with a frown.

Robert Ludlow, senior partner of Ludlow and Ludlow, did not react with amusement. Cristo, a leading investment banker specialising in venture capital, and richer than Croesus, was not a man to be teased. Indeed, if he had a sense of humour Robert had yet to see it. Cristo, unlike his late and most probably unlamented father, Gaetano Ravelli, took life very seriously.

'I'm afraid it's not a joke,' Robert confirmed. 'Your father had five children with a woman in Ireland—'

Cristo was stunned by the concept. 'You mean, all those years he went on his fishing trips to his Irish estate—?'

'I'm afraid so. I believe the eldest child is fifteen years old—'

'*Fifteen?* But that means…' Cristo compressed his wide sensual mouth, dark eyes flaring with anger, before he could make an indiscreet comment unsuited to the ears of anyone but his brothers. He wondered why he was even surprised by yet another revelation of his father's notorious womanising. After all, throughout his irresponsible life Gaetano had left a trail of distraught and angry ex-wives and three legitimate sons in his wake, so why shouldn't there have been a less regular relationship also embellished with children?

Cristo, of course, could not answer that question because he would never ever have risked having an illegitimate child and was shaken that his father could have done so five times over. Particularly when he had never bothered to take the slightest interest in the sons he already had. Cristo's adult brothers, Nik and Zarif, would be equally astonished and appalled, but Cristo knew that the problem would fall heaviest on his own shoulders. Nik's marriage breakdown had hit him hard and his own part in that debacle still gave Cristo sleepless nights. As for their youngest sibling, as the new ruler of a country in the Middle East Zarif scarcely deserved the huge public scandal that Gaetano's immoral doings could unleash if the easily shocked media there got hold of the story.

'Fifteen years old,' Cristo mused, reflecting that Zarif's mother had evidently been betrayed throughout her entire marriage to his father without even being aware of the fact. That was not a reality that Zarif would want put out on public parade. 'I apologise for my reaction, Robert. This development comes as a considerable shock. The mother of the children—what do you know about her?'

Robert raised a greying brow. 'I contacted Daniel Petrie, the land agent of the Irish estate, and made enquiries. He said that as far as the village is concerned the woman, Mary Brophy, has long been seen as something of a disgrace and an embarrassment,' he framed almost apologetically.

'But if she was the local whore she would've been right down Gaetano's street,' Cristo breathed before he could bite back that injudicious opinion, his lean, darkly handsome face grim, but it was no secret to Gaetano's family that he had infinitely preferred bold and promiscuous women to clean-living ones. 'What provision did my father make for this horde of children?'

'That's why I decided to finally bring this matter to your attention.' Robert cleared his throat awkwardly. 'As you will be aware, Gaetano made no mention of either the woman or the children in his will.'

'Are you telling me that my father made *no* provision for these dependants?' Cristo prompted incredulously. 'He had five children with this…this woman over the course of many years and yet he settled no money on them?'

'Not so much as a penny piece on any of them… *ever*,' Robert confirmed uncomfortably. 'I thought he might have made some private arrangement to take care of them but apparently not as I have received an enquiry concerning school fees from the woman. As you know, your father always thought in terms of the present, not the future, and I imagine he assumed that he would be alive well into his eighties.'

'Instead of which he died at sixty-two years old, as foolish as ever, and tipped this mess into *my* lap,' Cristo ground out, losing all patience the more he learned of the situation. 'I'll have to look into this matter personally. I don't want the newspapers getting hold of the story—'

'Naturally not,' Robert agreed. 'It's a given that the media enjoy telling tales about men with multiple wives and mistresses.'

Well aware of that fact, Cristo clenched his even white teeth, dark eyes flaming pure gold with rage at the prospect. His father had been enough of an embarrassment while alive. He was infuriated by the idea that Gaetano might prove even more of an embarrassment after his death.

'It will be my hope that the children can be put up for adoption and this whole distasteful business quietly buried,' Cristo confided smooth as glass.

For some reason, he noted that Robert looked a little disconcerted by that idea and then the older man swiftly composed his face into blandness. 'You think the mother will agree to that?'

'If she's the usual type of woman my father favoured, she'll be glad to do as I ask for the right… compensation.' Cristo selected the word with suggestive cool.

Robert understood his meaning and tried and failed to imagine a scenario in which for the right price a woman would be willing to surrender her children for adoption. He had no doubt that Cristo had cause to know exactly what he was talking about and he was suddenly grateful not to be living a life that had made him that cynical about human nature and greed. But then, having handled Gaetano's financial dealings for years, he knew that Cristo came from a dysfunctional background and would be challenged to recognise the depth of love and loyalty that many adults cherished for their offspring.

Cristo, already stressed from his recent business

trip to Switzerland, squared his broad shoulders and lifted his phone to tell his PA, Emily, to book him on a flight to Dublin. He would get this repugnant business sorted out straight away and then get straight back to work.

'I *hate* them!' Belle vented in a helpless outburst, her lovely face full of angry passion. 'I hate every Ravelli alive!'

'Then you would also have to hate your own brothers and sisters,' her grandmother reminded her wryly. 'And you know that's not how you feel—'

With difficulty, Belle mastered her hot temper and studied her grandmother apologetically. Isa was a small supple woman with iron-grey hair and level green eyes the same shade as Belle's. 'That wretched lawyer hasn't even replied to Mum's letter about the school fees yet. I hate the whole lot of them for making us beg for what should be the children's by right!'

'It's unpleasant,' Isa Kelly conceded ruefully. 'But what we have to remember is that the person responsible for this whole horrible situation is Gaetano Ravelli—'

'I'm never going to forget that!' her granddaughter swore vehemently, leaping upright in frustration to pace over to the window that overlooked the tiny back garden.

And that was certainly the truth. Belle had been remorselessly bullied at school because of her mother's relationship with Gaetano Ravelli and the children she had had with him. A lot of people had taken exception to the spectacle of a woman carrying on a long-running, *fertile* affair with a married man. Her mother, Mary, had been labelled a slut and, as a sensitive adolescent, Belle had been forced to carry the shadow of that humiliating label alongside her parent.

'He's gone now,' Isa reminded her unnecessarily. 'And so, more sadly, is your mother.'

A familiar ache stirred below Belle's breastbone for the loss of that warm, loving presence in her family home and her angry face softened in expression. It was only a month since her mother had died from a heart attack and Belle was still not over the shock of her sudden passing. Mary had been a smiling, laughing woman in her early forties, who had rarely been ill. Yet she'd had a weak heart, and had apparently been warned by the doctor not to risk another pregnancy after the twins' difficult birth. But when had Mary Brophy ever listened to common sense? Belle asked herself painfully. Mary had gone her own sweet way regardless of the costs, choosing passion over commitment and the birth of a sixth child triumphing over what might have been years of quiet cautious living.

Whatever anyone had said about Mary Brophy— and there had been all too many local people with a moral axe to grind about her long-term affair with Gaetano—Mary had been a hardworking, kind person, who had never had a bad word to say about anyone and had always been the first to offer help when a neighbour was in trouble. Over the years some of her mother's most vociferous critics had ended up becoming her friends when they finally appreciated her gentle nature. But Belle had never been like the mother she had seen as oppressed: she had loved her mother and hated Gaetano Ravelli for his lying, manipulative selfishness and tight-fisted ways.

As if sensing the tension in the air, Tag whined at her feet and she stretched down a hand to soothe the family dog, a small black and white Jack Russell whose big brown adoring eyes were pinned to her. Straightening again, her colourful hair spilling across her slim shoulders, Belle pushed a straying corkscrew curl from her Titian mane out of her strained eyes and wondered when she would find the time to get it trimmed and how on earth she would ever pay for it when money was required for far more basic necessities.

At least the Lodge at the foot of the drive winding up to Mayhill House was theirs, signed over by Gaetano years earlier to give her mother a false sense of security. But how much use was a roof over their heads when Belle still couldn't pay the bills? Even so, homelessness would have been far worse, she acknowledged ruefully, her generous mouth softening. In any case, in all likelihood she would have to sell the Lodge and find them somewhere cheaper and smaller to live. Unfortunately she was going to have to fight and fight hard for the children to receive what was rightfully theirs. Illegitimate or not, her siblings had a legal claim to a share of their late father's estate and it was her job to take on that battle for them.

'You *must* let me take charge of the children now,' Isa told her eldest granddaughter firmly. 'Mary was my daughter and she made mistakes. I don't want to stand by watching you pay the price for them—'

'The kids would be too much for you,' Belle protested, for her grandmother might be hale and hearty but she was seventy years old and Belle thought it would be very wrong to allow her to take on such a burden.

'You attended a university miles from here to escape the situation your mother had created and you planned to go to London to work as soon as you graduated,' Isa reminded her stubbornly.

'That's the thing about life…it changes without warning you,' Belle fielded wryly. 'The children have lost both parents in the space of two months and they're very insecure. The last thing they need right now is for me to vanish as well.'

'Bruno and Donetta both go to boarding school, so they're out of the equation aside of holiday time,' the older woman reasoned, reluctant to cede the argument. 'The twins are at primary school. Only Franco is at home and he's two so he'll soon be off to school as well—'

Shortly after her mother's death, Belle had thought much along the same lines and had felt horribly guilty to admit, even to herself, that she felt trapped by the existence of her little brothers and sisters and their need for constant loving care. Her grandmother, Isa, had made her generous offer and Belle had kept it in reserve in the back of her mind, believing that it could be a real possibility. But that was before she got into the daily grind of seeing to her siblings' needs and finally appreciated the amount of sheer hard graft required and that any prospect of her grandmother taking charge was a selfish fantasy. It would be too big a burden for Isa to take on when some days it was even too much for Belle at the age of twenty-three.

Someone rapped loudly on the back door, making both women jump in surprise. Frowning, Belle opened the door and then relaxed when she saw an old friend waiting on the step. Mark Petrie and Belle had gone to school together where Mark had been one of her few true friends.

'Come in,' she invited the slimly built dark-haired man clad in casual jeans. 'Have a seat. Coffee?'

'Thanks.'

'How are you doing, Mark?' Isa asked with a welcoming smile.

'I'm doing great. It's Belle I'm worried about,' Mark admitted heavily, throwing Isa's granddaughter a look of unvarnished male admiration. 'Look, I'll just spit it right out. I heard my father talking on the phone this morning and he must've been talking to someone from Gaetano Ravelli's family. I think it was the eldest one, Cristo—'

Tensing at the sound of that familiar name, Belle settled a mug of coffee down on the table for Mark. 'Why do you think that?'

'Cristo is the executor of Gaetano's estate and my father was being asked about your mother and, of course, he doesn't even know Mary's dead yet. Nobody's bothered to tell him that she passed while he and Mum were staying with my uncle in Australia—'

'Well, your father and my mother weren't exactly bosom pals,' Belle reminded Mark bluntly. There had been a lot of bad blood over the years between the land agent, Daniel Petrie, and Mayhill's housekeeper, Mary Brophy. 'So why would anyone mention it to him?'

Cristo Ravelli, Belle was thinking resentfully. The stuffed-shirt banker and outrageously good-looking eldest son, who never ever smiled. Over the years she had often researched Gaetano's tangled love life on the Internet, initially out of curiosity but then more often to learn the answers to the questions that her poor trusting mother had never dared to ask. She knew about the wives, the sons and the scandalous affairs and had soon recognised that Gaetano was a deceitful, destructive Svengali with the female sex, who left nothing but wreckage and regrets in his wake. Furthermore, as Gaetano had only ever married *rich* women, her poor misguided mother had never had a prayer of getting him to the altar.

'The point is, evidently Ravelli's family have decided they want Gaetano's children with Mary to be adopted—'

'Adopted?' Belle interrupted, openly astonished by that suggestion coming at her out of nowhere.

'Obviously the man's family want the whole affair hushed up,' Mark opined with a grimace. 'And what better way to stage a cover-up? It would keep the story out of the papers and tidy up all the loose ends—'

'But they're *not* loose ends—they're children with a family and a home!' Belle argued in dismay. 'For goodness' sake, they belong together!'

Uncomfortable in receipt of that emotional outburst, Mark cleared his throat. 'Are you the children's legal guardian?'

'Well, who else is there?' Belle asked defensively.

'But it's not down legally on paper anywhere that you're their guardian, is it?' Mark prompted ruefully as her clear green eyes lifted to his in sudden dismay. 'I didn't think so. You should go and see a solicitor about your situation as soon as you can and get your claim to the children recognised with all the red tape available…otherwise you might discover that Gaetano's family have more legal say on the subject of what happens to them than you do.'

'But that would be ridiculous!' Belle objected. 'Gaetano had nothing to do with the kids even when he was here.'

'Not according to the law. He paid the older children's school fees, signed the Lodge over to your mother,' Mark reminded her with all the devotion to detail inherent in his law-student studies. 'He may have been a lousy father in the flesh but he did take care of the necessities, which could conceivably give Gaetano's sons a bigger say than you have in what happens to the children now.'

'But Gaetano left all five of them *out* of his will,' Belle pointed out, tilting her chin in challenge.

'That doesn't matter. The law is the law,' Mark fielded. 'Nobody can take their birthright away from them.'

'Adoption…' Eyes still stunned by that proposition, Belle sank heavily back down into her chair. 'That's a crazy idea. They couldn't have tried this nonsense on if my mother were still alive!' she exclaimed bitterly. 'Nobody could have said their mother didn't have the right to say what should happen to them.'

'If only Mary had lived long enough to deal with all this,' Isa sighed in pained agreement. 'But maybe, as the children's granny, I'll have a say?'

'I doubt it,' Mark interposed. 'Until you moved in here after Mary's death, the children had never lived with you.'

'I could pretend to be Mum…' Belle breathed abruptly.

'*Pretend*?' Isa's head swivelled round to the younger woman in disbelief. 'Don't be silly, Belle.'

'How am I being silly? Cristo Ravelli doesn't know Mum is dead and if he thinks she's still alive, he's very unlikely to try and interfere in their living arrangements.' Belle lifted her head high, convinced she was correct on that score.

'There's no way you could pretend to be a woman in her forties!' Mark protested with an embarrassed laugh at the idea.

Belle was thinking hard. 'But I don't need to look like I'm in my forties…I only need to look old enough to have a fifteen-year-old son and, at the age women are having children these days, I could easily only be in my early thirties,' she reasoned.

'It would be insane to try and pull off a deception like that,' her grandmother told her quellingly. 'Cristo Ravelli would be sure to find out the truth.'

'*How?* Who's going to tell him? He's a Ravelli—he's not going to be wandering round asking the locals nosy questions. He would have no reason to question my identity. I'll put my hair up, use a lot of make-up… that'll help—'

'Belle…I know you're game for anything but it would be a massive deception to try and pull off,' Mark said drily. 'Think about what you're saying.'

The kitchen door opened and a thumb-sucking toddler with a mop of black curls stumbled in. He steadied himself against Belle's denim-clad thigh and then clambered up clumsily into his sister's lap, taking his welcome for granted. 'Sleepy,' he told her, the words slurring. 'Hug…'

Belle cradled her youngest half-sibling gently.

Franco was very affectionate and he was quick to curve his warm, solid little body into hers. 'I'll take him upstairs for a nap,' she whispered, rising upright again with difficulty because he was a heavy child.

Belle tucked Franco into his cot beside her bed and for a moment stood looking out of the rear window, which provided a picturesque view of Mayhill House, a gracious grey Georgian mansion set in acres of parkland against the backdrop of the ancient oak woods. Her mother had been a widow and Belle only eight years old when Mary had first started work as Gaetano Ravelli's housekeeper.

Belle's own father had been a violent drunk, renowned for his foul-mouthed harangues and propensity for getting into fights. One night he had stepped out in front of a car when under the influence and few had mourned his demise, least of all Belle, who had been terrified of her father's vicious temper and brutal fists. Mother and daughter had believed they were embarking on a new and promising life when Mary became the Mayhill housekeeper. Sadly, however, Mary had fallen madly in love with her new boss and her reputation had been destroyed from the instant Belle's eldest half-sibling, Bruno, had been born.

Someone like Cristo Ravelli, Belle reflected bitterly, could have absolutely no grasp of how other less fortunate mortals lived. Cristo was handsome, brilliant and obscenely successful. He had grown up in a golden cocoon of cash, the son of a very wealthy Italian princess who was renowned as a leading society hostess. His stepfather was a Hungarian banker, his home a Venetian palace and he had attended an exclusive school from which he had emerged literally weighed down with academic and athletic honours. It was hardly surprising that Cristo was a dazzling star of success in every corner of his life. After all, *he* didn't know what it was to be humiliated, ignored or mocked and she'd bet he had never had to apologise for his parentage.

On the other hand Bruno had only been thirteen when Gaetano first accused his son of being gay because that was the only way Gaetano could interpret Bruno's burning desire to be an artist. Belle's little brother had been devastated by that destructive indictment from a father whom he had long been desperate to impress. His growing unhappiness at school where he was being bullied had resulted in a suicide attempt. Belle still got the shivers recalling it, having come so terrifyingly close to losing her little brother for ever. Bruno *needed* his family for support. Bruno, just like his siblings, needed love and commitment to grow into a contented, well-adjusted adult. There was nothing Belle would not have done to ensure that her siblings remained happy and together.

Having delivered his warning, Mark was taking his leave when she returned downstairs.

'I'll get supper on,' Belle's grandmother declared.

'You're not serious about trying to pretend to be Mary, are you?' Mark pressed on the doorstep.

Belle straightened her slight shoulders. 'If that's what it takes to keep the family together, I'd do it in a heartbeat!'

The evening light was fast fading when Cristo's car finally turned up the long driveway to Mayhill.

He had never visited Gaetano's Irish bolt hole before because Gaetano had never invited any of his relatives to visit him there or, indeed, anywhere else. His father had never bothered to maintain relationships and the minute he was bored he had headed for pastures new and wiped the slate clean of past associations.

A woman with a little dog running at her heels was walking across the sweeping front lawn. Cristo frowned; he didn't like trespassers. But a split second later he was staring, watching that cloud of colourful curls float back from a stunning heart-shaped face, noting the way her loose top blew back to frame her lush full breasts and a sliver of pale flat stomach, exposing the denim shorts that hugged her derriere and accentuated her long, long shapely legs. She took his breath away and the pulse at his groin reacted with rampant enthusiasm. He gritted his teeth, trying to recall when he had last been with a woman, and when he couldn't blamed that oversight for his sudden arousal. In reality, Cristo always chose work over sex for work challenged and energised him while he regarded sex as a purely stress-relieving exercise.

He unlocked the massive wooden front door and stepped over the top of a pile of untouched post into a large black-and-white-tiled hall. His protection team composed of Rafe and John moved past him. 'We'll check the house.'

A fine layer of dust coated the furniture within view and Cristo was not surprised when Rafe confirmed that the house was vacant. But then, what exactly had he expected? Mary Brophy and her five children occupying the property? Yes, that was *exactly* what he had expected and why he had used his keys to emphasise the fact that he had the right of entry. He strode through the silent rooms, eventually ending up in the kitchen with its empty fridge standing wide open, backed by the sound of a dripping tap. His handsome mouth curved down as he noted the phone on the wall. One of the buttons was labelled 'housekeeping'. Lifting the phone, he stabbed the button with exasperated force.

'Yes?' a disembodied female voice responded when he had almost given up hope of his call being answered.

'It's Cristo Ravelli. I'm at the house. Why hasn't it been prepared for my arrival?' he demanded imperiously.

At the other end of the phone, Belle went on all systems alert at the vibrating tone of impatience in that dark, deep accented drawl and her green eyes suddenly glinted as dangerously as emeralds in firelight. 'Do you think maybe that could be because the housekeeper's wages were stopped the same day Mr Ravelli crashed his helicopter?'

Cristo was not accustomed to smart-mouthed replies and his wide sensual mouth hardened. 'I didn't make that instruction.'

'Well, it doesn't really matter now, does it? Regrettably nobody works for free,' Belle told him drily.

Cristo bit back a curse. He was tired and hungry and in no mood for a war of words. 'I gather you're the housekeeper?'

It was the moment of truth, Belle registered, and for a split second she hesitated. An image of her siblings rehomed in an orphanage on the slippery slope to a foster home gripped her tummy and provoked nausea. 'Er...yes,' she pronounced tightly.

'Then get yourself up to the house and do your job. I can assure you that you will be well paid for your time,' Cristo informed her grittily. 'I need food and bedding—'

'There's several shops in the village. You must've driven past them to get to the house,' Belle protested.

'I'm happy to pay you to take care of those tasks for me,' Cristo fielded smoothly before returning the phone to the wall and wondering if it had been wise to recall an insolent housekeeper to her former duties. Reminding himself that he only planned to stay a couple of days before arranging to have the house sold, he dismissed the matter from mind. The housekeeper, he reflected, would be a useful source of local knowledge to have on hand.

Following that call, Belle was in an infinitely more excitable state. After all, it was now or never. She couldn't introduce herself as Mary's daughter and then change her mind. Either she pretended to be her mother or she went up to Mayhill and told Cristo Ravelli that his father's former housekeeper/lover was dead. But when she thought of the influence she could potentially wield for the children's benefit by acting as their mother, her doubts fell away and she hurried upstairs, frantically wondering how she could best make herself look more mature.

The first thing she did was take off her shorts and top. Rustling through her wardrobe, she found a short stretchy skirt and a long-sleeved tee. Her mother had never ever worn flat heels or jeans and Belle owned only one skirt. Clinging to those Mary Brophy habits as if they might prove to be a good-luck talisman, Belle pulled out a pair of high heels and hurriedly got dressed. That achieved, she went into the bathroom, pushed her hair back from her face and grimaced at her porcelain-pale complexion, which she had often suspected made her look even younger than her years. Surely if she put her hair up and went heavy on the make-up it would make her look older? Brows pleating, she recalled the smoky eye treatment that a friend had persuaded her to try on a night out and she dug deep into her make-up bag for the necessary tools.

She stroked on the different shadows with a liberal hand, blurred the edges with an anxious fingertip and added heaps of eyeliner. Well, she certainly looked different, she acknowledged uneasily, layering on the mascara before adding blush to her cheeks and outlining her mouth with bright pink gloss.

'I was about to call you down for supper...' Isa Kelly froze in the tiny hall to watch her granddaughter come downstairs. 'Where on earth are you going got up like that?'

Belle stiffened. 'Why? Do I look odd?'

'Well, if you bent over you could probably treat me to a view of your underwear,' Isa commented disapprovingly.

An awkward silence fell, interrupted within seconds by the noisy sound of the back door opening and closing. Children's voices raised in shrill argument broke the silence and a dark-haired boy and girl of eight years of age hurtled into the hall still engaged in hurling insults.

'If you don't stop fighting, it will be early to bed tonight,' Belle warned the twins, Pietro and Lucia.

The twins closed their mouths, ducked their tousled heads and surged up the stairs past their eldest sister.

'You can tell me now why you're wearing a skirt,' Isa pressed Belle.

'Cristo Ravelli phoned…in need of a housekeeper.' Belle quickly explained what had transpired on the phone. 'I need to look at least ten years older.'

As Belle spoke, Isa studied the younger woman in consternation. 'You can't possibly pretend to be Mary… It's an insane idea. You'll never get away with it.'

Belle lifted her chin. 'But it's worth a try if it means that Cristo Ravelli has to listen to what I have to say. He obviously knows nothing about Mum. I don't think he even realises that she was his father's housekeeper.'

'I doubt if he's that ignorant,' Isa opined thoughtfully. 'It could be a shrewd move. Naturally he's going to want to meet the children's mother as soon as possible. But I don't want you going up there to run after the man, doing his shopping and cooking and making up his bed, especially dressed like that!'

'What's wrong with the way I'm dressed?'

'It might give the man the wrong idea.'

'I seriously doubt that,' Belle responded, smoothing her stretchy skirt carefully down over her slim hips. 'As far as I'm aware he's not sex-mad like his father.'

Isa compressed her lips. 'That kind of comment is *so* disrespectful, Belle.'

'It's a fact, not a nasty rumour.'

'Gaetano was the children's father. He may not have been much of a father but you still shouldn't talk about him like that where you could be overheard,' her grandmother rebuked her firmly.

Aware that the older woman was making a fair point, Belle reddened with discomfiture. 'May I borrow your car, Gran?'

'Yes, of course.' Belatedly aware that Belle had successfully sidetracked her concern about the deception she was preparing to spring on Cristo Ravelli, Isa planted a staying hand on the front door before Belle could open it. 'Think about what you're about to do, Belle. Once you try to deceive this man, there's no going back and he'll have every right to be very angry with us all when he discovers the truth...as eventually he must,' she reasoned anxiously.

'Cristo is a Ravelli, Gran...shrewd, tricky and unscrupulous. I need an advantage to deal with him and the only way I can get that advantage is by pretending to be Mum.'

CHAPTER TWO

BELLE DROVE DOWN to the garage shop in the village to stock up on basic necessities for the Mayhill kitchen and was taken aback by the cost of the exercise.

Cristo Ravelli was expecting her to cook but she couldn't cook, at least not anything that required more than a microwave and a tin opener. She pondered her dilemma and decided on an omelette, salad and garlic bread. Surely even she could manage a meal that basic? She had often watched her mother and her grandmother making omelettes. Bruno was also a dab hand in the kitchen. They always ate well when he was home at weekends.

Tense as a steel girder, she drove round to the back of the house, noting that the lights weren't on. The back door was still locked and with a groan she lugged her carrier bags round to the front, mounted the steps and pressed the doorbell.

Cristo was on the phone when the bell echoed through the hall. Brows drawing together, he went to answer the door, stepping back in surprise when a slender redhead in sky-high heels tramped in past him. The housekeeper? Not his idea of a housekeeper, he conceded, swiftly concluding his call, his brilliant

dark eyes flaring over one of the shapeliest bodies he
had ever seen and very probably the best ever legs.
Legs that put him in mind of the girl he had seen
walking across the lawn, his gaze rising to the woman's face to note the huge anxious green eyes lost in
the heavy make-up and the ripe full mouth. She was
not his type, no way was she his type, too obvious,
too loud, hair too red. Indeed Cristo knew to his cost
that he was most attracted to tiny ice-cool blondes
with big blue eyes. His conscience sliced through that
thought instantaneously, reminding him that that particular image was forbidden for very good reasons.
Lush black lashes shielding his grim and guilty gaze,
he rested his attention quite deliberately on the redhead's remarkable breasts. Now, those were truly a
work of art like her legs, he conceded abstractedly.

Sadly accustomed to the effect her full bosom
tended to have on the male sex, Belle studied Cristo
Ravelli at her leisure. By any estimate, he was drop-
dead gorgeous. He had luxuriant black hair closely
cropped to his arrogant head, spectacular bone structure and quite stunning dark-as-charcoal eyes enhanced by absurdly long sooty lashes. A light shadow
of stubble roughened his olive-skinned jaw line, adding to an already overpoweringly masculine presence.

Her pupils dilated, her heart began hammering
an upbeat tempo and her tummy performed acrobat-
ics. It was nerves, she told herself, nerves and adrenalin reacting to the challenge of the deception she
was embarking on. It didn't help that Cristo was also
extremely tall, actually tall enough to make her feel
small even though she was an easy five feet eight
inches in height and stood even higher in heels. His

shoulders were broad below the tailored jacket of his no doubt expensive business suit, his chest wide, his lean hips tapering down to legs that were very long and powerful.

'I'll take these down to the kitchen and start cooking,' Belle told him, raising her arms to display the bulging carrier bags.

Her rounded breasts shimmied below the fine jersey top and Cristo's mouth ran dry. 'You're my father's housekeeper?' he prompted because she was not at all what he had expected, having dimly imagined some feisty but sensible countrywoman of indeterminate age.

Abandoning her attempt to walk right by him, Belle set the bags on the floor at her feet and lifted her head high. 'I'm Mary Brophy,' she announced, thrusting up her chin in challenge.

Both disconcertion and disbelief assailed Cristo and his dark deep-set eyes narrowed to increase their searching intensity as he scrutinised her. 'You were my father's…mistress?' he asked.

Nausea stirred in her tummy at that label but she could think of no more accurate description for the compromising position her late mother had occupied in Gaetano's life and colour fired her cheeks. 'Yes.'

A split second earlier, Cristo had been mentally undressing her and that awareness now revolted him as the ultimate in inappropriate activities now that he knew who she was. This was the woman who had occupied his father's bed for at least fifteen years, earning a longevity that no other women had contrived to match in Gaetano's easily bored existence. And looking at her, suddenly Cristo was not surprised by that fact because self-evidently this woman worked at her appearance. Even after giving birth to five children she still had the slender waist of a young girl and, below the make-up she seemed to trowel on as thick as paste, her fine pale skin was unlined and still taut. She was too young, way too young-looking though to match the woman he had expected to meet, he decided, his ebony brows pleating in perplexity.

'You were also Gaetano's housekeeper?' Cristo questioned.

'Yes.' With determination, Belle bent down to lift the bags again. 'Omelette and salad all right for you?' she asked, heading for the kitchen at speed.

A very decorative housekeeper, Cristo thought numbly, still quite unable to picture her as the mother of five children. *Five!*

'You must have been very young when you met my father,' Cristo commented from the kitchen doorway.

Belle stiffened as she piled the perishable food into the fridge. 'Not that young,' she fielded, wanting to tell him to mind his own business but reluctant to cause offence. After all, she needed his support to secure a decent future for her siblings. Although what realistic chance did she have of gaining it? At worst, Cristo Ravelli might despise and resent his father's illegitimate children, and at best, he might be simply indifferent to them. Adoption, for goodness' sake, she reflected in lingering disbelief. How many people would even *dare* to suggest such an option?

'I assumed you would be living here in the house,' Cristo remarked, his attention clinging of its own volition to the amount of slender thigh on view as she crouched down to pack the fridge.

'I only…er…lived in when Gaetano was here,' Belle said awkwardly.

'And the rest of the time?' Cristo enquired, because as far as he knew his father had only come to Ireland three or four times a year and had never stayed for longer than a couple of weeks at most.

'I live in the lodge at the gates,' Belle admitted grudgingly, straightening to set out lettuce and eggs on the granite work counter.

Cristo gritted his teeth at the news because she and her children would have to vacate the lodge house before he could put Mayhill on the market. Of course he would have to pay her for the inconvenience of finding another home. Her hair shone bright as a beacon below the lights, displaying varying shades of gold, auburn and copper, tiny curls of hair adorning the nape of her long, elegant neck. She had very curly hair, the sort of hair he had once seen on a rag doll, he mused absently, irritated by the random nature of the thought. He studied the smooth line of her jaw and the full lush softness of her bold red-painted mouth with a persistent sense of incredulity. She had to be a lot older than she looked to be the parent of a teenager, although perhaps he was being naïve. It was perfectly possible that Mary Brophy looked so amazingly youthful because his father had paid for her to have plastic surgery.

Belle unwrapped the garlic bread and shoved it on an oven tray to cook. She wished he would go away. Standing there, all looming six feet four inches or so of him, he made her feel nervous and clumsy. She had to search through cupboards to find the utensils she wanted because she had rarely visited Mayhill since childhood. Indeed she had avoided it on principle whenever Gaetano was in residence. Her green eyes darkened as she recalled the way she and her ever-growing band of siblings would go and stay with her grandmother in the village even before Gaetano arrived, leaving her mother free to make her preparations for his arrival. Mary had always, *always* put Gaetano Ravelli first.

Belle remembered her mother's excitement when Gaetano was due to arrive, the frantic exercising, hair appointments and shopping trips to ensure that Mary could look her very best for her lover. Belle had long since decided that she would rather die than want to please any man to that extent. Certainly Mary's rather pathetic loyalty and devotion had not won her any prizes.

Belle prepared the salad quickly, heaping it into a bowl and then making up her mother's favourite salad dressing as best she could because she couldn't quite recall the proportions of the different ingredients. That achieved, she embarked on the omelette. Cristo had vanished by then and she heaved a sigh of relief as she walked through to set the table in the spacious dining room across the hall.

He had accepted that she was Mary Brophy without protest and why shouldn't he? It meant nothing to him that her poor mother was gone. Mark's father, the land agent Daniel Petrie, would eventually catch up on the local gossip and learn that the woman he had long despised was dead and buried. But Belle thought it was unlikely that Daniel would bother making an announcement of that fact to Cristo Ravelli as, not only would he feel foolish about having misinformed his employer, but he would also most likely assume that Cristo had already found out the truth. Soothing herself with such reflections, Belle returned to her cooking and struggled to control the gas burners because she was accustomed to cooking with electric.

Cristo surveyed his meal with an appetite that very quickly vanished. He prodded the omelette with a fork. It had the solid consistency of a rubber mattress but lacked the bounce. The salad had been drowned in a vat of oil. Even the garlic bread was charred although valiant attempts had been made to cut away the most burnt bits. He swallowed hard and pushed the plate away. She couldn't cook, but presumably she and his father had dined out. Distaste suddenly filled Cristo and he stood up in a lithe movement, his lean strong face hard and taut. He didn't want to be in Ireland. He didn't want to deal with the wretched woman and the consequences of her sordid long-term affair with his father. But he knew that he didn't have a choice. Mary Brophy and her children were not a problem he could afford to ignore. In any case, there was no one else to deal with the situation.

Belle was digging into the linen cupboard on the upper landing when she heard a noise behind her and whirled round to stare in dismay at the tall square-featured young man leaning back against the bannister. He was built like a solid brick wall.

'So this is where the bedding is hidden,' he remarked.

'Who are you?' Belle demanded nervously.

'Rafe is one of my two bodyguards,' Cristo interposed, strolling up onto the landing. 'Rafe and John are staying here with me.'

'John and I need bedding. We can take care of ourselves though,' Rafe declared, stepping past her to peruse the tidy, labelled shelves just as she emerged clutching the linen she required for the master bedroom. Conscious of Cristo Ravelli's stare, and feeling somewhat harassed, Belle walked stiffly down the corridor. Damn the man! Why was he watching her like that? Did she have two heads all of a sudden? And why hadn't he told her he had companions? She hadn't bought enough food and that thought reminded her that she had to get him to settle up with her for the shopping she had done on his behalf. Dropping the linen on the bed, she dug into her pocket for the till receipt and turned to offer it to him.

'This is what you owe me,' she told him.

Cristo dug out his wallet and extended a banknote while still engaged in frowning at the gilded furniture and mirrors and the fantastically draped red king-size bed. 'Is this my father's room?'

'Yes.'

'I'll sleep somewhere else. The Victorian brothel design doesn't appeal to me,' he informed her curtly.

The décor was dark, fussy and horrible, Belle was willing to concede. She lifted the linen again and trudged across the corridor to one of the few guest rooms that enjoyed an en suite. Mayhill was badly in need of updating.

'When I said that about the decoration, I didn't intend to insult you,' Cristo remarked, standing poised by the window, thinking that at this early stage it would be most unwise to offend her. He swore to himself that he would make no cheap cracks about her role as his father's mistress, not least because it was becoming clear that it had not been a profitable position, he reflected wryly, which was hardly surprising when Gaetano had been renowned for his stinginess. Indeed in every one of his three divorces Gaetano had made money off his ex-wives in spite of the fact that in each case the women had been the injured parties. That Gaetano's secret mistress had still been working as his housekeeper and wore cheap off-the-peg clothing should really not come as a surprise. For that reason he found it hard to believe that Gaetano had stumped up for plastic surgery to keep his mistress looking young but, of course, he reminded himself, it was perfectly possible that there had been no cosmetic enhancement. Mary Brophy could simply be, and probably was, a very lucky woman who looked much younger than her years.

'I'm not offended. I wasn't involved in choosing the furnishings here. About ten years ago, Gaetano hired an interior decorator,' Belle explained, recalling how very hurt her mother had been not to be trusted with that responsibility by her lover. But then good taste had not been her mother's strong point either. The Lodge rejoiced in every shade of pink known to man, pink having been Mary's favourite colour.

Cristo watched Belle crush the pillows into pillow slips, her slender figure twisting this way and that, allowing him to notice her ripe, pouting curves at breast and hip from every angle. His wide sensual mouth slowly settled into a harder and harder line as he studied her delicate flushed profile, scanning her fine brows, her subtle little nose and full pink mouth.

And his body reacted accordingly, stirring with forbidden interest until he angrily turned his back on her, castigating himself for viewing his father's mistress as if she were some kind of sex object. But then he reminded himself that she was dressed to attract in an outfit and shoes that accentuated her long legs and shapely figure, and, when all was said and done, he was still a man with all that entailed and almost guaranteed to look.

Belle shot a sidewise glance at Cristo from below her lashes. His detachment, his air of command and superiority reminded her of his father, who had barely acknowledged Belle's existence on the rare occasions when he had seen her. Suddenly she regretted agreeing to play housekeeper because no doubt as intended it made her feel inferior. Her soft mouth tightened as she shook out the duvet with unnecessary violence and then carried the towels into the bathroom. Unfortunately she carried the image of Cristo Ravelli with her, those penetrating eyes dark as sin, that sleek bred-in-the-bone sexiness that lent him such charismatic appeal. She could feel her nipples pushing hard against the scratchy surface of her lace bra, a tightening, sliding sensation of warmth between her thighs and she was deeply disturbed by her reaction. But there was no denying it: *he* appealed to her; *he* attracted her on the most basic level. Did that mean that at heart she was as foolish as her mother had once been about Gaetano?

'I'd appreciate the opportunity to have a private word with you here tomorrow morning,' Cristo murmured smoothly as she emerged again. 'Shall we say at ten?'

LYNNE GRAHAM   37

Belle nodded agreement. 'When will you want to
meet the children?' she prompted.

Cristo froze, his facial bones locking tight. 'I
don't...wish to meet them, that is,' he extended unapologetically, dark eyes cold as black ice.

Belle paled, uncertain of how to take that statement.
Was his lack of interest good or bad news for her siblings? Did that mean that the adoption idea was just
a silly rumour? She scrutinised his lean, handsome
features with frowning green eyes, unnerved by his
icy reserve and lack of humanity. Did he think nothing of the blood tie? A lot of people would just have
agreed to meet the children for the sake of it, even if
they weren't particularly interested in them, but Cristo
Ravelli had chosen to spurn even that polite pretence.

In acknowledging that, Belle felt sheer loathing
suddenly leap through her in a fierce wave of antago-
nism because she was gutted on her siblings' behalf
by his detachment. Was he refusing to accept that the
children were part of the Ravelli family? *Obviously.*
Clearly, Mary Brophy's children were not good enough
to make the grade, just as Mary had never been good
enough for Gaetano to marry. Bile scoured Belle's
throat as she sped downstairs to clean up the kitchen
and go home. She hoped he wasn't expecting her to
come up and cook breakfast when she found the meal
she had cooked thrown in its entirety into the bin. Her
face burned but her chin came up. So, it hadn't been
one of her best efforts but in her opinion it had been
as much as he deserved!

After spending half the summer with Mary over
twenty years earlier, Gaetano had confided that he
was unhappily unmarried and Mary's hopes of a happy

ending for her romance had risen high. But Gaetano
had not asked his Arabic wife for a divorce or even
a separation. Over the years the media had published
several stories about his extramarital affairs. Her
mother had refused to believe the stories, even after
Belle had shown her revealing pictures on the Internet.
Mary had always been very quick to make excuses in
Gaetano's defence.

'He feels trapped and lonely in his marriage. It's
only a business arrangement. She was a friend for
years before he married her and he doesn't love her.
He needed a hostess to entertain his business colleagues and she comes from an old-fashioned country
where a woman needs a husband if she wants any freedom,' Mary had reasoned. 'I can't hold his marriage
against him, Belle. I'm not even an educated woman.
I couldn't do what his princess can do for him.'

Mary Brophy had been hopelessly infatuated with
Gaetano Ravelli from the moment she first met him
and she had allowed nothing to interfere with her rosy
view of their relationship. Her grief in the wake of the
helicopter crash that had taken Gaetano's life had been
all-consuming.

'I know you don't understand,' she had said to
Belle, 'but Gaetano was the love of my life. I know
he wasn't interested in marrying me but nothing's perfect. I wasn't his match in money or background and
I can't blame him for that. When you love someone,
Belle, you accept their flaws and he was too much of
a snob to want to marry an ordinary woman like me.'

A woman like me, Belle recalled painfully. It was
little wonder that Mary had suffered from low self-
esteem. She had travelled from a shotgun wedding

at the age of seventeen straight into an abusive marriage and had finally ended up as a married man's mistress. Life had always been tough for her mother, but then, as Isa was prone to reminding Belle, Mary had *always* made the wrong choices when it came to the men in her life.

Isa was waiting up for Belle when she got back to the Lodge.

'Well?' her grandmother pressed. 'Did he actually credit the idea that you were a woman in her forties?'

'No, he assumed I must have got involved with his father when I was very young,' Belle advanced with a dismissive toss of her head. 'He did do a lot of staring, though. He's invited me up to the house to talk to him tomorrow at ten, so presumably the kids' future will be discussed then.'

The older woman released a heavy sigh. 'I don't like the way you're going about this, Belle. Honesty is always the best policy.'

'But I won't be dealing with a nice, honest guy.'

'You hated Gaetano. Don't take it out on his son.'

Belle folded her lips at that unwelcome advice. 'He doesn't even want to meet the kids.'

Her grandmother shook her greying head, her unhappiness at that news palpable. 'If only your mother had thought about what she was doing and how much the children would be resented by the rest of Gaetano's family.'

Cristo had a troubled night of sleep. He dreamt that he was pursuing a woman with the longest legs possible across a misty landscape. Every time he got close she pulled away and laughed and her resistance made him want her more than ever, lust pounding through his veins like an explosive charge. But when he finally caught up with her, she was a different woman, pale blonde hair falling back from her piquant face to highlight big blue enquiring eyes and instantaneous recoil wakened him. He had broken out in a cold sweat, angry frustration and guilt slicing through him for the one woman he couldn't enjoy having even in his dreams…Betsy, his brother Nik's estranged wife. His jawline rigid, Cristo sprang out of bed and went for a shower.

His eyes closed tight shut below the refreshing blast of the power shower. He hadn't meant to wreck his brother's marriage. There had been no intent on his part to inflict damage, he reasoned painfully. Betsy had come to him for support, devastated by what she had learned from Zarif. But, unhappily, it had been Cristo who first gave Zarif the destructive news that had ruined Nik's relationship with his wife. Cristo had broken his brother's confidence and spoken out of turn, but he had never ever at any stage planned to harm Nik or hoped to steal Betsy from him.

For his own benefit, however, he listed the sins he had committed. He *had* thought that Nik didn't deserve a woman like Betsy. He *had* stood by watching while his brother took his wife for granted and he had *not* warned him of what he was doing. With the basest disloyalty, he *had* cherished feelings for his brother's wife. That was why Gaetano's mess in Ireland was *his* mess to clean up, Cristo reflected grimly. Nik already had enough on his plate to deal with and Zarif was still suffering the fallout from the loose-tongued confession that had wrecked Nik's marriage because ever since then the three brothers had barely spoken to each other.

'Very mumsy,' Isa pronounced the next morning with a raised brow when she saw what Belle was wearing. 'Did that skirt belong to your mother?'

Belle paled. 'Yes, I kept a couple of things just to remember Mum by. It's a little big but it looks all right with the belt.'

'Which is more than you can say about that flapping cardigan and the beads round your neck with that fussy blouse,' Isa groaned disapprovingly. 'You look like a young woman trying to look older.'

'Yes but that's because you know the truth. It's daylight now and I need to make a better impression than I did last night,' Belle pointed out anxiously.

'Even daylight couldn't penetrate the amount of make-up you've got on,' her grandmother said drily. 'But you're right—it does age you.'

'Look, I accept that Cristo is eventually going to find out the truth but I want that adoption idea off the table first,' Belle told her.

'Even at the cost of infuriating him?' Isa asked. 'Gaetano had a very low threshold for provocation.'

'Whatever happens, I'll deal with it.'

'I can't see how,' Isa said bluntly. 'You're pretty much powerless up against his wealth and intellect.'

Belle trudged up the drive in her high heels, striving not to feel like someone got up in fancy dress. She was *not* powerless. Money wasn't everything, nor was intellect. She was not stupid. She had a first-class degree in business and economics and she had the power of the unexpected on her side. He thought she was who she had said she was and, whether he knew it or not, that meant he would be fighting with one hand tied behind his back. Where her mother would have rolled over on command for a Ravelli and said thank you very much for the attention, Belle was programmed to fight dirty.

Cristo watched her approach from the window in the drawing room. No miniskirt in evidence today, but high-heeled court shoes with pointy toes embellished those award-winning legs. He gritted his even white teeth together, stamping out that inappropriate thought. So, she was an attractive woman. It was par for the course: his father's lovers had always been beauties even while his wives were more of the plain variety. Gaetano had always rated wealth and class above looks. Cristo wondered how much money it would take to persuade the older woman into his way of thinking. He was a skilled negotiator and envisaged few problems because Mary Brophy had not been enriched in any way by her relationship with his father and was currently penniless. Furthermore she couldn't be the brightest star in the firmament when she had given the wily older man five children he could never have wanted and kept on slogging away for him as a humble housekeeper.

Surprisingly a rare shard of pity stabbed Cristo at that acknowledgement, making him register that where Mary Brophy was concerned he didn't want to use a sledgehammer to crack a nut. He didn't want to threaten or intimidate her into doing his bidding; he simply wanted a neat and tidy solution to a very messy and potentially embarrassing problem for *all* their sakes.

CHAPTER THREE

'MR RAVELLI IS in the drawing room,' Rafe informed her.

Breathing in deeply and slowly to maintain her calm front, Belle walked into the over-furnished room where the ornate drapes and blinds cut out much of the daylight. Cristo swung round to study her and instantly her every sense went on high alert, her backbone stiffening, her slim legs bracing, her soft pink lips parting as she dragged in a sudden extra shot of oxygen.

Cristo scanned her appearance, his nostrils flaring with sudden impatience. She was dressed in a frumpy skirt and cardigan that a maiden aunt might have worn and she had inexplicably teamed that look with the kind of bold make-up a streetwalker might have flaunted like a signpost. And he realised then that there was something he wasn't seeing, something he wasn't grasping about this woman, because so far her long-term affair with his father wasn't adding up at all. Whatever else might have been said about Gaetano, he had been a connoisseur of women and a sophisticate and there was no way his father had returned again and again to Ireland in order to take advantage of the charms of the woman currently standing in front of him.

'Mr Ravelli...' she said breathily and she turned her head away to glance out of the window, her hair a sunburst of colour, her fine profile delineated against the light, soft, glossy mouth full and pouting peach pink, long lashes fluttering up on big eyes as green and verdant as Irish grass.

And Cristo ground his perfect white teeth together on the smoulderingly sexual pull of her in that instant, recognising that she had buckets of that inexpressible quality that reduced the male mind to mush and turned a man on hard and fast. For a split second, he wanted to snatch her up into his arms and crush every line of the remarkable body concealed by the unattractive clothing to his own while he discovered if that voluptuous mouth of hers tasted as impossibly good as it looked. His hands closed into fists of restraint while he fought off the erection threatening, struggling to think of something, *anything*, that would take his thoughts off her mouth and her breasts and her legs and, even worse, what lay between them. That she could be affecting him on such a level outraged his every principle.

Trying to avoid direct contact with those spectacular dark-as-night eyes of his, Belle could feel her colour heightening, awareness of him leaping and pounding through her in an uncontrollable surge. She stared at him, breathless, frozen like someone cornered by a wild animal, and all the time she was noticing things about him: the way his sleek ebony brows defined his eyes, the way the faint line of colour accentuated the hard masculine angle of his high cheekbones, the way the pared-down hollows below enhanced his wide, sensual mouth. Very, very good-looking but, yes, she had noticed that before, certainly didn't need to keep *on* noticing it. The atmosphere thickened and the silence screamed at her nerves as every muscle in her body tightened defensively. It was as if there were nobody else in the world but them and what she was feeling: the insidious warmth blossoming in her pelvis, the sudden tightening discomfort of her nipples.

Lean, strong face rigid, Cristo expelled his breath in a sudden hiss and took a measured step back from her and away from such treacherous ruminations as to what she might *taste* like, what her skin would *feel* and smell like. He was appalled that she could drag such a strong physical reaction from him against his will, but even more annoyed that she could somehow cloud his usual crystal-clear clarity of thought.

'Miss Brophy.'

'It's Mrs actually.'

Cristo frowned. 'You're married?'

'I've been a widow for many years,' Belle replied tightly, straying over to the window, partially turning her back to him while she fought to regain her mental focus. The deception she had entered on demanded her whole concentration. She was Mary Brophy, Gaetano's former mistress and the mother of five of his children, she reminded herself doggedly.

'I invited you here today to discuss your future and your children's,' Cristo delivered smoothly.

Lifted by that solid assurance, Belle's spirits perked up. 'Yes…Gaetano has left us in a pretty awkward position.'

'Naturally, you're referring to your financial situ-

ation. My father was most remiss in not making provision for you in the event of his death.'

'Yes…but he *did* sign the house over to me,' Belle
pointed out, keen to sound like a loyal woman in
Gaetano's defence because she could not afford to let
an ounce of her loathing for the man betray her true
identity in his son's presence.

Cristo went very still, allowing her to take in the
faultless cut of the dark business suit he wore teamed
with a bland white shirt and blue silk tie. His brows
drew together in a frown. 'Which house?'

'The Lodge…he signed it over to me years ago to
ensure that we would always have a home.' Belle's
voice faltered slightly because he seemed so taken
aback by the news, yet surely he should've known
that already as the executor of the estate. 'But bearing in mind the running costs and the children's current needs I'll probably be selling it now.'

'Excuse me for a moment,' Cristo urged, striding
out of the room into the one next door and pulling out
his phone to call his father's lawyer, Robert Ludlow.
If she owned part of the property, he should've been
informed of the fact.

Robert's initial disconcertion over Cristo's query
trailed away as he trawled through Gaetano's files and
then emerged with the facts of a minor legal agreement
drawn up about fifteen years earlier, which Robert's
elder brother had apparently handled shortly before
his retirement. Robert was volubly apologetic for the
oversight. Brought up to date, Cristo was triumphantly
aware that he knew something Mary Brophy did not
appear to know. Under no circumstances would she
be selling the Lodge.

Conscious that Cristo Ravelli clearly had not known about the ownership of the Lodge, Belle paced and wondered anxiously why he had not been aware of the fact. She was trying not to recall the fact that the solicitor who had dealt with her mother's estate had found no paperwork confirming the older woman's ownership. He had brushed off the matter and said he would look into it, and at the time Belle had had so many other things on her plate that she hadn't pursued it.

Cristo strolled back into the drawing room with the lithe, unconscious grace of a male who was confident that he was in the strongest position. 'I'm afraid you don't own the Lodge,' he spelt out softly, his Italian accent edging his vowel sounds.

'That's not possible,' Belle countered, her chin rising in challenge. 'Your father told me it was mine—'

'But for your lifetime only, after which it reverts back to the Mayhill estate,' Cristo qualified smoothly.

Suddenly Belle felt as if the ground below her feet had opened to swallow her up. 'That's not what Gaetano led me to believe.'

'My father had a way with words and may have wished you to believe that you *owned* the Lodge but, in fact, you only have the *use* of it.'

A shot of rage flamed through Belle like a lightning strike. That hateful, manipulative man whom her wretched mother had loved! How could he have misled her like that over something so important? Hot colour sprang into her cheeks as she parted her dry lips. 'And this right to live there while…er I am alive, does it devolve to the children after my…er death?' she prompted sickly.

'I'm afraid not.' Cristo Ravelli gave her a specious

smile of sympathy, which wouldn't have fooled her in
any mood, least of all the one she was in. 'But to all
intents and purposes, the Lodge does belong to you
for the present. You can't, of course, sell it, use it as
security for a loan or indeed make any extensive al-
terations to it, but you do have the right to live there
for as long as you wish.'

Belle had lost every scrap of her angry colour by the
time he had finished speaking. It was appalling news,
the very worst she could have heard. Her mother was
dead and the right to live in the Lodge had died with
her, which meant that Belle and her siblings were il-
legally occupying the house. Indeed, her pretence that
she was her mother could be seen by some people as
an attempt to defraud. She had taken their ability to
live at the Lodge for granted, she registered, stricken.
Now she was being punished for it because, in reality,
they were about to be made homeless.

'My father was very…astute with regard to money
and property,' Cristo murmured softly, watching her
standing there, white with shock below the garish
make-up, eyes wide and stunned by what he had revealed. 'But I'm willing to find you another property
and put it into your name.'

With difficulty, Belle struggled to concentrate.
'And why would you be willing to do that?'

'It will be easier to sell this estate without what
would be…in effect…a sitting tenant in the Lodge,'
Cristo admitted.

'That…' Belle made a valiant attempt to swallow
the massive surge of fury heating her to boiling point
and utterly failed to hold it in. 'That…bastard! How
could he do that to his own children?' she gasped.

'My father wasn't a sentimental man,' Cristo said drily. 'And he has left a mess in his wake. I have a proposition to put to you which *could* solve all your problems…'

Belle was rigid, furious that she had cursed Gaetano to Cristo's face but unable to overcome the bitter resentment threatening to consume her like a living flame. He was so calm, so assured, so very much in control that she hated him with every fibre in her straining body.

Cristo watched her snatch in another audible breath, eyes green as emeralds in sunlight and literally alight with fury. She was highly volatile, a woman with strong emotions she couldn't hide and everything he had always avoided in her sex. But she looked magnificent and the seductive shimmy of her lush rounded breasts below the silky blouse every time she moved was incredibly attention-grabbing.

'Pro-proposition?' Belle framed shakily, fighting like mad to maintain control over her temper. So, she'd had bad news and she was going to have to deal with it. She stared stonily back at Cristo, clashing with stunning dark eyes nailed to her with unsettling intensity. In the rushing silence that had fallen, her throat closed over and her mouth ran dry.

'I want to ask you to consider the idea of having your children adopted,' Cristo suggested quietly. 'It would surely be best for them to leave their troubled and questionable parentage behind them and have the opportunity to live a normal life.'

'I can't believe you just said that to my face,' Belle confided between gritted teeth of restraint.

'I would make the sacrifice very well worth your

while,' Cristo continued evenly as if what he was suggesting were perfectly normal and acceptable. 'My father should have ensured that you have a home and an income but since he hasn't done it, I will take care of it instead.'

'No decent mother would surrender her children for financial gain,' Belle declared in a raw undertone while shooting him a look of scorn that he could even suggest otherwise. 'What sort of women are you used to dealing with?'

'That's not your affair. I am not my father and I have no children,' Cristo replied with cold dignity.

'And don't deserve any either!' Belle lashed back at him. 'For goodness' sake, those children you're talking about are your own brothers and sisters!'

'I do not, and *will* not, acknowledge them as such,' Cristo retorted with icy hauteur.

'Why? Aren't they good enough to be Ravellis?' Belle shot back at him resentfully. 'The housekeeper's kids...not very posh, is it? Not quite the right background, am I right? Well, let me tell you something—'

'No. I don't want you to tell me anything while your temper is out of control,' Cristo cut in with the cutting edge of an icy scalpel.

'And you pride yourself on being an iceberg, don't you?' Belle launched back fearlessly, her generous mouth curling with contempt. 'Well, I'm not ashamed to be an emotional person and ready to do what's right no matter how unwelcome or difficult it is!'

'Does your ranting ever get you to the point?' Cristo enquired witheringly.

Belle's slender hands coiled into tight fists. She had never wanted to hit another living person before and she was shocked by the fact that she would very much have liked to slap him. How dared he stand there looking down on her and her siblings as if they were so much lesser than him? How dared he suggest that her brothers and sisters be torn away from the people they loved and settled in another home with adoptive parents? Couldn't he appreciate that the children were living, breathing people with emotions and attachments and a desperate need for security after the losses they had already sustained? And couldn't he accept that while Mary Brophy might have had her flaws when it came to picking reliable men, she had also been a wonderful loving mother every day of Belle and her siblings' lives?

'The point is...' Belle breathed in a voice that literally shook with the force of her feelings. 'My mother may only have been a housekeeper and she may have been your father's mistress for years, but she was also a very special, kind and caring person and, having lost her, her children deserve the very best that I can give them.'

'Your...*mother*?' Cristo repeated flatly. 'Mary Brophy was your mother?'

And Belle froze there, her skin slowly turning cold and clammy with shock as she realised what she had revealed in her passionate attempt to bring Cristo round to her point of view. For a moment, she had totally forgotten that she was pretending to be her mother in her desperate need to defend the older woman's memory.

'So, if you're not Mary Brophy...where is she? And who are you?' Cristo framed doggedly, incensed that she had dared to try and fool him.

'I'm Belle Brophy. My mother died about a month after your father. She had a heart attack,' Belle admitted with pained green eyes, accepting that she could no longer continue the pretence and that her own unruly temper had betrayed her when she could least afford for it to do so. Unfortunately Cristo Ravelli's unfeeling detachment and innate air of command and superiority were like vinegar poured on an already raw wound.

'You had no intention of telling me that your mother was dead… You lied to keep the Lodge,' Cristo condemned without hesitation.

Dismay assailed Belle at how quickly he had leapt to that unsavoury conclusion and had assumed she had had a criminal motivation for her masquerade. 'It was nothing to do with the Lodge. Until I came here today I believed my mother owned it and that as her children it became ours after her death,' she reminded him. 'But I didn't think you'd listen to what I want for the children if you knew I was only their sister and not their mother.'

Cristo had a very low tolerance threshold for people who lied to him and tried to deceive him. He was remembering the long-legged redhead crossing the lawn the evening before and guessing that that had been Belle Brophy all along. Outrage swept through his big powerful body, sparking his rarely roused temper. Anger fired his dark eyes gold and he took a sudden livid step towards her. 'You pretended to be your mother… Are you crazy? Or simply downright stupid?'

Her heart suddenly thumping very fast at the dark masculine fury etched in his lean, strong face, Belle sidestepped him and raced for the door. She never hung around long when a man got mad in her vicinity; her childhood had taught her that rage often tumbled over the edge into physical violence.

Cristo closed a hand round her slender forearm as she opened the door. 'You're not going anywhere yet.'

'Let go of my arm!' Belle slung up at him furiously, feeling intimidated by the sheer size of him standing that close. 'I made a mistake but that doesn't give you the right to manhandle me!'

'I'm not manhandling you!' Cristo riposted in disgust. 'But you do owe me an explanation for your peculiar behaviour!'

Her green eyes flared with anger and she yanked her arm violently free of his hold. 'You're a Ravelli! The day I owe you anything there'll be two blue moons in the sky!'

For a split second, Cristo watched her stalk across the hall, stiletto heels tap-tapping, slender spine rigid, red corkscrew curls beginning to untidily descend from her inexpertly arranged chignon. 'Come back here!' he roared at her, out of all patience.

Belle spun round angrily, watching him move towards her, and then she spun out a hand and grabbed up a heavy vase from the table beside her and brandished it like a weapon. 'Don't you dare come any closer!' she warned him.

'Is it normal for you to act like a madwoman?' Cristo asked softly, mastering his fury and his exasperation with the greatest of difficulty.

'I'm going to take you to court, *force* you to recognise the children!' Belle spat back at him in passionate challenge. 'They have legal rights to a share of your father's estate and you can't prevent them from receiving it. And I am not a madwoman.'

An inner chill gripped Cristo at the threat of a court case in which every piece of Gaetano's dirty linen would be aired with the media standing by happy to scoop up and publicise every sordid detail. 'Calm down,' he advised tersely. 'And we'll talk.'

'I don't trust you!' Belle hurled back. 'Let me leave or I'll throw this at you!'

An instant later, Cristo could not comprehend that he had walked forward in the face of that warning instead of just letting her go, particularly when it was clear that he wouldn't be able to get a sane word out of her until she had calmed down.

Belle flung the vase at him and fled, cringing from the sound of breaking porcelain hitting the tiled floor as she hauled open the front door and raced down the front steps.

'Technically that was an attempt to assault you,' his bodyguard, Rafe, remarked from the stairs as Cristo brushed flakes of porcelain from his suit, his handsome mouth compressed and lean, dark face a grim mask.

'She couldn't hit a barn door at ten paces. Next time, I won't jump out of the way,' Cristo breathed from the steps as he watched her stalk down the driveway, her head held high like an offended queen. She was mad, completely and utterly mad, nutty as a fruitcake. How was he supposed to negotiate with a woman like that? But he *had* to deal with her or face a very public and embarrassing court case.

'There'll *be* a next time?' Rafe could not help responding in surprise.

Cristo's smile was as cold and threatening as a hungry polar bear's. 'Oh, there'll be a next time all right.'

CHAPTER FOUR

'IT'S ALL OUT in the open now, which is much better,'
Isa told Belle comfortably. 'Now we all know where
we stand.'

Belle dashed a stray curl from her hot brow with a
forearm, finished wiping the work surface and dried
her hands. She had indulged in an orgy of cleaning
since returning to the Lodge. She had needed a physical outlet to work off her excess energy. Her grandmother always reacted to stressful situations with calm
and acceptance and when Belle had mentioned worst-
case scenarios in the homeless field, Isa had quietly reminded her that it would be a few weeks before Bruno
and Donetta returned home for the summer and that
that was ample time in which to find somewhere to
rent. Belle had had to swallow back the thorny question of how she would *pay* rent because she didn't have
the money and Isa didn't either.

Tag began to bark noisily a split second before the
doorbell went. Belle walked out to the hall with Tag
bouncing excitably at her heels.

Cristo Ravelli stood on the step, six feet four inches
tall at the very least and Belle had no heels on, so he
towered over her, radiating raw energy and power. His

lean, darkly beautiful face was hard and forbidding. 'Miss Brophy?'

'Belle,' she corrected curtly.

Cristo looked his fill from the mane of colourful curls tumbling round her shoulders to the porcelain-pale delicate features that provided the perfect frame for grass-green eyes and a full pink mouth. Out of disguise and bare of the tacky make-up she was absolutely breathtaking.

Belle flushed and parted her lips to ask what he wanted and her grip on the door loosened, allowing Tag to take advantage and dart outside to spring an attack on the visitor.

Cristo got off the step fast as the little dog snarled and attacked his ankles. Belle squatted down, saying not very effectively, 'No, Tag, no!'

Cristo received the impression that the dog was welcome to eat him alive if he chose to do so.

'Grab Tag!' an older woman snapped from the hall.

Belle gathered the frantic little dog into her arms. 'I'm sorry. He's suspicious of men.'

'Come in, Mr Ravelli,' Isa Kelly invited politely over her granddaughter's crouching figure.

Belle's head came up fast, green eyes stormy. 'I wasn't going to ask—'

'Mr Ravelli is a guest,' her grandmother decreed. 'He will visit and you will talk like civilised people.'

Tag growled at Cristo from the security of Belle's arms. 'Your father kicked him…so did mine,' she confided grudgingly. 'That's why he doesn't like men. He's too old now to change his ways.'

The older woman studied Cristo, hostility creeping into her voice, despite the civility of her words.

Cristo strolled into a hideous lounge with pink walls, hot-pink sofas and embellished with so many pink frills and ostentatious fake-flower arrangements that it was as if his worst nightmare had come to life. 'I've never liked dogs,' he confided.

A curly-haired toddler clamped both arms round his leg before he could sit down.

'No, Franco,' Belle scolded.

'Or kids,' Cristo added unapologetically.

Franco looked up at him. He had Gaetano's eyes and Cristo found that sight so unnerving that he sat down with the kid still clamped awkwardly to one leg.

'Man,' Franco pronounced with an air of discovery and satisfaction.

'He's a wee bit starved of male attention,' Belle breathed, setting down the dog to grab the toddler in his place and convey him struggling and loudly protesting into the kitchen with her.

'Cristo drinks black coffee,' her grandmother told her from the doorway.

Belle gritted her teeth but she knew that the older woman was talking sense; she *did* have to talk to Cristo and, having set out her expectations, at least he already knew her plans.

Cristo ignored the dog snarling at him from below the coffee table. It was little and grey around the muzzle and should have known better in his opinion than to embark on a battle it couldn't possibly win. Cristo never wasted his time on lost causes or thankless challenges but Belle would, no doubt, have been pleased to learn that her threat had focused his powerful intellect as nothing else could have done.

The instant the tray of coffee and biscuits arrived,

Cristo rose back upright, feeling suffocated amidst all that horrible pinkness. 'I don't want you to take the question of the children's parentage into court.'

'Tough,' Belle said succinctly, not one whit perturbed by his statement because she could hardly have expected him to be supportive on that score. 'My brothers and sisters have been ignored and passed over far too many times. I want them to have what they're entitled to.'

'A few years ago, Gaetano sold up most of his assets and he salted away the proceeds in overseas trusts, which no Irish court will be able to access,' Cristo volunteered. 'With the exception of the sale of the Mayhill estate there is very little cash for you to demand a share of on behalf of your siblings.'

'I'm not looking for a fortune for them.'

'I have a better idea,' Cristo told her.

'I imagine that you *always* have a better idea,' Belle quipped helplessly, leaning back against the kitchen door with defensively folded arms while she wondered how any man could look so fit and vital clad in a tailored business suit that belonged in a boardroom.

She was slim as a whip in her tight faded jeans and an off-the-shoulder black tee that revealed an entrancing glimpse of a narrow white shoulder bisected by a black strap that Cristo savoured, glorying in the fact that he was now free to appreciate her glowing beauty while he speculated as to whether or not she was that pale all over, her skin in vibrant contrast to her bright hair and eyes. The instant he developed an erection, he regretted that evocative thought.

'I will make a settlement on your siblings in compensation for their not pursuing their rights through the courts,' Cristo delivered, half turning away from her to look out of the window overlooking the drive.

'We don't want Ravelli charity,' Belle traded, lifting her chin.

'But it wouldn't be charity. As you said, they're my father's children and I should make good on that for all our sakes. My family would find a court case embarrassing,' Cristo admitted tight-mouthed.

Belle didn't shift an inch. 'Why should I care about that?'

'Publicity is a double-edged sword,' Cristo warned her. 'The media loves sleaze. Your mother won't emerge well from the story. At least three of the children were born while Gaetano was still married.'

At that blunt reminder, a veil of colour burned up below Belle's fair complexion. 'That can't be helped and Mum can't be hurt now. I have to consider the children's future. I want them to have the right to use the Ravelli name.'

'No court that I know of has the ability to bestow that right when no marriage took place between the parents,' Cristo countered, exasperated by her pigheadedness. 'You're being unreasonable. If you keep this out of court and allow me to handle things discreetly, I will be generous. It's the best offer you're going to get.'

'Forgive me for my lack of trust. As I learned today with regard to the ownership of this house, your father was a good teacher.'

'I will not allow you to take this sordid mess into a public courtroom,' Cristo spelt out harshly. 'If you do that I will fight you every step of the way and I warn you—you don't want me as an enemy.'

'Fight me all you like…it's still going to court,' Belle replied thinly. 'We have nothing to lose and everything to gain.'

'What would it take for you to drop this idea?' Cristo growled, almost shuddering at the threat of how much damage a media smear campaign could do to his brother. Zarif's standing in Vashir was delicate, his having only recently ascended the throne. The last thing Zarif needed right now was a great big horrible scandal that would give all too many people the impression that he was from a sleazy family background and was far from being the right ruler for a very conservative country. Zarif, Cristo reminded himself grimly, had already taken the fall for revealing Nik's biggest secret to Nik's estranged wife, Betsy, when the first careless spilling of that secret was entirely Cristo's fault.

'I'd probably be asking for the impossible,' Belle admitted ruefully, 'but I want my siblings to have the lifestyle they would have enjoyed had Gaetano married my mother. It's very unfair that they should have to pay the price for the fact that he didn't marry her.'

'You're being irrational,' Cristo condemned, impatiently, moving out of the room. 'You can't change the past.'

'I don't want to change the past. I simply want to right the wrongs that have been done to my siblings.'

'Leave the past behind you and move on.'

'Easy for you to say,' Belle quipped. 'Not so easy in practice. And I'm not irrational—'

In the hall, Cristo swung round, surprisingly light on his feet for so large and powerfully built a man. 'You're the most irrational woman I've ever met.'

Belle collided with his stunning dark eyes and for a timeless moment the world stopped turning and she stopped breathing.

'And for some reason I find it incredibly sexy,' Cristo purred the admission, his accent roughening his dark deep drawl as he flicked her tee shirt back up over her exposed shoulder with a long careless forefinger.

'You can't get round me. I'm not as naïve as my mother was,' Belle told him tartly.

'Wake up and smell the roses, *cara*. You're a child trying to play with the grown-ups,' Cristo told her thickly, his intimate intonation vibrating down her taut spinal cord.

Suddenly, Belle was short of breath and she stared up at him, her eyes very wide and scornful. 'A child? Is that the best you can do on the insult front?'

'I wasn't trying to insult you.' Up that close his dark eyes had tiny gold flecks like stars. His hand curved to her shoulder and the scent of clean, warm male overlaid with a faint hint of cologne ignited a burst of heat low in Belle's tummy. Just as suddenly she was locked into his eyes and it was as though her feet were encased in concrete and she literally *couldn't* move. He lowered his handsome dark head and took her parted lips with a scorching urgency that sent something frighteningly wild and alive flying through her like an explosive charge. It was a fiery kiss and like no other she had experienced. The minute his tongue plunged into the tender interior of her mouth, it sent a wave of violent response crashing through her, and she was lost. Her hands roamed from his broad shoulders up into his luxuriant dark hair while she rejoiced in the taste of him, the unique sexual flavour of a dominant and surprisingly passionate male. His arms tightened round her, long fingers smoothing down her spine to pin her into uncompromising awareness of his erection. She gasped beneath the thrust of his tongue, mind flying free to picture a much more sexual joining and craving that completion with a strength that started an ache between her thighs.

The sheer intensity of what she was feeling totally spooked Belle. With a startled sound of rejection, she pushed him back from her. 'No, we're not doing this!' she told him furiously.

Dark eyes veiled, Cristo stepped back and drew in a long, deep, steadying breath. *Maledizione!* He was too aroused to be comfortable with the sensation or the woman who had got him into that condition. 'I seem to recall that I was trying to persuade you not to take private family business into a court of law,' he murmured flatly.

Belle shot him a disconcerted glance, unable to credit that he could act as frozen as ever in the wake of that passionate kiss. Passion, it seemed, didn't control Cristo Ravelli. All in the space of a moment she resented his assurance, was insulted by his cool indifference and furious that she hadn't fought him off. But, my goodness, he could kiss. That mortifying thought crept through her mind no matter how hard she tried to kill it dead.

Belle had done a lot of kissing and not much else as a student, very much hoping to experience a volcanic reaction that would signal that all-important spark of true, overwhelming physical attraction. Now fate was having the last laugh by finally serving up that long-awaited, miraculously special kiss and it was happening with the *wrong* man. She had no doubt that Cristo Ravelli was wrong in every way for her. He was stuffy and cold and unfeeling and she was a warm, emotional and impulsive individual.

'I'm sorry. I'm going to do what's best for my siblings and take this matter to court to get it sorted out,' Belle told him curtly.

'You can't,' Cristo countered with chilling bite. 'It will damage other people. You and your siblings are not the only individuals likely to be affected by this.'

'I don't care about anyone else,' Belle admitted truthfully. 'I want my brothers and sisters to be able to hold their heads high and know who they are without shame.'

'You want the impossible,' Cristo derided, turning on his heel.

'No, I want justice.'

Justice! Cristo reflected contemptuously, a deep sense of frustration ruling him, for Cristo never backed down and never failed to find solutions to problems. Damage limitation was his speciality. How could it be justice that Zarif's throne would be rocked by the extent of Gaetano's infidelity and the revelation of his secret family in Ireland? Like father, like son, Zarif's critics would sneer. Mary Brophy had made her choices when she chose to get involved with a married man and have his children. Her daughter, Belle, had too much pride and her resentment of the Ravelli family, or, more specifically, his father, had persuaded her that she could somehow rewrite history. But washing the family dirty linen in public was *not* going to make those children feel that they could raise their heads high. No, it was much more likely to shame them by depicting their parents in ways they would never forget. No child of Gaetano's had *ever* been proud of him or his name. Gaetano had been a cruelly selfish and uninterested parent.

Ironically, Cristo had always believed growing up that he would be a better man than his father and now he wondered what had happened to that dream and at what point cynicism had killed that honourable goal stone dead. He knew that he had not once considered the plight of Mary Brophy's children from any viewpoint other than his own. He was a pragmatic man and he knew he was selfish. But even *he* recognised that Belle Brophy was too young and her grandmother too old to take on full responsibility for Gaetano's children. Cristo was suddenly very conscious that those kids, right down to the little one with his father's eyes, were his flesh and blood too, even though he didn't want to recognise that unwelcome fact.

And then the answer to the problem came to him in a sudden shocking moment of truth. He recoiled from the prospect at first, but as he filtered through the list of challenges he currently faced and that solution ticked every box he began to mull it over as a genuine possibility. It was not as though he were ever likely to fall in love again. Indeed it was a wonder it had happened even once to a male as detached from emotion as he was, he reasoned grimly. Gaetano and Mary's affair could be decently buried and the children's antecedents concealed from the media. As for Belle, in the role he envisaged, which was frankly Belle reclining wearing only a winsome smile on his bed in London, well, she would be perfect there, he reflected with the very first flicker of enthusiasm for the challenge of sacrificing his freedom for the greater good.

Belle suffered a restless night of sleep. She relived the kiss again and again and got hot and bothered while tossing and turning in guilty discomfiture. Cristo was a Ravelli just like Gaetano and the very last man alive she should enjoy kissing. In the morning, she made breakfast for the children on automatic pilot because her brain felt fuzzy and slow. There had been too much agonising over whether or not going to court was the right thing to do for the children, she decided irritably. She did not have a choice. There had never been a choice and there was no way on earth that she planned to trust in any promises made by Cristo Ravelli, who would undoubtedly be every bit as slippery in such delicate negotiations as his late father had proved to be. Exasperated by the constant parade of anxious thoughts weighing her down, Belle saw the twins off to school and then told her grandmother that she was taking Franco down to the beach.

When he reached the beach, Cristo had the pleasure of seeing Belle looking relaxed for the first time. Her wild mane of curls was blowing back from her face in the breeze that plastered her jeans and her blue tee to her lithe, shapely body. She was engaged in throwing a stone into the sea while the leg-clinging toddler bounced up and down in excitement and the dog circled them both barking noisily. Espying Cristo first, the Jack Russell raced across the sand to attack.

'*No!*' Cristo thundered as he strode across the sand.

Tag cringed and rolled over and stuck his four little legs up in the air, beady eyes telegraphing terror.

'You didn't need to shout at him,' Belle criticised, rushing over to crouch down and pet the little animal. 'Look how frightened he is! He's very sensitive.'

'I'm a little sensitive to being bitten,' Cristo murmured drily.

'Man!' the toddler exclaimed and immediately went for Cristo's left leg. Cristo froze, wondering if he could *do* it—actually take on the whole bunch of them and survive with his dignity and sanity intact. He wasn't a family man, he hadn't a clue how a normal family functioned and didn't really want to find out.

Belle was looking up at him, her lovely face flushed and self-conscious, clear green eyes wide above her dainty freckled nose, and her vibrant beauty in that instant scoured his mind clean of all such thoughts. She made him think about sex, lots and lots and lots of sex, and on one level that unnerved him and on another it turned him so hard it literally hurt.

Belle stood up. Tag, the terrified dog, was clasped to her bosom, and now giving Cristo a rather smug look. 'Did Isa tell you where I was?'

'I could be down here for a walk.'

Belle raised a fine auburn brow, scanning his lean, powerful body with assessing eyes. It amazed her that a man who spent so much time in a business suit could be so well built but there he was: broad of shoulder and chest, lean of hip and long of leg with not even the hint of jowls or a paunch. Clearly, he kept fit. And although she had long thought business suits were boring Cristo's dark, perfectly tailored designer suit screamed class and sophistication and was cut close to his powerful thighs and lean hips, directing her attention to areas she didn't normally appraise on men. Her colour heightening, she tore her attention from the prominent bulge at his crotch and dropped it down to his highly polished shoes, which were caked with sand, and she wondered why he couldn't just admit that he had come looking for her.

'You didn't come down here for a walk dressed like that.'

'Sand brushes off,' he fielded carelessly as she settled the dog down on the beach and he scampered off.

In silence, Belle studied Cristo's lean, extravagantly handsome features, heat blossoming in her pelvis and butterflies flying free in her tummy. She felt as clumsy and ill at ease as a schoolgirl in the presence of her idol. But then was it any wonder that she was embarrassed? She had looked at his body and positively delighted in the strikingly strong muscular definition inherent in his build. She could not recall ever doing that to a man before. But the need to look at Cristo felt as necessary as the need to breathe. In reaction to that humiliating truth she flushed to the roots of her hair, mortified by her failure to control her reaction to his looks and dark, charismatic appeal.

Cristo reached down to detach the toddler's painful grip from his leg. *Starved of male attention*, he recalled, thinking that he could certainly understand that. Neither in childhood nor adulthood had Gaetano ever touched him or, indeed, enquired after his well-being. 'We have to talk,' he said succinctly.

'There's nothing more to talk about. We said it all last night,' Belle tossed over a slim shoulder as she started down the beach again and extended her hand. 'Franco, come here!'

'No!' the toddler said stubbornly and, deprived of Cristo's leg, grasped a handful of his trousers instead, making it difficult for Cristo to walk.

Cristo expelled his breath in a slow measured hiss. 'I placed the Mayhill estate on the market this morning,' he fired at her rudely turned back.

Belle came to a dead halt, her narrow spine suddenly rigid as panic leapt inside her at the prospect of losing the roof over their heads. There was certainly no room for them all to squeeze into Isa's one-bedroom apartment in the village. She stared out to sea but the soothing sound of the surf washing the sand smooth failed to work its usual magic. She turned her bright head, green eyes glittering. 'Couldn't that have waited for a few weeks?'

Cristo took his time crossing the sand to join her, her little brother clinging to whatever part of Cristo he could reach and finally stretching up to grip the corner of his suit jacket with sandy fingers. 'No. I want the property sold as soon as possible. I want Gaetano's life here to remain a secret.'

'And what about us? Where are we supposed to go?' Belle demanded heatedly, her temper rising. 'It takes time to relocate.'

'You'll have at least a month to find somewhere else,' Cristo fielded without perceptible sympathy while he watched the breeze push the soft, clinging cotton of her top against her breasts, defining the full rounded swells and her pointed nipples. The heavy pulse at his groin went crazy and he clenched his teeth together, willing back his arousal.

'That's not very long. Bruno and Donetta will be home from school for the summer soon. Five children take up a lot of space... They're your brothers and sisters too, so you should *care* about what happens to them!' Belle launched back at him in furious condemnation.

'Which is why I'm here to suggest that we get married and *make* a home for them together,' Cristo countered with harsh emphasis as he wondered for possibly the very first time in his life whether he really did know what he was doing.

'*Married?*' Belle repeated aghast, wondering if she'd missed a line or two in the conversation. 'What on earth are you talking about?'

'You said that you wanted your siblings to enjoy the Ravelli name and lifestyle. I can only make that happen by marrying you and adopting them.'

Frowning in confusion, Belle fell back a step, in too much shock to immediately respond. 'Is this a joke?' she asked when she had finally found her voice again.

'Why would I joke about something so serious?'

Belle shrugged. 'How would I know? You thought it was acceptable to suggest to their mother that she give them up to be adopted,' she reminded him helplessly.

'I'm not joking,' Cristo replied levelly, a stray shard of sunlight breaking through the clouds to slant across his lean, strong face.

All over again, Belle studied him in wonder because he had the smouldering dark beauty of a fallen angel. His brilliant dark eyes were nothing short of stunning below the thick screen of his lashes and suddenly she felt as breathless as though someone were standing on her lungs.

'I'm a practical man and I'm suggesting a practical marriage which would fulfil *all* our needs,' Cristo continued smoothly. 'You're aware that I don't want a court case. I also want to prevent the squalid story of Gaetano and his housekeeper leaking into the public domain. You would have to agree not to discuss the children's parentage with anyone but nobody need tell any lies either. As far as anyone need know, the children are simply your orphaned brothers and sisters.'

Belle breathed in deep and slow but it still didn't clear her head. 'I can't believe you're suggesting this.'

'You didn't give me a choice, did you? The threat of a court case piled on the pressure. *Are* you prepared to settle this out of court?' Cristo studied her enquiringly.

Belle didn't hesitate. 'No.'

Cristo raised a sleek ebony brow. 'Then what's your answer?'

'It's not that simple,' Belle protested.

'Isn't it? I'm offering you everything you said you wanted.'

Her lashes flickered above her strained eyes. She felt cornered and trapped. 'Well, yes, but...*marriage*? I could hardly be expecting that development!'

Annoyance lanced through Cristo. It was his very first proposal of marriage and he had never before even considered proposing to a woman. Without a shade of vanity he knew he was rich, good-looking and very eligible and yet she was hesitating and he was grimly amused by his irritation.

'Look, I'll think it over until tonight,' Belle muttered uncomfortably.

'*Di niente*...no problem,' Cristo fielded, his wide,

sensual mouth compressed. 'By the way…I mean a *real* marriage.'

'Real…?' Belle spluttered to a halt, the tip of her tongue stealing out to wet her dry lower lip. His intent dark gaze flashed pure naked gold to that tiny movement. Heated colour swept her face as she grasped his meaning in growing disbelief. 'You'd expect me to *sleep* with you?'

'Of course,' Cristo murmured with an indolent assurance that suggested that that idea was entirely normal and acceptable. 'I have no plans to emulate my father and entertain mistresses while I'm married. And I don't want a wife who plays around behind my back either. That kind of lifestyle would not provide a stable home for the children.'

Belle got his point, she really did, but she flushed scarlet at the thought of sharing a bed with him, suddenly very conscious of her own lack of sexual experience. Growing up, she'd had to combat the expectations of the local boys who saw her mother as free and easy in that department and she had had to prove over and over again that she was different. Saying no had been a matter of pride and self-preservation, but as she got older that conditioning along with other needs and insecurities had influenced her and *trusting* a man enough to drop her guard and make love had proved to be even more of a challenge for Belle.

Cristo settled a business card into her limp hand and she stared down at it blankly.

'My private cell number. Let me know by seven

this evening, *bellezza mia*,' he instructed with unblemished cool. 'That way I can make an immediate start on the arrangements.'

CHAPTER FIVE

'DON'T DO THIS...*don't do this...*' Isa's constant refrain was still sounding like a death knell in Belle's ears as she climbed out of the car Cristo had sent to collect her and mounted the steps that led up into the chapel of St Jude's. She was wearing an elegant but rather plain vintage dress with a boat-shaped lace neckline. It was her late mother's wedding gown.

The symbolism of that gesture had appealed to her and in the three weeks that had passed since she last saw Cristo she'd had the dress lengthened to suit her greater height. Mary might never have got her Ravelli to the altar but her daughter was succeeding where she had failed, Belle could not help reflecting with guilty satisfaction. She knew it wasn't right to feel that way because Cristo was not Gaetano and he had not committed his father's sins but she couldn't help it. She was the talk of the neighbourhood, for nobody was quite sure how she had hooked a husband who had only set foot in Ireland for the first time less than a month ago. Indeed there was a crowd of well-wishers waiting outside the old church, quietly ignoring Cristo's request that the wedding be regarded as a private affair.

Of course, Cristo definitely knew how to garner

support and respect in the locals, Belle conceded rue-fully. He had decided not to sell Mayhill but to instead gift the historic house to the village as a community centre and endow it for the future. Money talked, money certainly talked *very* loudly in an area where incomes were low and jobs were few. Mayhill would put the village on the map by becoming a tourist at-traction and its maintenance and the business pros-pects it would provide would offer many employment opportunities. And naturally, it was tacitly and silently understood by the recipients of Cristo's extraordinary largesse that his father's affair with Mary Brophy and the birth of their children were matters to be buried in the darkest, deepest closet never to see the light of day again.

Her sisters, thirteen-year-old Donetta and eight-year-old Lucia, were beaming at her from a front pew. Her brothers Bruno, Pietro and little Franco were be-side them. Bruno was frowning, too intelligent to be fooled by the surface show and still suspicious of what was happening to his family.

'Do you really *want* to marry Gaetano's son?' Bruno had demanded the night before when he had returned from school with Donetta, both teenagers granted special leave for the occasion of their sister's wedding.

'It was love at first sight,' Belle had lied, deter-mined to remove the lines of concern from his brow and the too anxious look from his sensitive gaze. 'And how can you ask me that?'

'I'm not saying I don't believe you…but it seems very convenient in the circumstances. I mean, here we are, broke, virtually homeless and sinking fast and along comes Cristo Ravelli *in* the rescue boat and suddenly our every dream is coming true,' Bruno had recited thinly. 'It doesn't *feel* real to me—it's too good to be true. How did you finally bury the hatchet?'

'What hatchet?'

'You grew up hating the Ravelli family and now all of a sudden you're *marrying* one of them?'

'He's your brother,' Belle had reminded the teenager stubbornly.

'He's a super-rich banker and as sharp as a whip. It's you I'm concerned about. What do you know about being married to a guy like that?' Bruno had asked worriedly. 'He lives in a different world.'

But right now, Cristo was in Belle's world, she savoured helplessly, finally allowing herself to look at the tall, well-built male waiting for her at the altar. Not an iota of the traditional bridegroom's nervous tension showed on his lean, darkly handsome features. In fact he might just have been an attendant at someone else's wedding for all the awareness he was showing. Unconsciously, Belle's chin lifted as if she had been challenged; her heart was pounding fast as a hammer blow behind her ribs and her spine was rigid with all the tension he lacked. After all, she had barely slept since texting him a single word, 'Yes', on the day he had proposed to her on the beach.

Accepting had taken a massive amount of courage and she had garnered that courage only by focusing on the advantages of marrying Cristo Ravelli and suppressing all awareness of the downsides. Her family would finally be safe, absolutely *safe and secure* and that was the bottom line and the only important thing she should concentrate on. What it cost her personally wasn't important and couldn't be weighed on the scale of such things.

After all, she had never been in love and was even more certain that she didn't want to fall in love with anyone. Her memories of her mother's unhappiness during Gaetano's long absences were still fresh as a daisy. Mary had only really come alive when Gaetano was around. Every time he departed it had broken Mary's heart afresh and he would leave her pining and lifeless with only the occasional brief phone call to anticipate while she counted the weeks and days until his next visit. Belle had kept one of those painstakingly numbered calendars as a reminder of what such unstinting, unhesitating love, loyalty and devotion could do to wreck a woman's life. Mary had *lived* for Gaetano. Belle only wanted to live for her family and ensure that they enjoyed a much happier and more stable childhood than she had received.

Isa was staying on in the Lodge for the summer and had insisted that Bruno, Donetta and the twins stay on there with her, leaving only Franco to stay with Belle because her little brother was too attached to her to be separated from her for weeks on end. 'You get your marriage sorted out before you uproot the kids to London and new schools and all the rest of it,' her grandmother had told her bluntly. 'You know I don't approve of what you're doing and if there's a risk that this marriage will only last as long as it takes you to come to your senses, you shouldn't drag the children into it with you.'

Belle had argued until she was finally forced to acknowledge that the older woman was talking good sense. Of course there was a chance that she and Cristo

wouldn't make a go of their 'practical' marriage. She
would have to make a success of their relationship
before she could risk disrupting the children's lives
and bringing them to London to live on a permanent
basis. That was a pretty tall order when she had, more
or less, agreed to marry a complete stranger.

Thinking along those lines, Belle decided she had
to have been insane to say yes with so little thought. It
was not that she had not thought about things, simply
that she had avoided considering the negative aspects.
Going to bed with Cristo had to be one of the more
intimidating negative aspects, she conceded, turning
hot and cold at the very thought of it, but just *living*
with Cristo, indeed with *any* man, would surely be the
ultimate challenge.

Wintry dark eyes slashed with gold by the sunlight piercing the stained-glass window behind him,
Cristo watched his bride approach. She looked absolutely amazing in white, red gold curls tumbling round
her narrow shoulders, her bright head crowned by a
simple seed-pearl coronet. Lust engulfed Cristo in a
drowning wave and his wide, sensual mouth compressed hard. *Maledizione!* He was convinced that
he had never wanted a woman as much before yet he
was equally convinced that she would ultimately prove
as disappointing as her predecessors. Of course she
would, he reflected impatiently, being no fan of optimism or fairy stories. But at least he already knew the
worst of her, which was that she was a virtual blackmailer, a gold-digger and a social climber. Better the
devil you know than the one you don't, he conceded
sardonically and he was exceptionally well versed on
the habits and needs of mercenary women.

Her hand trembled in his when he slid on the wedding ring. A nice touch, he thought cynically, a bridal display of nerves and modesty and utterly wasted on Cristo, who was the last man alive likely to be impressed or taken in by such pretences. He was gaining a very beautiful and desirable wife, he reminded himself doggedly, and putting a lid on the threat of an unsavoury scandal. Even his brothers didn't know what he was doing, for the last thing he would have risked was bringing either of them to the scene of Gaetano's reckless shenanigans in this little Irish village.

Cristo pretty much ignored Belle on the short drive back to the Lodge, where a small catered buffet and drinks had been laid on for the family and the few friends invited. It had not escaped Belle's notice that Cristo had not invited a single person and it bothered her, making her wonder if he was ashamed of her and her humble background and lack of designer polish.

Bruno walked up to Cristo in the hall. 'Could we have a word?' he asked, youthful face taut and pale.

Bruno was the living image of Zarif as a teenager and that likeness had unsettled Cristo at their first brief and awkward meeting the evening before. It seemed that Gaetano had stamped the Ravelli genes very firmly on all his offspring.

'Is there a problem?' Cristo enquired, a fine ebony brow lifting.

The teenager backed into the small space at the foot of the stairs and said gruffly, 'If you hurt my sister like your father hurt my mother, I swear I'll kill you.'

Cristo almost laughed but a stray shard of compassion squashed his amusement when he recalled his own turbulent teenaged years. In any case the warning had all the hallmarks of a prepared speech and, having delivered it, Bruno was backing off fast, troubled brown eyes nervously pinned to Cristo as though he was expecting an immediate physical attack. Before the boy could leave, Christo called him back.

'We're family now and I'm not like my father in any way,' Cristo responded very quietly to the teenager. 'I have no desire to hurt any woman.'

From a tactful distance, Belle absorbed that little interplay. Although she hadn't heard the conversation, she suspected that Bruno had probably been very rude in his outspoken need to protect her and she recognised with a sense of unfamiliar warmth that Cristo had handled her kid brother with surprising sympathy. *Their* kid brother, she mentally corrected, yet there it was—Cristo might not be ready yet to acknowledge that blood tie, but he had restrained both his cutting tongue and his temper when he dealt with Bruno and she was grateful for his kindness.

As Bruno moved hurriedly away, his goal evidently accomplished, Cristo studied the slim dark man whose eyes were welded to Belle's vibrant face as she talked to her grandmother's friends. Cristo stiffened, aggression powering through him as he recognised the son of the land agent, Petrie. Petrie's son, Mark, was attracted to his wife. *His* wife. The shock of that designation ricocheted through Cristo as well and he suppressed his awareness of both strange reactions. He concentrated on Belle instead and watched when she fell still the instant she saw him looking at her, enabling him to clearly see her sudden tension and insecurity.

The golden power of Cristo's gaze was almost mesmeric in its intensity and Belle gulped down the rest of the wine in her glass.

'Eat something,' Isa instructed. 'You didn't have any breakfast.'

Belle accepted the sandwich extended for the sake of peace, for although her tummy felt hollow it had nothing to do with hunger. 'I'll go and get changed,' she said uneasily, ruffling Franco's curly head where he stood by her side.

Cristo was still in the hall, detached from the small crowd by a barrier of reserve that chilled her.

'He's not very friendly, is he?' her sister Donetta whispered in her ear.

Belle forced a smile, cursing Cristo's detachment and his clear reluctance to use the opportunity to get to know his younger siblings. 'He's just shy.'

'Shy?' Donetta gasped in surprise.

'*Very* shy,' Belle lied, wanting to lay the teenager's concerns to rest. 'It'll be different when he gets to know all of you properly.'

And the burden of ensuring that it would be different was on *her* shoulders, Belle acknowledged apprehensively, registering what a challenge she had set herself. Cristo had been raised an only child and a family the size of hers had to be a shock to his reticent nature. Franco was tugging at his jacket, looking up at Cristo with adoring brown eyes, and Cristo was at least tolerating the child, she reasoned ruefully, wondering if that was the most she could hope for from him when it came to the children. And her? Would he only be *tolerating* her as well? A shiver of distaste at that image ran down her back until she was warmed by the recollection of his considered response to Bruno.

'Where are you going?' Cristo enquired when she brushed past him to head for the stairs.

'I'm getting changed…for the flight you mentioned,' she extended awkwardly, lashes screening her strained green eyes.

He was her husband, for goodness' sake, and he had decreed that they would be flying out of Ireland within hours of the ceremony. She had thought about arguing but then had seen no point in trying to put off the inevitable. She had given up her life to enter his and leaving home was the first step in that process.

'No. I like the dress. Don't take it off.'

Thoroughly taken aback by the command, Belle glanced up at him in astonishment at the request. 'I can't trudge through an airport dressed like this.'

'I have a private jet and we won't be trudging anywhere. Don't take the dress off, *bellezza mia*,' Cristo instructed sibilantly, a strong dark forefinger curling below her chin to lift it so that she collided with smouldering golden eyes. '*I* want to be the one who takes it off.'

Face burning, breath coming in tortured bursts, Belle fled upstairs, barely able to credit that he had said that to her. She had read about male fantasies and he had just told her his with a lack of embarrassment that made her all the more conscious of her own ignorance. He was already fantasising about removing her bridal gown. It was a useful message as to what went on in Cristo's arrogant head. While she was worrying about him getting to know and like their brothers and sisters *he* was thinking about sex. Was that all their marriage meant to him? Sex and the threat of a big scandal removed?

And if it was, what on earth could she do about it? All her gran's warnings and dire predictions came crashing down on her at once. What if he was cruel? Unfaithful? Belle swallowed hard, mastering her tumultuous emotions. You made your bed, now you have to lie on it...*literally*, she told herself sternly as she checked that she had packed the most essential things for herself and Franco.

Franco cried and begged to get out of his car seat all the way to the airport. Aware of the irritation Cristo couldn't hide and with her own spirits low at having left home and everything and almost everyone familiar behind her for goodness knew how long, Belle tried to distract the child.

'Why did your mother have so many children with my father?' Cristo asked suddenly.

'She always wanted a big family and I think the kids were her compensation for not seeing much of your father,' Belle opined and then, hesitating, added, 'Gaetano wanted nothing to do with them though. When he was here they went to stay with Isa and maybe only saw him once for about ten minutes and it would be very strained. He just wasn't interested.'

'He was the same with me and my brothers.'

'I *hated* him!' Belle admitted in a driven undertone. 'I felt guilty about that when he was killed in the crash.'

'You shouldn't, *cara*,' Cristo parried. 'He was a very selfish man, who lived only for his pleasure and his profit. Nothing else mattered to him.'

Belle settled into her seat on Cristo's opulent private jet. Franco was in the sleeping compartment and, once she had settled her little brother down for his nap, Cristo had informed her that he had hired a nanny for the child, who would be waiting when they reached their destination.

'Which...*is*?'

'Italy. I'm taking you to my home in Italy.'

'Venice...we're going to Venice?' Belle carolled in sudden excitement.

'No, that is where my mother and stepfather live. I inherited a house in Umbria, which has belonged to my mother's family for generations. Sorry, it's not Venice,' Cristo quipped.

'Won't your mother be upset that she wasn't at your wedding?' Belle prompted, shooting him a look of wide-eyed curiosity.

'I doubt it. Anything that reminds Giulia of Gaetano puts her in a very bad mood,' Cristo admitted, compressing his lips. 'She never recovered from what he put her through. You couldn't be in her company for five minutes before she told you that he stole the best years of her life, robbed her blind and slept with— among others—her best friend and her maid.'

'Good grief...' Belle breathed, reeling from that blunt admission.

During the flight, even with his laptop open in front of him, Cristo found his attention continually straying from the financial report he was checking. He studied Belle's delicate profile from below his dense lashes, marvelling at the display of innocence and vulnerability that she continued to exude. Was he supposed to be impressed? Did he strike her as that stupid? After all, Mary Brophy's daughter was considerably shrewder than her mother had ever been because she had not hesitated to use Gaetano's children as a weapon to enrich herself. But his awareness of that aspect of her less than stellar character faded whenever Cristo looked at her, appreciating the vibrancy of her Titian curls against her porcelain-pale skin, the clarity of her beautiful green eyes, the feminine elegance of the fingers and unpainted nails adorning the slim hands that held a magazine. She always looked so amazingly natural, he registered, black brows drawing together in a bemused frown as he questioned the depth of his fascination and hurriedly returned to his financial report, trying and singularly failing to rustle up an immediate image of Betsy's face.

The nanny, Teresa, a middle-aged woman with a warm smile, greeted them at the airport and gathered up Franco with enough appreciation to persuade Belle that her little brother would enjoy the best of attention. Though quite what Cristo expected her to do with her time while someone else looked after Franco, she had no idea. After driving through miles of extensively cultivated agricultural land the sun was going down fast when the limousine began to climb mountain roads with hairpin bends that soon slowed the speed of their passage.

'It feels as if we're travelling to the end of the world,' Belle commented.

'As far as my mother was concerned, the Palazzo Maddalena, named for one of her ancestors, might as well have been. It was never her style.'

And as the car travelled slowly towards to the massive stone building presiding over the hill tops, Belle knew it wasn't her style either and her heart and her courage sank to their lowest ever level. For the first time it really hit her exactly what marrying Cristo entailed and the little girl whose earliest home had been a tiny house was ready to surface again because the adult woman was overpowered by the sheer size and grandeur of the property confronting her. Ancient mellowed stone encased the three-storeys-tall palazzo, which had graceful wings spreading to either side. Elaborate terraced gardens in an ornamental pattern spread down the hill in front of it and behind the solid bulk of the building loomed the imposing snow-capped tops of the Sibillini mountain range.

As pale as a newly created ghost, Belle climbed out of the car, her lovely face frozen and expressionless, her wedding gown glimmering eerily in the twilight. Cristo surveyed her with a level of satisfaction that disconcerted him. *His* wife, *his* home where he was free to be himself. *Her* tension, though, was not a surprise because Cristo was convinced he knew precisely why Belle would have preferred Venice. What was the point of marrying a billionaire if she couldn't enjoy the expected rich advantages that came with the wedding ring? In Venice she could have partied with his mother's wealthy and famous friends and shopped in expensive boutiques and jewellery stores. An ancestral palazzo in the mountains was no fair exchange.

'It's a great place for a honeymoon,' Cristo informed her with something that just might have been amusement glimmering in his keen gaze.

A honeymoon? Well, she *was* married. But why was he laughing at her? Did he also see the ludicrous gulf between a boy raised in a gilded Venetian palace and the housekeeper's daughter? How could he fail to? A tide of self-conscious colour washed Belle's complex-

ion as they entered the enormous palazzo. She knew
time was running out. They had dined on the plane,
so not even the need to eat could be stretched out to
lengthen the evening ahead. For goodness' sake, she
urged herself, lighten up, *wise* up. This was the deal;
this was the agreement that would ensure her siblings
received everything that should have been theirs from
birth. They would grow up secure and safe as Ravellis and nobody would have an excuse to mock them
or sneer at them. They would have the best of educa-
tions and opportunities to equip them to enter adult
life. They would never have to worry about where their
next meal was coming from. As she listed the countless benefits of having married Cristo Ravelli, Belle's
breathing slowly steadied and she steeled her spine.

Franco clutched at her dress as they mounted the
stairs and the manservant who had let them in showed
them first to a nursery suite where the nanny tried
to detach Franco from Belle. But Franco didn't like
strange places and he started to sob and clutch at his
sister and it took Cristo to detach him from her.

'Kiss-do,' Franco warbled mid sob, ready to smile
until Cristo handed him over to the nanny, and then in
desperation stretching his arms out to Belle instead.

Belle moved forward to go to Franco but Cristo
forestalled her with a hand on her arm. 'It's our wedding night,' he reminded her drily and the very dry-
ness of his tone disturbed her.

In her opinion only people who loved each other
had wedding nights, but that wasn't what she had
signed up for, she reminded herself squarely as Cristo
led the way along the corridor and cast open a door
across yet another landing into a huge bedroom. In

spite of her nervousness, the thrill of desire began to build within her.

Belle's attention centred on the giant gilded four-poster bed topped with a gilded coronet and stayed there as if a padlock had snapped her into place. Suddenly she was regretting the innate shyness and mistrust that had kept her out of other men's beds. A little sexual experience would have felt better at that moment when ignorance felt more like a threat.

Cristo closed his arms round her rigid figure from behind and the scent of him engulfed her. He smelled so good, a citrusy mix of designer cologne and aromatic male that did something strange to her senses. Her heartbeat kicked up pace as he tugged her hair back from her shoulders and bent his mouth to her nape. His chest was against her spine and as solid as rock, and lower down against her bottom she was suddenly startlingly aware that he was aroused and that had the oddest effect on her. Even as her nervous tension heightened, she couldn't help being pleased that she could have that much influence over a male who tended to reveal very little on the surface, and who had stood at the altar in the chapel as though he were an innocent bystander on the brink of boredom.

'I love you in that dress, *gattina mia*,' he growled against her skin, and buried his mouth there in a place she hadn't even known could be sensitive. Every cell in her body pulled taut with anticipation as he laved her flesh with the tip of his tongue and grazed her with the edges of his teeth in an incredibly erotic approach she had certainly not expected from Cristo Ravelli. She was already trembling, her nipples tingling, a sliding sensation of warmth rising between her thighs. A slice of cooler air feathered her spine and her wedding gown slid down her arms without any warning. A gasp of surprise was wrenched from her but ten seconds later the dress was pooled round her feet and he was lifting her out of it.

He spun her round, swiftly engulfing her hands in his before she could make any move to cover the lacy bra, knickers and hold-up stockings she wore beneath. Shimmering eyes, dark as Hades, flared naked gold as they scanned the full curves of her breasts cupped in the bra, sliding down to her narrow waist and the flare of her hips before seguing down the long, shapely length of her legs.

'You were definitely worth waiting for,' Cristo told her with hungry conviction lacing every syllable. 'You're gorgeous, *cara.*'

Belle sucked in a shaken drag of oxygen and then he kissed her with a heat and strength that consumed her. He caressed the seam of her lips, parted them, delved deep and sent a shudder of excitement racing through her that startled her. Yes, as she had noted before, Cristo knew how to kiss and his mouth on hers was deeply addictive and intoxicating. He teased her with his tongue and she shivered and dimly recognised that she was being very efficiently seduced by a man she had once written off as a stuffy banker. Her fingers laced into the thick black hair at the back of his neck and an appreciative growl escaped low in his throat. Just as quickly she became airborne when he scooped her up and settled her down on the bed.

Green eyes dazed, Belle stared back at him, nerves beginning to rise again as he undressed, shedding his tie, his jacket and shoes with a careless haste that flattered her. With his scorching golden eyes pinned to her as intently as though she were Helen of Troy, she realised that he truly did appear to find her very attractive, and when he shed his shirt to reveal six-pack abs and a torso straight out of a male centrefold Belle's mouth ran dry because for the first time ever *she* was appreciating the male body. With his every movement sleek muscles flexed below smooth golden skin. A thin furrow of dark hair ran from below his navel and disappeared beneath his waistband and then just as quickly he was skimming off the trousers as well, displaying tight buttocks and a…and a massive bulge in the front of his boxers.

At that point, all of Belle's virginal concerns surged to the forefront of her mind. Was he supposed to be that big? Was that normal? She could hardly ask.

Cristo wondered why she was blushing as red as a tomato. He had never seen anything more beautiful or more innately satisfying than the sight of her on top of his bed, clad only in delicate lace lingerie. He tugged off his boxers and left them in a heap, on fire for the climax his body craved.

The full-frontal effect caused Belle to edge back up towards the headboard. He didn't seem to have a single inhibition in his entire body. Her lashes lowered to screen her expression, heat and what she didn't immediately recognise as hunger snaking through the secret places of her body.

'You're very quiet,' Cristo remarked, tugging her back into the shelter of his arms and reaching behind her to unhook her bra.

'And you're very…single-minded.' Belle selected

the word shakily because she thought he had a lot in common with a bullet aimed at a target.

'I've had three weeks to think about this moment,' Cristo growled low in his throat. 'Three weeks too long...I wanted you the first moment I saw you.'

'When you thought I was my mother?' she parried incredulously.

'You were crossing the lawn with the dog in tow and looking exactly like yourself,' Cristo contradicted, raising almost reverent hands to the spill of pale breasts he had unveiled, long fingers tracing the underside of the full round swells. 'You are totally magnificent, *cara mia.*'

Her breath was feathering in and out of her lungs in insufficient drags while he played with her straining nipples, teasing and plucking the tender crowns and sending trickles of fire flaming down into her pelvis. He smoothed his hands down over her quivering frame.

'Are you cold?' he asked in surprise.

'Just a bit nervous,' she gasped, her voice strangled at source as he rested his palm on her inner thigh and then hooked a finger below the lace edge of her knickers and stroked so that a current of pure tingling warmth ran through her veins.

He tipped up her face with his other hand and burning golden eyes assailed hers. 'Why would you be nervous?'

'I haven't done this before.'

'With me,' he filled in.

'With anyone!'

Cristo froze in the midst of trailing off her last garment. 'Are you trying to tell me you're a virgin?'

The heat of mortification flushed her fair skin like a flaming tide and she couldn't find her voice and was forced to nod affirmation with a jerk of her head.

'And this is not a tease?' Cristo prompted. 'Not a stupid idea to give me what you think could be a wedding-night fantasy?'

Belle focused on him with disconcerted eyes, striving to imagine how he could even suspect such a thing.

Cristo collided with those clear green eyes and discarded his plans of a wedding-night sex marathon. She wouldn't be able to handle that. A virgin. He was good at reading people. He was convinced she wasn't lying and he was shell-shocked because it was not at all what he had expected from her and he did not know whether he liked the idea or not.

'No, not a tease, *cara*,' Cristo said for himself.

'You're disappointed, aren't you?' Belle guessed.

'No, I'm not. You're my wife,' Cristo pointed out with a sudden sense of satisfaction that she would never be able to compare him to another man in bed, never know anything other than what he showed her. A possessive vibe he didn't know he had pulsed through him at that awareness.

'I don't see what difference that makes. I'm not what you expected,' Belle protested.

Still taut with arousal, Cristo was tired of talking. He kissed along her delicate jaw bone and then crushed her generous mouth urgently beneath his, shifting over her to lower his mouth to her generous breasts and then string a line of kisses down over her straining midriff to the very heart of her. He eased a finger into her tight channel and she bucked up her hips and he smiled, loving her responsiveness, parting her thighs for a more intimate caress.

'No…no,' she began, trying to move away.

Glancing up to meet dismayed green eyes, Cristo made a soothing sound he was sure he had never had to make in the bedroom before. 'Trust me…I'll take care of you.'

Belle rested her head back against the pillows and closed her eyes tight, trembling with a crazy mix of mortification laced with tingling sexual awareness and anticipation. He touched her and she gasped out loud because she was so sensitive there and the more he licked and nibbled and tormented her, the more frantically excited she became, all control wrested from her, her body moving in a new feverish rhythm like an instrument being strummed by an expert. Incomprehensible moans and sounds fell from her lips as she writhed and the unbearable ache at her core rose to a crescendo and her whole being was straining towards a climax.

And that was when Cristo lifted over her and eased slowly into the slick, wet welcome of her body. Her eyes flew wide at that shock of sensation, of sudden fullness and stretching inside her.

'This could hurt,' he told her gently.

'I know…' she said breathlessly. 'I'm not a baby.'

For the first time in his life Cristo was more concerned about his partner than himself, which felt strangely alien to him. 'You're so tight,' he bit out, flexing his hips, tipping her up to him for a deeper connection and then sliding home to the very heart of her, causing a stinging, fleeting pain that made her grimace.

'Not too bad,' she told him shakily. 'Just do it.'

Just do it? Cristo laughed out loud and grinned down at her preoccupied face. She looked up at him, rocked by the dark beauty of him at that moment wearing that flashing brilliant smile she had never seen before. And then he moved again, sliding back and delving into her again until he was seated to the hilt and strong sensation was exploding like fireworks inside her. The delicious friction as his hips pounded against hers and the speed of his breathtaking thrusts consumed her with wild excitement. It was electrifyingly intense and passionate and so was he, she registered as her body stiffened and clamped tight around him, and wave after wave of pleasure cascaded through her in a climax so powerful she felt utterly drained in the aftermath but decidedly floaty and full of well-being.

'Well, that was definitely worth getting married for, *bellezza mia,*' Cristo groaned hoarsely in her ear. 'You might be a blackmailer, a gold-digger and a social climber but you're fabulous in bed.'

Belle's eyes flew wide in shock and suddenly she was pushing against those brown muscular shoulders and levering out from underneath him in a rage of disbelief at what he had dared to say to her.

She slid out of the bed like an electrified eel and raced into the bathroom in search of a weapon of mass destruction but there was no club, no gun, no whip, nothing with which to thump him good and hard as pride demanded she must. In desperation she filled a glass by the sink with water and stalked back into the bedroom and slung the contents of the glass at him.

Astonished, Cristo sat up dripping in the tumbled

bedding, looking extraordinarily and quite irresistibly
handsome with his golden skin and bright eyes and
tousled black hair and her awareness of the fact only
inflamed her more. 'What the hell?' he demanded,
wiping away the water dripping from his face.

'Don't you dare speak to me like that, you pig!' his
bride screeched at him like a harpy from his worst
nightmares.

'Speak to you...?' For a split second, Cristo
frowned. 'Oh...didn't you like me being honest?'

'I am not a blackmailer, a gold-digger or a social
climber!' Belle fired at him furiously. 'How dare you
accuse me of those things?'

Cristo shot her a derisive look. 'I hate drama
queens.'

'You think I care about that? You think I'm ever
going to get into that bed again with you after what
you called me and the way you spoke to me?' Belle
screamed across the depth of the bedroom, so outraged
she could barely frame the words.

Cristo lounged back against the banked pillows
looking remarkably unconcerned by that threat. 'I
think you will because if you *don't*, I'll be asking for
a divorce,' he spelt out without hesitation.

'Right then...I want a divorce!' Belle spat at him
before flouncing back into the bathroom and locking
shut the door with a loud click.

Well, didn't you handle that well? Cristo reflected,
very much in shock himself at what he had divulged
to her of his opinions. After all, it wasn't as though
such frankness came naturally to him. In fact, Cristo,
a man of few words, invariably kept his convictions
to himself, but somehow something about that fantas-

tic sex had clashed with his opinion of her inside his head and he had found himself delivering judgement there and then. Had he *wanted* her to know what he thought of her? he queried with a bemused frown. Had he wanted her to prove him wrong or endeavour to develop her character into something more acceptable to him? And why was he even thinking along such lines? He had meant every word he said and he wasn't taking it back or apologising for telling the truth as he saw it.

CHAPTER SIX

ALMOST TWO HOURS later, Cristo scrutinised the empty four-poster bed as if further attention might magically conjure Belle up from below the tossed bedding. His even white teeth clenched so hard his jaw ached. He had gone for a shower in another room, giving her time to settle down, but Belle being Belle, both impulsive and tempestuous, had evidently emerged from the sit-in in the bathroom to take off instead. But to where? It was eleven at night and the palazzo lay several kilometres from the main road.

Cristo expelled his breath with an audible hiss. He had screwed up, screwed up spectacularly and for a reserved and clever male, who rarely ever miscalculated with women, that was a bitter and maddening acknowledgement. Why had he told her what he thought of her and in such terms? That he couldn't answer his own question only made him more angry and unsettled by the experience. It was their wedding night and his bride had run away, not what anyone would call a promising start and for Cristo, who was an irretrievable perfectionist, it was a slap in the face and an unwelcome reminder that he was only human and that humans made mistakes.

At the bottom of the terraced gardens, Belle swung her legs up on her stone bench, striving for a comfort that was unattainable on such an unyielding surface. Unfortunately she could not think of anywhere else to go, certainly not back to the grand building on the top of the hill with its vast and intimidating heavily furnished rooms where she felt like an old-style kitchen maid roaming illicitly from her proper place in the servant's quarters. Oh, Gran, why *didn't* I listen to you? Belle was thinking with feverish regret and an intense sense of self-loathing.

She had married a man who clearly despised her. And worst of all, she had *slept* with him, which just then felt like the biggest self-betrayal of all. Tears dripped silently down Belle's quivering cheeks because she had never felt so alone and out of her depth in her life, at least not since the teenaged years when she had been horrendously bullied. Now she felt trapped, trapped by the marriage, trapped by the promises she had made to her siblings about the wonderful new life ahead of them all. She couldn't just walk away; it wasn't that simple. Telling him she wanted a divorce had been sheer bravado and he had probably recognised it as such.

Cristo Ravelli. He got to her as no other man ever had, rousing feelings and thoughts and reactions she couldn't control. She had become infatuated with him, she decided, mentally and physically infatuated and, as a result, she had acted every bit as foolishly with him as her late mother had once behaved with Gaetano, unable to keep her distance and failing to count the costs of the relationship. How was she supposed to handle Cristo? He was streets ahead of her in the sophistication stakes. He was a Ravelli, taught from birth that he was a superior being. She hugged her knees, rocking her hips against the hard stone beneath her in an unconscious self-soothing motion, her fingers clenching convulsively together as she fiercely blinked back tears.

Well, the infatuation was dead now. He had *killed* it stone dead. She hated him, absolutely hated him for what he had said within moments of using her body for his pleasure. All right, she reasoned guiltily with herself, it had been *her* pleasure as well. She couldn't pretend to have been an unwilling partner in what had transpired, but then she had not been prepared for that level of passion or pleasure. She had dimly imagined that something much less exciting awaited them in the bedroom.

Mercifully it was a clear night, Cristo conceded grudgingly, tramping down the multitude of steps that featured in the gardens. He was in a filthy mood. Telling Umberto, who ran the palazzo, that his bride was missing had embarrassed him and very little, if anything, embarrassed Cristo. But if he couldn't find Belle, he knew that calling the police in would be considerably *more* embarrassing. He didn't know what he was going to say to her if he *did* find her either. Was he supposed to lie and pretend he hadn't meant his indictment? Apologise for speaking the truth? He was damned if he was going to apologise when she was forcing him to tramp all over his extensive property in search of her in the middle of the night. *Dio mio!* Obviously he was worried about her. Suppose she had come down here in the dark and she had fallen? Hitched a lift out on the country road from some cruising rapist or pervert? Her temper might make her do something self-destructive or dangerous, he reasoned grimly. Cristo's imagination was suddenly travelling in colourful directions it had never gone in before.

And then he heard a noise, the human noise of feet shifting across gravel. *'Belle?'* he called.

Dismay gripping her at the sound of Cristo's voice, Belle returned to her stone bench, having stretched and glued her lips together, but he kept on calling and her silence began to feel childish and selfish and eventually she parted her lips to shout back. 'Go away!'

Relief assailed Cristo. She was safe, would no doubt live to fight many another day with him, a reflection that sent a wash of something oddly like satisfaction through his tall, well-built frame. He followed the voice to its most likely source: the garden pavilion at the very foot of the garden, sited beside a craggy seventeenth-century-built rushing stream and waterfall. Rounding a corner on one of the many paths, he saw her there sitting in darkness, long legs extended in front of her along a stone bench, eyes reflecting the moonlight.

'I was worried about you,' Cristo declared, coming to a halt a couple of feet from the pavilion steps, intimidatingly tall, outrageously assured. 'You didn't answer your cell phone.'

'I don't have it with me and I'm sure you weren't that worried about my welfare,' Belle remarked curtly while quietly noting that he looked more amazing than ever when clad in faded jeans and a casual tee, bare brown feet thrust into leather sandals. 'Not after the way you spoke to me.'

'It was the wrong place, wrong time,' Cristo admitted, mounting the steps to lift the lighter from its hook on the wall and ignite the fat pillar candle in the centre of the stone table.

Not even slightly soothed by that comeback, Belle tilted her chin as the candle flame illuminated his darkly handsome features while he looked down at her from the opposite side of the table. 'But it was obviously what you thought...*blackmail*?'

'I did tell you that other people could be seriously embarrassed by you taking such a story to court on your siblings' behalf,' Cristo reminded her stubbornly. 'You told me you didn't care.'

Your siblings, not his as well, she noted in exasperation, since he was clearly still set on denying that blood tie. 'Why should I have? Neither you nor your brothers care about them.'

'Neither Nik nor Zarif even know of your siblings' existence as yet,' Cristo pointed out. 'Nik's not into children though. For Zarif, however, the news that throughout the whole of his parents' marriage Gaetano was sleeping with another woman and having a tribe of children with her would be deeply destructive and damaging. He's the new King of Vashir.'

Belle rolled her eyes, unimpressed or, at least, *trying* to seem unimpressed. 'I know that.'

'Vashir is a very devout and conservative society and Gaetano's behaviour would cause a huge scandal there, which would engulf Zarif's image in Gaetano's sleaze. Every ruler has opponents and it would be used against him to remind people that his father was a foreigner with a sordid irreligious lifestyle. He doesn't deserve that. Like all of us, he paid the price of having Gaetano as a father while he was still a child,' Cristo informed her grimly. 'I offered to marry you and adopt those children to prevent that from happening.'

'But you didn't tell me that, so you can hardly

expect me to be sympathetic now,' Belle told him roundly. 'It's not only a little late in the day to start calling me a blackmailer, it's also darned unfair when you never gave me those facts in the first place!'

At that spirited retort, Cristo gritted his teeth again in smouldering silence.

'I did *not* blackmail you!' Belle exclaimed, sliding off the bench to stand up and walk down the steps before turning back to face him while his attention lingered on her slender leggy proportions in the denim shorts and camisole she wore. 'Evidently my plans to go to court on the children's behalf put you between a rock and a hard place but *you* made the decision to propose marriage!'

Lean, strong features set in forbidding lines in the shadowy candlelight, Cristo stared broodingly back at her. 'I did but even now I know that your plans to have your day in court would have damaged those children more than you can possibly appreciate.'

'You don't know what you're talking about!'

'I know *exactly* what I'm talking about—in fact nobody knows better!' Cristo parried with unexpected rawness, his dark eyes glittering like stars. 'Gaetano trailed my mother through court in a supposed attempt to gain custody of me when I was a child. Of course what he really wanted was a bigger payoff from the divorce. He didn't want me; he never wanted me. All the dirty secrets of my parents' marriage were trailed out in court and made headlines across Europe and you can *still* read about it online if you know where to look. Do you really think those children would thank you either now or years from now for seeing their parents' less than stellar private life splashed across the tabloids and the net?'

That angle hadn't occurred to Belle and she gulped. 'Naturally I didn't want your charity when the children were legally entitled to a share in their own name.'

'It wouldn't have been charity.'

'No, but you would've been buying my silence and theirs!' she lashed back at him angrily. 'I watched what you did with Mayhill—all aboard the Ravelli gravy train to keep everyone quiet about Gaetano, Mary and their kids.'

'Didn't you climb aboard the same train with a wedding ring?' Cristo taunted with sizzling derision.

'No, I darned well didn't!' Belle hurled back, temper leaping up in a surge of inner flame. 'Because no matter what you think I'm *not* a gold-digger or a social climber! I married you for the sake of my brothers and sisters, so that they would never have to go through what Bruno and I went through!'

'What did you go through?' Cristo demanded with galling impatience.

'When Mum started the affair with Gaetano and then later when she gave birth to Bruno, I think people were inclined to turn a blind eye to it all because everybody knew she'd had a rough time with my father until he died.' Belle breathed in deep, angry pain and mortification coursing through her slender length. 'Back then the locals felt sorry for her—my father was an abusive drunk.'

'And then?' Cristo's attention was locked to her beautiful face and the glistening lucidity of her wide green eyes.

'And then it went sour for all of us because Mum

continued the affair with Gaetano and went on having children. Everyone knew Gaetano had a wife abroad. They decided Mum was shameless and bold and stopped talking to her, wouldn't even serve her in some village shops,' Belle recounted unhappily. 'But she lived in the Lodge outside the village and shopped elsewhere so the hostility didn't really touch her...but I went to local schools with the children of those judgemental parents...'

Her voice momentarily ran out of steam and then picked up again as she shared a memory, a haunted look on her face as if she had drifted mental miles away, and in a way she had because she was back there, walking into a classroom as a vulnerable adolescent, being called a slut by a bunch of girls because everyone knew her mother was a woman who had just given birth to two more children by her married lover. Nobody had intervened when she was bullied because it was widely known and accepted that Mary Brophy was a wicked woman raising her children in a degenerate home where the most basic rules of morality and decency were being broken on a regular basis.

'I never had any friends apart from Mark,' she admitted curtly. 'The other mothers wouldn't let their daughters mix with me or come to my house. It got worse as I got older because then I had the boys calling me names as well and making approaches...well, you can imagine the approaches.'

Cristo, raised from an early age in a city that bred anonymity, was genuinely taken aback by what she was telling him. He'd had no suspicion of the moral rectitude in a small rural community where those who dared to defy public opinion and break the rules could be punished by exclusion and enmity.

'I didn't want my sisters or my brothers to go through that.'

'Obviously not, *cara*,' Cristo murmured ruefully, suddenly grasping one very good reason why his bride had been inexperienced because she had naturally been denied that outlet as a teenager and young woman when to give way to the desire to experiment could have surely seen her labelled as having followed in her mother's footsteps. 'And Bruno?'

'I'll tell you about that some other time but he was bullied as well. That's why he and Donetta were sent to boarding school in the first place.'

'Are you coming back up to the house?' Cristo enquired in the dragging silence that had fallen. 'It *is* two o'clock in the morning.'

Belle prayed for calm and restraint as she walked away from the pavilion. 'You were very offensive and insulting...and disrespectful too.'

'*Sì, bellezza mia*, but it is possible that complete honesty could be the best way forward in a marriage such as ours,' Cristo stated thoughtfully.

Belle mulled that concept over while she mounted yet another endless flight of steps. All the emotion and activity of the day were suddenly hitting her in one go and exhaustion was weighing her down. 'I haven't forgiven you, though,' she was quick to tell him, lest he be assuming that the slate had been wiped clean when it wasn't.

Having watched her pace flag, Cristo closed an arm round her slender spine to guide her up the steep incline. 'That's okay.'

Cristo felt surprisingly buoyant as he urged her

back upstairs to their bedroom. In the light he could see the marks of tearstains on her face and his conscience pierced his tough hide. She was so much more emotional than he was and that unnerved him. He would never forget the wounded expression on her face when she had told him about the bullying she had endured at school. To his way of thinking, her mother had been every bit as selfish in her own way as his father, he reflected grimly, but he knew better than to share that thought.

At the same time, he could only be impressed by how very protective Belle was of her brothers and sisters. He had never known that family intimacy, never appreciated that love could bond a family so tightly together, and he could not help wondering how different he might have been had he shared a similar experience. In spite of the misfortunes Gaetano had caused Mary Brophy's children, they remained a very closely connected unit.

'I'm not getting back into the same bed,' Belle announced one step inside the bedroom door.

Payback time, Cristo acknowledged. 'I'm not that insensitive. I wasn't about to make a move on you.'

Her eyes were prickling with the sudden heat of tears and she held them wide to hold the tears back. 'I know, but I still need my own space for a while,' she said tightly.

Cristo searched the pale, unhappy tightness of her lovely face and compressed his stubborn mouth, knowing without even thinking about it that he didn't want her away from him and, even worse, had a disturbing desire to keep her close. 'I'd prefer you to stay with me.'

Mere minutes later, having won that last battle, Belle settled heavy as a stone into the comfortable bed in the room next door and lowered her lashes on her damp eyes. She had wanted to be with him but had angrily denied herself that choice because common sense had told her it would be wrong. Wrong to let Cristo think he could do and say as he liked without consequences, wrong to let him hurt her and then put a brave face on it to the extent that he would think he might as well do it again. *Blackmailer, gold-digger, social climber?* Was it even possible for her to disprove such suspicions? And should she even want to? Did it really matter? After all, theirs was a marriage of convenience and she simply had to learn to keep a better hold on her emotions and stop looking for responses she was unlikely to receive. She couldn't afford to start caring about a male who didn't care about her but, regardless of every other factor, she was utterly determined that, at the very least, Cristo would give her respect.

Cristo lay sleepless in bed and expelled a groan. He knew Belle was treating him just as she treated Franco with the 'no means no' approach and the withdrawal of privileges until better behaviour was established. In the darkness he suddenly surprised himself when amusement surged over him and he laughed out loud. She had thrown him a challenge. No woman had ever done that to Cristo before and it bothered him to appreciate that he actually admired her nerve.

The next morning, Cristo wakened when something bounced hard on the bed and his eyes flew wide on the dawn light piercing the curtains.

'Kiss-do!' Franco carolled from below his mop of black curls and looked down expectantly at him. *'Belle?'*

'Belle's asleep,' Cristo responded, anchoring the sheet more firmly round his naked length as Franco threw his small solid body at him. 'Bekfast?' Franco asked hopefully, leaning over him with wide eyes.

Wondering where the nanny was, Cristo promised breakfast and Franco beamed. Indeed, Cristo was startled when his little brother wound his arms round his neck and bestowed a soggy kiss on him. The toddler accompanied him into the en suite, chattering endlessly but using few recognisable words. Cristo showered and shaved while Franco played with the contents of the drawers and cupboards and made an unholy mess. While he got dressed, Franco played under the bed with, 'Bekfast, Kiss-do?' a constant refrain to the activity.

Franco closed his hand into Cristo's as they left the bedroom and the flustered nanny appeared several doors further down the corridor.

'I'm so sorry, Mr Ravelli. I've been looking everywhere for him. He disappeared while I was in the bathroom,' Teresa confided.

'Relax, I'll ensure he gets breakfast.'

'Bekfast,' Franco repeated urgently, swinging on Cristo's hand and skipping with excitement. There was a definite charm to the child's open-hearted affection and liveliness, Cristo conceded reluctantly.

In the dining room, Umberto provided an ancient wooden high chair for Franco's use and Cristo advised the manservant to see that a new one was purchased with a safety harness because he was already aware that Franco was an escape artist and guilty of frequently climbing out of his cot. Whatever Cristo ate, Franco wanted to eat and Cristo was quietly appalled at the mess the child made. When he threw a piece of tomato, Cristo told him off and Franco burst into floods of tears, which had to be the exact moment when Belle entered the room.

'Oh, my goodness, I didn't know he was with you!' Belle gasped in dismay.

'He's a very determined little character,' Cristo remarked above the racket Franco was making. 'I told him off for throwing food.'

'No hug, then,' Belle ruled as Franco held out his arms to be comforted. 'You know you're not allowed to throw food.'

Franco sulked when his complaints were ignored and finally started eating again.

Belle grinned across the table at Cristo. 'Thanks for looking after him.'

The natural glory of her smile took his breath away and his dark eyes narrowed appreciatively. It was first thing in the morning and as far as he could tell she wasn't wearing much make-up but she still looked amazing, her translucent china skin flushed and freckled, green eyes bright, her mane of hair coiling round her slim shoulders with a life all of its own in every bouncy corkscrew curl of auburn. 'He's my brother as well,' Cristo murmured wryly. 'And quite a handful.'

'Yes, he is…far too much for Isa to cope with at this age.' Pleased by that long-awaited concession that Franco was *his* brother too, Belle stared at Cristo, trying to stop herself from doing it but quite unable to resist the temptation. Her gaze traced the line of his high-cut cheekbones, perfectly straight nose and wide shapely mouth. The perfect features of a dark fallen angel, which got to her every time. A rush of heat tightened her nipples and surged low in her pelvis in a betrayal she could not squash. She still found him irresistibly attractive, she conceded ruefully.

The thwack-thwack of noisy helicopter rotor blades somewhere nearby made Cristo frown and spring upright to stride over to the window. Still munching her toast, Belle followed suit. 'What is it?'

'I think you're about to make the acquaintance of one of my brothers,' Cristo murmured tautly. 'Nik. Make allowances for him if he's short with you. He's going through a tough divorce and it's unsettled him.'

'I'll just make myself scarce while you catch up with him,' Belle offered, hastily lifting Franco out of the elderly high chair.

'No, he should meet you now that he's here, *gioia mia*,' Cristo overruled without hesitation. 'You're my wife. I'm not ashamed of you, nor am I going to hide you.'

CHAPTER SEVEN

CRISTO STRODE OUTSIDE to greet his brother, Nik. The two men stopped on the terrace to talk. Belle hovered, hearing an animated exchange between the men in a foreign language. It didn't sound like Italian and she wondered if it could be Greek. When she heard the other man expostulate loudly several times she guessed that Cristo was telling him about her mother and the children and she winced uncomfortably, feeling agonisingly self-conscious.

Nik Christakis was a big man, even taller than her bridegroom, but he did bear a strong resemblance to Cristo. Nik frowned across the room at her and his frown only darkened more when he saw the young child standing by her side.

'My wife, Belle, and our youngest little brother, Franco,' Cristo imparted in calm explanation in response to his brother's interrogative look. 'My brother, Nik.'

'*Our?*' Nik queried straight away. 'The child's nothing to do with me. Five of them? You would have to be crazy to take that on, Cristo! Gaetano's dead and buried. What does it matter what comes out about him now?'

'It would matter to Zarif,' Cristo countered squarely.

'Like I care about that!' Nik quipped darkly, digging into an inside pocket on his jacket to extract a document, which he extended to his brother. 'Read it and weep. Learn what happens when you get married without a pre-nup.'

'We didn't have a pre-nup,' Belle remarked awkwardly, uneasy with the tension flowing around them, and Nik's reluctance to even acknowledge her, never mind make polite conversation.

Cristo raised his dark gaze slowly from the document to say, 'I have to admit that I'm surprised.'

'Are you? Are you still that naïve? Obviously Betsy married me for my money and now she's trying to steal half of everything I own!' Nik declared with raw, unconcealed bitterness.

'She *didn't* marry you for your money,' Cristo contradicted with quiet assurance. 'She fell in love with you.'

'Don't be naïve. I give you and your wife and her little bunch of Ravelli by-blows two years at most before she walks out and tries to take the shirt off your back!' Nik vented with ringing derision.

Belle flushed and lifted her chin. 'I wouldn't do that. Look, I'll leave you two to talk in private,' she completed, anchoring Franco's hand in her own.

As she left she heard Nik Christakis cursing, something that was instantly recognisable in many languages. She realised that she was very grateful not to be married to a man like that. Nik's hard-featured face, cold eyes, not to mention the smouldering bitterness that escaped every time he mentioned his estranged wife, Betsy, chilled Belle to the marrow. Nik was clearly tough, obstinate, furiously hostile and, she suspected, the sort of man who would make an implacable enemy, a man who saw only the worst in anyone who crossed him.

Cristo, she reasoned, was more reasonable, more civilised…wasn't he? She respected him for speaking up in defence of his sister-in-law. Furthermore the night before she had been surprised and reluctantly impressed when Cristo had suggested that complete honesty between them might well be the way to make their marriage work. That was a rational and mature attitude to take, she acknowledged thoughtfully. She liked and respected honesty, hated the lies and persuasive pretences that Gaetano had shamelessly employed to keep her mother content and make his own life smoother.

Two hours later, after Nik had finally departed and a second helicopter had flown in and deposited its colourful cargo, Cristo went off in search of Belle and found her sitting in the shade of a tree clutching a book. 'You own a massive library of books,' she complained as she heard his approach and lifted her head, auburn hair gleaming rich as silk in the shadowy light below the overhanging foliage, 'but I could only find a couple written in English.'

Cristo swiped the hardback from between her fingers and studied the spine. It was a heavy-duty tome on the history of his mother's family, written by one of his ancestors and translated by a more recent one. 'I'll order some English books for you. I'd suggest that you start learning Italian but it would hardly be worth your while.'

Her bone structure tightened, tension leaping

through her as she absorbed that reminder that their relationship was of a strictly temporary nature. Images of his passionate lovemaking the night before swam up through her mind and killed every sensible thought stone dead, making concentration impossible while sending a wave of unwelcome heat travelling through her slender length. Her face hot, she studied the book fixedly as he returned it to her with an elegant gesture of one long-fingered hand. Last night those hands had touched her with breathtakingly erotic expertise and had extracted more pleasure from her weak body than she had known it was capable of experiencing. His complete poise in the aftermath of their passionate argument the night before, however, set her teeth firmly on edge. Evidently, as far as he was concerned, everything was done and dusted but Belle still felt as though her reactions, emotions and even her thoughts were whirling around in a maelstrom and out of her control.

'Were you looking for me?' she asked curiously.

'Yes, *cara*. It's time for you to enjoy your wedding present.'

'Wedding present?' Belle parroted as she rose slowly to her feet in discomfiture. 'What on earth are you talking about?'

'Wedding presents go with the territory of getting married,' Cristo fielded smoothly, a lean hand settling to the base of her spine to steer her back in the direction of the villa.

'But not between us, not in *our* sort of marriage,' she parried with spirit.

'I promised to treat you as my wife and that is what I am trying to do.'

'So…' Belle murmured tightly in the echoing hall. 'This present…?'

'It's waiting for you in the ballroom,' Cristo informed her, nodding to Umberto to open the double doors.

Belle crossed the hall slowly, peering into the vast room to focus in astonishment on the catwalk now dissecting it. 'My goodness, what the heck—?' she began in confusion.

'Every woman wants a new wardrobe. I arranged to have a selection flown in along with the models to show the clothing off. All you have to do is choose what you want to wear.'

Every woman wants a new wardrobe? Most social climbing, gold-digging women would certainly fall into that category, Belle reflected with a helpless little moue of distaste that he should have assumed that she was that sort of a woman. But he hadn't given her a choice. This was what Cristo thought she wanted and, it seemed, he was happy to deliver on that score and it would be needlessly confrontational for her to deny him the opportunity. One step into the ballroom she was introduced to Olivia, who whisked a tape measure over her with startling speed and efficiency and announced that any garments she selected would be delivered sized to fit by lunchtime the next day.

Funky music kicked off in the background as Olivia took one of three comfortable seats awaiting them while urging Belle to define what Olivia described as 'her personal style'. Belle had to hinge her jaw closed at the question because she had no idea how to answer it. In any case Olivia had already embarked on a commentary on the first outfit while a brunette model wearing something floaty, purple and weirdly shaped like a lampshade strolled down the catwalk towards them. As a very tall blonde with a shock of almost-white chopped hair appeared in swimwear Olivia endeavoured to determine Belle's fashion preferences. But Belle had never had the budget to develop a taste for luxury. As a student, she had worn jeans in winter and shorts in summer with only the occasional cheap skirt or dress purchased for nights out. Money had always been in short supply in her life, clothing generally purchased from her part-time earnings as a bartender, and she had only ever shopped in chain stores.

'Don't you like any of it?' Cristo prompted, shooting his bride a questioning glance from his brooding dark eyes when she remained awkwardly silent.

As she connected with his stunning eyes her heart flipped inside her chest and turned a somersault. 'It's a bit overwhelming...all this,' she admitted breathlessly.

'Then I'll choose for you.'

And *what* Cristo chose was highly informative and Belle almost burst out laughing, for without fail every short skirt, backless gown and low neckline received Cristo's unqualified and enthusiastic vote of approval. On that score he was very predictable, very male and reassuringly human. Amused by the very basic male he was revealing beneath the sophisticated façade, Belle began to regain her confidence and started to quietly voice opinions, shying away from the more spectacular garments in favour of the plainer ones, insisting that she couldn't possibly wear shocking pink with her hair.

'I like pink,' Cristo argued without hesitation. Though as Olivia took up the conversation he sud-

denly remembered his feelings of horror at the many
shades of pink spun throughout the small home back
in Ireland. But his *wife* in pink…that was a different matter.

'There are only certain shades of pink which you
should avoid,' Olivia, ever the highly accomplished
saleswoman, assured her.

At that point the blonde appeared in a ravishing
set of ruffled turquoise lingerie and Cristo sprang upright and actually approached the catwalk. 'I want
that,' he spelt out without an ounce of discomfiture
in his bearing.

Belle's cheeks flamed while she noted the manner
in which the very leggy blonde was posing for Cristo
like a stripper, loving the attention as her breasts jig-
gled in the bra with her little dance movements, and
she spun round to display her almost bare bottom taut
in panties that were little more than a thong. Cristo
seemed mesmerised by the spectacle, his dark golden
eyes veiled, his sinfully seductive bronzed features
taut as if he was struggling to conceal his thoughts.

He was attracted to the blonde, Belle decided with
a sinking sick sensation in the pit of her stomach, and
he couldn't hide the fact.

'Thank you, Sofia,' the saleswoman said loudly as
she stood up and the music stopped mid-note, leaving a sudden uncomfortable silence in its wake. Olivia
said her goodbyes and took her leave through the rear
door of the ballroom.

'Well, wasn't that educational?' Belle remarked freez-
ingly when Cristo finally wandered back to her side.

His winged ebony brows drew together in bewilderment. 'How so?'

Her generous mouth compressed. 'You fancied the blonde,' she told him bluntly.

Cristo frowned.

'Oh, don't bother denying it. I saw you,' Belle told him thinly. 'You couldn't take your eyes off her!'

Cristo moved steadily closer in a slow stalking movement that was quite ridiculously sensual. Belle looked up at him, fearless in her condemnation, and collided with smouldering golden eyes so intense in focus that she was rocked back on her heels. All the oxygen in the atmosphere seemed to have dried up and she parted her lips to snatch in air.

'I have only one point to make. It wasn't her I was seeing...it was *you*,' he spelt out hoarsely, his brilliant eyes pinned to her with mesmerising force. 'It was *you* I was picturing in that get-up.'

Disbelief assailed Belle and she flicked him a scornful upward glance of dismissal. 'Like I'm going to believe that with a half-naked beauty cavorting in front of you!' she derided.

'*Believe*...' Cristo urged in a roughened undertone that vibrated with assurance in the stillness. 'When I've got a real woman like you, why would I want one with fewer curves than a coat hanger?'

Her mouth fell wide at that less than flattering description of the beautiful model. 'Not your type?'

'You're my type,' Cristo confided huskily. 'The erotic image of you bountifully filling those little blue scraps of nothing turns me on fast and hard.'

A *real* woman? Belle almost laughed out loud at that label. After all, the rigorous dieting she had tried in her teen years had failed to hone an inch off the solid bone structure that gave her defiantly curvaceous hips and voluptuous breasts. Back then she would have given her right arm to be one of the more fashionable 'skinny-minnies' at school. But she was not fool enough as an adult to instantly dismiss the idea that some men actually preferred curves to more slender proportions. It simply hadn't entered her head before that Cristo might be one of those men.

He brushed a straying curl from her cheek and tucked it behind her ear with a casual intimacy that unnerved her. It said that he had the right to touch her, a right she had already denied him. An alarm bell shrieked in her brain, warning her to back off and enforce her boundaries yet again. But he was close, *so* temptingly close that she could smell the evocative scent of cologne and masculine musk that he emanated. He smelt so unbelievably good to her that her senses swam and she felt light-headed. Her knees wobbled beneath her while warmth snaked down from the breasts straining below her camisole to the very core of her, leaving her feeling hot and achy and dissatisfied. Even staying still in that condition was a challenge.

He touched her face, a long tanned forefinger gently tracing the line of her jaw to the cupid's bow above her upper lip while a thumb stroked the soft fullness of her lower lip. Belle trembled, scarcely able to breathe for the rush of excitement that had come out of nowhere at her. Her body raced up the scale in reaction, temperature rising, heart pounding, pulse hammering. Her lashes lowered to a languorous half-mast as she gazed up at him in helpless silence, for she had no words to describe what he was doing to her. He was so beautiful, so devastatingly beautiful that she hadn't even

blamed the models for concentrating their attention on
him while they displayed their wares. Not only was he
the buyer, but also a male so handsome that he made
women stare while they struggled to comprehend what
it was about those lean, darkly dazzling features that
exercised such sinful power and magnetism over their
sex. Belle didn't know; she only knew that the minute
she stopped looking at him, she *needed* to look again.
It was a compulsion she couldn't fight.

'You can put on that blue set just for me,' Cristo
murmured hungrily, stunning dark eyes flaring wicked
gold at that prospect.

'In your dreams,' Belle warned him without hesitation, thinking he would wait a very long time if he
hoped to see her tricked out in provocative underwear
for his benefit. Playing the temptress wasn't her style
and in her opinion he didn't need the encouragement.
That conviction in mind, she walked into the drawing room, where at least their conversation would be
unheard by the staff.

'Don't tell me that you don't have the same dream,'
Cristo chided, shifting in front of her to clamp his lean
hands possessively to her hips.

Belle was about to hit him, push him away, stamp
on his foot, loudly lodge a protest to physical contact
of any kind. She really was going to do at least one of
those things and then his mouth plunged down hungrily on hers and her hands spread against the hard,
warm contours of his chest and slowly fisted into the
fabric of his shirt as she fought herself and fought the
craving he induced.

In that split second between her thinking and acting, his tongue snaked into her mouth to taste her and

she was lost while he nipped and teased at her lips and delved deep. The hot, throbbing sensation between her legs rose in intensity until she was rocking her hips against his, wanting more, *needing* more with an urgency that unnerved her. She could feel the long, hard ridge of his arousal against her belly and their clothes were an obstruction she couldn't bear, overwhelming physical hunger surging through her quivering body with a force she couldn't withstand.

Cristo lifted his handsome head, eyes hot and bright with sexual heat, black hair tousled by the fingers she had dug into the luxuriant strands, an edge of colour accentuating his hard cheekbones. 'Shall we take this upstairs?' he murmured thickly.

No was on Belle's lips but yes was in her heart because her body was drenched with treacherous longing for his. She took in a slow steadying breath and struggled to clear her head, fighting the wanting clawing at her with all her strength.

'I want you…you want me, *cara,*' Cristo said drily. 'What's the problem? Are you still suspicious about that model? Do you really think I'd be that crass?'

'No,' Belle conceded reluctantly, for she would have used that as an excuse had she been able to do so. Unfortunately, her brain was in free fall. He had spoken the truth: the attraction between them was explosive. Furthermore, had he not been strongly attracted to her in the first place, he probably wouldn't have offered her marriage. Even so the bond that was being created between them solely on a physical level was too superficial for her to accept and she wanted more.

Cristo elevated a sleek black brow. '*Then?* Are you still judging me as if I'm my late father?' he demanded impatiently. 'Or is it something in your own past which makes you so suspicious of men?'

Belle stiffened. 'I don't know what you're talking about—'

'I think you do. You watched Gaetano run rings round your mother and hated him for it,' Cristo contended. 'But I'm *not* him.'

Belle bridled and gritted her teeth. 'I know that and I didn't say you were.'

'Why else would you accuse me of coming on to that model right in front of you?' Cristo slung back, tension etched along the hard line of his cheekbones and the angle of his strong jawline. 'What sort of a man would behave like that?'

'I overreacted. I'm sorry.' Belle turned her vibrant head away, guilt and mortification piercing her. There was a certain amount of truth to his condemnation. She did distrust men but not *all* men. During her years at university she had been hurt by boyfriends who were offended by her refusal to get straight into bed with them before she even got to know them. The same boys had deceived her with other girls and let her down but no more so than any of her friends, who had suffered similar wake-up calls from young men who wanted nothing more lasting from a woman than physical release.

'If you want this marriage to work, this isn't the way to go about it,' Cristo delivered in a measured undertone.

'You said honesty was the best policy,' Belle reminded him, walking away a few steps and then turning back to face him, her lovely face flushed and tense. 'Then I'll *be* honest. For this to work for me, I want something more than just sex with you. I want us to get to know each other. You can't build a relationship purely on sex.'

'I've never known anything else,' Cristo growled.

'Do you have any female friends?'

When he nodded with a faint frown, Belle smiled. 'Well, then, you have known something else.'

'Why didn't you make these demands *before* you married me?' Cristo derided.

'I didn't think it through until now,' Belle confided truthfully. 'I was desperate to make the children secure and marrying you was the price. I didn't think beyond that. I didn't think about how I would *feel...*'

Marrying you was the price. Not a statement he had expected to hear from Belle, not one he was even sure he could believe, Cristo mused grimly, dark eyes shielded by his lush lashes. She wanted more. Why did women always want more than was on offer? Were they programmed to want more at birth? All this and five children too, he reflected heavily—had he really thought about what he was doing either?

The forbidding look tensing his lean, dark features stirred Belle's conscience. 'I realise this is coming out of nowhere at you and you have a right to be irritated.'

'That's not quite the word I would've chosen,' Cristo countered curtly.

Belle steeled herself to be more honest than she really wanted to be. 'I *did* have thoughts I shouldn't have had when I agreed to marry you,' she admitted gruffly, her pale skin suddenly blossoming with mortified colour. 'But none of those thoughts related to personal enrichment or social advancement.' Feeling more uncomfortable than ever, she hesitated. 'Although I wouldn't go as far as to say that I had thoughts of getting revenge for what Gaetano put my family through over the years, I certainly had an inappropriate sense of satisfaction when you offered to marry me and I quite deliberately wore my mother's wedding dress to get married in. I'm ashamed of those feelings now. After all, it was very unfair that you should have to pay in any way for your father's mistakes. But then we're both doing that now,' she completed ruefully.

Cristo was violently disconcerted by her complete honesty. He hadn't expected that, hadn't been prepared for her to admit any reactions that might reflect badly on her motivation in marrying him. Getting a rich and powerful Ravelli to the altar had briefly thrilled her but she had owned up to it and that impressed a male who was rarely impressed by the women he met.

'*La via dell'inferno è lastricata di buone intenzione*…the road to hell is paved with good intentions,' Cristo translated sibilantly. 'Do you ever do anything for the sheer hell of it?'

'No.' Belle stiffened as she made that admission. 'And it doesn't have to be hell,' she pointed out uncomfortably. 'We can make the best of the situation. You said you wanted to treat me like a proper wife, wanted to show me respect…'

The reminder hung there like a dark cloud between them, with Cristo finally registering that his partiality for that lingerie set had evidently caused offence. Last night he had become her first lover and she had been *amazing*, he recalled, arousal slivering through him at even the memory. He was expecting too much too soon and he gritted his perfect white teeth together. 'I'll try harder,' he told her in a driven undertone.

'I'll try too,' Belle responded with a tentative smile.

But it was too late because Cristo had already turned away and could not have seen her smile, which had combined both regret at her inability to be the purely sexual object he so clearly wanted her to be and her hope for a better understanding between them in the future. Spirits low, she went upstairs to find her little brother and give Teresa a break. Franco's warm affection and trusting acceptance that he would be loved back were wonderfully soothing to her troubled state of mind. She played hide and seek with the little boy and the upper floor rang with laughter and thudding feet.

Umberto paused in Cristo's office doorway to say warmly, 'It is a joy to hear a child playing here again.'

'There's another four of them—a boy and a girl of eight and a pair of teenagers,' Cristo confided, for he had known the kindly manservant since he was a child.

'Your late father's children?' Umberto prompted.

Cristo's brows drew together. 'How did you know?'

'I heard rumours over the years. My cousin flew Mr Gaetano's helicopter right up until his retirement,' the older man reminded him gently.

'Let's hope the rumours stay buried,' Cristo commented wryly.

'No one in my family will gossip,' the older man assured him with pride. 'But Mr Gaetano had other staff who may not be so discreet.'

A current of uneasiness assailed Cristo, who had ensured that his father's surviving employees were paid off with adequate remuneration for their years of service. Was it possible he had got married for no good reason? And inexplicably, at that point, he thought of

Franco, who demonstrated such a desperate need for
male attention. Franco definitely needed a father figure, Cristo reflected, his stern mouth softening as the
toddler's gales of laughter echoed down from above.

'No…no…*no*, Franco!' Belle gasped in dismay
when she found her little brother picking in delight
through the collection of items lying on the dressing
table in Cristo's bedroom. 'Don't touch those.'

Jingling the car keys still in his hand, Franco
dropped the wallet he had been investigating and it
fell to the floor. Belle knelt down to gather up the
banknotes that Franco had crumpled, smoothing them
out before returning them to the wallet along with
credit cards, a couple of business cards and…a tiny
photograph. Belle lifted the photo and stared down at
it in surprise, recognising Nik Christakis's estranged
wife, Betsy. She was a little blonde sprite of a beauty
with delicate features and big blue eyes. Her brow furrowed. Had the photo fallen out of the wallet or had it
just been lying there forgotten on the floor? The rug
beneath her knees, however, bore the ruffled evidence
of recent vacuuming. So, assuming the photo *had* been
inside Cristo's wallet, why was her husband carrying
round a photo of his brother's wife?

And was she even going to ask him why? Belle
came out in a cold sweat at the very prospect of so
embarrassing a conversation. After her misjudgement
of his behaviour with the model, he would never believe that she had accidentally seen the photograph.
He would think she had been snooping in his wallet
and he would naturally assume that she was one of
those madly jealous, distrustful women, who would
always be scheming to check his cell-phone messages

and his pockets for evidence of infidelity. Cringing at that likelihood, Belle slotted the photo back into his wallet and returned it circumspectly to the dressing table. No, she wasn't about to ask him any more awkward questions.

Matters were tense enough between them. And yet so many important things hinged on the success of their marriage, she thought wretchedly. If she and Cristo couldn't make a go of it, what would happen to her siblings? She had made promises, not least those in the chapel, which she had to, at least, *try* to keep. Unless she was prepared to let Cristo go free, she had to make more of an effort.

But please, no, she prayed, let not the only avenue to success demand the sporting of saucy underwear....

CHAPTER EIGHT

BELLE SAT ALONE at the breakfast table out on the terrace, which overlooked the glorious gardens and, beyond them, the beautiful panorama of the idyllic Umbrian landscape, and decided that nobody would ever credit how miserable and insecure she was. Here she was, all dressed up in gorgeous surroundings, married to an even more gorgeous man and already she had made a mess of things! Although, to be fair, expecting her to be willing to put on provocative lingerie for his benefit had scarcely been calculated to soothe her misgivings.

Do you ever do anything for the sheer hell of it? Cristo had asked. And the truthful answer would have been, no, *never*. So, how on earth had she managed to leap into marrying Cristo without fully considering what she was doing? She still couldn't answer that question to her own satisfaction. Had her treacherous attraction to him destroyed every single one of her brain cells? Why hadn't she listened to her grandmother's warnings? After all, nobody knew better than Belle that relationships between men and women were often difficult and prone to unhappiness.

Her mother's over-hasty marriage at a young age to

Belle's drunken father followed by Mary's long affair with Gaetano Ravelli had taught Belle to be very cautious and sensible and to carefully reason out every move she made in advance with men, *except* when it came to the opportunity to marry Cristo when she had—inexplicably to her—jumped right in with both feet. And her current wary attitude to intimacy was creating friction with Cristo. Could she blame him for his outlook?

What, after all, had Cristo *gained* from their marriage? Her silence, no court case and five pretty needy children he had promised to adopt into the Ravelli family. Her tense mouth down-curved on the discouraging suspicion that he had sacrificed much more than she had and that few people would feel sorry for her having given up her freedom to work and instead live in the lap of luxury with her fancy designer wardrobe. That thought made her eyes sting fiercely with tears because she had very little interest in the luxury and the vast selection of new clothes that had been delivered in garment bags to her room before she even got out of bed. In fact, she had only donned one of the outfits, a silky top and skirt, because she hadn't wanted Cristo to think that she was ungrateful for the gesture he had made.

But unfortunately, Cristo wasn't even around to notice what she was wearing. That was the problem of separate bedrooms in a massive house and two people who didn't know each other's habits very well, Belle reflected wretchedly. Cristo had been absent at dinner the night before and now he was absent again. Was he avoiding her? Fed up with her immature outlook? It seemed pretty obvious to her that she was getting absolutely everything in their marriage wrong, and to achieve that at such an early stage suggested that she had cherished completely unreasonable expectations of what being married to Cristo would entail. He had assumed she was a gold-digger and, having brooded over that accusation, she wasn't sure she could blame him for his cynicism. After all, he didn't know her and possibly connecting on a physical level was the only way Cristo knew *how* to get to know a woman, so her coming over all prudish and standoffish because he had hurt her feelings wasn't helping the situation…

And worst of all, Belle knew she couldn't even phone her grandmother. Isa Kelly's sensible advice would have been very welcome even though Belle could not have brought herself to mention the bedroom side of things to the older woman. Indeed even the sound of Isa's voice and those of her siblings would have been a comfort. Belle was horribly homesick and missed the family dog, Tag, almost as much. But Belle knew that if she phoned home within days of the wedding her grandmother would be astute enough to suspect that things weren't working out and it would be very, very selfish to lay yet another worry on her grandmother's already overburdened shoulders.

Disgusted at her self-pitying mood and lack of activity, Belle suddenly pushed her chair back and stood up. Sitting here feeling sorry for herself and agonising over her possible mistakes wasn't *fixing* anything, was it? It was time to go and find Cristo.

Questioned, Umberto smiled and indicated a door at the foot of a short corridor off the main hall. 'Mr Cristo has been working round the clock in his office since news of the banking crisis broke…'

What banking crisis? Belle had not seen a television or a newspaper since the morning of her wedding. She had noticed that the nanny, Teresa, had a TV in her room but had drawn a blank when she looked for access to one for her own benefit. Perspiration breaking on her brow, she knocked on the door of Cristo's office and then opened it.

Dark eyes flying up from his laptop screen, Cristo swung round in his chair. Belle's appearance shocked him on two levels. *Dio mio,* he had a wife and he had forgotten about her, and then his next thought was that forgetting about her should have been impossible when she was such a beauty, standing in the doorway, a slender, wonderfully leggy figure taut with uncertainty in a peach-coloured top and skirt that toned in perfectly with her torrent of vibrant spiral curls. Wide grass-green eyes assailed his.

'I wondered where you were,' she said awkwardly, transfixed as she always was at first glimpse of his tousled dark head, perfect bronze profile and striking eyes. The fact he hadn't shaved merely added a raw-edged masculinity to his charismatic appeal and she could feel her face warming up, her tummy flipping, her heart rate skipping upbeat: all standard reactions to Cristo. 'Then Umberto mentioned a banking crisis of some kind. I'm afraid I haven't seen a newspaper since I arrived and I didn't know about it. Do you need any help?'

'Help?' Cristo queried, ebony brows rising in surprise. 'How could you help?'

'I have a first-class degree in business and economics and I worked as an intern for a year in a Dublin bank as part of the course,' Belle confided hesitantly.

A line of colour flared across Cristo's cheekbones as it crossed his mind that he should've known such elementary facts about the woman he had married, and rare discomfiture sliced through him. 'I had no idea.'

Her eyes sparkling with genuine amusement, an involuntary grin slanted Belle's wide and generous mouth. 'So, you just assumed you were marrying an uneducated Irish peasant, did you?'

'If you're willing to help, I'd be grateful, *bella mia,*' Cristo admitted, smoothly, gratefully ducking that issue entirely. 'I'm trying to work with my London staff remotely and it's complicated but this is supposed to be our honeymoon.'

'I've got nothing else to do,' Belle pointed out gently, convinced that a couple of their ilk scarcely qualified for the itinerary or the behaviour of a normal honeymoon couple.

Cristo immediately recognised yet another screaming indictment of his behaviour as a new husband and hurriedly sidestepped that awareness by offering Belle the laptop beside his own and springing upright to ask Umberto to go and find another chair. His conscience reacted as though someone had given it a good hard kick. Marriage, he was learning by slow and painful steps, would demand much more of him than he had imagined and would entail considering Belle's needs as well as his own.

For the first time, he appreciated that he had had absolutely no right to judge his brother, Nik, for the mess he had made of his marriage to Betsy. After all, he only knew *one* side of that story and tiny, fragile Betsy weeping out her heartbreak on Cristo's chest had definitely cornered the sympathy vote as far as appearances went. His lip curled as he skimmed a glance across Belle's composed and lovely face and he almost smiled in relief. There was nothing helpless about Belle and at least she wasn't crying hysterically, complaining, condemning...

'Yes, she's amazing,' Cristo agreed in Italian with his chief finance officer in the London branch of his investment bank. 'If I wasn't married to her, I'd hire her!'

Cristo studied his wife with an involuntary sense of pride. Belle was curled up in a chair with a laptop, long incredible legs in shorts on display, auburn hair spiralling down round her shoulders, enhancing porcelain-pale freckled skin while her fingers flew over the keyboard. It was the pivotal moment when he realised that he had struck literal gold and had seriously underestimated her worth when he married her. For a woman of her beauty to have retained qualities of such natural likeability and unpretentiousness was extraordinary. She was also intelligent, resourceful and hardworking. Not once had she complained over the past three days about the very long hours they were putting in and she had kept pace with him every step of the way. He winced when he recalled the lingerie episode at the fashion show.

Belle stood up to stretch and set the laptop down. The banking crisis was over and she was almost disappointed by that reality since it had acted as a brilliantly positive antidote to the friction between them. They could work together now, talk to each other. He had stopped treating her like some sort of glorified sex doll expected to offer him entertainment and she had learned to her own satisfaction that Cristo was as smart as a whip while being as stubborn and impatient as she was.

Her clear gaze wandered over him while he sprawled back against the edge of the desk, long powerful thighs sheathed in denim splayed, a crisp lemon shirt open at his strong tanned throat. She looked at his wide, sensual lips and recalled the passionate intoxication of his kiss and momentarily felt dizzy. Her mouth ran dry, hunger stirring at the core of her as it had so often in recent days when her body reacted to the presence of his. She leant slightly forward, willing him to make a move to hold her, touch her, kiss her...*anything*!

'Put on something fancy. I'm taking you out to dinner, *bella mia*,' Cristo volunteered, glancing up to transfix her with spectacular dark golden eyes heavily fringed with lush black lashes.

Belle flushed to her hairline, mortified by her thoughts and drawn up short by the unexpected invitation. 'Only if you want to.'

'*Dio mio!* Of course I want to,' Cristo countered with a frown.

'You don't need to thank me for helping out,' Belle told him stubbornly.

Cristo expelled his breath in a slow hiss. 'Is it so hard for you to accept that I might want to take my beautiful wife out and show her off?'

Belle laughed at the idea. 'Not when you put it that way, you smoothie!' she teased.

Cristo winced. 'Don't call me that...it makes me think of Gaetano.'

Belle wrinkled her nose in agreement. 'You don't remind me of him in any way.'

'*Grazie a Dio*...thank God,' Cristo retorted with visible relief.

Belle collided with Franco on the way into the office. Her little brother pushed past her to throw himself at Cristo with a shout of satisfaction. Although they had been incredibly busy in recent days, Cristo never turned Franco away and she appreciated that, glancing back as Cristo tickled Franco and engaged in the kind of rough, noisy, masculine play that the toddler adored. While she hovered, Cristo answered the buzz of his cell phone.

At supersonic speed she registered that something bad had happened and she moved back into the office because Cristo's lean, strong face had clenched into rigid lines, his eyes darkening, his mouth compressing as he finished the call in clipped Italian. He released Franco and the little boy scampered off into the hall, already in search of fresh amusement.

Cristo settled dark eyes now flaming accusing gold on Belle and asked harshly, 'Have you been talking to the press?'

Astonishment furrowed her brow. 'No, of course not! What on earth are you talking about?' she parried, instantly cast on the defensive.

'A friend who's a journalist in London just called me to warn me that the story of Gaetano, your mother and the kids will be appearing in print some time soon in a British tabloid!' Cristo bit out furiously.

Belle paled at that news but rallied fast because her own conscience was clear. 'Well, that's very unfortunate.'

Cristo sprang upright, six feet plus inches of enraged, darkly powerful masculinity. '*Unfortunate?* Is that all you think this is?'

Infuriated by his attitude and wounded by the speed with which he had leapt to distrust, Belle squared her slight shoulders against the wall, her lovely face flushed and taut with strain. 'Keep this in proportion, Cristo, and try to be reasonable.'

'*Reasonable?*' he growled as if he didn't recognise the word. 'I married you to keep that sleazy story out of the newspapers!'

And just then, Belle could have done without the reminder of that fact.

'I always thought it was unlikely that you could prevent that story from *ever* coming out,' she admitted reluctantly. 'My mum was with your father for almost twenty years and everyone for miles around, who enjoyed a bit of gossip, knew about their relationship and the children. All it would have taken was for *one* person to talk to the wrong person, who saw some chance of profit in the information and the secret would have emerged.'

Lean tanned hands clenching into fists by his side, Cristo jerked his arrogant dark head in grudging acknowledgement of that possibility, his innate intelligence warring with his equally natural aggressive instincts to persuade him that she was talking sense.

Belle prowled forward like a stalking tigress and flicked his shirtfront with an angry finger. 'But how dare you even *think* that it might have been me who leaked the story to the press?' she launched at him, green eyes bright with indignation. 'I wouldn't do that to my brothers and sisters. They've already paid a high enough price for the sins of their parents and the very last thing I would ever want to do is upset them more!'

'I didn't accuse you.'

'You *asked* me if I had been talking to the press. What sort of a question was that to ask your wife? What reason would I have to expose all of us to that kind of unpleasant public attention?' Belle demanded.

'Revenge? Gaetano may be dead but you hate his guts and never got the chance to tell him so. In fact I suspect you distrust and dislike anyone called Ravelli!' Cristo slammed back at her in condemnation.

'I've changed.' Yet Belle wanted so badly to slap him that her palm tingled. Only the knowledge that *before* she met him she had had that attitude burned her deep with shame, for one thing she had learned to appreciate since then was that Gaetano's hedonistic lifestyle had damaged almost every life he touched, not least those of the children he had fathered without parenting. 'Well, then I'd have a real problem with my identity, wouldn't I?' she fired back with ringing disdain. 'Considering that now I'm a Ravelli too.'

'*Sì,* and my wife, *cara mia.*' Cristo found himself suddenly savouring that reality as he looked at her, aggression switching into another similarly testosterone-driven reaction, his attention surging from her beautiful defiant face down to her heaving breasts shimmying below the light tee she wore, arousal roaring through him like an engine revving up.

'But not so happy to be your wife right now!' Belle hissed a split second before Cristo cornered her by the wall, closing an ensnaring hand into her tumbling curls to tip up her mouth and then silencing any objection she might have made with the heat of his own.

Belle pushed against his chest but it was, at most, a half-hearted protest because, as fired up by emotion as she was, she couldn't fight the overwhelming rush of sexual hunger that assailed her the instant Cristo touched her. His kisses were ravenous, both of his hands fisted in her hair, his lean, powerful body pinning her to the wall while his tongue teased and delved inside her mouth with ravishing force. A moan was wrenched from her lips as he squeezed the straining bud of one tender nipple through her clothing and the sensation ran like dynamite to the aching heart of her. She felt frantic, possessed, needy way beyond anything she had ever experienced before.

Belle wrenched at his shirt, struggling with the buttons and then finally yanking in frustration at the barrier between them, so that the buttons flew and the shirt parted and he drew back for an instant. She was shocked by what she had done, her colour high but, regardless, she succumbed to the overpowering desire to mould her palms to the hard planes of his hair-roughened chest and feel the wild heat and strength of his very masculine body.

'I've never wanted any woman as much as I want you,' Cristo bit out, taking a long stride away from her to slam the door shut, turn the lock and stalk back to her with clear devastating intent in his devouring gaze.

And Belle had never known what hunger felt like until she met him and, even though she was shaken by her own primitive urges, her passionate desire was stoked higher by the boldly visible erection he sported below his chinos. 'Take off the shirt,' she told him.

'Getting bossy now?' Cristo quipped as he dropped it on the floor.

'Oh, you have no idea,' she murmured, relishing the sight of his powerfully muscled chest and impressive abs, helpless anticipation lancing through her as she curled her fingers into his belt and hauled him back to her.

At that point, Cristo flung back his handsome dark head and laughed, lowering his head to kiss her again in the midst of lifting her silk top up and up and finally, somewhat clumsily for a man of his sophistication, off over her head. She was not wearing a bra and he shaped the firm full globes he had revealed with reverent hands, thumbs and fingers stroking over the swollen tips. 'I *love* your curves,' he confided with husky emphasis, skating his palms down admiringly over the sloping softness of her hips before his hand slid below the skirt and ran unerringly up the hot skin of her inner thigh. Lost in the grip of urgent need, she angled away from the wall towards him, wanting, inviting, and truly *needing* his touch.

Her eyes slid shut as he teased the swollen hot flesh already damp with desire at the heart of her and, with a little sound of impatience, he knelt down to dispose of her panties and lingered to appreciate that most tender part of her with his tongue and his sensually skilled mouth.

'Cristo!' Belle gasped.

'For the last three nights while you went to your bed and I went to mine, I've been dreaming about doing this,' Cristo confessed with carnal boldness, the low growl of his roughened intonation vibrating down her spine.

He tasted her and savoured her as though she were the finest wine and intoxicating waves of sensation

engulfed Belle until she was trembling and only the
wall and his arm at her hips were keeping her upright
against that seductive onslaught. Only when she literally couldn't take any more of the taunting, delirious
pleasure that he wouldn't allow to progress to its natural conclusion did he sweep her up in his arms and
sit her down on the edge of the desk. Once she was in
position, he stepped between her spread thighs and
crushed her reddened mouth below his again with a
primal insistence that consumed her like an adrenalin
shot injected straight into her veins.

'I didn't see us doing this...*here*,' Belle muttered
shakily.

'I don't know how I kept my hands off you the last
few days, *bellezza mia*,' Cristo confided hoarsely, nuzzling his cheek down the extended length of her throat
with a deeply expressive masculine groan of agreement. 'I didn't want to rock the boat.'

'Rock it!' Belle urged him on breathlessly as he
began to push inside her, her inner walls initially protesting the unflinching demand of his entrance and
then slowly stretching around him with a delicious
sensation of fullness that made her moan in elated
response.

His hands firm on her hips, Cristo tipped her back
and then he drove home to the hilt with a power and
immediacy that was even more thrilling for her highly
aroused body. He pulled back and then slammed home
again, jolting her with an excitement that ran like a
river of fire through every erogenous zone she possessed. Her heart was racing, her entire body straining and pleading for the ultimate climax while he
increased the speed of his strokes, driving faster,

deeper while the frenzy of her need and exhilaration combined into a wild roller-coaster ride of ever-increasing pleasure. Her body clenched and she convulsed, crying out and quivering as the pleasure burst like shooting fireworks inside her, sending surge after surge of breathtaking ecstasy travelling through her trembling body.

Cristo wasn't quite sure he could stay upright as his own climax engulfed him and he held her close, groaning out loud as he spilled his seed inside her, and the very newness of that sensation sent him back on full alert. '*Che diavolo!*' he exclaimed in consternation, immediately imagining the worst possible scenario. 'I didn't use a condom!'

Taken aback by the sudden admission, Belle blinked uncertainly as he wrapped both arms round her and steadied them both. 'Oh…' she framed against his chest, his heart thundering against her cheek, the musky male scent of his skin wonderfully familiar and extraordinarily soothing to her now.

'I've never ever *not* used one before,' Cristo assured her in a driven undertone. 'You got me so worked up.'

'It's all right,' she mumbled, hiding a smile of satisfaction at the awareness that she could be responsible for exciting him to the extent that he failed to exercise his usual self-discipline. 'I started taking the pill before the wedding, so there shouldn't be any consequences.'

Cristo pictured Franco purely in terms of a consequence and was quite astounded to recognise the tiniest pang of disappointment when she reassured him that there was no risk of such a development. He shook his handsome dark head as if to clear it of such an insane thought, seriously rattled by it and where it might have come from. He had no desire for a child, had never had a desire for one and yet there was something about Franco...

'You're incredible, *bellezza mia*,' he husked, blanking out those unsettling weird reflections in favour of kissing her brow, the tip of her nose and finally her luscious mouth. 'You have a passion and an ability to excite me that most men can only dream about finding with one woman.'

Slowly, carefully he lowered her back down to the floor before helpfully lifting her top to slide over her head and back over her torso. Dazed, she leant back against the desk again, cheeks as hot as coals, eyes screened by her lashes as she absorbed that last statement with pleasure but also because she was shockingly disconcerted by the wildness they had shared and the sheer screaming intimacy of the experience.

A couple of hours later and groomed to within an inch of her life, those tumultuous emotions and sensations carefully tamped down, Belle scrutinised her reflection with a sharply critical gaze. It was a beautiful dress and her youngest sister would have told her that she looked like a princess in it because Lucia, in common with their late mother, adored feminine frills. Pale pink and full length, the gown was bare at the shoulder and moulded to her figure at breast and hip. Did she look just a little *too* busty? She hitched the bodice and then almost laughed, pretty much convinced when she thought about it that Cristo would enjoy the view.

Betsy rang Cristo as he emerged from the shower in his own room next door. He listened as he always did but he felt strangely detached from his sister-in-law and her problems. It occurred to him that he had never lusted after Nik's wife the way he did after his own and he marvelled at that reality, wondering if some internal censor button had somehow prevented it or whether indeed she didn't appeal to him quite that much on that more basic level, which struck him as an extraordinary possibility.

He was *still* listening to Betsy recount the latest hostile moves his brother had made in the divorce battle when Belle came downstairs and his mind went totally blank because Belle looked fantastic and he couldn't think of anything else. He ended the call with an apologetic mutter.

'Who were you talking to?' Belle asked, her attention locked to the unusually distracted expression on his lean dark features.

'Betsy.'

'Nik's wife?'

Cristo struggled not to sound defensive. 'We're friends.'

'That must be awkward,' Belle remarked. 'Were you friends before they got married?'

Cristo tensed, a muscle pulling taut at the corner of his shapely mouth. 'No. It happened because of the way they broke up.'

Like a bloodhound on the trail, Belle was in no mood to settle for less than she wanted to know. 'And why *did* they break up?'

'For very private reasons. But something I let slip when I should have kept quiet and minded my own business contributed to it.' Cristo framed that admission of guilt in a harsh undertone. 'I'm sorry I can't tell you more but I caused a lot of trouble by once care-lessly revealing a secret which Nik had shared with me and...I definitely have lived to regret it.'

Belle wanted to drag the whole truth out of him there and then because all her suspicious antennae were now waking up to full alert. Exactly what did his 'friendship' with Betsy Ravelli entail?

Outside the limousine awaited them. 'Where are we going?' she asked to fill the strained silence, which confirmed for her that there had to be a very good rea-son why Cristo was quite so wary and uncomfortable when it came to discussing his brother's estranged wife. Was she being fanciful in being so suspicious? *Was* his reaction simply the result of his guilty con-viction that he might have contributed to the break-down of the couple's marriage? But if that was true, why did he carry a photo of Betsy in his wallet? That lent an all too personal dimension to the relationship that could only make Belle feel troubled.

'We're going to Assisi. There's a very special restaurant there,' Cristo imparted, relieved she had dropped the touchy subject of Nik's marriage break-down.

'Assisi...as in the birthplace of St Francis?'

Cristo gave her a droll look. 'There is only one.'

'To be actually going there just feels so weird. It was my mother's lifelong dream to visit Assisi. She was a great believer in the power of St Francis,' Belle explained, a certain amount of embarrassment at that unsophisticated admission mingling with the very real sadness that claimed her when something touched on her many memories of the older woman.

'And Gaetano never brought Mary to Italy?' Cristo prompted in surprise.

'Are you kidding? He never took Mum anywhere,' Belle countered between compressed lips of grim recollection. 'Their relationship only existed behind closed doors.'

'And your mother didn't object to that?'

'No and what's more she *still* thought the sun rose and fell on him. Gaetano didn't take her money, knock her around or get drunk, so in her opinion he was perfection. She wasn't very bright or well educated,' Belle proffered in a guilty undertone because she felt disloyal making that statement about the parent she had loved. 'But she was a very loving, loyal and kind person.'

'She must also have been very tolerant and forgiving. That's probably why their affair lasted so long,' Cristo commented with a wry twist of his mouth.

Belle's throat thickened with tears and she swallowed with difficulty. 'Sometimes I miss her so much it *hurts*,' she admitted quietly.

Cristo tensed when he noticed the glimmer of moisture on her cheeks. He breathed in slow and deep, unfroze his big powerful body with difficulty and pushed himself to close a hand over her tightly clenched fingers where they rested on her lap. 'I can't even say that I can imagine how you feel because it would be a lie,' he conceded ruefully. 'I'm not particularly close to my mother and I had no relationship with Gaetano to mourn when he died. You're fortunate to be a part of such a close family.'

In silence, Belle nestled her fingers beneath the warmth of his and marvelled at that unexpectedly thoughtful gesture of comfort and the sentiment from his corner.

They dined at a table set for two on a massive terrace surrounded by amazing views of the picturesque hillside town. The streets they had driven through had been a geranium-hung blaze of flowering colour and she had caught glimpses of medieval back lanes and piazzas adorned with ancient fountains.

'Where are all the other customers?' Belle asked, surveying the empty tables around them.

'Tonight, we're the *only* customers and one of Italy's most famous chefs is cooking solely for us, *bella mia*.'

'And you arranged it that way?' Belle prompted in amazement.

'This is the very first time I've taken you anywhere,' Cristo pointed out bluntly. 'And we've been married a week, which basically tells me that I owe you a decent night out. I also owe you for all the work you put in for me without complaint.'

'I like working. I like feeling useful,' Belle confessed truthfully, green eyes sparkling, generous mouth warming into an unrestrained smile because simply sitting there in her beautiful dress with her even more beautiful husband opposite made her feel ridiculously spoilt and contented.

Hungry desire flaming through him afresh and coalescing in an ache of raw need so eager to stir at his groin, Cristo studied his wife, marvelling at the explosive effect she had on his libido. Although he didn't consider himself to be either an emotional or sentimental man, he found her natural warmth and liveliness amazingly attractive.

The waiter brought the menu and the chef came out

to greet them and offer recommendations. By then dusk was falling and the candles were lit. Belle cradled her wine and sipped, rejoicing in the fact that she could at last relax in Cristo's company.

'You still haven't explained why Bruno and Donetta were sent to boarding school,' Cristo drawled lazily.

Her fingers tightened round the glass in her hand. 'Bruno was never an athletic boy and he finally admitted to Gaetano that he was only interested in art. Your father asked him if he was gay…he was only thirteen at the time,' she completed in a tone of disgust.

Cristo swore under his breath.

'Then Gaetano decided to make that a running joke and whenever he saw Bruno after that he called him "gay boy". Eventually someone else overheard and talked and Bruno started getting bullied at school but he didn't tell us what was happening,' Belle explained heavily, having to pause to breathe in deep before she could continue to tell the distressing truth. 'Bruno tried to kill himself but, very fortunately for us and him, we found him in time and he recovered.'

Cristo was honestly appalled by the confession while he recalled that skinny-wristed boy with the anxious eyes who had cornered him on the day of the wedding. 'I was remarkably lucky, it seems, to escape Gaetano's concept of how to be a good father.'

'Well, after that Donetta finally picked up the courage to tell us what had been going on at school and that's why they both went into boarding,' Belle advanced. 'Bruno's experience with Gaetano is the main reason why I hated your father. And my brother, by the way, is *not* gay.'

'It wouldn't have made any difference to me if he

was,' Cristo remarked as the first course was deferentially laid before them. 'The poor kid.'

'He's a very talented artist and the change of environment was exactly what he needed, even if it does mean he and Donetta are separated from the family.'

'When they move to London, they won't be separated any longer,' Cristo reminded her. 'They can attend a day school or even board and come home at weekends—whichever they would prefer... It's up to them.'

'I know. I wanted us all to be together again,' she confided ruefully. 'But you might find it a little crowded with all of us around.'

Cristo dealt her a wicked look teeming with all the passion that simmered so close to the surface of his apparently controlled exterior. 'I think I will enjoy being crowded by you.'

CHAPTER NINE

WITH A GROWING sense of awe, Belle studied the laptop pictures of the latest London property details sent for their perusal by the consultant hired by Cristo. Cristo had told Belle simply to pick a house, as his penthouse apartment was too small to house her family. He had very little interest in what his new home would be like, having merely specified a room to house an office and sufficient space in which to entertain. Belle was staggered, not only by the sheer meteoric cost and superb appointments of the elite properties tendered to them, but also by the level of responsibility Cristo had entrusted her with.

At the same time, she would have been the first to admit that during the past weeks in Italy their relationship had changed out of all recognition. Most mornings she helped Cristo catch up in the office. After that they would spend the rest of the day exploring, eating out, swimming, generally just relaxing and often with Franco in tow. And equally often they would sit out until very late talking over guttering candles on the terrace where they usually dined. A dreamy expression clouded Belle's eyes in tune with the increasing sense of security that she was feeling in her new life.

Nothing seemed that daunting with Cristo by her side. No, not even his mother, Princess Giulia, who had arrived with his stepfather, Henri Montaldo, with very little warning only the day before. Belle's mother-in-law had literally shrieked in infuriated horror once she finally grasped the identity of the woman whom her one and only child had married.

'What are the children of this unscrupulous Irish woman to do with you?' the princess, an imperious, ageless little brunette dressed in the latest fashion, had demanded in outrage of her son.

'They are my family,' Cristo had responded quietly and Belle's chest had swelled with pride, for she knew what an achievement it was that he had now moved beyond his original feelings to regard her siblings in that just and unselfish light.

And the battle between mother and son had then switched to incomprehensible volleys of furious Italian while Belle offered Cristo's stepfather, Henri, a mild-mannered man, coffee and tried to pretend that she wasn't aware that his wife was undoubtedly engaged in attacking Belle's late parent, Mary, for the reckless choices she had made in life.

'Gaetano is Giulia's one blind spot,' Henri had remarked ruefully under cover of the argument raging back and forth between mother and son. 'He was the love of her life.'

'Yet you've been together…?' Belle had begun awkwardly.

'Since Cristo was a toddler,' Henri had confirmed in the same even, accepting manner. 'Don't worry about this. Cristo will settle it. He knows how to handle his mother.'

By the time the coffee was being served, the argument had become a much less tense discussion laced with Henri's soothing comments, and Belle swiftly recognised that Cristo both liked and respected his stepfather. Indeed by the time the volatile princess had departed, the older woman had recovered her mood to the extent of ruffling Franco's black curly hair, remarking what a very handsome little boy he was and kissing Belle on both cheeks and welcoming her to the family. The threat of lingering bad feelings that Belle had feared might result from such an encounter had been successfully averted.

'So, as you witnessed this afternoon, everybody gets embarrassed when it comes to family members,' Cristo had remarked in bed the night before while she still lay boneless and weak with drowning contentment in the circle of his arms. 'My mother has a very short fuse. She loses her head and throws scenes.'

'But she calms back down again and she doesn't hold spite,' Belle pointed out lightly. 'That's a plus.'

'I didn't want her to upset you, *bellezza mia*,' Cristo admitted. 'It's more than a quarter of a century since she divorced Gaetano and, let's face it, what he did after that and who he did it with is none of her business.'

'But at one time she obviously cared a lot for him,' Belle mused, drowsily settling her head down on his smooth bronzed shoulder, breathing in the scent of him in a state of sublime relaxation. 'And his infidelity and his lies must have hurt her enormously. A woman would've needed to be hard as a rock or wilfully blind like my mother to handle Gaetano without getting chewed up into little pieces.'

'I'll always be honest with you,' Cristo declared, long tanned fingers skimming her tousled curls back from her brow as he looked down at her, dark eyes sexy gold below the stunning black of his luxuriant lashes. 'I can promise you that much.'

That was a big promise and an even bigger temptation, Belle reflected sleepily. She knew she ought to ask him about the photo in his wallet but just at that moment when she felt deliciously happy and comfortable felt like the wrong moment and she kicked the idea back out of her head with relief. No man had ever made her feel secure the way Cristo did, she conceded blissfully. She would ask him some time soon and would no doubt quickly learn that she had been agonising over nothing. Perhaps he had had the photo for some reason and had simply forgotten he still had it...

Recalling that thought, Belle drifted back to the present to find Cristo on the pool terrace regarding her where she reclined in the shade with an abandoned book, his amusement unhidden. 'You were a thousand miles away.'

'So, I daydream sometimes,' Belle parried, studying him with helpless appreciation: a lithe sun-bronzed god of a male, lean, powerful frame garbed in black jeans and a white tee. His breathtaking good looks still enthralled her but then *she* wasn't the only one looking, she recognised with pleasure as Cristo's gaze whipped with flattering appreciation over her bikini-clad curves. 'Were you looking for me?'

'*Sì.*' Cristo hesitated. 'I'm flying the rest of your family here this afternoon.'

Brow furrowed in surprise, Belle sat up. 'What are you talking about?'

'I've been warned that the story about Gaetano and his children by your mother will be published tomorrow, so I'm taking your grandmother and the children out of harm's way and over here where no one will bother them.'

Thrown off balance by that terse explanation, Belle exclaimed, 'When did you decide to do that? My gran as well? They won't want to come at such short notice, for goodness' sake.'

'Bruno's bored stiff at home over the summer and counting the hours. I Skyped him and he believes he will like the Umbrian landscape,' Cristo supplied with a decided hint of one-upmanship.

'You *Skyped* him?' Belle gasped in complete disconcertion.

'I alerted your grandmother to the situation last week. She's now only awaiting your call to reassure her that they won't be intruding on us,' Cristo completed.

'But she never said a word when I last spoke to her...' Belle's voice trailed away, for she could scarcely recall what she had discussed with the older woman during that call and would have been the first to admit that her concentration hadn't been what it was of late. More and more her entire world seemed to be defined by the closed little world she inhabited with Cristo, where nothing else seemed to matter very much.

'She didn't want to worry you, so will you ring her and assure her they're all welcome and that we have plenty of space for them?' Cristo prompted. 'The experience of having the paparazzi on the doorstep would be traumatic for the children.'

Pale and dismayed at the threat of her family being

exposed to that kind of rude and humiliating attention, Belle was propelled straight off the lounger and back indoors.

When she phoned her grandmother, Isa was her usual calm and logical self. 'Whatever happens we'll weather it the way we've weathered everything else. You don't *have* to bring us to Italy,' she declared staunchly.

'I'm dying to see you all again. I know it's only been a few weeks but it feels more like months,' Belle confided truthfully. 'And Franco keeps on asking for you all.'

'Newly married couples need privacy and five children and a granny are going to put quite a dent in that,' Isa forecast ruefully.

'You're family—that's different,' Belle protested. 'And I've missed you all so much.'

And that was true, regardless of her contentment with Cristo, she acknowledged. In fact her time away from the family had already taught her how much she had taken their presence for granted before her marriage and how much she had since missed the warm hurly-burly of their home and her grandmother's soothing support.

With her family's coming visit confirmed, Belle went off to consult Umberto about where everyone was to sleep and discovered that Cristo had already spoken to him on the subject the week before. Isa suffered from arthritic knees and sometimes found stairs a challenge and Belle was further disconcerted to learn that a room downstairs that opened out on a seating area on the terrace had already been set up for the older woman's occupation.

'When did you organise the room for Isa?' Belle asked Cristo curiously as she came to a halt in the doorway of his office.

'As soon as I knew she was coming, *bellezza mia*. My grandmother also preferred ground-floor accommodation,' Cristo told her quietly.

Belle collided with his spectacular dark heavily fringed eyes and her heart hammered behind her breastbone. 'Is your grandmother still alive?'

'No. She died the summer after I graduated but she was very much a part of my life when I was younger,' Cristo admitted.

'How does your brother Zarif feel about the news article that's about to be published?' Belle asked worriedly. 'I know how worried you were about the effect it might have on him.'

'Zarif never panics and he believes that such a juicy story was always going to escape into the public domain. He says he'll ride it out.'

In receipt of that assurance, Belle felt a little of her tension evaporate. She wanted to ask Cristo if he now felt that he had married her for nothing. After all, he had married her to bury that story and the safeguard hadn't worked. 'That's good.'

Cristo sprang upright, his attention pinned to Belle's pensive face, the sparkle in her eyes and the ripe curve of her mouth. 'You're happy your family's coming to stay, aren't you?'

Belle cast off her insecurities and a grin relaxed her mouth. 'Yes. I've missed them a lot.'

'I really didn't appreciate how close you all were. Growing up, I was strictly an only child. I first met my half-brothers when I was a teenager and only then because my stepfather argued in favour of it.'

Within hours, Cristo received an emailed copy of the article that was to be published in a leading tabloid newspaper the following day.

'You've been immortalised in print!' Cristo growled from the doorway of the bedroom where Belle was putting a pile of fashion magazines in place for her younger sister, Lucia. A dark flush had overlaid his hard cheekbones and his eyes were bright with anger.

Belle whirled round to study him the instant she glimpsed the papers that he was angrily burnishing. 'I beg your pardon?'

Her heart in her mouth, she stared down at the email he'd printed out, spread flat on the table beside her. The headline *'Ravelli's Secret Irish Family'* spelt out the facts and shock reverberated through Belle when she saw the number of photos in the spread, not least the one of her clad in her wedding gown, which looked rather as though it might have been taken by a camera phone outside the chapel on the day. The main picture, however, was of her pregnant mother and her siblings taken at a local fair shortly before Franco's birth. There was even a small snap of her grandmother.

'So, the story really is going to be printed... I'm so sorry. I know how you felt about this,' Belle breathed heavily.

'But how *dare* they publish a photo of you?' Cristo demanded in a raw undertone, stabbing the offending item with a blunt forefinger. 'Smearing you with

Gaetano's sleaze as if *you* had anything to do with your mother's choices!'

Disconcerted by the focus of his rage, Belle swallowed hard. 'Who was it who talked to the press?'

'Gaetano's former driver.'

Belle was hurriedly reading the article, noting with relief that her grandmother was referred to as 'well-respected' and that she was merely mentioned as Mary's 'recently married' daughter. 'Luckily nobody seems to have made the connection that I got married to a Ravelli,' she remarked in astonishment. 'In fact there's no reference to you at all—'

'Isn't there?' Frowning in surprise at that news, Cristo bent to scan the blurred newsprint. 'Well, that's something at least.'

'And it doesn't say anything that isn't true. I mean, Gaetano *was* married throughout most of their affair and my mother wasn't the only woman in his life at the time.' Belle breathed in deep, colliding head-on with his burnished gaze and feeling her tummy flip in response. 'You know, I think the article could have been a lot nastier in tone than this is.'

'I just don't like you being soiled with Gaetano's sleaze,' Cristo admitted in a roughened undertone while he ran an admiring finger along the softened line of her generous mouth. 'But I suppose you're right and if Zarif can handle the fallout, we certainly can.'

Almost of their own volition her lips parted and she laved his fingertip with the tip of her tongue. His lashes lowered, his semi-screened eyes flashing burning gold and scorchingly light against his bronzed skin as he hauled her into his arms and covered her mouth hungrily with his own. Excitement flared through Belle's slender body like a storm warning and the instant surge of desire stirred a sharp ache between her thighs.

'I want you,' Cristo ground out against her swollen lips, arching her into him with an imprisoning hand splayed across her hips, ensuring that she was fully aware of his arousal.

Belle lifted an unsteady hand to his lean dark face and her fingertips traced a hard masculine cheekbone in a helpless caress. 'Well, I'm not doing anything else...' she whispered teasingly, hot as an inferno inside her own skin and literally weak with longing.

He took that invitation with a thoroughness she could only appreciate. Lifting her in his arms, he took her back to their bedroom. Her heated bare skin revelled in the brush of the cool, crisp linen on the bed when he tossed the sheets back. She was excited by the crushing weight of her lover and his forcefulness as he stretched her arms above her head, her wrists gripped between the fingers of one strong hand, and ravished her mouth erotically with his own. Between the sheets, Cristo was dominant and she rejoiced in that aspect of him. Her heart thundered in her ears as he stroked and teased the tender tissue between her thighs, her slender spine arching in helpless delight as he took advantage of the welcome offered by the honeyed dampness of her sensitive flesh.

When Cristo flipped her over onto her knees, a sound of surprise was wrenched from her and then, before she could say or do anything, he was driving into her hard and fast, stretching her with shocking fullness, every entry and withdrawal perfectly timed to deliver the maximum possible pleasure. Insane excitement roared through Belle like a hungry fire, burning up every thought in the heat of the flames. She was out of control, lost in sensation, a slave to the delight. Her body raced to the climax it craved and she cried out in pure ecstasy, hearing his answering groan. Afterwards she collapsed in a heap on the bed, her muscles like jelly, her breath still hissing in and out of her gasping throat as she struggled to reason and speak again.

'Did I ever tell you how fantastic you are in bed, *bella mia*?' Cristo husked, pulling her back against his hard, damp body, his broad chest still heaving from the exertion of their encounter.

'Maybe you've mentioned it once or twice.' A smile as old as Eve curved Belle's reddened mouth because it made her feel good that he could think that even in the light of his much greater sexual experience.

Black hair wildly tousled, Cristo rubbed a stubbled jaw across a slim, smooth shoulder and murmured earthily, 'I can't keep my hands off you…you're killing me.'

Belle laughed softly and curved round him, every possessive urge in her body thrumming on full charge. She was happy, so happy that the horrible newspaper article hadn't rocked their relationship as she'd once feared, but still a sense of unease niggled in the back of her mind. The moment she looked for it, that tiny little seed of doubt about Cristo and Betsy refused to stay buried any longer. She wanted, no, she *needed* to know the truth, which she was convinced would be entirely non-threatening in reality.

'Why do you carry a photo of your brother's wife in your wallet?' Belle lifted her head to ask, the question as bold and instinctive on her lips as it was in her mind.

CHAPTER TEN

CRISTO'S BIG, POWERFUL frame froze and, that fast, Belle knew she had made a fatal mistake in assuming that she had nothing to worry about.

Dark blood rose in a revealing banner across Cristo's cheekbones. His spectacular bone structure had hardened into taut angles and hollows overlaid with the rigidity of fierce self-control while his dark golden eyes remained carefully shielded. 'What are you talking about?'

No longer warm and relaxed in the intimate circle of his arms, Belle rolled away and sat up against the tumbled pillows, tugging the sheet up to cover her breasts with hands that now felt clumsy. 'Franco got hold of your wallet one day and the photo fell out of it. I wasn't snooping, I *swear* I wasn't, but naturally I wondered why you had it.'

'Franco,' Cristo groaned, raking the long fingers of one tanned hand through his black hair and sitting up while he played for time and considered his options. That blasted photo, which he had forgotten he still had! He could lie, of course he could lie to her, but the memory of Gaetano's frequent lies and deceptions had left his son with an ineradicable desire never to follow in the older man's footsteps. Besides, lying was not only a weakness but also an act of deceit. Belle was his wife and she was entitled to the truth, he reasoned grimly, even if it was a truth he was in no hurry to share or recall. But where there was honesty, he believed there would be no future misunderstandings or grey areas.

He breathed in deep and slow and then released his breath again in an impatient hiss, his handsome mouth compressing. 'Betsy turned to me for support after her marriage to Nik broke down…for a while I thought I'd fallen in love with her…'

Belle was already in the grip of mental turmoil because his visible reaction to her question had immediately betrayed that she had stumbled onto a sensitive issue. Her head ached with the ferocity of her tension and her conflicting thoughts and incipient panic made her a poor listener. *I fell in love with her* was all Belle took from that fractured speech and his confession had the same impact on her as the announcement of a sudden death. *I fell for her.* Her mouth ran dry, her heartbeat accelerated and her tummy performed a sick somersault. *I fell for her.* She could feel the blood draining from her face, the clawing clench of her fingertips on the edge of the sheet and the resulting ache in her knuckle bones. For a truly dreadful moment she was scared she might throw up where she sat, and then mercifully the tide of sickness receded while her brain kicked feverishly back into action.

Cristo had fallen in love with little fairy-like Betsy, who was so tiny and exquisite that Belle was convinced that she herself would look like a comic-book character standing beside her. Belle was taller, cur-

vier, and physically larger in every way, her hair rau-
cous red to Betsy's pale, subtle blonde. No two women
could have been more diametrically opposed in the
looks department. Did he try to fantasise that she was
Betsy in bed? That cruel suspicion pierced Belle like
a knife in her chest, shock still winging through her
in blinding waves while her mind leapt on to make
even more offensive connections. Cristo had actually
dared to marry her when he was in love with another
woman! Appalled at this knowledge that sucked out
every atom of her former happiness and contentment
in her role, Belle slid out of bed and swept up her wrap.
She folded herself into it in a jerky motion because her
limbs still felt oddly detached from her body.

'Why on earth did you marry *me*?' Anger was roaring through Belle in a giant floodtide that drowned
every rational thought and controlled every response.
'I mean, you were in love with another woman, so why
the heck would you ask me to marry you?'

Taken aback by her behaviour, his incomprehension
growing at her overreaction to what he now saw as a
comparatively insignificant mistake on his own part
that had caused no one any harm, Cristo frowned in
bewilderment. 'Why should it bother you?'

'It doesn't bother me. I'm not one bit bothered!'
Belle proclaimed in furious vehement denial, her pride
answering for her. 'But obviously I don't like what it
says about *you*. What sort of man gets involved with
his brother's wife?'

Understanding crossed Cristo's sleek dark face,
swiftly followed by an unmistakeable expression of
distaste. 'I wasn't sexually involved with Betsy. I didn't

make a single move that crossed the boundaries of friendship with her.'

'Are you trying to tell me that you *haven't* had an affair with her?' Belle demanded incredulously. 'Do I look that stupid?'

Honesty, it suddenly struck Cristo for the first time, could be a poisoned chalice. His gift of honesty, offered with the best of intentions, had simply stirred up more serious suspicions. He sprang out of bed and reached for his jeans, pulling them on commando style in a fluid motion. Stunning dark eyes met unflinchingly with Belle's accusing stare.

'There was never any question of an affair. For a start, I never told Betsy how I felt, and naturally there was no physical intimacy. *Dio mio*, she's my brother's wife. I couldn't possibly cross that line.'

'But they're getting a divorce!' Belle cut in furiously.

'Nik will always be my brother. I could still *never* go there and from the outset I accepted that there was no future in my feelings for her.'

'Yet you married me even though you *loved* her!' Belle reminded him painfully, scarcely able to frame the words through her chattering teeth. She felt cold and clammy and nauseous. She had never felt so hurt and rejected in her entire life and it was as though a great well of anguish deep inside her was threatening to drag her down and swallow her alive. Suddenly the world looked dark, her future empty and full of threat.

'Why shouldn't I have married you? How I believed I felt about Betsy is pretty much irrelevant now. There was no way I was ever going to have anything but a friendship with her, and let's not forget that you and I agreed to a marriage purely based on practicality.'

That reminder was brutally unwelcome. Belle's nails bit painfully into the flesh of her hands as she knotted them together. A *practical* marriage. When had she contrived to forget that revealing description of his expectations and her own agreement on that basis? When had she developed expectations of something a great deal more emotionally satisfying than a detached marriage of convenience? And whatever the answer to those questions was it didn't really matter at a moment when she was in so much pain that she could barely bring herself to look at him. Just then she was too worked up to argue with Cristo and she was desperate to make an escape lest she embarrass herself by saying something she shouldn't.

'Excuse me,' Belle breathed curtly, sidestepping Cristo to stalk into the bathroom.

The door closed, the lock turning with a fast and audible click.

In frustration, Cristo swore under his breath. Why was she so angry? Why the hell was she so angry with him? Blasted relationships, he reflected with brooding resentment. He was no good at them, and never had been. He had always settled for sex and got out before anything more complex was required. But he couldn't walk away from Belle and their marriage any more easily than he could escape the fallout from what appeared to be a disastrous error of judgement on his part. He pictured Belle's face when he had truthfully answered her question. She had turned pale as snow, her eyes blank while immediate constraint tightened her features. One minute she had been in his arms, smiling and happy and affectionate, the next angry and distant and...*hurt*. His wide sensual mouth compressed grimly at that awareness. Every natural instinct told him he should have lied in his teeth and made up an excuse for still having that photo in his wallet. But although he had told her about Betsy, it had decidedly not been the moment to tell her the rest of that story because she would never have believed him in the mood she was in, he reasoned bitterly.

Trembling with reaction, Belle splashed her face with cold water. Tears were running from her eyes and she washed them away with punitive splashes of more cold water, finally burying her chilled face with a shudder in a soft warm towel. Cristo was in love with Betsy and nothing had ever hurt Belle so much as that discovery. Why was that? she asked herself wretchedly; why was she taking the news so badly, so...*personally*?

They had married for convenience and her main motivation before the wedding had been the welfare of her brothers and sisters. That goal had been achieved most successfully for Cristo was already accepting that her siblings were also his and therefore family to them both. He wasn't going to turn round and suddenly desert the children, he was too honourable for that, she reflected heavily. To date he had also kept his promises to her. To say the very least, he treated her with warmth and respect.

Had she hoped he felt more than that where she was concerned? Belle nibbled at her lower lip, afraid to meet her own eyes in the mirror because, on her terms, their relationship had very quickly become intensely personal both in and out of bed. The limits of practicality had been bypassed and forgotten by her within days of the wedding. She had learned to care for Cristo, to enjoy his company, his sense of humour, his kindness to Franco, his thoughtfulness whenever it came to a question of what made her happy. In short she had travelled all the way from initial admiration and appreciation to falling madly in love with her husband, which was why hearing that he loved someone else had caused her such pain. Stupid, *stupid* man—why on earth had he told her? And, even worse, why had he looked at her as though she was insane when she reacted with furious condemnation? Didn't he understand *anything* about women? About her? Maybe she should have framed the experience in terms he would have understood...

'*Cristo!*' Belle bawled across the bedroom on her noisy return, the bathroom door still shuddering behind her from her aggressive exit.

Cristo emerged from the dressing room in the act of buttoning a shirt and fixed enquiring dark eyes on her with exaggerated politeness. 'You called, *bella mia*?'

Belle reddened fiercely. 'All right, I shouted. I'm sorry. It's just you don't seem to understand how I feel, so I thought I should give you an example.'

A winged ebony brow elevated. 'An example?'

'Try to imagine how you would feel if I was to tell you right now that I was in love with Mark Petrie,' she urged.

Before her very eyes, Cristo froze into an icy bronzed statue. '*Are* you?'

'You see, the boot's very much on the other foot now, isn't it?' she fired back. 'No, of course I'm not in love with Mark, but you don't like the idea, do you?'

'Of course, I don't—you're my wife.' Dawning comprehension slivered through Cristo and his shrewd gaze veiled but he remained stubbornly silent, wary as he was of setting her temper off again.

'No wife would want to hear that her husband *ever* loved another woman,' Belle pointed out with dignity. 'It's not personal, it's simply a matter of what's… what's…acceptable. You're my husband. I'm possessive about you. I can't help that.'

'We're both possessive by nature, *bella mia,*' Cristo husked, relieved that the storm had been weathered and she appeared to be calming down.

But Belle was simply putting on an act to save face. She had her pride. She didn't want him to know how she felt about him. Determined to act normally, she shone a light smile of acceptance in his direction before returning to her own room where her clothes were still kept. While she dressed for lunch, she concentrated her rushing thoughts on the knowledge that her family were arriving within hours. Family, that was what *really* mattered. There was absolutely no point in tearing herself apart over what went on in Cristo's dark, complex head because she couldn't change that.

No doubt, though, he had Betsy on a pedestal. Betsy would always be the unattainable perfect woman in his eyes while Belle would have to settle for being the much more convenient, accessible and real-world wife, who would dutifully help him raise their orphaned brothers and sisters. Well, she could live with that unromantic reality, couldn't she? Of course she could, she told herself urgently, while in the back of her mind furious objections flared. It wasn't a matter of being second-best, she told herself. That was a degrading label and she would go insane if she started picturing herself as some kind of martyr.

Keep it simple, she urged herself sternly. She loved her husband. How had that happened? She had once been so afraid of falling in love and getting hurt, yet miraculously those concerns had been overwhelmed by the powerful emotions Cristo drummed up inside her. He was very generous, very attentive and absolutely breathtaking in bed. What's not to like, she asked herself accusingly. To want or expect more than she was already getting was downright greedy. He couldn't help what he felt. She should respect his privacy, she reasoned in an even more frantic loop of planning; she shouldn't concern herself with his emotions. And telling him that he was never to see or even speak to Betsy again would not be a winning move...*would it*?

Cristo watched Belle across the lunch table, utterly distrusting her demure expression as she fed Franco from her own plate, breaking her own rules and using the child as a distraction every time Cristo spoke. Franco, of course, lapped up the extra attention and would throw a merry tantrum the next time he was refused a selection from someone else's plate. Cristo was torn between a strong desire to shake Belle and an even stronger desire to drag her back to bed and stamp her as *his* again. Suspecting that he might strike out in that field, he decided to throw in the towel. Belle was in a mood and she would get over it but he was exasperated by the way she was behaving and the wedge she was driving between them. His chair scraped across the terrace tiles as he pushed it back and plunged upright.

'I have a couple of calls to make. I'll see you later,' he said drily.

Targeted by shrewd dark-as-night eyes, Belle went pink and then parted her lips. 'I was planning to sleep in my own room tonight. If the article is to be published tomorrow, I want to be really rested so that I can be with my family,' she muttered uncomfortably.

Cristo gritted his perfect white teeth. It wasn't as if he kept her up *all* night *every* night! Was he a little too demanding in the bedroom? Wouldn't she have complained before now? Belle was no human sacrifice and indeed had a whole repertoire of delightful approaches calculated to wake him up hot and hard at dawn. It was an unfortunate recollection when every basic instinct he possessed craved a renewal of the very physical connection they shared. Handsome mouth set in a steely stubborn line, Cristo strode away.

'Now Cristo's annoyed with me,' Belle mumbled into Franco's tousled hair as he sat on her lap. 'He never says anything. He just gives me this sardonic look and it makes me cross and it makes me sad and for some peculiar reason it makes me want to run after him and say sorry.'

'*Kiss-do*,' Franco slotted with emphasis into that confused flood of confidence and the little boy began wriggling off her lap, suddenly keen to be free.

Belle watched her brother race after Cristo and her mouth down-curved; it promised to be a long and lonely afternoon.

In the echoing hall of the palazzo, Tag leapt straight out of his travel box and flung himself in a passionate welcome at Belle, pink tongue lolling, ragged tail wagging like mad, his little white and black body wriggling frantically. No sooner had he achieved that reunion and more than a few hugs of reciprocal affection, he glanced at Cristo and growled long and low in his throat.

'*No*, Tag!' Bruno stepped forward to say forcefully, casting his older sister a look of reproach as he scooped up the little dog and walked to the door with him to let him out to run off his over-excitement. Pietro and Lucia, the eight-year-olds too wound up to stay still after hours of travelling confinement, hurtled back outside in the dog's wake. 'You have to be very firm with him, Belle. He doesn't understand anything else.'

'She's the same with Franco,' Cristo remarked wryly. 'Lets him get away with murder.'

'Well, thank you both for that vote of confidence,' Belle countered as her grandmother laughed and folded her into a warm hug. 'How have you been, Gran?'

'I missed you,' Isa confided, her shrewd gaze searching her granddaughter's pale face and shadowed eyes with a frown. 'Missed that little scamp, Franco, as well. We all did.'

'Bruno says there's no shops near here.' Donetta sighed, her pretty face troubled and self-pitying. 'And I've got nothing to wear in this heat.'

'We'll go shopping,' Cristo promised.

'Well, don't expect me to come, especially not if Lucia is going as well.' Bruno winced and shot Cristo a rueful look. 'Lucia only likes the colour pink and won't wear anything else. Getting her into a school uniform will be a nightmare.'

'It's only a phase. She'll get over it,' Belle told him soothingly.

'Mum never did,' Bruno reminded her wryly, his mobile face shadowing with a sudden stark grief that he couldn't hide and which made him hurriedly study the floor with fixed attention.

Belle tensed and tried and failed to think of something comforting to say. Isa grabbed her hand to draw her attention back to her. 'You can start the official tour by showing me to my room,' she suggested. 'And a cup of tea would be even more welcome.'

Isa was tireless in the questions she asked about the Palazzo Maddalena and astonished to be told that Cristo's aristocratic mother didn't care for her former family home.

'The princess grew up here and much prefers life in the city,' Belle explained. 'Cristo only comes here for the occasional holiday so the place does need updating, but I don't like to wade in and start talking about changes when we're only just married.'

'You sounded so happy when you phoned me ,' Isa remarked thoughtfully as she sank with an appreciative sigh into a comfortable wicker armchair on the terrace and reached for the tea Umberto had brought. 'What's happened since then?'

Belle forced a smile. 'Nothing,' she swore with determination. 'I am very happy with Cristo.'

'A man and a woman can find it a challenge to live together at first,' Isa commented gently. 'Being part of a couple entails compromise.'

'Cristo is really, really good to me,' Belle muttered in a rush, keen to settle any concerns her grandmother might be cherishing. 'I really do have nothing to complain about.'

'Then why aren't you happy?' Isa prompted bluntly. 'I can see something's not right.'

'But it's not something I can discuss... It's something I need to talk about with Cristo,' Belle declared, recognising in that moment that she had actually spoken the truth. Much as she would like to, she could not avoid the subject of Betsy. That had to be discussed and she had to come to terms with it, she registered unhappily. The worst possible stance she could take would be to hold Cristo's feelings against him and poison every other part of their relationship with her bitterness. But it was so very hard to suppress the resentment, jealousy and hurt bubbling up inside her every time she looked at him.

'That sounds sensible,' her grandmother commented with approval and deftly changed the subject to bring Belle up to date on what had been happening in her family since her wedding.

Dinner was served out on the terrace at a big table Umberto had retrieved from a storeroom. The meal was an uproarious affair with all the children talking together, exchanging insults, pulling faces at Franco's table manners, and Belle could see that Cristo was disconcerted by the sheer liveliness of their over-excited siblings. Pietro and Lucia could barely spare the time to eat before they, with Tag in hot pursuit, chased off to explore the gardens again, with Franco trying desperately to keep up with them and breaking down into floods of tears when he was left behind. Cristo went to retrieve the toddler left sobbing at the top of the steps.

'Time for bed, I think,' he murmured quietly. 'I'll call Teresa.'

'No, I'll take him up,' Belle interposed, holding out her arms to take her little brother. 'A bath will soothe him.'

'I'll carry him,' Cristo countered flatly, stunning dark eyes hard and challenging as he studied her set face. 'I'll be back down in—'

'Oh, don't worry about us,' Isa cut in hastily, glancing at Bruno and Donetta. 'The three of us have a date with the television Umberto has most kindly set up for our use.'

Belle stomped upstairs in Cristo's wake, wondering what was wrong with him, her face still burning from that hard, impatient look he had angled at her.

Teresa greeted them on the landing and lifted Franco from her employer's arms. 'Poor little pet... he's exhausted. I'll put him straight in the bath,' she announced.

Belle turned on her heel but a strong tanned hand closed round her forearm to prevent her hurrying back downstairs. 'I'd like a word in private,' Cristo breathed.

Temper sparking fast in the strained mood she was in, Belle rounded on him, her green eyes flashing a fiery warning. 'What on earth is the matter with you?' she hissed.

'You've been avoiding me and ignoring me since this morning,' Cristo pointed out.

Belle's face flamed. 'I'm only trying to keep things polite for the family's benefit.'

'Then you can't act worth a damn,' Cristo told her succinctly, his hand on her forearm sliding down to engulf her fingers instead in a firm grip as he dragged her down the corridor with him. 'And we need to clear the air.'

'I don't want to talk…I'm not ready yet,' Belle exclaimed with more honesty than she had intended, because she had not yet reached the desirable stage where she could consider his feelings for Betsy without raging resentment infiltrating her every thought and reaction.

'Too bad. I'm ready now,' Cristo decreed, shoving wide the door of his bedroom and urging her in ahead of him.

'Is that why you're suddenly acting like a cave man?' Belle demanded furiously.

'No, that's entirely your fault,' Cristo fielded without hesitation. 'If you want to argue with me, argue with me, don't go all passive-aggressive and do it from behind a fake smile.'

'That is not what I've been doing!' Belle protested angrily.

'That's exactly what you've been doing and I've had enough of it. I made the mistake of admitting that at one stage I thought that I had fallen for Betsy—'

'No, you said you *had* fallen for her!' Belle contradicted.

'You mustn't have been listening,' Cristo told her severely. 'For a while before I met you I did believe I'd fallen for her, but once I met you I soon realised that I'd misconstrued my response to her.'

Belle abandoned her angry pacing round the room and fell still. *'Misunderstood?'* she questioned sharply, turning her head back to look at his darkly handsome face.

His lean, strong features taut, Cristo expelled his breath in a rueful hiss. 'You have to understand how I felt at the time Nik and Betsy's marriage broke down. I felt unbearably guilty and accountable because—'

'You told some secret of Nik's to Zarif and he talked when he shouldn't have and let the cat out of the bag,' Belle interposed impatiently. 'Yes, I remember—'

'And Betsy was devastated and she turned to me as Nik's brother, believing that I might know or understand why Nik had done what he had done. That was why she came to me. Unfortunately I didn't know or understand, and I couldn't help, but I felt extremely sorry for her. For whatever reasons, Nik had treated her badly. I felt very protective towards her and angry with Nik and I honestly assumed that those feelings were love.'

While she listened to what Cristo had to say, Belle was slowly breaking out in a cold sweat of relief because she was finally recognising that somehow in her hot-headed emotional response she had got the wrong end of the stick. Cristo had misinterpreted his feelings for Betsy and then recognised his mistake. Belle could understand how confused Cristo must've felt at the time, torn between guilt and responsibility for his brother's marriage breakdown while feeling both disloyal to his brother and strongly sympathetic towards Betsy's plight.

'I can understand that. You felt responsible so you tried to be helpful and provide a supportive shoulder.'

'I did still think I loved her when I asked you to marry me even though I'd never been attracted to Betsy the way I was to you,' Cristo admitted with a twist of his mouth. 'That sounds ludicrously naïve, doesn't it?'

Belle was frowning in surprise. 'You *weren't* attracted to her?'

'No. I assumed that was because I still thought of her as my brother's wife but I think it was more because she wasn't my type and didn't appeal to me on that level.'

'But...I've seen photos of her and she's incredibly pretty!' Belle fired back at him in ridiculous challenge.

'I've discovered that tall, curvy redheads are much more my style, *amata mia*,' Cristo quipped. 'Particularly ones who can give as good as they get in a row and can function as my intellectual equal.'

Belle dragged in a steadying breath before she could ask uncertainly, 'Are you talking about me?'

'Who else?' Dark golden eyes locked to her bemused face and lingered. 'After all, it was only because I fell in love with you that I learned to appreciate that I'd *never* been in love with Betsy.'

Mouth running dry, eyes wide, Belle was suddenly feeling very short of breath and even slightly dizzy, as if the floor below her feet were rocking. And indeed it might as well have been because it seemed that most of her pessimistic assumptions had been glaringly wrong. 'You fell in love with me?'

'And it was almost love at first sight,' Cristo teased with a charismatic smile. 'Before you decided to try and convince me that you were your mother and a forty-odd-year-old woman, I saw you crossing the lawn, wearing a pair of shorts, and you have curves and legs to die for,' Cristo told her with a wicked grin.

'You're so superficial,' Belle mumbled in a pained

tone of amusement. So superficial but *mine*, she was thinking lovingly.

'Not at all. I love your legs but I love your brain and your ready tongue more,' Cristo confided without hesitation. 'In fact there's a whole host of things I like about you that have nothing to do with your very sexy appearance.'

'Like...?' Belle pressed shamelessly.

'Your loyalty and love for your family, your kindness, your lack of greed,' Cristo enumerated, moving closer step by step while Belle continued to survey him with wonder. He loved her, not Betsy, and her brain was struggling to process that alien conviction. She was not second-best; she was his *first* choice and he genuinely cared about her. The first heady spur of joy surged through her like a rejuvenating drug.

'I like lots of things about you too,' Belle burbled. 'But I fell in love with you without knowing I was doing it. It was only when I thought you loved Betsy that I realised how I felt about you.'

'Great minds think alike,' Cristo purred, stroking the side of her face with a gentle forefinger. 'You love me, I love you. We're a perfect match.'

'No, we're imperfect but that's okay...we're only human,' Belle mumbled unsteadily, her heart leaping behind her breastbone as Cristo drew her into his arms and eased her wonderfully, reassuringly close to his lean, powerful frame. 'Oh, I can't believe this...I was *so* miserable today!'

'I would've told you how I felt about you then if you hadn't been so angry I was afraid that you wouldn't believe me,' Cristo confessed. 'Let's face it, neither of us was looking for or expecting love in this marriage, but you turned out to be the best thing that's ever happened to me and I think the family we already have will be the icing on the cake.'

Belle dealt him an anxious upward glance, afraid he was being too optimistic in his outlook. 'But you can get lots of little problems too with family.'

'And together we'll deal with them,' Cristo asserted huskily as he brushed his mouth very tenderly over hers, lifting his handsome dark head to stare down at her with tender love and appreciation softening his stunning gaze. 'You're mine, my love, my wife, my future…'

'I like the sound of that very much,' Belle admitted, snuggling into his broad chest with a happy sigh. 'But you know when you said that it wouldn't be worth my while learning Italian, I assumed you only saw me as a short-term prospect.'

'*Ma no*…certainly not,' Cristo chided huskily. 'I only meant that these days I don't spend a lot of time in Italy.'

'I'd still like to learn.'

'I love you,' he told her in Italian and she repeated the words faithfully back with a little giggle as he backed her down on the bed with a clear agenda in mind.

Belle greeted her family with a shining smile the following morning. Isa beamed and said nothing. Franco was scolded for trying to steal off Cristo's plate and Tag for snarling at Cristo's ankles. Pietro and Lucia squabbled as usual. Donetta wanted to know when they were going shopping and Bruno was making rapturous comments about the quality of the light.

Below the level of the table, Cristo gripped Belle's hand in his and breathed, 'Family is what it's all about, *amata mia*. My father missed out on so much.'

EPILOGUE

FOUR YEARS LATER, Belle stood at a cheval mirror and pulled her stretchy dress away from the very small bump she sported.

'You're pregnant. You're supposed to be that shape,' her grandmother told her reprovingly.

'I'm putting on a lot of weight though,' Belle groused, checking the generous curve of her bust and hips in the mirror as she turned round and pulled a face.

'Not too much,' Isa contradicted. 'You're very active and naturally you need to eat. At least you're not as sick as your mother was when she was expecting.'

'There is that,' Belle conceded reluctantly. 'Now, are you sure you're going to be all right while we're away?'

'Belle, you and Cristo will only be away for five days, of course we'll be all right,' the older woman declared lightly. 'Stop fussing.'

Cristo and Belle were celebrating their fourth wedding anniversary in Venice where they would be visiting the princess and Henri in their palazzo on the Grand Canal but staying in a small intimate hotel that Cristo had carefully selected for them. Belle could barely credit that so much time had passed since their wedding and that soon she would be a mother in her own right.

Cristo had bought a fabulous house for them in Holland Park. Bruno was now studying art at college and Donetta was planning to do fashion design. Pietro and Lucia were both in secondary school and fought a little less often now that they were so conscious of being almost teenagers. Franco was a sturdy six-year-old in primary school, who insisted on having his curls cropped the minute they became visible and who modelled his every masculine move on Cristo, whom in common with the twins he called, 'Dad.'

Although they had started out with a ready-made family, who had been officially adopted by Cristo and Belle within months of their first wedding, Cristo had never overlooked their personal relationship or taken it for granted. They had, after all and at his insistence, had their marriage blessed in an Italian church service shortly before the first Christmas they had shared, both of them feeling the need to exchange their vows with rather more sincerity and emotion than had figured when they had initially married. They also enjoyed regular weekend breaks and holidays as a couple.

It had been during their last romantic break that Cristo had admitted that he would love her to have his child. That development had taken place far sooner than either of them had expected because Belle had fallen pregnant within a month of that decision. She smiled, hand splaying across her tummy as she thought of the little girl on the way to joining the Ravelli family. She could hardly wait and her brothers and sisters were equally excited at the new addition in the offing.

Indeed, Belle was happier than she had ever dreamt of being with Cristo and her family. And she had never been so busy. The palazzo, where they usually spent their summers on a family holiday, had been modernised. The whole family circle had drawn closer. Cristo's brother, Nik Christakis, still intimidated Belle but his life had taken some surprising turns since their first meeting and he had definitely warmed up from the driven workaholic he had once been.

Zarif's life was still a story under development and Belle loved visiting Vashir with its colourful vibrant culture and fabulous history. Cristo's younger brother had weathered the storms over the scandal of his father's secret double life because the rumours about Gaetano's misbehaviour had once been so wild that the truth was no more shocking to the populace, who could only marvel that Zarif was such a conservative male in comparison.

Belle clambered into the limo that was to whisk her to the airport to meet Cristo and smiled, looking forward to the promise of having her husband's undivided attention for a few days. An hour and half later, she boarded the private jet, her attention switching straight to Cristo's tall, well-built figure as he pushed aside his laptop and sprang upright to greet her in the aisle.

'You look beautiful, *amata mia*,' he told her huskily.

Belle slid self-mocking hands down over her bust and hips and quipped, 'Well, you are getting a more generous portion of me with every month that goes past...'

'And I *love* it,' Cristo growled, bending down to

kiss her ripe peach-tinted mouth with hungry appreciation. 'I think you look incredibly sexy.'

'Tell me more,' she urged as he settled her down in a comfortable seat beside his and fastened her belt for take-off.

'Later. Right now it's time for this...' Cristo slowly slid an emerald ring onto her wedding finger. 'It's the same colour as your eyes and it is to signify my gratitude and appreciation for four very happy years of marriage.'

'Thank you, it's absolutely gorgeous. Unfortunately my gift is unavailable right at this moment, so you'll have to wait.'

'What is it?' Cristo asked curiously.

'Well, it might be turquoise and frilly and exactly the sort of thing you like but you'll just have to wait and see,' she warned him with an irreverent grin. 'It has to be love, Cristo. It really has to be love I feel for you.'

'I adore you, *amata mia*,' Cristo murmured, holding her hand in his. 'And if you're talking about what I think you are, I can hardly wait.'

Belle rolled her green eyes teasingly and her colour heightened. 'You don't have to wait. I'm wearing it. Have you ever heard of the Mile High Club?'

* * * * *

ENTHRALLED BY MORETTI

CATHY WILLIAMS

To my three wonderful daughters.

Cathy Williams is originally from Trinidad, but has lived in England for a number of years. She currently has a house in Warwickshire, which she shares with her husband Richard, her three daughters, Charlotte, Olivia and Emma, and their pet cat, Salem. She adores writing romantic fiction, and would love one of her girls to become a writer – although at the moment she is happy enough if they do their homework and agree not to bicker with one another!

CHAPTER ONE

CHASE EVANS PUSHED aside the folder in front of her and glanced at her watch. For the fourth time. She had now been kept waiting in this conference room for twenty-five minutes. As a lawyer, she knew what this was about. Actually, even if she hadn't been a lawyer she would have known what this was about. It was about intimidation. Intimidation by a juggernaut of a company that was determined to get its own way.

She stood up, flexed her muscles and strolled over to the floor-to-ceiling panes of glass that overlooked the teeming streets of the city.

At this time of year, London was swarming with tourists. From way up here, they appeared to be small little stick figures, but she knew if she went down she would join foreigners from every corner of the globe. You couldn't escape them. You couldn't escape the noise, the crowds and the bustle although here, in the opulent surroundings of AM Holdings, you could be forgiven for thinking that you were a million miles away from all that. It was deathly quiet.

Yet another intimidation tactic, she thought cynically. She had seen a lot in the past few years since she had been a practising lawyer, but the antics of this company took some beating.

She thought back to meeting number one, when they

had imagined that buying up the women's shelter would be a walk in the park. For meeting number one, they had sent their junior lawyer, Tom Barry, who had become embroiled in a tangle of logistics with which he had patently been unable to cope.

For meeting number two, they had dispatched a couple of more experienced guys. Alex Cole and Bruce Robins had come prepared, but so had she. Out of all the pro bono cases in which she specialised, the women's shelter was dearest to her heart. If they had come prepared to wipe it out from under her feet, then she too had upped the stakes, pulling out obscure precursors and covenants that had sent them away scratching their heads and promising that they would be back.

Chase had had no doubt that they would. The shelter, or Beth's House, as it was nicknamed, sat on prime land in West London, land that could earn any halfway canny speculator a great deal of money should it be developed. She knew, through contacts and back doors, that it had been targeted for development by the AM group. An ambitious transformation—from a women's shelter to an exclusive, designer shopping mall for the rich and famous.

Well, over her dead body.

Staring down as the minutes of the clock ticked past and no one appeared, she knew that there was a very real possibility that she would have to let this one go, admit defeat. Yet for so many reasons she refused to let herself think that way.

After Alex and Bruce, her next meeting—this time with her boss by her side—had been with their top guy, Leslie Swift. He had cleverly countered every single magic act they had produced from their rapidly shrinking hat. He had produced by-laws, exemptions and clauses that she knew had been designed to have them running back to the drawing board. Now, alone in this sprawling conference room, Chase knew that she was in the last-chance saloon.

Once again she glanced at her watch before moving back to her seat at the thirty-seater table. Lord only knew who they would send this time to take her on. Maybe they would realise that she was mortally wounded and see fit to delegate her right back to the junior lawyer so that he could gloat at the woman who had sent him packing.

But she had one more trick up her sleeve. She wasn't going to give up without a fight. The memory of giving up without fighting was too embedded in her consciousness for her ever to go down that road again. She had dragged herself away from a dark place where any kind of fighting had never been a good idea and she wasn't about to relinquish any of the grit and determination that had got her where she was now.

Banishing all thoughts of a past that would cripple her if she gave it a chance, Chase Evans returned her attention to the file in front of her and the list of names and numbers she had jotted down as her final attempt to win her case.

'Shall I tell Ms Evans how long she might be expected to wait?'

Alessandro Moretti glanced up at his secretary, who stared back at him with gimlet-eyed steeliness. She had announced Chase Evans's arrival half an hour ago, longer, and had already reminded him once that the woman was waiting for him in the conference room. From anyone else, a second reminder would have been unthinkable. Alicia Brown, however, had been with him for five years and it had been clear from the start that tiptoeing around him wasn't going to be on the cards. She was old enough to be his mother and, if she had never tiptoed around any of her five strapping boys, then she certainly wasn't going to tiptoe around anyone. Alessandro Moretti included. He had hired her on the spot.

'You can't keep her waiting for ever. It's rude.'

'But then,' Alessandro countered drily, 'you've been with me long enough to know that I'm rude.' But he stood up and grabbed his jacket from where he had earlier flung it on the long, low, black leather sofa that occupied one side of the office.

In the concrete jungle where fortunes were made and lost on the toss of a coin, and where the clever man knew how to watch his back because the knives were never far away, Alessandro Moretti, at the tender age of thirty-four, ranked as one of the elite pack leaders.

Well, you didn't get to that exalted position by being soft and tender-hearted. Alessandro understood that. He was feared and respected by his employees. He treated them fairly; more than fairly. Indeed they were amongst the highest paid across the board in the city. In return, the line they trod was the line he marked. If he wanted something done, he expected it to be done yesterday. He snapped his fingers and they jumped to immediate attention.

So he was frankly a little put out that his team of lawyers had, so far, singularly failed in nailing the deal with the shelter. He couldn't imagine that it was anything but routine. He had the money to buy them out and so he would. Why then, four months down the line, was he having to step in and do their job for them?

He had elaborate plans to redevelop the extensive land the place was sitting on. His price was more than fair. Any fool should have been able to go in, negotiate and come out with the papers signed, sealed and delivered.

Instead, in a day which was comprised of back-to-back meetings, he was having to waste time with a two-bit pro bono lawyer who had set up camp on the moral high ground somewhere and was refusing to budge. Did he really need to take valuable time out to demolish her? Because demolish her he most certainly would.

He issued a string of orders as he left his office and threw over his shoulder, as he was about to shut the door behind him, 'And don't forget how good I am at sacking people! So I'd better not find that you've forgotten any of what I've just told you! Because I don't see your trusty notepad anywhere...' He grinned and shut the door smartly behind him before his secretary could tell him what she thought of his parting shot.

He was carrying nothing, because as far as he was concerned he didn't need to. He had been briefed on the woman's arguments. He didn't anticipate needing to strong-arm her at all into giving up. He had managed to unearth a couple of covenants barely visible to the naked eye that would subvert any argument she could put forward. Additionally, she had now been waiting for over forty minutes in a conference room that had deliberately stripped bare of anything that could be seen as homely, comforting, soothing or in any way, shape or form, designed to put someone at ease.

He briefly contemplated summoning those losers who had not been able to do their job so that they could witness first hand how to do it, but decided against it.

One on one. Over and done with in fifteen minutes. Just in time for his next conference call from Hong Kong.

Having had plenty of time to mull over the intimidation tactics, Chase was standing by the window waiting for a team of lawyers. In bare feet, she was five-eleven. In heels, as she was now, she would tower over her opponents. The last one had barely reached her shoulders. Maybe, as a last resort, she could stare them down into submission.

She was gazing out of the window when she heard the

door to the conference room opening behind her and she took her time turning round.

If they could keep her waiting in a room that had all the personality of a prison cell, then she could take her time jumping to attention.

But it wasn't a team of lawyers. It wasn't Tom Barry, Alex Cole, Bruce Robins or Leslie Swift.

She looked at the man standing by the door and she felt the colour drain from her face. She found that she couldn't move from her position of dubious advantage standing by the window. Her legs had turned to lead. Her heart was beating so violently that she felt on the verge of a panic attack. Or, at the very least, an undignified fainting spell.

'You!' This wasn't the strong, steady voice of the self-confident twenty-eight-year-old woman she had finally become.

'Well, well, well…' Alessandro was as shocked as she was but was much more adept at concealing his response and much faster at recovering.

And yet, as he moved slowly towards her, he was finding it almost impossible to believe his eyes.

At the speed of light, he travelled back in time, back to eight years ago, back to the leggy, gloriously beautiful girl who had occupied his every waking hour. She had changed, and yet she hadn't. Gone was the waist-long hair, the jeans and sweater. In its place, the woman standing in front of him, looking as though she had seen a ghost— which he supposed she had—was impeccably groomed. Her shoulder-length bob was the same blend of rich caramel and chestnut, her slanting eyes were as green and feline as he remembered, her body as long and willowy.

'Lyla Evans…' He strolled towards her, one hand in his trouser pocket. 'Should I have clocked the surname? Maybe I would have if it hadn't been preceded by Chase…' He was standing right in front of her now. She looked as though she was about to pass out. He hoped she wouldn't expect him to catch her if she fell.

'Alessandro… No one said… I wasn't expecting…'

'So I see.' His smile was cold and devoid of humour. Of their own accord, his eyes travelled to her finger. No wedding ring. Not that that said very much, all things considered.

'Will you be here on your own, or can I expect the rest of your team…?' Chase tried desperately to regain some of her shattered composure but she couldn't. She was driven to stare at the harsh, sinfully sexy contours of a face that had crept into her head far too many times to count. He was as beautiful as she remembered. More so, if that were possible. At twenty-six, he had been sexy as hell but still with the imprint of youth. Now he was a man, and there was nothing warm or open in his face. She was staring at a stranger, someone who hated her and who was making no attempt to mask his hatred.

'Just me. Cosy, as it turns out. Don't you think? So many years since last we saw one another, Lyla…or Chase, or whoever the hell you really are.'

'Chase. My name is Chase. It always was.'

'So the pseudonym was purely for my benefit. Of course, it makes sense, given the circumstances at the time…'

'Lyla was my mother's name. If you don't mind, I think I'll sit.' She tottered over to the chair and collapsed on it. The stack of files in front of her, her briefcase, her laptop, they were all reminders of why she was in this conference room in the first place, but for the life of her she couldn't focus on them. Her thoughts were all over the place.

'So, shall we play a little catch-up, Lyla? Sorry…Chase? A little polite conversation about what we've been doing for the past eight years?' Alessandro perched on the edge of the sprawling conference table and stared down at her:

the one and only woman he had wasted time chasing, only to be left frustrated when she'd failed to fall into his bed. For that reason alone, she occupied a unique spot in his life. Add all the other reasons and she was in a league of her own.

'I'd rather not.'

'I bet. In your shoes, I'd plead the fifth as well.'

'Alessandro, I know what you must think of me, but—'

'I really don't need to hear any sob stories, Lyla.'

'Stop calling me that. My name is Chase.'

'So you became a lawyer after all. I take my hat off to you—although, thinking about it, you did prove you were the sort of girl who would get what she wanted whatever the cost...'

Chase's eyes flickered up to him. The expression on his face sent the chill of fear racing up and down her spine, yet how could she blame him? Their story had been brief and so full of things that had to be hidden that it was hardly surprising.

'And I notice that there's no telling wedding ring on your finger,' he continued in the same mildly speculative voice that wouldn't have fooled an idiot. 'Did you dispose of the hapless husband in your ever-onwards and upwards climb?'

When he had met her—sitting there in the university canteen with a book in front of her, a little frown on her face, completely oblivious to everyone around her—she had knocked him sideways. It was more than the fact that she'd stood out, that she possessed head-turning looks; the world was full of girls who could turn heads. No, it had been her complete and utter indifference to the glances angled in her direction. He had watched as she had toyed with her sandwich before shoving it to one side and heading out. She had looked neither right nor left. The canteen could have been devoid of people.

Standing here now, looking at her, Alessandro could recreate that feeling of intense, incomprehensible attraction that had swept over him then as though it had been yesterday.

Significantly, she hadn't been wearing a wedding ring then either.

'I'm not here to talk about my past,' Chase said, clearing her throat. 'I've brought all the paperwork about the shelter.'

'And I'm not ready to talk about that yet.' He sat on one of the chairs alongside her and angled it away from the table so that he had a bird's eye view of her as she stared down at the bundle of files and papers in front of her and pretended to concentrate. 'So...' he drawled. 'You were about to tell me where the wedding ring's gone...'

'I don't believe I was,' Chase said coolly, gathering herself. Eyes the colour of bitter chocolate bored straight through her, bypassing the hard, glossy veneer she had taken so much time and trouble to build like a fortress around herself. 'You might be curious about what I've been up to for the past few years, Alessandro, but I have no intention of satisfying your curiosity. I just want to do what I came here to do and leave.'

'You came here to lose to me,' Alessandro told her without preamble. 'If you had any sense, you would recognise that and wave the white flag before I start lowering the price I've offered to pay for that place.' He drew her attention to the clock on the wall. 'With every passing minute, I drop my price by a grand, so make sure your argument's a winning one, because if it's not you're going to find that you're not working on behalf of your client.'

'You can't do that.'

'I can do whatever I like, Lyla...Chase...or shall I call you Mrs Evans? Or perhaps *Ms*...?'

'This isn't about *us,* Alessandro.' She tried to claw the

conversation back to the matter at hand, back to the shelter. 'So please don't think that you can use empty threats to—'

'Look around you,' Alessandro cut in lazily. 'And tell me what you see.'

'Where are you going with this?'

'Just do as I ask.'

Chase looked around nervously. She could feel the jaws of a trap yawning around her, but when she tried to figure out what sort of trap she came up empty. 'Big, bland conference room,' she told him in a voice that hinted that she was already bored with the subject. When she looked around her, her eyes kept wanting to return to him, to look at his face and absorb all the small changes there. Seeing him now, she was beginning to realise that she had never entirely forgotten him. She had buried him but it had obviously been in a shallow grave.

'I like it bland. It doesn't pay to provide distractions when you want the people seated at this table to be focused.'

'*You* like it bland...'

'Correct. You see, I am AM Holdings. I own it all. Every single deal is passed by me. What I say goes and no one contradicts me. So, when I tell you that I intend to drop my price by a grand for every minute you argue with me, I mean it and it's within my power to do it. Of course, you're all business and you think you can win, in which case my threat will be immaterial. But if you don't, well, after a couple of hours of futile arguing... Do the maths.'

Chase looked at him, lost for words. In view of what had happened between them, the deceit and the half-lies that had finally been her undoing, she was staring at a man who had been gifted his revenge. She should have done her homework on the company more thoroughly, but she had been handed the case after her boss had done the preliminaries himself, only to find that he couldn't follow through for personal reasons. She had focused all her energies on trying to locate loopholes that would prevent the sale of the shelter to *anyone* rather than specifically to AM Holdings. Even so, would she have recognised Alessandro had his name cropped up? They hadn't afforded much time for surnames.

'Sounds ungentlemanly.' Alessandro gave an elegant shrug and a smile that was as cold as the frozen wastelands. 'But, when it comes to business, I've always found that being a gentleman doesn't usually pay dividends.'

'Why are you doing this? How could you think of punishing those helpless women who use the shelter because we…we…?'

'Had an ill-fated relationship? Because you lied to me? Deceived me? Does your firm of lawyers know the kind of person you really are?'

Chase didn't say anything but she could feel her nervous system go into overdrive. She had inadvertently stepped into the lion's den; how far did revenge go? What paths would it travel down before it was finally satisfied? Alessandro Moretti owned this place. Not only was it within his power to do exactly as he said, to reduce the amount he was willing to pay for the shelter with each passing minute, but what if he decided actively to go after *her*?

'Things weren't what they seemed back then, Alessandro.'

'The clock's ticking.' He relaxed and folded his hands behind his head. Against all odds, and knowing her for what she really was, he was irritated to discover that he could still appreciate her on a purely physical level. He had never laid a finger on her but, hell, he had fantasised about it until his head had spun, had wondered what she would look like underneath the student clothes, what she would feel like. By the time he had met her, he had already bedded his fair share of women, yet she had appealed to him on a level he had barely comprehended.

He hadn't gone to the university intending to get involved with anyone. He had gone there as a favour to his old don, to give a series of business lectures, to get students inspired enough to know that they could attempt to achieve in record time what he had succeeded in achieving. Six lectures charting business trends, showing how you could buck them and still come out a winner, and he would be gone. He hadn't anticipated meeting Lyla—or, as she now called herself, Chase—and staying on to give a further six lectures.

For the first time in his very privileged life, he had found himself in a situation with a woman over which he'd had little control and he had been prepared to kick back and enjoy it. For someone to whom things had always come easy, he had even enjoyed the hard-to-get game she had played. Of course, he had not expected that the hard-to-get game would, in fact, lead nowhere in the end, but then how was he to know the woman he had been dealing with? She had left him with the ugly taste of disillusionment in his mouth and now here she was…

Wasn't fate a thing of beauty?

'You're not interested in reliving our…exciting past. So, sell me your arguments… And, by the way, that's one minute gone…'

Feeling that she had stepped into a nightmare, Chase opened the top file with trembling fingers. Of course she could understand that he was bitter and angry with her. And yet in her mind, when she had projected into a future that involved her accidentally running into him somewhere, his bitterness and anger had never been so deep, nor had he been vengeful. He could really hurt her, really undo all the work she had done to get where she had.

She began going over some of the old ground covered

in the past three meetings she'd had with his underlings, and he inclined his head to one side with every semblance of listening, before interrupting her with a single slash of his hand.

'You know, of course, that none of those obstructions hold water. You're prevaricating and it won't work.'

Chase involuntarily glanced at the clock on the wall and was incensed that the meeting—all the important things that had to be discussed, things that involved the lives of other people—had been sidelined by this unfortunate, unexpected and worrying collision with her past.

And yet she lowered her eyes and took in the taut pull of expensive trousers over his long legs, the fine, dark hair that liberally sprinkled his forearms... Not even the unspoken atmosphere of threat in his cool, dark eyes could detract from the chiselled perfection of his face. He had the burnished colour of someone of exotic blood.

When she had first laid eyes on him, she had been knocked sideways. He hadn't beaten about the bush. He had noticed her, he said, had seen her sitting in the university canteen. She had instinctively known that he had been waiting for a predictable response. The response of a woman in the presence of a man who could have whoever he wanted, and he wanted her. She had also known that there was no way she could go there. That she should smile politely and walk away, because doing anything else would have been playing with fire. But still she had hesitated, long enough for him to recognise a mutual interest. Of course, it had always been destined to end badly, but she hadn't been able to help herself.

She tightened her lips as she realised just how badly things could go now, all these years later.

'Okay, so you may have all the legalities in place, but what do you think the press would make of a big, bad company rolling in and bulldozing a women's shelter? The public has had enough of powerful people and powerful companies thinking that they can do exactly as they like.' This had been her trump card but there was no hint of triumph in her voice as she pulled it out of the bag.

'I have names here,' she continued in the gathering silence, not daring to risk a glance at him. 'Contacts with journalists and reporters who would be sympathetic to my cause...' She shoved the paper across to him and Alessandro ignored it.

'Are you threatening me?' he asked in a tone of mild curiosity.

'I wouldn't call it threatening...'

'No? Then what exactly *would* you call it?'

'I'm exercising leverage.' It had seemed an excellent idea at the time, but then she hadn't banked on finding herself floundering in a situation she couldn't have envisaged in a million years. His dark eyes focused on her face made her want to squirm and she knew that her veneer of self-confidence and complete composure was badly undermined by the slow tide of pink colour rising to her face. 'If you buy the shelter in a cloud of bad publicity, whatever you put up there will be destined to fail. It's quite a small community in that particular part of London. People will take sides and none of them will be on yours.'

'I bet you thought that you'd bring that out from up your sleeve and my lawyers would scatter, because there *is* such a thing as bad publicity being worse than no publicity. It's a low trick, but then I'm not surprised that you would resort to low tricks.' He leaned forward, rested both arms on the shiny conference table and stared directly at her. 'However, let's just turn that threat on its head for a minute...'

'It's not a threat.'

'I have offered an extremely generous price for the purchase of the shelter and the land that goes with it. More than enough for another shelter to be built somewhere else.'

'They don't *want* to build another shelter somewhere else. These women are accustomed to Beth's House. They feel safe there.'

'*You* can wax lyrical to your buddies at the press that they're being shoved out unceremoniously from their comfort zone. My people will counter-attack with a long, detailed and extremely enticing list of what they could buy for the money they'll be getting from me. A shelter twice the size. All mod cons. An equal amount of land, albeit further out. Hell, they could even run to a swimming pool, a games room, a nursery...the list goes on.

'So, who do you think will end up winning the argument? And, when it comes to light that I will be using the land for a mall that will provide much-needed jobs for the locals, well, you can see where I'm going with this...' He stood up and strolled lazily towards the very same window through which she had been peering earlier.

Chase couldn't tear her eyes away from him. Like an addict in the sudden presence of her drug of choice, she found that she was responding in ways that were dangerously off-limits. She shouldn't be reacting like this. She couldn't afford to let him into her life, nor could she afford to have any deep and meaningful conversations about their brief and ruined past relationship. Heck, it had only lasted a handful of months! And had never got off the starting block anyway.

'So.' Alessandro turned slowly to face her. With his back to the window, the light poured in from behind, throwing his face into shadows. 'How are you feeling about your ability to win this one now?'

'It's Beth's place; she's comfortable there. Why do you think people fight to stay in their homes when a developer comes along promising to buy them out for double what their place is worth?' But he would be able to sell it across the board. He had the money and the people to make sure that whatever message they wanted to get across would be successful. She knew Beth. Was she fighting to preserve something for reasons that were personal?

'I can tell from your expression that you already know that you're staring defeat in the face. By the way, it's been nearly forty-five minutes of unconvincing arguing from you... So how much have you lost your client already? The games room? The nursery? The giant kitchen with the cosy wooden table where all those women can hold hands and break bread?'

'I never thought that you were as arrogant as I now see you are.'

'But then you could say that we barely knew anything about each other. Although, in fairness, I didn't lie about my identity...' He was unconsciously drawn to the way the sunlight streaming through the panes of glass caught the colours of her hair. Her suit was snappy and business-like and he could tell that it had been chosen to downplay her figure. In his mind's eye, he saw the tight jeans, the jumpers and trainers, and that tentative smile that had won him over.

Chase stared down at the folder in front of her. There was nothing left to pull out of the hat. Even if there was, this was personal. He was determined to win the final argument, to have the last word, to *make her pay*.

'So I'm guessing from your prolonged silence that you'll be breaking the happy news to... What's her name? Beth?'

'You know it is.'

'And can you work out how much I'll be deducting from my initial offer?'

'Tell me you don't really mean to go through with that?'

'Lie, in other words?' Alessandro walked towards her and perched on the edge of the table.

'You can't force them to sell.'

'Have you had a look at their books? They're in debt.

Waiting to be picked off. It may be a caring, sharing place, but what it gains in the holding hands and chanting stakes it lacks in the accountancy arena. A quiet word in the right banker's ear and they'll be facing foreclosure by dusk. Furthermore, if it becomes widespread knowledge that they're in financial trouble, the vulture developers will swoop in looking for a bargain. What started out as a generous offer from me would devolve into an untidy fire sale with the property and land going for a song.'

'Okay.' Chase recognised the truth behind what he was saying. How could this be the same man who had once teased her, entertained her with his wit, impressed her with the breadth of his intelligence…driven her crazy with a longing that had never had a chance to be sated?

'Okay?'

'You win, Alessandro.' She looked at him with green eyes that had once mesmerised him right out of the rigidly controlled box into which he had always been accustomed to piling his emotional entanglements with the opposite sex. 'But maybe you could tell me whether you would have been as hardline if I hadn't been the person sitting here trying to talk you out of buying the shelter.'

'Oh, the sale most certainly would have gone ahead,' Alessandro drawled without an ounce of sympathy. 'But I probably wouldn't have tacked on the ticking clock.'

He strolled round to his chair and sat back down. His mobile phone buzzed, and when his secretary told him to get a move on because she could only defer his conference call for so long he informed her briefly that she would have to cancel it altogether. 'And make sure the same goes for my meetings after lunch,' he murmured, not once taking his eyes off Chase's downbent head. He signed off just as Alicia began to launch into a curious demand to know why.

'I don't want to keep you.' Chase began stacking all her files together and shoving them into her capacious brief case. She paused to look at him. *Last look*, she thought. *Then I'll never see you again.* She found that she was drinking in his image and she knew, with resignation, that what she looked at now would haunt her in the weeks to come. It was just so unfair. 'But I would like it if you could reconsider your…your…'

'Lower offer? And save you the humiliation of having to tell your client that you single-handedly knocked the price down?'

Chase glared at him. 'I never took you for a bully.'

'Life, as we both know, is full of cruel shocks. I'll admit that I have no intention of pulling out of this purchase, but you could recoup the lost thousands.'

'Could I? How?' She stared at him. At this point, the images of those wonderful additions to any other house Beth might buy vanishing in a puff of smoke, because of her, were proliferating in her head, making her giddy. She knew that the finances for the shelter were in serious disarray. They would need all the money they could get just to pay off the debts and wipe the slate clean.

'We have an unfinished past,' Alessandro murmured. 'It's time to finish it. I wouldn't have sought out this opportunity but, now it's here, I want to know who the hell you really are. Satisfy my curiosity and the full price is back on the table…'

CHAPTER TWO

So WHERE WAS the jump for joy, the high five, the shriek of delight? For the sake of a little conversation, she stood to claw back a substantial amount of money. He might have expected some show of emotion, even if only in passing.

Alessandro didn't take his eyes off her face, nor did he utter a word; the power of silence was a wonderful thing. Plus, he didn't trust her as far as he could throw her. If she thought that she could somehow screw him for more than the agreed amount, then let her have all the silence in the world, during which she could rethink any such stupid notion.

'I would need any assurances from you in writing,' Chase finally said. He wanted to finish business between them? Didn't he know that that was impossible? There were no questions she could ever answer and no explanations she could ever give.

'You will be getting no such thing,' Alessandro assured her calmly. 'You take my word for it or you leave here with your wallet several shades lighter.'

'There's no point rehashing what happened between us, Alessandro.'

'Your answer: yes or no. Simple choice.'

Chase stood up and smoothed down her grey skirt. She knew that she had a good figure, very tall and very slender. It was a bonus because it meant that she could pull off

cheap clothing; she felt she needed simply to blend in with
the other lawyers and paralegals in the company where she
worked. Fitzsimmons was a top-ranking law firm and it
employed top-ranking people; no riff-raff. Nearly everyone there came from a background where Mummy and
Daddy owned second homes in the country. She kept her
distance from all of them, but still she knew where they
came from just by listening to their exploits at the weekends, the holidays they booked and the Chelsea apart-
ments they lived in.

Thankfully, she was one of only two specialising in
pro bono cases, so she could keep her head down, put
in her hours and attend only the most essential of social
functions.

She didn't want her quiet life vandalised. She didn't
want Alessandro Moretti strolling back into it, asking
questions and nursing a vendetta against her. She just
couldn't afford to have any cans of worms opened up.

Likewise, she didn't want to feel this scary surge of
emotion that made her go weak at the knees. Her life was
her own now, under control, and she didn't want to jeop-
ardise that.

But where were the choices? Did she make Beth pay for
what *she* didn't want? Did she risk her boss's disapproval
when she turned up and recounted what had happened?

More than that, if she kept her lips tightly buttoned
up, who was to say that Alessandro would conveniently
disappear? The way those hard, black eyes were watching her now...

She sat back down. 'Okay. What do you want to talk
about? I mean, what do you want me to say?'

'Now, you don't really expect us to have a cosy little
chat in a room like this, do you?'

He began prowling around the conference room: thick
cream carpet aided and abetted the silence; cream walls;

the imposing hard-edged table where the great and the good could sit in front of their opened laptops, conversing in computer-speak and making far-reaching decisions that could affect the livelihoods of numerous people lower down the food chain, often for the better, occasionally for the worst.

'I mean, we have so much catching up to do, Lyla… Chase…'

'Please stop calling me Lyla. I told you, I don't use that name any more.'

'It's approaching lunchtime. Why don't we continue this conversation somewhere a little more comfortable?'

'I'm fine here.'

'Actually, you don't have a vote. I have five minutes' worth of business to deal with. I trust you can find your way down to the foyer? And don't…' he positioned himself neatly in front of her '…even think of running out on me.'

'I wouldn't do that.' Chase tilted her chin and stood up to look him squarely in the eyes. As a show of strength, it spectacularly backfired because, up close and personal like this, she could feel all her energy drain out of her, leaving behind a residue of tumultuous emotions and a dangerous, scary *awareness*. Her nostrils flared as she breathed in the clean, woody, aggressively masculine scent of his cologne. She took an unsteady step back and prayed that he hadn't noticed her momentary weakness.

'No?' Alessandro drawled, narrowing his eyes. 'Because right now you look like a rabbit caught in the headlights. Why? It's not as though I don't already know you for a liar, a cheat and a slut.' He had never addressed a woman so harshly in his life before but, looking at her here, taking in the perfection of a face that could launch a thousand ships and a body that was slender but with curves in all the right places, the reality of their past had slammed

into him and lent an ugly bitterness to every word that
passed his lips.

'I notice you're not defending yourself,' he murmured.
He didn't know whether her lack of fight was satisfying
or not. Certainly, he wished that she would look at him
when he spoke, and he was sorely tempted to angle her
face to him.

'What's the point?' Chase asked tightly. 'I'll meet you
in the foyer but...' she looked at him with a spurt of angry
rebellion '...I won't be hanging around for an hour while
you take your time seeing to last-minute business with
your secretary.'

Alessandro's eyes drifted down to her full, perfectly
shaped mouth. He used to tease her that she looked as
though she was sulking when it was in repose, but when
she smiled it was like watching a flower bloom. He had
never been able to get his fill of it. She certainly wasn't
smiling now.

'Actually, you'll hang around for as long as I want you
to.'

'Just because you want to...to...pay me back for...'

'Like I said, let's save the cosy chit-chat for somewhere
more comfortable.'

Only when he left the room did Chase realise how tense
she had been. She sagged and closed her eyes, steadying
herself against the table.

She felt like the victim of a runaway truck. In a heartbeat, her life seemed to have been derailed, and she had
to tell herself that it wasn't so; that because Alessandro
was the man with whom she was now having to deal, because their paths had crossed in such a shadowy manner,
it didn't mean that he was out to destroy her. His pride had
been injured all those years ago and what he wanted from
her now was answers to the questions he must have asked

himself in the aftermath of their break-up. Not that they had ever really had a *relationship*.

Of course, she would have to be careful with what she told him, but once he was satisfied they would both return to their lives and it would be as if they had never met again.

She left the conference room in a hurry. It was almost twelve-thirty and there were far more people walking around than when she had first entered the impressive building. Workers were going out to lunch. It was a perfect summer's day. There would be sandwiches in the park and an hour's worth of relaxing in the sun before everyone stuck back on their jackets and returned to their city desks. Chase had always made sure to steer clear of that.

In the foyer, she didn't have long to wait before she spotted Alessandro stepping out of the lift. As he walked towards her, one finger holding the jacket that he had tossed over his shoulder, she relived those heady times when she had enjoyed kidding herself that her life could really change. Every single time she had seen him, she had felt a rush of pure, adrenaline-charged excitement, even though all they ever did was have lunch together or a cappuccino somewhere.

'So you're here.'

'You didn't really expect me to run away?' Chase fell into step alongside him. It was a treat not to tower over a guy but she still had to walk quickly to match his pace as they went through the revolving glass doors and out into the busy street.

'No, of course I didn't. You're a lawyer. You know when diplomacy is called for.' He swung left and began walking away from the busier streets, down the little side roads that gave London such character. 'And, on the subject of your career, why don't we kick off our catch-up with that?'

'What do you want to know?'

Alessandro leaned down towards her. 'Let's really get

into the spirit of this, Chase. Let's not do a question-and-answer session, with me having to drag conversation out of you.'

'What do you expect, Alessandro? I don't want to be here!'

'I'm sure you don't, but you're here now, so humour me.'

'I…I…got a first-class degree. In my final year I was head-hunted by a firm of lawyers—not the ones I work for now, but a good firm. I was fast-tracked.'

'Clever Chase.'

Chase recognised that it hadn't been said as a compliment, although she could only guess at what he was implying. He loathed her so, whatever it was, she had no doubt that it would be offensive.

Yet, she *was* clever. In another place and another time, she knew that she would have been one of those girls who would have been said to 'have it all': brains and looks. But then, life had a way of counter-balancing things. At any rate, she had relied far more on her brains than she ever had on her looks. She had worked like a demon to get her A-levels, fought against all odds to get to a top university, and once there had doggedly spared no effort in getting a degree that would set her up for life. And all that against a backdrop that she had trained herself never to think about.

'Thank you.' She chose to misinterpret the tone of his voice. 'So, I got a good job, did my training, changed companies…and here I am now.'

'Fitzsimmons. Classy firm.'

'Yes, it is.' She could feel fine prickles of nervousness beading her forehead.

'And yet, no designer suit? Don't they pay you enough?'

Chase cringed with embarrassment. He had never made any secret about the fact that he came from money. Was that how he could spot the fact that her clothes were off the peg and ready to wear from a chain store? 'They pay me more than enough,' she said coolly. 'But I prefer to save my money instead of throwing it away to a high-end retailer.'

'How noble. Not a trait I would tend to associate with you.'

'Can't you at least try and be civil towards me?' Chase asked thinly. 'At any rate, most of my work is pro bono. It's sensible not to show up in designer suits that cost thousands.' It was what she had laughingly told someone at the firm ages ago and her boss had applauded her good sense.

They were now in front of an old-fashioned pub nestled in one of the quieter back alleys. There were gems like this all over London. When they entered, it was dark, cool and quiet. He offered her a drink and shrugged when she told him that she would stick to fruit juice.

'So...' Alessandro sat down, hand curved round his pint, and looked at her. He honestly didn't know what he hoped to gain from this forced meeting but seeing her again had reawakened the nasty questions she had left unanswered. 'Let's start at the beginning. Or maybe we should pick it up at the end—at the point when you told me that you were married. Yes, maybe that's the place we should start. After we'd been meeting for four months... Four months of flirting and you gazing at me all convincingly doe-eyed and breathless, then informing me that you had a husband waiting in the wings.'

Chase nursed her fruit juice. She licked her lips nervously. Her green eyes tangled and clashed with cold eyes the colour of jet. 'I don't see what the point of this is, Alessandro.'

'You know what the point of it is—you're going to satisfy my curiosity in return for the full agreed price for your shelter. It's a fair exchange. Tell me what happened to the husband.'

'Shaun...was killed shortly after I got my first job. He... he was on his motorbike at the time. He was speeding, lost control, crashed into the central reservation on the motorway…'

'So you didn't ditch him in the impersonal confines of a divorce court.' Nor would she have. Alessandro downed a mouthful of beer and watched her over the rim of the glass. Not, as she had told him on that last day in exhaustive detail, when he'd been her childhood sweetheart and the love of her life. 'And I take it you never remarried.'

'Nor will I ever.' She could detect the bitterness that had crept into her voice, but when she looked at him his expression was still as cool and unrelenting as it had been.

'Is that because there's no room for a man in the life of an ambitious, high-flying lawyer? Or because you're still wrapped up with the man who was…let me try and remember… Oh, yes, I've got it: the only guy you would ever contemplate sleeping with. *Sorry if you got the wrong idea, Alessandro. A few cappuccinos does not a relationship make, but it's been a laugh…*'

'We should never have seen each other. It was a terrible idea. I never meant to get involved with anyone.'

'But you didn't get involved with me, did you?' Alessandro angled his beautiful head to one side as he picked up an unspoken message he wasn't quite getting.

What was there to get or not get? he thought impatiently. The woman had strung him along, led him up the garden path and then had casually disappeared without a backward glance. Hell, she had made him feel things… No, he wasn't going to go there.

'No! No, I didn't. I meant…'

'I'm all ears.'

'You don't understand. I shouldn't even have even to you. I was married.'

'So why did you? Were you riding high on the knowledge that you'd managed to net the rich guy all the groupie students were after?'

'That's a very conceited thing to say.'

'I value honesty. I lost track of the number of notes I got from girls asking for some "extra tuition".'

If there hadn't been notes, she thought, then he surely would have clocked the stares he'd garnered everywhere he went. The man was an alpha male with enough sex appeal to sink a ship. Throw in his wealth, and it was little wonder that girls were queuing up to see if they could attract his attention. She'd never, ever been at the university longer than was strictly necessary but, if she had been, she knew that she would have become a source of envy, curiosity and dislike.

'So was that why you decided to keep your marital status under wraps? To take the wedding ring off? To string me along with the promise of sex?'

'I never said we would end up in bed.'

'Do me a favour!' He slammed his empty glass on the table and Chase jumped. 'You knew exactly what you were getting into!'

'And I didn't think… I never thought…'

'So you lied about the fact that you weren't single or available for a relationship.'

'If I remember correctly, you once told me that you weren't interested in commitment, that you liked your relationships fast and furious and temporary!'

Alessandro flushed darkly. 'Weak reasoning,' he gritted cuttingly. 'Did you lie because you thought that you might try me out for size? See whether I wasn't a better bet than the stay-at-home husband? Is that why you strung me along for four months? Were you hedging your bets?' He shook his head, furious with himself for losing control of the conversation, for actually caring one way or another what had or hadn't been done eight years previously.

'No, of course not! And Shaun was never a *stay-at-*

home husband.' Again, that bitterness had crept into her voice.

'No? So what was he, then?' Alessandro leaned forward, the simple shift of body weight implying threat. 'Banker? Entrepreneur? If I recall, you were a little light on detail. In fact, if my memory serves me right, you couldn't wait to get out of my company fast enough the very last time we met.'

Alessandro was surprised to find that he could remember exactly what she had been wearing the very last time he'd laid eyes on her: a pair of faded skinny jeans tucked into some cheap imitation-suede boots and a jumper which now, thinking about it, had probably belonged to the 'childhood sweetheart' husband. On that thought, his jaw clenched and his eyes darkened.

It hadn't taken her long to spill out the truth. Having spent months of innocent conversation, tentative advances and retreats and absolutely no physical contact—which had been hell for him—she had sat down opposite him at the wine bar which had become their favourite meeting place; at a good bus ride away, it was far from all things university. With very little preamble, and keeping her eyes glued to his face while around them little clusters of strangers had drunk, laughed and chatted, all very relaxed in the run-up to Christmas, she'd informed him that she would no longer be seeing him.

'Sorry,' he recalled her saying with a brittle smile. 'It's been a laugh, and thanks for all the help with the economics side of the course, but actually I'm married...'

She had wagged her ring finger in front of him, complete with never-before-seen wedding band.

Shaun McGregor, she had said airily. Love of her life. Had known him since they were both fifteen. She had even pulled out a picture of him from her beaten-up old wallet and waxed lyrical about his striking good looks.

Alessandro had stared long and hard at the photo of a young man with bright blue eyes and a shaved head. There was a tattoo at the side of his neck; he'd probably been riddled with them. It had been brought home to him sharply just what a fool he had been taken for. Not only had she strung him along for fun, but he had never actually been her type. Her husband had had all the fine qualities of a first-rate thug.

'Shaun did lots of different things,' Chase said vaguely. 'But none of that matters now, anyway. The fact is, I'm sorry. I know it's late in the day to apologise, but I'm apologising.'

'Why did you use a different name?'

'Huh?'

'You used the name Lyla. Not just with me, with everyone. Why?'

'I…' How could she possibly explain that she had been a different person then? That she had had the chance to create a wonderful, shiny new persona, and that she had taken it, because what she could create had been so much better than the reality. She had still been clever, and she had never lied about her academic history but, she had thought, what was the harm in passing herself off as just someone normal? Someone with a solid middle-class background and parents who cared about her? It hadn't been as though she would ever have been required to present these mysterious and fictitious parents to anyone.

And she had always made sure never to get too close to anyone—until Alessandro had come along. Even then, at the beginning, she had had no idea that she would fall so far, so fast and so deep, nor that the little white lies she had told at the beginning would develop into harmful untruths that she'd no longer be able to retract.

'Well?' Alessandro prompted harshly. 'You lied about your single status and you lied about your name. So let's take them one at a time.' He signalled to a waitress and ordered himself another glass of beer. There went the afternoon, was the thought that passed through his mind. There was little chance he would be in the mood for a series of intense meetings and conference calls later. He was riveted by the hint of changing expressions on her face. He felt that he was in possession of a book, the meaning of which escaped him even though he had read the story from beginning to end. Then he cursed himself for being fanciful, which was so unlike him.

'Lyla was my mother's name. I like it. I didn't think there was anything wrong in using it.'

'And so you stopped liking it when you decided to join a law firm?'

'You said we weren't going to do a question-and-answer session!' Her skin burned from the intensity of his eyes on her. Alessandro Moretti, even as a young man in his mid-twenties, had always had a powerful, predatory appeal. There was something dangerous about him that sent shivers up and down her spine and drew her to him, even when common sense told her it was mad. He certainly hadn't lost that appeal.

'It was easier to just use my real name when I joined Edge Ellison, that first law firm. I mean, my Christian name.'

'Why am I getting the feeling that there are a thousand holes in whatever fairy story you're spinning me?'

'I'm not spinning you a fairy story!' Chase snapped. Bright spots of colour stained her cheeks. 'If you want, I can bring my birth certificate to show you!' Except that would suggest a second meeting, which was not something that was going to be on the cards.

But what would he do if he found out where she really came from? What would he do if he discovered that the solid, middle-class background she had innocently hinted at had been about as real as a swimming pool in the middle of the Sahara?

He might be tempted to have a quiet chat with the head of her law firm, she thought with a sickening jolt. Of course, she hadn't lied about any of her qualifications, and she knew that she was a damned good lawyer. There was no way she could be given the sack for just allowing people to *assume* a background that wasn't entirely true, yet...

Wounded pride and dislike could make a person do anything in their power to get revenge. What if he shared all her little white lies with the people she worked with— the posh, private-school educated young men and women who weren't half as good as she was but who would have a field day braying with laughter at her expense? She was strong, but she knew that she was not so strong that she could survive ridicule at the work place.

'I should be getting back to work.' She drained the remainder of her orange juice and made to stand up.

Without thinking, Alessandro reached out and circled his hand around her wrist.

Chase froze. Really, it was the most peculiar sensation...as if her entire body had locked into place so that she was incapable of movement. His fingers around her wrist were as dramatic as a branding iron and she felt her heart pick up speed until she thought it might explode inside her.

'Not so fast.'

'I've answered all your questions, Alessandro!'

'What the hell was in it for you?'

'Nothing! I...just made a mistake! It was a long time ago. I was just a kid.'

'A kid of twenty and already hitched. I didn't think that kind of thing happened any more.'   .

'I told you...we were in love...' Chase looked away and

shook her hand free of his vice-like grip. 'We didn't see the point of waiting.'

'And your families both joined in the celebrations?'

She shrugged. 'He's dead now, anyway, so it doesn't matter whether they joined in the celebrations or not.'

'Spoken like a true grieving widow.' Why did he keep getting this feeling that something was out of kilter? Was his mind playing tricks on him? Had his ego been so badly bruised eight years ago that he would rather look for hidden meanings than take her very simple tale of treachery at face value?

'It's been years. I've moved on.'

'And no one else has surfaced on the scene to replace the late lamented?'

'Why is this all about me?' Chase belatedly thought that she might turn the spotlight onto him. If there was one thing to be said for going into law whilst simultaneously detaching yourself from most of the human race, it was that it did dramatic things to your confidence levels. Or maybe it was just her 'flight or fight' reflex getting an airing. She stared him squarely in the face and tried not to let the steady, speculative directness of his gaze get to her.

'What about *you*?' she asked coolly. 'We haven't said anything about what *you've* been up to…'

'What's there to say?' Alessandro relaxed back, angling his body so that he could cross his legs. She really did have a face that made for compulsive watching. It was exquisite, yet with a guarded expression that made you wonder what was going on behind the beautiful mask. Even as a much younger woman, she had possessed that sense of unique mystery that had fired his curiosity and kept it for the duration of their strange dalliance.

And now, yet again, he could feel his curiosity piqued.

'I'm an open book.' He spread his arms wide. 'I don't

hide who I am and I don't make a habit of leading anyone down the garden path.'

'And is there a special someone in *your* life? Is there a Mrs Moretti dusting and cleaning in a house in the country somewhere and a few little Moretti children scampering around outside? Or are you still only into the fast and furious relationship without the happy ending?'

'My, my. You've certainly become acid-tongued, Chase.'

Chase flushed. Yes she had. And there were times when she stood back and wondered if she really liked the person she had become. Not that she had ever been soft and fluffy, but now...

'I don't like being trampled.'

'And is that why you think I brought you here? To trample over you? Is that what you think I'm doing?'

Chase shrugged. 'Isn't it?'

'We're exchanging information. How could that possibly be described as trampling all over you? And, in answer to your question, there is no Mrs Moretti in a country house—and if there were, she certainly wouldn't be dusting or cleaning.'

'Because you have enough money to pay for someone to dust and clean for you. Are you still working twenty-four-seven? Surely you must have made enough billions by now to kick back and enjoy life?'

She used to listen, enraptured, as he'd told her about his working life: non-stop; on the go all the time. The lectures, he had said, were like comic relief, little windows of relaxation. She had teased him that, if giving lectures was his form of relaxation, then he would keel over with high blood pressure by the time he was thirty-five. She was annoyed to find herself genuinely curious and interested to hear what he had been up to. Having anything to do with Alessandro Moretti was even more hazardous now than it had been eight years ago.

'None of my business,' she qualified in a clipped voice. 'Am I free to go now?'

Alessandro's lips thinned. He had found out precisely nothing. None of his questions had been answered. His brain was telling him to walk away but some other part of him wanted more.

'Why did you decide to concentrate on pro bono cases?' He asked softly. 'Surely with a first-class degree, and law firms head-hunting you, there were far more profitable things to do?'

'I've never been interested in making money.' He had stopped attacking her and she realised that she had forgotten how seductive he could be when he was genuinely interested in hearing what she had to say. He would tilt his head to one side and would give the impression that every word she uttered was of life-changing importance.

'I'd always planned on becoming a lawyer, although the two other options that tempted me were Social Services and the police force.' She blushed, because she didn't think that she had confided that in anyone before—not that she did a lot of confiding anyway.

'Social Services? The police force?'

'So please don't accuse me of being materialistic.'

'I can't picture you as a social worker, even less a policewoman.'

'I should be getting back to work. I have a lot to do, and I'll have to visit the shelter later today and tell them what the outcome of my meeting with your company was. They'll be disappointed because they honestly don't want to move premises, not when they've been such a reliable fixture in the area for such a long time, and not when the majority of the women who use their services are fairly local to the area. A big place with a swimming pool and a games room in the middle of nowhere is no good for anyone.'

'What made the decision for you?'

Hadn't he been distracted from asking her personal questions? Having lowered her guard for three seconds, Chase now felt as though she was handing over state secrets to the enemy, and yet what was the big deal? Was she so defensive because Alessandro was on the receiving end of her confidences? And wasn't it possible that, the more secretive she was, the more curious he would become? She forced herself to relax and smile at him.

'The hours,' she confessed in a halting voice. 'I didn't want to think that I might be called out at any time of the day or night. I might work long hours at Fitzsimmons but I can control the hours I work.'

'Makes sense. More to the point, I suppose both other options would have involved an element of danger, and even more so for someone like you.'

'Someone like me?' Immediately, Chase bristled at the implied insult. 'And I suppose you're going to launch into another attack on me? More criticism of me that I'm a liar and a cheat? Although I have no idea how that would have anything to do with being in the police force or working for the council! I get it that you're angry and bitter about what happened between us, but attacking me isn't going to change any of that!'

'Actually,' Alessandro murmured, 'I meant that those two professions are the ones that are possibly least suited to a woman with your looks. You're sexy as hell; how would that have played out for you if you had found yourself in a dangerous situation…?' The lips he had never kissed and the body he had never touched…

Suddenly, his body jackknifed into sudden, shocking arousal. The sheer force of it took him by surprise. It pushed its way past his bitterness and anger and made a mockery of the answers he had told himself he demanded to hear. As his erection throbbed painfully against the zip of his trousers, his mind took flight in a completely different direction. He imagined her hand down there, her mouth wrapped around him…

Who the hell cared about answers when he was consumed with lust? He had to shift in the chair just to release some of the urgency that was becoming painful.

He was suffused with anger at his physical response to her. She represented everything he found most repellent, yet how was it that she could still manage to turn him on? Was his libido so wayward that it could defy cool judgement and rise to the challenge of the unavailable, the unacceptable…the out of bounds? He had never lost control when it came to any woman and he had dated some of the most spectacularly beautiful women in the world. So what the hell was going on here?

'I never gave that side of things any thought at all.' Chase was determined not to let that description of her take their conversation in a direction she most certainly didn't want.

Her voice was cool, Alessandro noted, yet her colour was up. And she couldn't meet his eyes. Now, wasn't *that* telling?

He knew that the last thing he should contemplate doing was to pay any credence to whatever her expression was saying or, more to the point, whatever his disobedient body was up to, and yet…

'You know what? I think I might like to see this shelter. Evaluate just how the land will play out for what I have in mind. I'm taking it you'll be my escort…?'

CHAPTER THREE

FOR THE FIRST time in years Chase felt helpless. Three days ago she had walked into the imposing glass building that housed AM Holdings with a simple mission: save the shelter. She had been in control—the career woman, successful in what she did, in command of the situation. She had hoped for a favourable outcome but, had there not been one, she would have left with a clear conscience—she would have done her best.

And now here she was, hanging around by the window in her house, peering out at regular intervals for Alessandro, who had made good on his request to be shown the shelter.

'What for?' she had demanded at the time. 'I don't see the point. You're just going to demolish it anyway so that you can put up a mall catering for rich people.'

'Be warned,' he had said, eyebrows raised, those midnight eyes boring straight through her, making her feel as though her whole body had been plugged into a socket. 'Do-gooders and preachers have a monotonous tendency to become self-righteous bores. Naturally, I have details of the land somewhere but I want to see for myself what the layout is. Since you're the one handling the deal, I can't imagine that would be a problem. Or is it? Does our past history make it a problem for you?'

Yes. Yes, it does, she had thought with rising desperation. 'No. Of course not. Why should it?' she had answered with an indifferent shrug.

So here she was now and she felt as though control was slipping out of her grasp. She knew that under normal circumstances a lapse in her self-control would be easily dealt with but with Alessandro...

Her frustration and anger was underlined by a darker, more insidious emotion, a swirl of excitement that scared her. It felt like a slumbering monster slowly reawakening. Even though she had taken care to dress as neutrally as possible, in a navy-blue suit that was the epitome of sexlessness—and an impractical colour, given the wall-to-wall blue summer skies and hot sunshine—she still felt horribly vulnerable as she hovered in the sitting room waiting for him to show up.

She had informed him that she would meet him at the premises, but he had insisted on collecting her.

'You can fill me in on the history of the place on the way,' he had said smoothly. 'Forewarned is forearmed.'

She had bitten her tongue and refrained from telling him that there was no point being forearmed when the net result would be a demolition derby. He was the guy with the purse strings and she had already seen first-hand how he could use that position to his own advantage. She had no desire to revive the ticking clock.

A long, sleek, black Jaguar pulled up outside the house just as she was about to turn away from the window and her attention was riveted at the sight of him emerging from the back seat, as incongruous in this neighbourhood as his car was.

He was dressed in pale-grey pinstriped trousers, which even from a distance screamed quality, and a white shirt, the sleeves of which he had rolled to the elbow.

For a few heart-stopping seconds, Chase found that she literally couldn't breathe, that she was holding her breath.

The mere sight of him was a full-on assault on all her senses. She watched as he looked around him, taking in his surroundings. She felt sure that this was the sort of neighbourhood he would be accustomed to telling his chauffeur to drive straight through and to make sure the car doors were locked. By no means was it in a dangerous part of London but neither was it upmarket. Well paid though she was, she wasn't so well paid that she could afford to buy a house in one of the trendier areas and, unlike many of her associates, she didn't have parents who could stick their hands in their pockets and treat her to one.

She dodged out of sight just as he turned to face the house and, when the doorbell rang, she took her time getting to it. Her heart was beating like a sledgehammer as she pulled open the door to find him lounging against the doorframe.

'Right. Shall we go?' she asked as her eyes slid away from his sinfully handsome face, returned to take a peek and slid away again. She gathered her handbag from where she had hung it on the banister and bent to retrieve her briefcase from the ground.

'In due course.' Alessandro stepped into the hallway and shut the front door behind him.

'What are you doing?'

'I'm coming in for a cup of coffee.'

'We haven't got time for that, Alessandro. The appointment has been made for ten-fifteen. With rush-hour traffic, heaven only knows how long it will take for us to get there.'

'Relax. I got my secretary to put back the visit by an hour.'

'You *what?*'

'So this is where you live.'

Chase watched in horror as he made himself at home, strolling to peer into the sitting room, then onwards to the kitchen, into which he disappeared.

'Alessandro…' She galvanised herself into movement and hurried to the kitchen, to find him standing in the centre doing a full turn. It was a generous-sized kitchen which overlooked a small, private garden. It had been a persuading factor in her purchase of the house. She loved having a small amount of outdoor space.

'Very nice.'

'This is not appropriate!'

'Why not? It's hardly as though I'm a stranger. Are you going to make me a cup of coffee?'

Chase gritted her teeth as he sat down. The kitchen was large enough for a four-seater table and it had been one of the first things she had bought when she had moved in three years previously. She had fallen in love with the square, rough, wooden table with its perimeter of colourful, tiny mosaic tiles. She watched as he idly traced one long finger along some of the tiles and then she turned away to make them both some coffee.

'Is this your first house?' Alessandro queried when she had finally stopped busying herself doing nothing very much at the kitchen counter and sat down opposite him.

He hadn't laid eyes on her in three days but he had managed to spend a great deal of time thinking about her and he had stopped beating himself up for being weak. So what if she had become an annoying recurring vision in his head? Wasn't it totally understandable? He had been catapulted back to a past he had chosen to lock away. Naturally it would be playing on his mind, like an old, scratched record returned to a turntable. Naturally *she* would be playing on his mind, especially when she had remained just so damned easy on the eye.

'What do you mean?' Everything about Alessandro Moretti sitting at her kitchen table made her jumpy.

'Is this the family home?'

'I have no idea what you're talking about.'

'The dearly departed... Is this the marital home?'

'No, it's not.' She looked down. 'Shaun and I... We, er, had somewhere else when we were together... When he died I rented for a couple more years until I had enough equity to put in as a deposit on this place.'

Alessandro thought of the pair of them, young love-birds renting together, while she had batted her eyelashes at him and played him for a fool. He swallowed a mouth-ful of instant coffee and stood up, watching as she scram-bled to her feet.

'Are you going to give me a tour of the place?'

'There isn't much to see. Two bedrooms upstairs; a bathroom. You've seen what's down here. Shall we think about going?'

Alessandro didn't answer. He strolled out of the kitchen, glancing upstairs before turning his attention to the sit-ting room. Why was she so jumpy? She had been as cool as a cucumber eight years ago when she had walked out on him, so why was she now behaving like a cat on a hot tin roof? Guilt? Hardly. A woman who could conduct an outside relationship while married would never be prone to guilt. Or remorse. Or regret.

Perversely, the jumpier she seemed to be, the more in-trigued he became. He shoved one hand in his trouser pocket, feeling the coolness of his mobile phone.

'For a cool-headed lawyer,' he mused as he stared round the sitting room, 'you like bright colours. Anyone would be forgiven for thinking that the decor here suggests a com-pletely different personality.' He swung round to look at her as she hovered in the doorway, neither in the room nor out of it. 'Someone fun...vibrant.' He paused a fraction of a second. 'Passionate...'

Chase flushed, and was annoyed with herself, because she knew that that was precisely the response he had been courting. He was back and he was intent on playing with her like a cat playing with a mouse, knowing that all the danger and all the power lay exclusively in his hands.

'And yet,' Alessandro drawled as he prowled through the room before gazing briefly out of the window which overlooked the little street outside, 'there's something missing.'

'What?' The question was obviously reluctantly spoken. As he began to walk towards her, she felt panic rise with sickening force to her throat. All at once she was over-come with a memory of how desperately she had wanted him all those years ago. Her eyes widened and her mouth parted on a softly indrawn breath.

Getting closer and closer to her, Alessandro thought he could *touch* the subtle change in the atmosphere between them. It had become highly charged and, for the first time in a very long time, he felt sizzlingly *alive*. Not one of the catwalk-model beauties he had slept with over the past few years had come close to rousing this level of forbidden excitement. The immediacy of his response shocked him, all the more so because he recognised that the last time he had felt like this was when he had been in the process of being duped by the very same woman standing in front of him now. Hatred and revulsion were clearly inadequate protection against whatever it was she had that was now pushing an erection to the fore.

The bloody woman had been elusive then, for reasons which he had later understood, and she was elusive now, this time for reasons he couldn't begin to understand.

'Are you afraid of me?' he demanded harshly and Chase roused herself from the heated torpor that had engulfed her to stare up at him.

'What makes you think that I'm afraid of you?' She tried to insert some vigour into her voice but she could hear the sound of it—thin, weedy and defensive, all the things she didn't want him to imagine she was for a second.

'The way you're standing in the doorway as though I might make a lunge for you at any minute!'

'I can't imagine you would do any such thing!'

Couldn't she? It was precisely what he wanted to do: behave like a caveman and take her, because she was tempting the hell out of him!

'I'm afraid of what you could do.' She backtracked quickly as her mind threatened to veer down unexpected, unwelcome paths. 'You've already shown that you'd be willing to punish Beth because you… Because of me.'

'And yet here I am now. Do you think I'm the sort of man who reneges on what he's said? I've told you that I intend to pay the full, agreed price. I'll pay it.' Not afraid of him? *Like hell.* She might not be afraid of him, but he was certainly making her feel uncomfortable. Uncomfortable enough to try and shimmy further away from him.

He extended one lean hand against the wall, effectively blocking any further scarpering towards the front door. He could smell her hair. If he lowered his head just a little, he would feel its softness against his face. Of their own accord, his eyes drifted to the prissy blouse and the even prissier navy-blue jacket. He was well aware that she was breathing quickly, her breasts rising and falling as she did her utmost to keep her eyes averted.

Just as quickly he pushed himself away, retreating from her space, and he watched narrowly as she relaxed and exhaled one long breath.

He wasn't going to lose control. He had lost control once with her and he wasn't about to become the sort of loser who made a habit of ignoring life's lessons and learning curves.

'I was going to say…' He led the way to the front door and paused as she slung her handbag over her shoulder and reached for the case on the ground. 'There's something missing from your house.' He opened the door for her and stood back, allowing her to brush past him. 'Photos. Where are the pictures of the young, loving couple, from before your husband died? I thought I might have seen the happy pair holding hands and gazing adoringly up at one another...'

Chase walked towards the waiting car, head held high, but underneath the composed exterior she felt the ugly prickle of discomfort.

'We didn't do the whole church thing.'

'Who said anything about a church?'

'Why are you asking me all these questions?' she burst out as soon as they were in the car. She had kept her voice low but she doubted the driver would have heard anything anyway. A smoked-glass partition separated the front of the car from the back. Presumably it was completely soundproof. The truly wealthy never took chances when it came to being overheard, not even in their own cars. Deals could be lost on the back of an overheard conversation.

Alessandro shifted his muscular body to face her. 'Why are you getting so hot under the collar?'

'I...I'm not. I...I don't like to be surrounded by memories. I think it's always important to move on. There are photos of me and Shaun, just not on show. Do you want to talk about the shelter? I...I've brought all the relevant information with me. We can go over it on the way.' Sitting next to him in the back seat of this car induced the feeling of walls closing in. She fumbled with the clasp of her briefcase and felt his hand close over hers.

'Leave it.'

Chase snatched her hand away. 'I thought you wanted to pick me up so that we could talk about this deal.'

'I'm more interested in the lack of photos. So, none of the husband. Presumably you have albums stashed away somewhere? But none of your family either. Why is that?'

Chase flushed. The adoring middle-class parents who

lived in the country. She was mortified at how easily the lie had come to her all those years ago, but then she had been a kid and a little harmless pretence had not seemed like a sin.

Who wanted a rich, handsome guy to know that you have no family? That your mother had died from a drugs overdose when you were four and from that point on you'd been shoved from foster home to foster home like an unwanted parcel trying to find its rightful owner. How wonderful it had been to create a fictitious family, living in a fictitious cul-de-sac, who did normal things like taking an interest in the homework you were set and coming along to cheer at sports days, even if you trailed in last.

She had loved every minute of her storytelling until it had occurred to her that she had fallen in love with a man who didn't really know a thing about her. The fact that she had been married was just one of the many facts she had kept hidden. By then, it had been too late to retract any of what she had said, and she hadn't wanted to. She'd been enjoying their furtive meetings too much. Okay, so she knew that they would never come to anything, but she still hadn't wanted them to end.

And now…

'My parents…er…moved to Australia a few years ago.' She hated doing this now but for the life of her she didn't know what to do. At least, she thought, sending her non-existent parents on a one-way ticket to the other end of the world would prohibit him from trying to search them out.

Although, why on earth would he do that? The answer came as quickly as the question had: revenge. Find her weak spots and exploit them because he hated her for what he imagined she had done to him. She felt sick when she thought of the number of ways he could destroy her if he set his mind to it and if he had sufficient information in his possession.

'Really?'

'It was…um…always a dream of theirs.'

'To leave their only child behind and disappear half-way across the world?'

'People do what they do,' she said vaguely. 'I mean, don't *you* ever want to disappear to the other end of the earth?' Although she was making sure to stare straight ahead, she could feel his probing eyes on her, and she had to resist the temptation to lick her lips nervously.

'I disappear there quite often, as it happens. But only on business.'

Chase could think of nothing worse than travelling the globe in the quest for more and more money and bigger and bigger deals. Stability, security and putting down roots had always been her number one priority. She had managed to begin the process, and she shuddered to think of him pulling up any of the roots she had meticulously put down over the past few years.

'I'm surprised that after all these years you haven't become tired of trying to make up for your parents' excesses.' It slipped out before she could think and Chase instantly regretted the momentary lapse. The last thing she wanted to do was establish any kind of shared familiarity. 'My apologies,' she said stiffly. 'I shouldn't have said that.'

The reminder of just how much she knew about him underscored his bitterness with a layer of ice. He had never understood how that had managed to happen, how he had found himself telling her things he had never told anyone in his life before.

But then, she had been different. He had never met anyone like her in his life before. Still and yet wryly funny; guarded and yet so open in the way she gazed at him; composed and brilliant at listening. Between the inane yakking of the students—who, at the end of the day, were only a few years younger than him, even though he had

been light years removed from them in terms of experience—and the pseudo-bored sophistication of the people
he mixed with in his working life, she had been an oasis
of peace. And, yes, he had told her things. For a relationship that struggled even to call itself a 'relationship', he
had confided and, hell, where exactly had it got him?

He clenched his jaw grimly. 'I'm really not interested
in psychobabble,' he told her.

'That's fair,' Chase returned. 'But if I'm not allowed to
talk about *your* history then I don't see why you should
talk about *mine*.' For starters, the last thing she needed was
detailed questions about her so-called parents and where
exactly they lived in Australia. And how dared he imply
that they somehow didn't care about her simply because
they had fulfilled their lifelong dream of emigrating? She
almost felt sorry for them...

She half-grinned at that and Alessandro's eyes narrowed. What was going through her head? He had a fierce
desire to know.

'So the shelter...' He interrupted whatever pleasant
thought had made her smile.

'The shelter...' Chase breathed an inward sigh of relief
because this was a subject she was more than happy to talk
about. He ceased being a threat as she began to describe
life at Beth's House. She smiled at some of the anecdotes
about the women who came and went. She told him about
the plans Beth had had for upgrading the premises, and
then assured him that he could see for himself what she
was talking about as soon as he got there. She told him
that he had a heart of stone for wanting to knock it down
to build, of all things, a stupid mall for people who had
more money than sense, but found it was impossible to
generate an argument because he hadn't taken her to task
for voicing her opinion.

As a professional, a lawyer in charge of the brief, voicing opinions was not within her remit but she hadn't been able to help herself.

By the time they made it to the shelter, her eyes were bright and there was colour in her cheeks. More to the point, her guard was down. Alessandro felt that he was watching the years falling away. He wasn't about to be sucked into believing that she was anything but the liar she undoubtedly was, but he was certainly enjoying the hectic flush in her cheeks and the lively animation on her face.

They made it to the shelter on time. He immediately understood its potential for investment.

The large Victorian house, clearly in need of vast sums of money for essential repair, sat squarely in the midst of several acres of land. For somewhere that was accessible by bus and overland rail, it was a gem waiting to be developed.

The car swung through iron gates that were opened for them only after they had cleared security and they drove up to the house which was fronted by a circular courtyard, in the centre of which stood a non-functioning fountain.

'Beth was left this property by her parents,' Chase told him. 'It's another reason why she's so reluctant to sell. It was her childhood home. She may have converted it into the shelter, but there are a truck load of memories inside.'

'Is this when you begin to repeat your mantra that I have no heart and that my only aim in life is to make money at other people's expense?'

'If the cap fits…' Chase muttered under her breath in yet another show of unprofessionalism that would have had her boss mopping his brow with despair.

Alessandro raised his eyebrows and she had the grace to blush before stepping out of the car into the sunshine.

Alessandro was more than happy to follow her lead. He had never been to a place like this before. They were greeted at the door by Beth, who was in her sixties, a woman with long, grey hair tied back in a ponytail and a warm, caring face. Whatever she felt for the big, bad developer who was moving in to sweep her inheritance out from under her feet, she kept it well hidden.

'Some of the girls who come to us are in a terrible way,' she confided as they toured the house which was laid out simply but effectively inside. 'Chase knows that.'

'And that would be because…?'

'Because I've taken an interest in the place from the very start,' Chase said quickly. 'This sort of thing appeals to me. As I told you, I was very tempted to go into Social Services or the police force, some place where I would be able to do good for the community.'

Alessandro personally thought that it was priceless that she could come over all pious and saintly in his presence but he kept silent. He made all the right noises as he was shown through the house and introduced to girls who looked unbearably young, many of whom had nowhere else to go and were either pregnant or with a child.

'I try and keep them busy,' Beth told him as they went from room to room. 'Most of them don't see the point of continuing their education and it's very difficult for a fifteen-year-old to go to classes when they have a baby to look after. Many of my dear friends are teachers and volunteer to hold classes for them. It's truly remarkable the goodness that exists within us.'

Alessandro's eyes met Chase's over the older woman's head and his lips twisted into a cynical smile. 'It's not a trait I see much of in my line of business,' he said.

'I'm sure,' Beth concurred with a sad shake of her head. 'Now, Chase tells me that you're a very busy man.'

'And yet,' Chase inserted blandly, 'he's managed to make time to come here and see what you're all about. Although, I guess that mostly has to do with him judging the potential for knocking down the house and developing the land as soon as the money changes hands.'

Alessandro was cynical enough to appreciate the underhand dig. No one could accuse her of giving up without a fight. Their eyes tangled and he gave a slight smile of amused understanding of where she was heading with that incendiary statement.

'I will personally see to it that your…operation is transferred to suitable premises,' he affirmed, raking fingers through his dark hair.

'Not the same. Is it, Beth?'

'I will certainly miss the old place,' Beth agreed. 'It may not seem much to you, Mr Moretti, but this is really the only house I've ever known. I've never married, never left the family house. You must think me a silly old woman, but I shall find it very difficult to move on. Well, in truth—and I haven't said this to you, Chase, and you must promise me that you won't breathe a word to anyone else—my thoughts are with retiring from the whole business once I move on. Of course, I shall make sure that some of the money I get from the sale goes towards another shelter—perhaps smaller than this—and Frank and Anne will run it.'

'Frank and Anne?' Alessandro made a point of avoiding the scathing criticism in Chase's eyes. He had absolutely nothing to feel bad about. He knew for a fact that there were vultures hovering over the place, waiting to pick it to pieces, and those vultures would not have parted with nearly as much cash as he was prepared to.

'My dear friends. They help me here. As for me, perhaps a retirement place by the coast… So, I expect you would like to see the land, Mr Moretti? There's a lot of it. My parents were both keen gardeners. Sadly, I haven't had the money to look after it the way it deserves, but if the place is to be redeveloped then I'm sure you won't find that a problem. Chase tells me you have grand plans for it to be an upmarket mall.'

Alessandro marvelled that 'an upmarket mall' could be made to sound like 'the tower of Babel', although when he looked at the older woman there was no bitterness on her face.

'It will bring a great deal of useful traffic to the community.'

So he made money. It was what he did. It was what he had always done. And he was still doing it. He frowned as he remembered Chase's barbed comment about his lifestyle.

He had enough money to retire for the rest of his life and still be able to afford what most people could only ever dream of. So was he trying to make up for his parents' excesses? He was angry and frustrated that he should even be thinking along these lines. His parents were long gone and he had barely known them. How could he have, when, from a toddler, he had been in the care of a succession of nannies who had all fallen by the wayside in favour of boarding school abroad?

His parents had both been products of ridiculously wealthy backgrounds and their marriage had provided them with a joint income that they had both happily and irresponsibly squandered. Untethered by any sense of duty, and riding high on the hippie mentality that had been sweeping through Italy at the time, they had zoned out on recreational drugs, held lavish parties, travelled to festivals all over the world and bought houses which they had optimistically called 'communes' where people could 'get in touch with themselves'. And then, to top it all off, they had seen fit to throw away yet more of their inheritance on a series of ill-advised schemes involving organic farming and the import of ethnic products, all of which had crashed and burned.

Alessandro, barely through with university, had had to grasp what remained of the various companies and haul

them back into profit when his parents had died in a boat-
ing accident in the Caribbean. Which he had done—in record time and with astounding success.

So what if he had learnt from his parents that financial
security was the most important thing in life? So what if
nothing and no one had ever been allowed to interrupt that
one, single, driving ambition?

A woman in whom he had once rashly confided things
that should have been kept to himself was certainly not
going to make him start questioning his ethos.

Beth was now chatting amicably about the wonderful
advantages of the place being developed, which would
bring much-needed jobs to the community. To Alessandro's finely tuned ears, it sounded like forced enthusiasm.
It was clear that she hated the thought of leaving the house,
and he couldn't help wondering what someone who had
always been active in community life in London would
do in the stultifying boredom of the seaside.

It was after midday by the time they were standing outside the house saying their goodbyes. His chauffeur had
returned for them but Chase pointedly made no move in
the direction of the car.

'I'll make my own way back,' she said politely.

'Get in.' Alessandro stood to one side and then sighed
with exasperation as she continued to look at him in stubborn silence. 'It's baking hot out here,' he said, purpose-
fully invading her space by standing too close to her. 'And
that outfit isn't designed for warm weather.'

'I'll take my chances on avoiding sunstroke.'

'Which is something I would rather not have on my
conscience.'

'You don't have a conscience!'

'And you do?'

Chase looked at him with simmering resentment. *He*
didn't look all hot and bothered. *He* looked as fabulous,

cool and composed as he always did. Plus, he had charmed
his way into Beth's affections. She could tell. He hadn't
come on too strong, he had pointed out all the benefits of
selling the place but in a perfectly reasonable way that
no one would have been able to dispute. He was just so...
damned *persuasive*! She hated it. And she hated the way
she had found herself staring at him surreptitiously, hated
the way her imagination had started playing tricks on her,
hated the way she had had to fight against being seduced
by the dark, deep, velvety tones of his voice.

'You can drop me to the bus stop. It's about a mile
from here.'

'Are you going back to your office? Perhaps I could go
in, meet all these people you work with... Tell your boss
what a great job you've done even though the shelter will
be sold. At least you've got me to thank for a reasonably
happy Beth.'

'She's not happy.' Chase slid into the back seat, barely
appreciating the terrific air conditioning as she grappled
with the horror of having him invade her work space as
well as having invaded her house. 'And I'm going home,
as a matter of fact. I have work I can do there.'

'I've noticed that you try and avoid looking at me as
much as possible,' Alessandro said softly. 'Why is that?'

As challenges went, that was about as direct as they
came. *Avoid looking at him?* She wanted to laugh at the
irony because all she seemed to do was look at him—it
was just that she was careful with her staring. She looked
at him now and the silence seemed to go on for ever as he
gazed right back at her. Her mouth had gone dry and, although she knew that she should be breaking this yawning silence with a suitably innocuous remark, her mind
refused to play along.

When he reached out and trailed one finger along her
lips, she gasped with shock. There was a sudden, ferocious

roaring in her ears and she couldn't breathe. All the strategies she had adopted to keep him at arm's length, to make him know that there was nothing whatsoever between them now aside from a brief, dubious past that no longer meant a thing, disappeared like mist on a hot summer's day.

She was no longer the lawyer with her life under control and he was no longer public enemy number one, the guy who could ruin everything she had built for herself in one fell swoop. She was a woman and he was a man and she still, against all rhyme or reason, wanted him with every incomprehensible, yearning ounce of her being.

'What are you doing?' She finally found her voice and pulled back.

Alessandro smiled. If he had had any doubts that she was still attracted to him, then he had none now. 'Maybe you're right,' he murmured, obediently removing his hand and observing her neutrally. 'Your friend really doesn't want to leave her home. The memories…the experiences… I don't see a bungalow on the coast cutting it, do you?'

'No.' Chase glared at him suspiciously. Her lips were burning from where he had touched them but she refused to cool them with her fingers.

'So I have an interesting proposal to put to you. You'd like me to believe that you're all bleeding heart and caring for the defenceless. Well, how would you like to prove it?'

CHAPTER FOUR

CHASE DIDN'T ANSWER immediately. Alessandro slid back the partition and told the driver to deliver them to a well-known French restaurant. By the time that sank in, the car had already altered course.

'What the heck do you think you're doing?'

'We're going to discuss my proposal over food. It's lunchtime.'

'And I've told you that I need to get back to do some work! Besides, I can't imagine what sort of proposal you have for me that involves you kidnapping me!'

'I like your use of language. Colourful.'

Chase was still burning from where his finger had touched her lips. Her mouth tingled.

'What made your friend decide to go into the good Samaritan business?'

Chase looked at him with unbridled suspicion. He was leaning indolently against the door and she got the feeling that it was all the better to see her. Like the big, bad wolf in the fairy story. 'I don't know what good it will do for you to hear Beth's potted history.'

'I've never known anyone who erects so many obstacles to complicate a perfectly harmless conversation.'

'That's because everyone kowtows to you, I imagine,' Chase offered ungracefully. While he was supremely relaxed, legs slightly open, one arm along the back of the seat, the other hanging loosely over his thigh, she was as tense as a block of wood. Her legs were tightly pressed together. Her lips were tightly compressed. Her fingers were interlinked and white at the knuckles.

'Rich people seem to have that effect,' she continued, avoiding his speculative eyes. 'I've seen it. They like throwing their weight around and they take it for granted that everyone is going to agree with everything they say.'

'You're getting all hot and bothered over nothing,' Alessandro murmured with mild amusement. 'The food at this restaurant is second to none. Have you been there? No? Then you should be looking forward to the experience. So why don't you relax? Tell me about your friend.'

'You didn't seem that interested in her when you were downgrading the price of the place by a thousand pounds per minute.'

'That was before I met her.'

Every argument she engineered seemed to crash into a brick wall. He wasn't interested in arguing with her. She, on the other hand, felt driven to keep arguing because something inside her was telling her that, if she didn't, she might find herself in dangerously unchartered territory. She might start remembering how funny he could be, how thoughtful, how engaging.

'She obviously comes from a fairly wealthy background,' Alessandro murmured encouragingly. 'And yet the road she decided to travel down wasn't exactly the predictable one.'

When he had first laid eyes on Chase after eight years, he had been shocked. And hard on the heels of that shock had come rage and bitterness. It seemed that he had badly underestimated the effect she had had on him. He hadn't put her behind him after all. Had he succeeded in doing that, he would have felt nothing but indifference and contempt. So, yes, revenge had been an option but why make a third party suffer? Weren't there other ways of handling a situation that had landed in his lap?

Rage and bitterness were corrosive emotions and there was one very good way of permanently eliminating them. He smiled with slow, deliberate intent.

Chase took note of that smile and wondered what the heck was going on.

'She hasn't had a…normal upbringing,' she said reluctantly. 'I know this because I knew her before this whole business with the shelter cropped up. Actually, she came to me when she was approached with your company's interference because we were already friends.'

'Interference? I'll overlook your take on my generous offer to buy her out. How did you become friends? Oh no, don't tell me—you were drawn to her because of your "care in the community" approach to life.'

'I'm glad you think it's funny to want to help other people!'

'I don't. I think it's admirable. Like I said, I just find the sentiments hard to swallow when they're coming from you.'

'If I'm such an awful person, why are you taking me out to lunch? Why didn't you let me find my own way back? The sale's agreed. Your legal team could take it from here on in.'

'But then I would miss out on the pleasure of watching you.'

Chase flushed and wondered whether he was being serious or not. She told herself that she didn't care and squashed the unwanted sliver of satisfaction it gave her when she thought of him watching her and *enjoying* it. Suddenly, it felt safer to talk about Beth than to sit in silence, as he looked at her, and speculate on all sorts of things that threw her into confusion.

'Her parents were both really well off,' she blurted out,

licking her lips nervously and wishing he would just stop looking at her in that pensive, brooding way that made the hairs on the back of her neck stand on end. 'They were missionaries. Beth says that as though it's the most normal thing in the world.'

She began to relax and half-smiled as she remembered the conversation they had had years ago when she had first met her. 'I mean, they didn't want to convert anyone, but they wanted to help people in the third world. They rented out their house, which is now the shelter, and took themselves off to Africa where they spent their own money on various irrigation and building projects. In fact, there's a plaque dedicated to them in one of the little villages over there.'

'Good people.' Alessandro thought of his own feckless parents and marvelled at the different ways money could be spent.

'They returned to London to live when Beth was a child. I think they wanted her educated over here. Maybe they thought that they had done what they had set out to do. At any rate, they found that they couldn't just do nothing once they'd come back, so they did lots of volunteer work at various places. They were both in their fifties by then. They'd had Beth when they were quite old. Beth went to university and studied to become an engineer, but found herself drawn to helping others, and when her parents died and she inherited the house and land, the stocks and shares and stuff, she turned the house into a shelter and hasn't looked back.'

'So effectively it's really the only house she's ever lived in and the only work she's ever done.'

'Yes. So there you have it. I don't suppose you can really understand what makes someone like Beth tick.'

'Do me a favour and stop trying to pigeon-hole me because I happen to have a bit of money.'

'A bit of money? You're as rich as Croesus.' They were now in front of the restaurant and Chase stared down at her formal working suit in dismay. 'I don't feel comfortable dining in a place like this wearing a suit.'

'Don't wear the jacket and undo the top three buttons of the shirt.'

'I beg your pardon?' She looked at him, her cheeks bright red, and he grinned at her. A full-on charming grin that knocked her sideways. It was that same grin that had turned her life on its head eight years ago and had made her continue to see him even though everything in her had been screaming at her to stop.

'You heard me.' He stepped out of the car and leaned through to give his driver instructions; when he straightened, it was to see that the prissy jacket, at least, had been left behind in the car.

'What about the buttons?' he asked, with the same sexy grin that made her toes curl and her skin feel tight and prickly.

He didn't give her time to think about it. With their eyes still locked, he undid the offending buttons. The softness of her skin under the starchy top... The glimpse of a cleavage... His breath caught sharply in his throat, mimicking hers.

'Don't do that!' Chase clasped the top and stumbled back a few steps.

'Much better. After you?'

Chase barely took note of the restaurant as they were ushered inside. She had been to a few fancy places since she had started working at Fitzsimmons. Her inclination to stare in awe had thankfully subsided. Nor was her mind in full working order just at the moment, not when her body was still in a state of heightened response at that intimate gesture of his undoing those buttons as though...as though she was his; as though they were the lovers they never, actually, ever had been.

'You said you had a proposal to put to me,' was the first thing she said tightly as soon as they were seated.

Alessandro perused the menu and made a few helpful suggestions which Chase ignored.

'This isn't a social occasion,' she said, choosing the first thing off the menu and shaking her head when he tried to entice her into a glass of wine.

'But it could be,' he returned smoothly. 'Couldn't it?'

'What do you mean?'

'I mean that eight years ago you were a married woman, albeit without my knowledge. Now, you're not. Your husband is no longer around and, unless you have another one stashed up your sleeve somewhere…?'

Caught unawares, Chase laughed shortly. 'Marriage isn't an institution I'll be going near again. Been there, done that, got the tee-shirt.'

Alessandro maintained a steady smile but his jaw hardened. 'Still in mourning?' he asked softly.

'Too wrapped up with my career,' Chase answered steadily.

'You haven't answered my question, but no matter. It really doesn't make any difference to the proposal I have in mind.' So she was still wrapped up in the ex. Why else would she have been at pains to avoid his question? He harked back to his image of the man, good-looking in a thuggish sort of way, her type of guy.

And yet, wrapped up or not in the past, she was still affected by *him*. He knew that with some highly developed sixth sense. As affected by him as he was, unfortunately, affected by her. She was an itch that needed to be scratched and he intended to do just that. Scratch the itch, and he would get her out of his system once and for all.

'So what's your proposal?' Had she ordered crab

mousse? It seemed so, as one was placed in front of her. She tucked into it without appetite.

'Do you get as personally wrapped up with all your clients as you do with this particular one?' Alessandro watched as she toyed with the starter in front of her.

'I told you. I knew her before... She's been a friend for years.'

'She's in her sixties.'

'What does age have to do with anything?' Chase looked at him defensively. Yes, she knew where this was going. Why was a young girl in her twenties friends with a woman in her sixties? Of course, age was no barrier to friendship. Many young people had friends who were much older than they were. What was the big deal? But Beth was one of her few friends, one of the few people in whom she had confided to some extent.

'Nothing. It's laudable. Although...'

'Although what? I suppose you're going to tell me that my friends should all be young and frivolous? That I should be spending my free time going to clubs and drinking instead of hanging out with a woman old enough to be my mother?'

'Although...isn't there something that suggests you shouldn't be working for someone with whom you're personally involved? I wasn't going to lecture you on hanging out with anyone. You choose your own friends, Chase. Interesting, however, that you never seemed to have a lot of those when I knew you eight years ago.'

'I...' She stared at him and, as their eyes tangled, she had the strangest sensation that he could see what was going on in her head. 'How would you know what friends I had or didn't have? You were only around part of the time. We met occasionally. You didn't know what I did in my spare time.'

Alessandro sat back as their food was placed in front

of them. He was surprised to see that he had eaten his starter although he couldn't even remember what he had ordered. She could barely meet his eyes and, again, he had the strangest feeling that there was something going on which he couldn't quite see.

He cursed himself for even being curious. 'True,' he concurred. 'And yet I remember a couple of occasions when kids from your course came up to you. You barely acknowledged them. Once they asked you if you were going to a party and you turned white and got rid of them as soon as you could.' The memory came from nowhere, as though it had been lurking there, just waiting to be aired.

'I…I had a husband.'

Alessandro found that he didn't like thinking about her husband. In fact, the thought of that shaved head, the tattoos, set his teeth on edge.

'Who would have been the same age as you were. Practically a teenager.'

It struck him that that was one of the things that had drawn him to her, the fact that she hadn't acted like a typical teenager. She had been old beyond her years in ways he couldn't quite pin down.

'I've never been into clubs and partying.'

'Never?'

'Why the thousand and one questions, Alessandro?' Her cheeks were bright red. Once upon a time she had actually enjoyed going out. She must have been fourteen or fifteen at the time, unsupervised, hanging out with older kids because most of the kids her age had had some form of parental control.

Schoolwork had been a breeze. She'd never had much need to bury her head in books. Absorbing information had come naturally to her. Oh yes, she had had plenty of time to go to clubs and parties. She frowned and wondered now whether she actually had enjoyed those parties, the dancing, the dim lights...and the confused, angry feeling that she shouldn't be there, that there should be someone in her life who cared enough to try and stop her.

'We're here. Why don't you just tell me what you want to say?'

'How does saving your friend's house sound to you?'

'Saving her house? What are you talking about?' Chase barely noticed that the starters had been removed, to be replaced with yet more exquisite food which she couldn't remember ordering. Despite having said no, her wine glass had been filled, and with a small shrug she sipped some of the cold white wine which tasted delicious. 'Are you going to build your mall around it?'

'Somehow I don't think that people on a quest for designer shoes would feel comfortable having to circumnavigate a shelter for women in need of help, do you?'

Chase thought about that and laughed. It was the first truly genuine laugh he had heard from her since they had met again and, God, how well he remembered the sound of it. Even back then, she hadn't laughed a lot, and when she had it was the equivalent of the sun coming out from behind a cloud. It was exactly the same now and he looked at her with rampant male appreciation.

'I know.' She grinned and leaned towards him confidingly. 'But wouldn't it be a great ploy? They'd all feel so guilty that they would contribute bags of money just to clear their conscience before they went to the shop next door to buy the designer shoes! Beth would never have any financial problems in her life again!'

'It would certainly be a solution of sorts to her financial problems,' Alessandro concurred.

'But you don't mean that, do you?' Her laughter subsided. She nibbled at the edges of her food and decided not to bother trying to second-guess what he had brought her here for.

'Not quite what I had in mind but the image was worth it just to hear the sound of your laugh.'

'Then what?' She ignored the tingling those words produced inside her. 'Will it involve getting any lawyers in? I can't honestly make any far-reaching decisions without reference to my boss.'

'How will he feel when you tell him that you'd had no option but to sell the place to me?' Alessandro asked curiously and Chase gave it some thought.

'A favourable outcome would have been for our client to hang on to the premises. The truth, however, is that our clients don't earn the firm money. The big money comes from our corporate and international clients. Intellectual property lawyers, patent lawyers, even some family lawyers…they earn the big money. I'm just a little cog subsidised by the big-fee lawyers, and I'm there because Fitzsimmons is a morally ethical law firm that believes in putting back some of what they take.'

Alessandro wasn't interested in hearing a long speech on the moral values of Fitzsimmons. 'Wonderful,' he said neutrally. 'But this particular decision won't require involvement from anyone else in your firm.'

'Okay.'

'Nor is it illegal.' Alessandro read the suspicion in her eyes and looked at her with wry amusement. 'However, yes, it will involve the house remaining in your friend's possession. More than that, what if I told you that I would be prepared to pay off all her debts and inject sufficient cash to make sure she can keep the shelter going for a very long time to come?'

Chase gaped at him. For a few seconds, she honestly believed that she had misheard what he had said. Then she thoughtfully closed her knife and fork, wiped her mouth with her linen serviette and searched his face to see whether this was some way of making a fool of her.

'So Beth...' she said slowly, giving him ample time to cut her short and rubbish what she thought he had said, 'gets to keep the house, plus you pay off her debts, plus you put money into renovating and updating the place... am I getting it right?'

'That would be about the size of it.'

'And you would do this because...?' Brow furrowed, she suddenly smiled at him with genuine delight. 'I know why. You were impressed with what you found at the shelter, weren't you? I don't suppose you were expecting it to be as well run as it was. Beth spares no effort when it comes to doing good for those girls. It's hard to go there and not be moved by what you find. I'm so pleased, Alessandro.' She reached out impulsively and covered his hand with hers.

Alessandro looked at the shining glow on her face and was extremely pleased with himself for being the one to put it there.

'Can I call and tell her?' Chase asked excitedly. 'No, perhaps I'd better not do that.' She flashed him an apologetic smile. 'You'll have to forgive the lawyer in me, but we'll have to get this all signed on the dotted line. But, once she knows, she'll be over the moon. Between you and me, I don't honestly think she was looking forward to a quiet retirement by the seaside.'

'So you agree with me that this is a good idea?'

'Of course I do! I'd be a fool not to.' Even with her defences up, knowing how he felt about her after what she had done to him, she knew that there was a blazingly good streak in him. Those lectures he had given had been given for free, and he had taken considerable time out to individually help some of the students, had actually offered internships to a couple of them. He hadn't just been as sexy as hell, he had shown her a glimpse of humanity that she had never seen before and that, amongst other things, had roped her in and kept her tethered in a place she had known was desperately dangerous.

'Naturally, there's no such thing as a free lunch in life.' Alessandro shook his head ruefully, the very picture of a man who regrets that there wasn't. 'I wish I could say that I was the perfect philanthropist, but you have to understand that all this will cost me a small fortune.'

The smile died on her face. The bill was brought to them and she automatically reached for her bag but it had been settled before she could rummage out her wallet and pay her fair share. 'Of course it will,' she agreed coolly. 'And you'll want to be repaid for your largesse. Will your rates be competitive?'

'Shall we go?'

Chase could feel disappointment rising inside her as he waited for her to gather her things, standing aside so that she could precede him out of the restaurant. Once outside, she didn't bother with her stupid jacket. He had been right when he had remarked that it was impractical for the weather.

What had he been playing at? Stringing her along with all manner of empty promises only to yank them all back at the last minute? Didn't he realise that, if Beth had wanted to borrow money so that she could clear her debts and get the shelter really going, she would have gone to the bank? Of course, Chase thought uncomfortably, she *had* tried that some time ago but to no avail. She simply hadn't had the collateral to get a loan of the size she required, even though the bank manager had known her parents. Money was just not being lent, not to ventures that had nothing to gain. Had Alessandro checked that out himself and come to the conclusion that he could provide her with the money but jack up the interest rates?

'I really believed you for a minute,' she simmered, barely noticing that she was being ushered into the back seat of his car. 'I really thought that you had been so impressed by what you saw that you decided to do the right thing. I really thought that there was a part of you that was the same guy who gave internships to those girls years ago, and the same guy who put in extra time helping that little group of Asian students through their language barriers with some of their papers.'

'You remember. Those girls have been promoted several times. One left a year ago to have a baby and returned a few months ago to resume work. Two of the Chinese students work in my Hong Kong offices.'

'You kept in touch with them.' She fought against the pull of a connection that threatened her valued self-control. She severed the incipient connection. 'Where are we going?'

'To discuss my proposal further. Out of public earshot.'

'Beth can't afford to pay you back for a loan.' Back to business, but her mind was still straying dangerously close to memories of the man she had once been so irresistibly drawn to—the man she knew still existed even if those complex sides, revealed all those years ago, would never again get an airing in her presence.

'Whoever mentioned loans?'

'You're confusing me, Alessandro.'

'Ditto,' he murmured under his breath. He looked at her in silence, his searing attraction laced with a poignant familiarity that wasn't doing his libido any favours, until she shifted uncomfortably and took notice of her surroundings. They were away from the hustle and bustle.

'And you haven't said where we're going. This isn't the way back to my house.'

'Well spotted. It's the way to mine.'

'What?' Chase immediately felt her pulses begin to race. She didn't want to be here, in this car! Far less heading to his place, wherever that was! He had just pulled a cheap trick, whatever he had said about his offer not being a loan. He had really shown his true colours, aside from which she knew that she should steer clear of him. But the memory of how much she had craved to see where he lived eight years ago slammed into her with the force of a freight train. 'Let me out of this car *immediately*.'

'Calm down.'

'I'm *perfectly* calm.'

'You're as perfectly calm as a volcano on the point of eruption. Relax. We'll be there in ten minutes.'

Chase felt ill at the thought of stepping foot into his private space. She had never thought that she would see him again and, now that she had, she should be laying down clear boundaries. Instead, the lines were blurring. He had come to her house, seen the way she lived, formed his opinions. Now she was going to his.

She watched with growing panic as the sleek, black car manoeuvred through quiet streets, finally turning into an avenue through imposing black wrought-iron gates. The houses here were beyond spectacular. No superlative could do justice to the pristine white-and-cream facades, the ornate foliage, the lush greenery, the air of indecently wealthy seclusion. The cars were all top of the range, high end.

So this was where he lived. Never in her wildest, twenty-year-old's dreams could she have come up with this.

'I'm not comfortable with this,' she said automatically as his driver opened the passenger door for her.

'I wasn't comfortable conducting a private conversation in a public place.'

'There was nothing private about our conversation. It was a business deal.' But she couldn't help staring at the enormous house in front of her, the perfectly shaped shrubs on either side of the black door, the highly polished brass of the knocker. Nor could she help feeling, in some deep,

dark part of her, that their conversation had been threaded
with undercurrents that were anything but businesslike.

'I love the way you constantly argue with me,' Alessandro remarked drily as he opened the front door and stood
aside so that she brushed past him. 'It's refreshing. You did
that eight years ago as well. And it was refreshing then.'

There had been times, countless times, when he had
just wanted to scoop her to him and silence those feisty
arguments with his mouth...just kiss them away. But he
had been prepared to bide his time. He had been prepared
to do way too much to attain the eventual goal of just having her. She had taught him the art of patience, damn fool
that he had been.

Chase didn't say anything. She was too busy being impressed. It wasn't just the size but the pristine perfection:
marble flooring, the colour of pale honey, was broken by
silky rugs. The paintings on the walls varied in size but
were recognisable—who on earth had paintings on their
walls that were *recognisable*? The impressive staircase
leading up gave onto a landing which was dominated by
a massive stained-glass window that did magical things
to the sunlight filtering through it.

She came back to planet Earth to find that Alessandro
was watching her, hands in his pockets.

'You have a beautiful place,' she said politely.

Alessandro dutifully looked around him, as though
taking stock of where he lived for the first time, then he
shrugged. 'It works for me. Come through.'

'I honestly don't see why you couldn't have laid out
your terms and conditions for this so-called "not a loan"
at the restaurant.' But she followed as he led the way towards a kitchen that looked as though it had never been
used. He didn't do cooking; she remembered him telling
her that way back when.

'Have you *ever* used this kitchen?' she asked, perching on one of the top-of-the-range chrome and leather bar stools by the counter and watching as he attempted to make sense of the complicated coffee machine.

'You don't want coffee, do you?' he eventually asked, turning to glance at her over his shoulder.

'If I did, would you be able to figure out how that thing works?'

'Unlikely.'

'Tea would be nice.' She hadn't appreciated just how rich he was. These were the surroundings of a man to whom money was literally no object. She bristled when she thought of him holding her to ransom by reducing his offer for the shelter just because he could.

'I'm very good with a kettle and some tea bags.' He hunted them down, opening and closing cupboards. 'I come in here very rarely,' he offered by way of explanation. 'I have a housekeeper who makes sure it's stocked and a chef who does all my cooking on the occasions when I happen to be in.'

'Lucky you.'

There wasn't a single woman on the planet, Alessandro thought, who would have offered that sarcastic response when confronted with the reality of his wealth. 'You don't mean that.'

'You're right. I don't.' She took the cup of tea from him. The cup was fine-bone china, weirdly shaped, with an art deco design running down one side. When she thought of him trying and failing to work out how his high-tech appliances worked, she could feel a smile tugging the corners of her mouth, but there was no way that she would be seduced by any windows of vulnerability in him.

'Why do you have all these gadgets in here if you don't cook and barely use the kitchen?'

'I remain eternally optimistic.'

Chase wished he wouldn't do that, wouldn't undermine

her defences with his sense of humour. She didn't want to remember how he had always been able to make her laugh. She didn't want him to make her laugh now.

'Well, now we're here, maybe you could explain this business with the shelter?'

Alessandro looked at her. He wondered what it was about her that just seemed to capture his imagination and hold it to ransom.

'You have no idea what goes through me when I think of what you did eight years ago,' he murmured.

'You brought me here so that you could talk about that?' Chase fidgeted uncomfortably. She wanted to drag her disobedient eyes away from him but somehow she couldn't.

'But the past belongs in the past. What's the good dredging it up every two seconds? The best thing I could do right now is send you on your not-so-merry way, out of my life once and for all. Unfortunately, I find that there's something holding me back.'

'What?' It was a barely whispered response. She cleared her throat and did her utmost to remember that this was just an opponent whom she happened to have known a long time ago. It didn't work. She still found herself hanging onto his every word with shamefully bated breath, watching him watching her, and letting those deep, dark looks penetrate every fibre of her being. Dampness pooled shamefully between her legs, physical proof of something she was loath to admit, and her nipples tingled, sensitive and taut against her lacy bra. 'What's holding you back?' She shifted, felt her slippery wetness making her panties uncomfortable.

'You.' Alessandro allowed that one word to ferment in the lengthening silence between them until it was bursting with significance.

'I have no idea what you're talking about.'

'Of course you do,' he drawled smoothly. 'We can both

waste a little time while I indulge your desire to feign ignorance but what would be the point? We'll end up getting to the same place eventually. Despite what happened between us, despite the fact that my levels of respect for you are lamentably non-existent, I find that I'm still sexually attracted to you. And I wouldn't be telling you this now if I didn't know that it was a two-way street.

'And don't bother trying to deny it. I've seen the way you look at me when you think my attention is somewhere else and I've seen the way you respond whenever I get within a two-foot radius of you. We had it once and we have it again. It's a shame but...' He shrugged with graceful elegance.

'You're...you're mad...' Her words said one thing; her treacherous body however, was, singing a different refrain.

'Am I? I don't think so.'

Chase watched, mesmerised, as he slowly stood up and breached the short distance separating them to plant his hands on either side of her chair, locking her into place so that she could only raise her eyes upwards to stare at him. She could feel the pulse in her neck beating wildly, a physical giveaway that every word he was saying struck home.

'I'm the lawyer working for Beth; sure, we know each other...' The word faltered and died in her throat as he cupped her cheek with his hand and stroked it with his thumb.

Years ago, their chaste relationship had pulsated with unexplored passion and unspoken, untested lust. Now, as his hand remained on her cheek, she shuddered and resisted the urge to sink into the caress.

'Please, Alessandro, don't.'

'Your body is telling me something different.'

'I don't want to start any kind of relationship with you.'

'Relationship?' Alessandro queried huskily. 'Who's talking about a relationship? I could no more have a relationship with you than I could with a deadly snake. No, I'm not interested in a relationship. I'm interested in having sex with you, plain and simple. Just like you're interested in having sex with me. Don't you want to touch what you spent months staring at eight years ago? Don't you want to finish what you started? I do. A lot.'

Chase opened her mouth to tell him to get lost but nothing emerged. His cool, brilliant dark eyes held her in a trance even though she knew that every word that left that perfect mouth was offensive and insulting.

And yet…her imagination was going crazy. The fantasies she had had of him touching her all those years ago sprang from the box into which they had been firmly locked and attacked her on all fronts. She weakened at the thought of his fingers stroking the wetness between her legs, his mouth kissing the twin peaks of her breasts, nipping the tight buds of her nipples, suckling on them while he continued to stroke her dampness…

'So here's the deal.' Alessandro was finding it hard to contain his excitement at the prospect of netting the prey that had once escaped him and putting to bed, once and for all, feelings that had no place in his life. Her skin was like satin beneath his fingertips. 'You sleep with me for as long as I want you to and the shelter stays. Renovated, updated and modernised. Your friend's debts will be cleared.'

'You want to *pay* me for services rendered?'

'I want to take what you want to give. In return, you get the shelter. And please don't try and tell me that you don't want to touch me. You do.' His mouth met hers and Chase braced her hands on his shoulders, determined to push him away. But instead she was horrified to find that she was caressing him; that her mouth was returning his kiss with equal urgency; that she was sinking into him like a person starved of nourishment; that she was whimpering, little mewling sounds that shocked and excited her in equal measure and, worse, when he finally pulled back that the sudden space between them felt cold and unwelcome.

'I think I've proved my point.' There was a betraying unsteadiness in his voice. He might not like her or respect her but, God, did he want her. More than anything or anyone. 'Let's finish this business. A couple of weeks, tops, and you can disappear back to whatever life you have, having made your friend a very happy bunny.'

Chase had withdrawn and was rising to her feet, arms tight around her body.

'I'll never do that, Alessandro!'

Alessandro shrugged and tried to wrestle back his self-control, even though just watching her was affecting him in ways he could barely quantify. 'You have forty-eight hours to give me your answer then the deal is off the table.'

'I've already given you my answer!'

'Forty-eight hours…' he repeated, his eyes roving over her flushed face and her defiant yet tellingly shaken expression. 'And let's just wait and see if your answer remains the same after you've…thought things through.'

CHAPTER FIVE

BETH TELEPHONED THAT evening. She could barely contain her excitement. She might be able to hang on to the shelter!

'What do you mean?' Chase asked tentatively. She had spent the past few hours unable to get down to work. Alessandro's offer kept playing in her head over and over again, like a tape recording on a loop. She had stalked out of his house, her head held high, and he had made no attempt to stop her. She thought that that, in itself, displayed a level of arrogance that should really have had her turning her back on him for ever. She loathed arrogance.

Unfortunately, along with her determination not to be browbeaten into making a pact with the devil, there lurked the uncomfortable awareness that, devil or not, he roused something in her she didn't want but couldn't resist. He had kissed her and her whole world had felt as though it had been tilted on its side. It was the same something that had been there eight years ago; the same something that had made her behave in a way she had known she shouldn't. Sexual attraction: he had put his finger on it. Sexual attraction and more...

'I had a call from Mr Moretti.'

'Ah...' She drifted over to the sofa and sat down.

'He's a lot more compassionate than I originally gave him credit for. You know, when this whole business started, well, I just thought of him as a human bulldozer, not caring what or who got in his way.'

Chase smirked. 'What did he say?'

'That he's spoken to you and you've both come up with a plan to secure the future of the shelter; you're both trying to iron out the creases. Chase, my dear, I can't tell you how overjoyed I would be if this worked out. I've been dreading telling the girls that they'll have to go, plus the waiting list is so long of people who need us. Not to mention the seaside idea. Never could quite see myself retiring by the coast and having coffee mornings with all the other retirees.'

'I'm sure there's more to life by the coast than coffee mornings.' Her mind was in a whirl. She was also incensed. So much for the forty-eight hours after which her decision would be final! How could she have been foolish enough to believe that Alessandro wouldn't exert influence over a decision he wanted? 'Lots of people go down there to…er…sail…' she said vaguely.

'Can't think of anything worse. Drive me mad!'

'Did he mention what this idea of…ours happens to be?' Chase prodded gently.

'Not a word!' Beth hooted. 'Said it was something he wanted kept up his sleeve. Probably to do with tax!'

'Sorry?'

'Well, don't these awfully rich people enjoy tax breaks by giving money to charity? We *are* a registered charity…'

Chase sighed and decided to lay off the details of any such scheme. Despite a sharp brain and her degree in engineering, Beth's interest in all things financial was sketchy at best.

'Sometimes,' she said, noncommittal.

'At any rate, it all sounds very promising. I know what you're going to say, my dear! Don't count your chickens… But I get a good feeling from that young man. Did the minute I met him. Showed a real interest in everything we do here at the shelter.'

Alternatively, Chase thought, the man was a skilled actor with a golden tongue. Take your pick.

She spent another twenty minutes on the line as Beth waxed lyrical about Alessandro, and as soon as her friend was off the phone she hunted down the business card he had given her and telephoned him on his mobile.

'Well, that was a low trick!' was the first thing she said the minute she heard his voice on the other end.

At a little after nine, Alessandro had just finished wrapping up a two-hour conference call and was about to leave the office, which was deserted aside from him. In the act of reaching for his jacket, he flung it down on the leather sofa instead and relaxed to take her call. 'So Beth called you,' he drawled without an ounce of shame. 'I thought she might. She certainly was over the moon when I spoke to her. Charming woman.'

'You're a low-down, sneaky rat!'

Alessandro grinned. Whatever Chase's downsides, she was by far and away the most outspoken, feisty woman he had ever met in his entire life. It would probably be a tiresome trait in the long run, but just for the moment it was certainly invigorating.

'Now, now, now…is that any way to speak to your friend's knight in shining armour?'

Chase detected the wicked grin in his voice and gritted her teeth in frustration. 'What did you tell her?'

'Long conversation. I'll fill you in when we next meet.'

'How could you?'

'How could I what? Make that delightful woman one very happy lady?'

'Try and twist my arm into accepting your…your… No, I take that back; I understand perfectly how you did that!'

'It's comforting to know that you can read me like a

book. That way, there will be no mixed messages between us. Now, why don't you carry on working and I'll call you in the morning?'

'I haven't been able to do a scrap of work today!'

'Too busy thinking about me?'

Chase made an inarticulate sound of pure frustration and racked her brains for a clever riposte.

'Well, why don't you get some well-deserved beauty sleep and we'll talk in the morning…or later, if you'd like. After all, your forty-eight hour deadline won't yet be up. Don't worry. I'll be in touch.'

She was left clutching the phone which had gone dead because he had hung up on her. He'd barely heard her out! She felt that there was a lot more anger to be expressed. Unfortunately, without an adversary at which to direct her attack, she was left simmering and fuming on her own as she flounced down in front of the television, having abandoned all attempts at reviewing her caseload.

She was barely aware of what she was watching. It appeared to be a crime drama with an awful lot of victims and an extremely elusive murderer. She had fully zoned out of the story line when, at a little after ten, she heard the insistent buzz of the doorbell and was jerked into instant red alert.

Alessandro.

Surely he wouldn't have the cheek to show up at this hour at her house?

Of course he wouldn't. Why would a shark bother to stalk a minnow when it knew full well that the minnow would swim into its gaping jaw of its own free will?

Much more likely that it was Beth; as she slipped on her bedroom slippers and padded out to the front door, she was already trying to work out what she might say to begin killing her friend's already full-blown optimism.

She pulled open the door to Alessandro and her mouth fell open in surprise.

'Rule one,' he said, strolling past her to take up residence in the sitting room before she had had a chance to marshal her thoughts into order. 'When living in London, never open the door unless you know who's going to be standing on your doorstep.' He turned towards her, which instantly made her feel like a guest in her own home. 'I could have been anyone.'

'And, unfortunately for me, you're not!' She folded her arms and looked at him with gimlet-eyed stoniness. 'What are you doing here?'

'You said that you were finding it impossible to get down to work because you were thinking of me, so I thought I'd drop by.'

'I never said any such thing!' He was not in work clothes but in a pair of black jeans and a grey polo-necked shirt. He looked drop-dead gorgeous, which did nothing for her composure, because she felt far from drop-dead anything in her tatty old jogging bottoms and a tee-shirt that had lost its shape in the wash years ago. She also wasn't wearing a bra and she was conscious of her nipples poking against the cotton of the tee-shirt.

'I must have misunderstood. My apologies. But I'm here now, so maybe you could offer me a cup of coffee? Nothing stronger. I'm driving.'

'I wasn't about to offer you anything!'

'Don't you want to let off steam? You were breathing brimstone and fire down the line less than an hour ago.'

'Because you went behind my back and led Beth to believe that you were going to save her shelter—worse, led her to believe that the decision lies with *me*!'

'Oh, but it does, doesn't it?' He stared at her with a mixture of cool certainty and mild surprise that she should question the obvious.

'What on earth did you tell her?'

'That you and I were working on a plan to see whether the place could be saved and money invested.'

'Because you're such a good guy, right?'

'Let's not go down the tortuous route of moral ethics, Chase. However non-existent you think mine are, you're not exactly in a position to point fingers.'

Chase chewed her lip and glared impotently at him. 'I'll make you some coffee.' She shrugged and turned away. He was here now, in her house, smug and self-satisfied at the awkward position into which he had shoved her; sooner or later they would have to talk, so why not make it sooner? She couldn't see herself getting to sleep in a hurry.

She returned with two mugs of coffee to find him ensconced in one of the deep chairs, the very picture of a man totally relaxed in his surroundings.

'You gave me your word that I would have forty-eight hours.'

'And nothing's changed on that front,' Alessandro said smoothly. 'You still do. I've just thrown an extra something into the mix.'

'And that wasn't fair.'

'Between us, the gloves are off. You're as scheming as I am, so don't even bother to try and play the wounded party with me.' He had not been able to get her out of his head and, the more he thought about her, the more urgent his need to have her became. The sooner he had her, sated this voracious lust, the faster he would be rid of her. He couldn't wait.

Nudging the back of his mind was the uncomfortable truth that he was not a vengeful man by nature, that this sort of revenge was born from emotions which he had handed over to her eight years ago only to find them thrown back in his face. She had shown him his vulnerability and the force of his reactions now lay in that one, unmentioned reality. It was something he could hardly stand to admit even to himself and it lay there, buried like a pernicious weed, even when he had told himself over the years that he had had a narrow escape; that getting involved with a woman such as she had turned out to be would have been an unmitigated disaster.

'You think you know me,' Chase muttered bitterly, and Alessandro narrowed his eyes to look at her.

'By which you mean… Tell me.'

'Nothing,' she said in a harried undertone. 'This is an impossible situation.'

'No, it's not. It's the sound of the wheel turning full circle.'

'You don't like me, you don't respect me, so why on earth would you want to sleep with me? You must be able to snap your fingers and have a thousand women standing to attention and saluting. Why bother with the one who doesn't want to fall in line?'

Chase projected into the future. So she turned him down and the shelter became a shopping mall with her friend retreating to the seaside, where she would live out the rest of her days, bored, grumbling and dissatisfied. Furthermore, what would happen to their friendship? Alessandro had put her in an invidious position, for would her friend ever forgive her for being the one who failed to 'iron out the crease' that would have enabled her to hang on to what she loved?

She would never be able to tell Beth what that particular crease was and eventually the wonderful friendship they had would wither and die under the weight of Beth's misunderstanding and simmering resentment. How could it not?

'I've always considered myself a man to rise to the challenge,' Alessandro said coolly.

'And I'm your challenge.' There was no point moaning

about the unfairness of fate. He had seriously upped the ante by involving Beth and now she had to step up to the plate one way or another. He might well consider himself a guy who couldn't resist a challenge, but when had *she* ever been the sort of woman to back down? Her days of doing that had been put behind her.

And he talked about unfinished business… Wasn't it the same for her? Over the years, through everything that had happened, hadn't he been the burr under her skin? Hadn't she had broken nights dreaming of him? Hadn't she replayed scenarios in her head during which what they had had came to fruition?

More to the point, hadn't all those scenarios sprung back into instant life the second she had laid eyes on him again? Common sense had wrestled with what she considered her stupid weakness, because he was as out of bounds now as he had ever been, despite the fact that Shaun was no longer on the scene. But common sense was failing to win the battle. She knew she looked at him, wondered…

'Are you going to tell me that I'm not yours?' Alessandro asked softly. Two adults, he thought, who wanted each other and this time no hidden obstacle lurking in the way. On top of that, so much for her to get out of it. So where was the problem? He had never had the slightest curiosity to plumb the hidden depths of any woman, yet now he had a sudden, urgent desire to reach into her head and discover what was going on behind that beautiful, enigmatic facade. The thrill of the unexplored was heady and erotic and it took a surprising amount of will power to remain where he was, holding on to silence as a weapon of persuasion.

'It feels…odd. Just not right.'

'But you can't deny that what I'm saying makes sense. If we cut through all the redundant emotion, if we leave bitterness and the past aside, don't we still fancy the hell out of one another?'

Chase thought of his hands on her body, touching her. She had stayed far away from the opposite sex over the past eight years. Offers had been plentiful, some of them horribly insistent, but there was no way she was going to get involved with any man ever again.

So here she was, nearing thirty, unattached, with barely any social life to speak of. Wasn't it time for her to rejoin the human race? And wouldn't she be able to do that once, as he had put it, business between them was finally finished? If she were brutally honest with herself, hadn't Alessandro been as much a reason for where she was now with her life, as Shaun had been? He had had such a dramatic hold on her all those years ago and the way things had ended between them had scarred her to the extent that she had just simply withdrawn.

'It just feels so…cold and detached. So businesslike.' She rubbed her lightly perspiring hands along the soft cotton of her jogging pants.

'You're looking for flowers and chocolates and courtship?' His mouth curled into a cynical smile. 'I believe I fell into that trap once before. I don't repeat my mistakes twice.'

Chase thought she could detect the rapid beating of her heart as he stared at her broodingly. She felt as though she had one foot raised over the edge of a precipice as she made her mind up as to whether to jump or not. Yet, she knew that that was a fallacy. She was older, wiser and tougher and, if this felt like a business arrangement, then it had to be said that business arrangements came with definite upsides. For starters, she would know all the parameters. She would not be hurt. She would be taking from him just as he would be taking from her and, when they walked away from each other, she would be freed from the strange half-emptiness of regret that had been her companion for the past eight years.

It was a tantalising thought.

As though she had opened a door to a gremlin, she was suddenly released from the constraints of having to fight the attraction that had been gnawing away at her. She *imagined*...and the images were so vivid that she felt faint.

'I can't think of anything I would want less than a court-ship,' she informed him with as much cool detachment as she could muster. Certainly not flowers or chocolate. He had given her those once before. He must have realised, in the aftermath of her dumping him, that those tokens had hit the bin before she had had time to make it back to her flat. Thank goodness she had bluntly refused to accept anything else. At least he would never be able to add 'gold-digger' to all the other bitter insults he had heaped on her.

Watching her closely, Alessandro knew that he had won. She was going to be his. And yet, instead of the satisfac-tion of accomplishment, he was irked by the notion that she didn't want a courtship because she had already had a courtship from the one guy who had really counted in her life.

Who gave a damn about the ex-husband? The bald fact was that the man was no longer around and the one woman who had eluded him was going to be his. He was not now, and never would be, in competition with a ghost. When he was through with her, he would discard her and she could return to the photo albums she had stashed in a drawer somewhere. He didn't care. He would have got the one and only thing he wanted from her and for which, essentially, he was prepared to pay a high price, bearing in mind all the money that would need pumping into that shelter if it was to achieve habitable status.

'Is that because you've decided to limit yourself to one and that role was filled by your dearest, departed ex—or because you've had so many in the intervening years that you're sick of them?'

'I've been so busy in the past few years that I haven't had time for…for any kind of relationship.' How strange it felt to be sharing this kind of confidential information! Over time, she had become defined by her need for privacy. She knew that most of her colleagues her age thought she was weird. She knew they thought that, with her looks, she should be putting herself out there instead of working all the hours God made before scuttling off to a house to which none of them had ever been invited. She didn't care, and she had become so accustomed to self-containment that she now looked at Alessandro, wide-eyed, startled by her outburst.

'You mean…?' Curiosity kicked in with cursed force.

'There's actually nothing out of the ordinary about that. Relationships require time and I haven't had a lot of that while I've been trying to climb up the career ladder.' Chase knew how she sounded: tough, hard, cold. This wasn't the person she had ever set out to be but she wasn't going to apologise for the fact that her life hadn't been a round of parties, late nights and sex with random men.

'So ever since your husband died…?' he encouraged.

Chase tilted her chin defensively. 'I know how it must sound to someone like you.'

'Someone like me?'

'I expect you have an active sexual life. Lots of women. You're rich, you're good-looking, you're self-assured. You wouldn't have a clue how I could…hold off on relationships for quite a long time.'

'I managed it eight years ago. With you.' He shook his head, impatient with himself. And he did, actually, understand. Grief and mourning could do all sorts of things and have all manner of consequences. That said…

'It's not healthy,' he said brusquely.

Chase reddened. 'I haven't asked for your opinion,' she

said defensively. 'And the only reason I'm telling you this is because you might want to have a rethink.'

'Not following you.'

'I'm a little rusty in that particular area.' She gave a brittle, nonchalant laugh, but inwardly every part of her felt exposed, vulnerable and uncertain. What on earth was she doing? She wasn't like the women she imagined him being drawn to; she lacked the finesse and the experience. Did she want to risk the humiliation of having him look at her with amusement and disappointment just because she needed to know what she had missed all those years ago? Because, sure, the shelter would be a happy bonus, but she was already yielding for reasons that were far more complex than the desire to save her friend's shelter. Shelter or no shelter, she would never have allowed herself to be manipulated into doing something she didn't want to do.

Alessandro frowned. He had been quick to assert that his proposal was a non-negotiable arrangement designed to assuage the inconvenient need he had to sleep with her and thereby get her out of his system. He had been even quicker to inform her that he would not be investing it with any bells and whistles. It would be sex, no more or less. Yet, he found that he didn't care for the cool approach she was taking. Hell, she was still sitting a million miles away from him!

'I'll cope. Does that mean that you've made your mind up?'

'Perhaps you're right. Perhaps I've been curious. Maybe we do need to…eh…take what we have a step further.' Her heart was beating like a drum. 'But if I accept,' she continued firmly, because it was important for him to know that she wasn't making a decision based on blackmail or unfair persuasion, 'it's not to do with the shelter. Much as I love Beth, I would never do something I didn't want to because of her.'

'Right now, the only thing that matters is that we're going to be lovers.' He gave her a slashing, sexy smile and patted the space next to him on the sofa. 'So why don't you come and sit next to me and we can continue *bonding* with a little less physical distance between us?'

Chase thought she could actually hear her own painful breathing. Fear and apprehension at touching him, being close to him, warred with unbridled excitement. She had stepped off the side of the precipice and she had no idea what she had let herself in for but it was an adventure she needed to have. It was a situation over which she could only hope to exercise control and, for someone who had constructed walls of control all around her, it was a daunting prospect. But she had done daunting before. Many, many times. She could handle daunting.

'How long do you think this will take?'

'Come again?' Alessandro had never had to fight this hard for anyone. Sexual attraction had proved stronger than his very justifiable bitterness and dislike. He had had to swallow a lot and yet, having done that, having got her to the place he wanted, surely the going should get less tough?

'How long do you think it will take before we get past this…thing? A night? A couple of days?'

'How the hell should I know?' Alessandro raked his fingers through his hair and frowned at her. 'And why are we talking about timelines, anyway? All I want to do right now is touch you, so why don't we dispense with the conversation and get down to business?' He sprawled back, arms extended on the back of the sofa, legs loose and open.

He was the very essence of man at his most physical, Chase thought with a shiver, utterly and beautifully masculine; she licked her lips cautiously. She wanted this so badly. It felt as though it was something she had never stopped wanting. She tentatively closed the distance between them to sit like a wooden doll next to him.

'I feel I should tell you,' she whispered as Alessandro lazily removed one arm from the back of the sofa to trail it along her neck.

'You talk a lot,' he growled and then, almost from no-where, plucked from thin air, 'You always did. As though you had too many words inside you that needed to get out.' He laughed softly, caught unaware by the memory. 'Do you remember the way you would mention a case file and then force me to have an opinion so that you could prac-tise shooting it down in flames?'

Hell, what was he going on about? He angled his body round and pulled her towards him and it was like the prom-ise of heaven. The undiluted thrill of having her in his arms was incomparable and he urgently sought her mouth, plun-dering it while his hands moved down to circle her waist. His erection was steel-hard and painful. More than any-thing else, he wanted to rip down those unattractive jog-ging bottoms, pull aside her panties and then just thrust into her, hard and fast, until he got explosive relief. There would be time enough to do the whole gentle foreplay stuff later.

Chase could feel the raw energy emanating from him in waves but that soft laugh, that nostalgic memory he had laid out bare for her without really thinking, was strangely seductive, strangely relaxing. Fingers that had been curled into his polo shirt suddenly splayed against his chest and she struggled back from him.

'Wait…'

'I'm not sure I can.' But he reluctantly drew back, his breathing ragged and uneven. She was stripped of her tough, outer shell, the consummate lawyer and assertive career woman. He glimpsed a uniquely feminine vulner-ability that startled him, because she was the last woman on the planet he would ever have labelled *'vulnerable'*.

Once upon a time, sure, but then once upon a time he'd been an idiot.

'I'm not into playing games,' he drawled just in case she got it into her head that she could string him along for a second time. 'And, just in case you think that you might be able to pull off any "one step forward, two steps back" tactic, then forget it. This time round, you're dealing with a different person, Chase. My levels of tolerance when it comes to you are non-existent.'

'I know they are!' Whatever the backdrop to what they had had eight years ago, it all seemed so innocent now in retrospect. 'It's just...'

'Just *what*, Chase?'

'Never mind.' She wasn't looking for sweet nothings whispered in her ear nor was she looking for any shows of affection. She told herself that she was perfectly comfortable with an 'arrangement', yet as she reached to hook her fingers under the tee-shirt to pull it over her head, she knew that she was breathing too quickly, close to freezing up.

'Oh for goodness' sake,' Alessandro groaned and caught her hands in his. 'Why tell me that this is what you want if you have to squeeze your eyes tightly shut and give every impression of a woman who has to grin and bear it?'

'I *do* want it,' Chase insisted but she could hear the give-away wavering in her voice and she hated it.

'Then what's the problem?' He took in the hectic flush in her cheeks. What was going on here? Shouldn't this be straightforward—two consenting adults getting something out of their system? 'Tell me.'

'You're not really interested.'

'Let me be the one who decides that.' He nuzzled her ear and smiled as she quivered, because it tickled.

'I'm... I've...' She took a deep, steadying breath. 'I've never really been into sex,' she said in a rush. 'I know you can't bear me, and your tolerance levels are low, but I can't just fall on this sofa with you and have wild sex.'

'Never really been into sex?' Alessandro's voice held accusatory disbelief. 'You were a married woman,' he pointed out with ruthless directness. 'Married at what age—eighteen? Younger? Are you telling me that you were a gymslip wife who didn't enjoy sleeping with her husband?'

'I don't want to talk about Shaun,' Chase said quickly. *Or,* she mentally tacked on, *anything to do with my past, the past you think you know but don't.*

Alessandro looked at her in silence for a long time. She was flustered as hell but trying hard to put on a show of strength and assertiveness. Did he need all of this? It was just sex and, yet again, that surge of curiosity that was more insistent than the cold logic he wanted to impose. 'Why don't you want to talk about him?'

'Because…there's no point. I'll just say that things are never what you think they are.' Too much information. 'But it's been a long time for me…' she concluded hurriedly.

'You just want me to take it slowly, do you?'

Chase nodded.

'In that case, what about a show of good faith?' He shot her a slow smile. 'Taking it slow is one thing,' he murmured, playing with a strand of her hair whilst he tried to halt his runaway mind, which wanted to ask her what she had meant by her enigmatic remark about things never being what you thought they were. 'A standstill pace, on the other hand, just won't do. So why don't we both get naked and see what happens next?' He watched her carefully, wanting her more than anything, prepared to do the complex if that was what it took. 'If you're not comfortable down here, then you could always give me a tour of upstairs and we can end up in your bedroom. How does that sound?'

Chase nodded. 'You might be disappointed at what you see.' She tried to make her voice as normal as possible but her pulse was racing as they quietly padded upstairs. 'The whole of my upstairs could probably fit into your downstairs cloakroom.'

He wanted a show of good faith and she couldn't blame him. She pushed open the doors to the small spare room, with its single futon, the desk at which she was accustomed to working until late into the night and the bathroom which was large and airy given the size of the house. They ended up in her bedroom.

Alessandro stood in the doorway and looked. The walls were a subdued cream but the four-poster bed was dressed and all romance. The prints on the walls were landscapes of deserted beaches. The dressing table, like the wardrobe, was old, doubtless bought at auction. He thought that he might be the first guy to step foot in this room and it gave him an unbelievable kick. Every single woman he had ever known had been keen to show him their bedrooms and the beds which promised inventive entertainment for as long as he wanted. Mood lighting had usually been a dominant theme. When he took in Chase's wary expression, he could see ambivalence there.

'Your sanctuary.'

'Not any longer. You're in it.'

'By invitation.' His hand reached to the button on his trousers, but first he removed the shirt in one easy movement.

Chase practically fainted. He was the stuff daydreams were made of and she had had enough of those over the years. His body was burnished gold and honed to perfection. When he moved, she could detect the ripple of muscle under skin. Her breathing picked up pace and her mouth went dry. Under her top, her bare breasts tingled, and she had the heady feeling that she wanted them touched, that she wanted her nipples played with.

'Your turn...' He liked the way her eyes skittered across his body as if helplessly drawn to stare at him. He remembered the way that used to do crazy things to him once and was uneasily aware that that should have changed—so why hadn't it? He found that he was holding his breath as her tee-shirt slowly rode up her belly, exposing her pale skin a slither at a time. She wasn't doing this because of undue pressure, yet there was an erotic hesitancy about her movements. The wealth of all her complexities crashed over him like a wave from which he had to fight to surface, to bring himself back in the moment.

He was a randy teenager all over again as he looked at her breasts, heavy and sexy and everything he had imagined. More. Her breasts were bigger than he had thought, tipped with perfect rosy-pink discs. She possessed a body that should never be constrained by a starchy lawyer's outfit. Her proportions were all feminine curves: bountiful breasts, a narrow waist and proper hips that swelled tantalisingly under the dreary track pants. He wanted nothing more than to stride over to her and feel her nakedness pressed against him.

With some sixth sense, though, he was aware of her skittishness. He didn't get it, but he could feel it. Any sudden moves and he got the feeling that she would take flight, even though she obviously wasn't embarrassed about her body, wasn't trying to be coy and hide her breasts behind her hands. He kept his eyes on her face as he removed his trousers and flung them to one side, still looking at her.

Chase felt her skin tighten at the glaring evidence of his arousal. His dark boxers could hardly contain it. She shakily reached to the elasticised waist of her joggers and stilled as he moved towards her.

'You look as though you want to run away,' he murmured. He swallowed hard because the tips of her breasts were almost brushing his chest and his hands itched to feel the weight of them. 'Believe it or not, this is taking it slow by my standards.'

'I believe you,' Chase said huskily. She touched his chest with one finger and felt his soft moan.

'Come to bed.' He stepped away from her. 'I'm not sure how long the slow plan can carry on for.'

When he turned his back to her, Chase knew that he was trying to hold himself back. She felt giddy with power. It was a wonderfully novel sensation and it afforded her a layer of strength she hadn't known she possessed. With Shaun, it had never been like this, never, not even in the very beginning. But she didn't want to think about her ex-husband. That was one very fast and very sure route to instant depression.

She slipped out of the jogging bottoms; his back was still turned when she crept into bed and under the covers.

'Now...' He wasn't used to taking sex slowly. He had never had to pace himself. He failed to consider that pacing himself with a woman for whom he harboured nothing more than a desire to even the score made no sense. 'Tell me...' he flipped onto his side so that they were lying under the covers, front to front, their bodies not touching but both of them vitally aware of their nudity under the duvet '...about the prints on your walls. And the four-poster bed...'

CHAPTER SIX

IF THERE WERE prizes for holding a man's interest, then Alessandro thought that Chase would be in line for all of them. He had planned on a straightforward conquest, aided and abetted by the trump card of saving the shelter. He would take her and, by taking her, he would rid himself of the allure of the inaccessible—which was the position to which she seemed to have been elevated over the years, apparently without him even having noticed. For him, the accessible had always had a short-lived appeal, especially when the quarry in question came with a truck-load of dubious cargo.

And she had played him at his own game, had not been browbeaten but had laid her cards on the table. But then that hesitancy, that tentative admission that sex wasn't her thing... She had lain in his arms but he could feel her tension and he had backed off, even though his body had been on fire for her.

The rapacious, lying, deceitful, manipulative woman had shown a shrinking violet side to her that had got under his skin. Since when had he become the sort of man who was content to hold off, especially in a situation like this, with a woman scarcely worth his time and attention? He had held off with her once and look at where that had got him! But had he done what he should have done? Had he sneered at her attempts to play the shy maiden and ploughed forward? Hell, no! He had lain with her in his arms like the virgin she most certainly was not, had *talked*, and then he had left to return to his apartment and a freezing-cold shower.

Then he had gone abroad for two days, giving himself time to figure out why he was behaving so out of character and giving her time to wise up to the fact that what they had was a deal—and one he intended to cash, because her time limit for playing shy had been used up. He had returned late last night with two flights to Italy booked and the decidedly uncomfortable realisation that there might just be a need to shift gears slightly—to woo her, despite everything he had said about what they had not being a courtship. Somewhere along the line the whole 'time limit' speech had been shelved.

He just knew that when she came to him she would come of her own volition. She would jettison whatever the hell it was that was holding her back. In the space of a heartbeat, it had become a matter of pride—actually in the space of time it had taken for the notion of a break in Italy to take root, which had been fairly instantaneous.

If she was holding back because she hadn't managed to put the premature death of her husband behind her, then she needed to move on from that place and come to him willingly. There was no way he was going to sleep with any woman unless her thoughts were focused one hundred per cent on him and, if it took some seduction to get her to that place, then he would play along with it. The end result would be the same, wouldn't it? And he was an 'end result' kind of guy.

He had phoned her from abroad and announced the whole Italy idea with far more conviction than he had been feeling at the time, but she had taken little persuading as it turned out in the end. She was due some time off and she would take it. A little more enthusiasm would have been appreciated but he had met his match in her. She hadn't pandered to him eight years ago and she wasn't going to pander to him now, even though she knew him for the billionaire that he was.

Now, standing in front of the check-in desk at Heathrow surrounded by crowds, he scowled as he felt himself inevitably harden at the tantalising prospect of having her; of touching that flawless body; of sinking against those breasts, feeling them against his chest, against the palms of his big hands, pushing into his mouth. He had once lost his head over a mirage and now he would take what he felt was his due, take the promised fruit and kill the bitterness inside him that made such an unwelcome companion.

Through the crowds he spotted her weaving and looking around for him and he gave her a brief wave.

'You're ten minutes late. You should have let my driver collect you instead of coming by public transport.'

Chase looked up at his frowning face and was tempted to snap because, however much she wore her hard-won independence like a badge of honour, he obviously had a Neanderthal approach to women in general. But she bit back the retort because she could remember the way he had always taken command when she had known him: paying for whatever they had before she could offer to go halves; impatient with second-rate service; intolerant of anyone in his lectures who'd failed to try.

'I told you. I had some work to finish before I left.' Left for a week in the sun. She had no idea where that idea of Alessandro's had sprung from. She had fought against going, because she was all too aware that their relationship was destined to crash and burn, and the last thing she needed was a plethora of memories she would later have to work out of her system, but he had been insistent. Maybe being out of the country would infuse this weird closure of theirs with an unreality that would be easy to box away.

Italy, he had told her, was his home and, hell, why not. It was a nice time of year over there and he had just closed a massive deal. She could see his house. His casual tone of voice down the end of the line had told her that it wasn't a big deal. He would be going over there himself, she figured, with her or without her, but he would take her along because, as far as he was concerned, she had yet to fulfil her side of the bargain. Lying naked in his arms, tense as a plank of wood, didn't count.

Had they had sex, she was sure that he would not have suggested the Italy trip. Revenge lay behind his motivation and revenge was an emotion that could be sated very quickly. Certainly, a week of her would be enough. Did she deserve that? Maybe she did, in his eyes, and she would never disabuse him of the complicated story behind her lies because that would open up a whole new can of worms far worse than the one she was dealing with.

'Isn't that the old hoary line used by men?' Alessandro queried, moving towards the check-in girl at the first class desk. It occurred to him that he would have quite enjoyed having her at his beck and call and put that down to a caveman instinct he'd never known he possessed. Or maybe he only possessed it when the chase was still on, and only with her because she hadn't followed the pattern of the women he slept with.

'You're very chauvinistic, Alessandro. Women who have careers can't just jettison them the second something better comes along. As it is, I'll have a mountain of work to get down to when I get back. I shouldn't really be here at all, even if I *am* due time off.'

'Are you telling me that being with me is more compelling than your career?'

'I'm not saying anything of the sort!'

'You work too hard.'

'How else am I expected to get on?'

'What are you expecting to *get on* to?' They had checked in and were now heading through Passport Control, towards the first class lounge. Years ago he had considered the possibility of a private jet, if only to cut down on the inconvenience of a bustling airport, but had ditched the idea, because who needed to be responsible for such a vast personal carbon footprint when it could be avoided? Shame, though, because, had he had one, he could have introduced her to some creative ways of passing time twenty thousand miles up without an audience of prying eyes.

'I'd like to head up my own pro bono department. Maybe even branch out on my own and concentrate on that area. Bring in a few other employees...who knows?'

'And what about another prance up the aisle? Is that up there on the agenda? Surely your parents would want to hear the patter of little feet when you visit them in Australia? Or do visits to Australia get in the way of your career?'

Chase temporarily froze. The passing lie was not one on which she wanted to dwell. She wanted no reminders of her non-existent family. She knew that the last thing he would want to discuss would be her ex or her past treachery. His only goal was to get her into bed; her only goal was to put this murky, tangled, haunting past to rest. He was motivated by revenge, she by a need for closure. It was a straightforward situation. She needed no reminders of white lies that had been told and could not now be un-told.

How would he react were he to know that, not only had she once lied to him about her marital status, not only had she dumped him in a way that now made her cringe with guilt and shame even though she knew that it just couldn't have been helped at the time, but that her entire past was as substantial as gossamer?

'Australia is a long way away...' she muttered vaguely.

'Yes. I know. I've been there. You've never told me which part of Australia they live in. It's a big place.'

'You wouldn't have heard of it.' She could feel beads of perspiration break out all over her body. 'It's just a small town on the outskirts of…um…Melbourne. Look, I really don't want to talk about this. Discussing personal issues isn't what we're about, is it?' Never had she realised how being trapped in a lie could prove as painful as walking on a bed of burning coals.

'No,' Alessandro said shortly. 'It's not.' He looked at her blank eyes and tight smile and felt a surge of rage that the thing most women gave naturally to him—the desperate openness which they always seemed to hope could suck him into something permanent and committal—was the one thing Chase steadfastly refused to give. It angered him that he was even going down the road of quizzing her because it reflected a series of inner challenges that he knew were inappropriate. The challenge to get her into bed so that he could assuage the treachery he felt had been done to him had been replaced by the challenge to get her into bed willingly and *hot for him*; the challenge to wipe her ex out of her head when they finally had sex, the challenge to get into her head, to know what made her tick.

Where the hell did it end? Did he need her to remind him that the rules of the game precluded certain things?

'Call it making polite conversation,' he offered with cool politeness.

'I overreacted. It's just that…'

'No need to explain yourself. I'm basically not interested in your past. Like I said, small talk…'

Chase was silenced. Of course he was basically not interested in her past. He was basically not interested in *her*. He was utterly focused on one thing and one thing only. She nodded, nonchalantly indicating that she understood, that she shared the same sentiment.

When he began telling her about some of the complex legalities of the deal he had just pulled off, she let herself slide smoothly into career-woman mode, and then the conversation flowed faultlessly onto the subject of Beth and the shelter. It was a happy story and Chase felt herself once again relax. This was an odd situation but she could handle it, just as long as she didn't start feeling angst over stuff, just as long as she maintained the composed exterior that was so much part and parcel of her personality. She couldn't let herself forget that she wanted this as much as he did. They both had their demons to put to rest.

They landed at Cristoforo Colombo Airport at Genova Sestri to a brilliant day. The wall-to-wall blue skies, which had no longer been in evidence in London after their brief appearance, were here in full force. As soon as they stepped into the waiting limo, she could feel a heady holiday spirit fill her.

'It's been ages since I've been away,' she confided as she settled back to watch the stunning scenery gallop past from the back of the car. 'In fact...' she turned to him '...my only trip abroad in the past few years has been a snatched week at a spa resort in Greece.'

'In that case, I shall make it my mission to see that you enjoy every second of my country...when and if we have the time; bed can be remarkably compulsive with the right companion in it.' His dark eyes roved over her face, encompassing her luscious body, enjoying the delicate bloom of colour that tinged her cheeks.

This holiday would put an end to the game playing which he had sworn he wouldn't tolerate, yet had ended up indulging that one night which should have seen this uncontrollable passion slayed. As she had pointed out in a timely reminder, this wasn't about getting to know one another, this was about sex. Getting to know one another had been a pointless game which he had mistakenly played a long time ago, little knowing that he had been the only participant.

This time round, there'd be no more messing around and taking things at a snail's pace. He would move only as slowly as he felt necessary to get her where he wanted her—which was out of his system so that he could return to normality.

Vaguely annoyed at the contrary drift of his thoughts, he was aware of telling her about the Italian Riviera, on autopilot, pointing out the grandeur of the mountainous landscape in such close and unusual proximity to the sea, giving her a little bit of history about the place. His voice warmed as he described the vast olive grove plantations stretching across the hills, vast tracts of which had once been owned by his ancestors, only to disappear over the years, mismanaged and sold off in bits and pieces—the last by his parents, who had needed the money in their quest for eternal fun.

'You could always come back here…buy more olive groves. It's so beautiful; I can't see why you would want to live in London.' Not even in her wildest, escapist fantasies could she ever have dreamt up somewhere as beautiful as this. The landscape was bold and dramatic, the colours bright and vibrant. Everywhere was bursting with incredible, Technicolor beauty. Alessandro might have had irresponsible parents but it had to be said that, whatever he had gone through, he had gone through it in some style.

'I have a house here. It's where we're going.'

'But how often do you visit it?'

'As you'll be the first to agree, taking time out gets in the way of a career.'

Chase bristled at the implicit criticism in his remark. It reminded her that what they shared was simply a truce but, behind that truce, there was a lot he just didn't like about her. 'My career is important to me.'

'I've gathered.'

'You say that as though you disapprove of women who work.'

'On the contrary. Some of the highest positions in my company are occupied by women.'

'But you would never actually go out with a woman who had a career…'

Alessandro shot her a sidelong glance. The car was air-conditioned but he had chosen to have the windows opened and the breeze blew through her hair, tossing it across her face in unruly strands. She was no longer the high-powered lawyer with the pristine appearance. She was the girl he had once known and he railed against the pull of memories. 'There's little I find attractive about a woman who puts her career first.'

Chase rolled her eyes and sighed, because the breeze was too balmy and the scenery too exotic for arguing. 'That is because you're a dinosaur.' He had old-fashioned ideas. Years ago she had teased him that that was a back-lash from his parents' excesses but she had liked those old-fashioned ideas, never having come across them before.

'And I take it that under normal circumstances you wouldn't choose to go out with a dinosaur? Tell me about your husband.'

'I no longer have a husband,' Chase said shortly, rousing herself from bittersweet memories of their brief, shared dalliance.

'I realise that. What was he like?' He was curious. He found that he wanted to know. This wasn't polite conversation, although the casual tone of his voice gave nothing away.

The last thing Chase wanted to do was to talk about Shaun but she had a sneaking suspicion that, if she backed away from the subject, it would arouse his interest even further. 'We met when we were young. I was only fifteen. Just. We met at the local disco.'

'Cosy. And was it love at first sight?'

'We found that we had a lot in common.'

'Always a good start to a healthy relationship. Even at the ripe old age of fifteen. Just.' He found that he didn't care for the idea of them having a lot in common at whatever the hell age they had happened to meet. Nor had he intended to get wrapped up in pointless conversations about the thug who had been lurking behind the scenes when she had taken him for a ride and played him for a fool.

'So they say,' Chase murmured tonelessly.

'I take it he wasn't sharp enough to make it to university?'

'Shaun was plenty sharp.' She couldn't help the bitterness that had crept into her voice but she kept it at bay. Talking about Shaun would inevitably lead to all sorts of questions about the sort of world she had really come from. Chase found that she had moved on from the fear of him discovering the truth about her and eking out some kind of belated revenge by spilling the beans to her work colleagues. She honestly couldn't see him doing that.

No, what she feared—and she hated herself for this— was to have him walk away in disgust at the lies she had told, at the person she really was and the life she had really led. His pedigree was impeccable and although she knew that they would be the archetypal doomed lovers— in it for the wrong reasons but driven to fulfil their destiny—she still found that she wanted him to believe her to be the sassy, smart lawyer with the perfectly ordinary background when they parted company.

Wasn't that to be expected? What if she bumped into him at a later date? What if he met some of the partners in her law firm and started talking about her? If he knew the truth about her, then wasn't it likely that it would slip out in conversation? And, even if nothing did slip out, surely he would never be able to disguise the contempt in his voice at the mention of her name?

'Sharp as in...?'

She snapped out of her daydreaming to find his eyes narrowed on her. 'Streetwise; sharp as in streetwise.'

'And did your streetwise late husband have a job?' He thought back to the picture she had shown him all those years ago.

'He...worked in transport but he...he lost his job shortly before the accident. I'd bought him that motorbike. I'd been putting aside some money and I wanted to celebrate getting my first promotion...'

'So you celebrated by buying him a motorbike. Shouldn't *he* have been the one doing the buying to congratulate you? Or am I just thinking like a dinosaur again?'

'Alessandro, please, let's move on from this. I honestly don't want to talk about Shaun. Tell me more about here. It's amazing to think that there can be snow on mountaintops that are just a short distance from the Med...'

Alessandro heard the soft plea in her voice. 'Why did you give me a second look if you were so clearly head over heels in love with your husband?'

'I...I'm sorry. I made a mistake.'

'Which doesn't answer my question.' He raked his hand impatiently though his hair and sat back with his eyes closed for a few seconds. 'Scrap that. Not sure I could stomach whatever fairy stories you decide to come out with.'

'Alessandro...'

He inclined his head towards her and linked his fingers loosely in his lap. She had the face of an angel, the body of a siren and he was furious with himself for wanting to probe deeper. He pointed to a spot behind her as the car turned left. 'My house.'

Chase turned just in time to glimpse a sand-coloured

mansion rising up from the cliffs, overlooking the placid turquoise sea with a backdrop of woods of chestnut trees. She forgot everything and her mouth dropped open.

'I have two housekeepers who live in, make sure everything is ticking over. Occasionally, it's used by some of my employees, a little bonus if they do well. The promise of an all-expenses-paid long weekend here generates a lot of healthy competition, and it does no harm for the place to get an airing now and again.'

'It's huge. What about family members?'

'Oh, completely off-limits to them. My parents ensured their place in the pecking order as the black sheep of the family and I've inherited their generous legacy. I have little contact with my extended family.

'My parents were both only children, so there are strangely few people who bear a belated grudge towards me. I see a couple of slightly less distant relatives now and again when I'm in Milan; a few more work in some of my associated companies, my way of making amends for my parents' appallingly hedonistic behaviour which was, if all accounts are to be believed, ruinous to both family names.'

He edged towards her and pointed. 'You can't see it, but there's a winding path that leads down to a private cove at the bottom of the cliff face. Excellent bathing. Once upon a time, fishing used to be big here. Not so much any more. Tourism pays better, it would seem. The wealthy find the sight of yachts far more uplifting than the reality of fishing boats.'

'What a shame you don't get here often,' Chase said. When he was like this—charming, informative, his voice as deep and as dark as the most pure, rich, velvety chocolate—she could forget everything. She could lapse back to the past where dangerous, taboo emotions still held a certain innocence, a time when he didn't hate her. 'Don't you sometimes long to have someone to share this with?'

'Oh, but isn't that what I'm doing now?' Alessandro drawled. 'Admittedly, only for a few days, and with a woman who is destined never to return, but it'll do for the moment.'

He reached across, pulling her towards him. 'I've given my loyal housekeepers time off,' he murmured into her hair. 'It's hot here. I thought it might be nice for us to live as naturists for a few days. Why bother with clothes? I want to be able to touch you anywhere...at any time... And you'll discover that my house is perfect for ensuring one hundred per cent privacy. I'll make you thaw, my sweet; on that count, you can trust me...'

Chase was still smarting from the insistent stab of hurt his words had generated. *Destined never to return.*

They approached the sprawling villa through wrought-iron gates which had been flung open, revealing perfectly groomed lawns stretching out on either side of the gravel drive.

'How many people does it take to look after these gardens?' She shouldn't have been, but she was still shocked by the splendour.

'A small army,' Alessandro admitted drily. 'I'm single-handedly trying to do my bit to keep the economy going. There's a very private pool to the side of the house. I have vague memories of my parents throwing some extremely wild parties there.'

'I had no idea the house belonged to them.' Chase turned to look at him and their eyes tangled. Instantly, she could feel her breasts begin to ache in expectation of his caresses. With Shaun, she had become conditioned to viewing sex as something that had to be done. But when she had lain next to Alessandro her body had been fired up in a way that was new and, whilst they hadn't made love, it now thrummed at the prospect of being touched by him. It was a heady, exciting feeling and she was sure that it was all wrapped up in the culmination of what had begun all that time ago, what had never come to fruition.

'It was their pride and joy. The one thing they both hung on to.'

'And you kept it for sentimental reasons?'

'I never do anything for sentimental reasons. It's a good, appreciating asset.'

It was dreamy. If she had been able to conceive of a place like this, she might have been more elaborate in her teenage fantasies about perfect lifestyles instead of just settling for average. Then she decided that it was just as well, because how much more awkward would life have been now had her naïve, happily married parents in their two-up two-down been turned into minor landed gentry living in a small castle?

They were greeted by an elderly housekeeper and her husband who had stayed on to welcome Alessandro, tugging him into the kitchen so that they could show him the freezer full of food that had been prepared and the well-stocked larder. He managed to shoo them away after an hour and they departed wreathed in smiles.

'They've been with me for longer than I care to think. As you know, my parents were firm believers in handing over care of their offspring to hired help,' he told her as he played tour guide, taking her from room to room. He absently thought how many of those little details of his past she had been privy to, courtesy of that small window in his life during which his self-control had gone on holiday.

'I'm treating them to a well-deserved rest in a destination of their choosing, which as it turns out happens to be France, where their eldest is a dentist. I tried to persuade them into somewhere a little further afield but they weren't having it. Mauritius, apparently, is no competition for two hyper grandchildren.'

Chase's heart fluttered. This was how he had managed

to get under her skin. This was why she never wanted to have him learn the truth about her. This was why the thought of what he could do to balance the scales of justice should he want to avenge past wrongs was no longer the only consideration. Underneath his ruthlessly cold exterior were these flashes of genuine thoughtfulness that kept reminding her of why she had risked so much just talking to him eight years ago; that ambushed all her good intentions to keep her distance. Whenever he made her laugh, her defences slipped just a little bit more.

This was a dangerous game because she would end up being hurt. She would end up losing her hard-won self-control. She would end up with someone else having power over her, someone who didn't care about her, who wanted her for all the wrong reasons. Maybe she had already ended up there.

She had walked into this with her eyes wide open but now she felt as though she had walked straight into a trap, having stupidly failed to take account of its power for destruction.

The whole sex thing… Yes, she had wanted it, had *craved* it, but she had been scared because of past experience and he had respected her when she had turned into a block of ice in his arms. That consideration he had shown her, as it turned out, was just something else that had nibbled away at the edges of her defences so that what had once been a fortress, protecting her from the slings and arrows of emotional involvement with the human race, was beginning to resemble a broken down old castle open to all the elements.

She felt exposed in a way she never had in her life before. She felt as she had eight years ago: like a woman *falling in love*.

'You've stopped using rapturous superlatives to describe my house.'

Chase blinked and realised that he was several metres ahead of her because she had stopped dead in her tracks. Her brain had been so wrapped up contemplating the horror of falling for this guy again that it hadn't had any room left to give messages to her legs to keep moving.

'I think I may have run out of them.' She blinked and took in the raw sexuality of the man lounging in front of her with that killer half-smile on his lips.

'Where is this famous pool you've been bragging about?' Her voice was normal but her brain was malfunctioning.

'I never brag.' Again that smile that hurled her back in time. He took her hand to lead her through the house, out to the kitchen and towards the sea-facing side of the house, which took her breath away. 'Except in this one instance.'

He gestured to the open view as though he owned it and then relaxed back to look at her response. He had never given a damn what women thought of his opulent lifestyle and was indifferent to their gasps of awe whenever they stepped foot into his house in London. Yet he rather enjoyed the way her mouth fell open as she stepped out to stand next to him.

The house looked down to the sea that was turquoise and as still as a lake. The garden on this side was just a strip of green, broken by distinctive Italian palm trees and bordered by thick shrubbery. To one side a gate announced the winding stone steps, which Chase imagined led to the cove he had told her about.

This was her dream come true. She had somehow been catapulted into the prints she had hung on her walls. The romance which had not been part of the plan clung to her in a miasma, giving her all sorts of stupid illusions that somehow what they had might be the beginning of something real. It was time to start unravelling that piece of fiction.

'Are you sure it's completely deserted here?' She

squinted against the sun to look up at him, shielding her eyes with one hand.

Alessandro looked down at her. She was in a flimsy sleeveless dress which was far too baggy for his liking but which, on the upside, provided terrific fodder for his imagination. 'As a ghost town. Why?'

'Because I think we should explore that pool area you were bragging to me about... Oh yes, I forgot: you never brag...' Her hand fluttered provocatively to the small top button of the dress. 'It's so warm. I think I might need to strip off, have a dip in that pool of yours, the one—'

'I keep bragging to you about even though I never brag?' He laughed under his breath and felt the bulge in his pants as that part of his body which had been in charge of his brain ever since she had reappeared to smash into his ordered existence rose to immediate attention.

He linked his fingers through hers and began leading her across the lawn, swerving to the side of the house where exuberant flora, lemon trees, shrubs sprouting with brightly coloured flowers and hydrangea enclosed an exquisite infinity pool. The air was aromatic.

'I feel as though I've stepped into a travel brochure.'

Alessandro frowned. A nagging thought occurred to him. Had he seen those prints on the walls and brought her here so that he could deliver her those dreams of sun, sea and sand that had clearly never been realised? Had that been some weird, unconscious motivation behind his invitation to bring her to his house? He irritably swept aside a suspicion with which he was not comfortable.

'You said you were hot...?'

'So I did.' She would have liked to enjoy the scenery a bit more. Well, a lot more. But business was business, wasn't it? The longer this game between them carried on, the deeper her scars would be when they parted company, when he had got what he wanted. She undid the small buttons of the dress and it fell to the ground, pooling at her feet.

Alessandro remained where he was, looking at her with lazy, predatory satisfaction. 'Will this be a full striptease?'

'I want you, Alessandro...' *And I love you. I loved you once and I think it would be very easy to love you again.* She schooled her features to conceal the chaos of her thoughts. 'And I think we've both waited long enough...' She walked towards him, reaching behind her as she did so to unhook her bra, which she tossed onto one of the low, wooden sun loungers, never taking her eyes off his face.

Alessandro found that he could barely control his breathing. The moment was electric. His jaw clenched when she was finally standing in front of him and he had to steel himself against an unruly, premature overreaction as she slipped out of her panties so that she was now completely naked.

'The sun's pretty fierce...' He curved his hand around her waist, idly caressing it and pulling her against him at the same time. 'And you're fair. Any doctor would tell you that you need to lather yourself in sunblock...' He kissed her slowly, tugging her bottom lip with his teeth, gently tasting her mouth, taking his time as their tongues melded, even though it was agony trying to keep his libido in check.

'So what do you want to do about it?' She wrapped her arms around his neck and flung her head back with a sigh as his lips traced a path along the slender column of her neck. She was wet and ready for him. She reached to fumble with the button of his trousers and he stayed her hand.

'One good striptease deserves another,' he murmured in a sexy, shaky undertone that sent her blood pressure skyrocketing. 'But first...'

He sauntered towards what she now saw was a vine-covered pool house and emerged a couple of minutes later with towels and various creams. He dumped them on one of the vacant loungers and she watched, heart beating wildly, as he did what she had done only moments before.

His shirt was tossed to join hers and he kept his eyes on her as he walked slowly towards her. Every inch that brought him closer did crazier things to her nervous system. Her breath caught in her throat as he removed his trousers, then, when she felt that swooning was a real possibility, the final item of clothing joined the rest and he was as naked as she was, his proud, impressive erection proclaiming that he was as turned on as her.

When he was inches away from her, she reached down and firmly circled it with her hand.

'Three days ago you were as tense as a violin string...' He led her towards one of the loungers which was shaded by an overhanging tree and he neatly spread one of the towels on it.

Three days ago, she thought, *I had no idea that my body could feel like this; three days ago it started to come alive. I may have been apprehensive then at what I was feeling but I'm not apprehensive now...*

'I'm not now,' she said huskily.

'Then lie down. I'm going to put sun cream on you and it'll be the best foreplay you've ever experienced...'

CHAPTER SEVEN

'IT MIGHT BE a little cold,' Alessandro murmured. He had to make sure to keep his eyes away from her breasts, away from her flat stomach, away from the soft, downy hair that lightly covered the triangular apex between her thighs. He would save himself. 'I keep the pool house air-conditioned. Lie on your stomach…'

'You honestly don't need to bother with sun lotion. It's perfectly safe here in the shade.'

'Doctor's orders. Safety first is the main thing.' She was on her stomach and very slowly he began to explore every exquisite inch of her body, rubbing the sun cream into her, feeling the silky smoothness of her skin and, with each stroke of his hand on her body, getting more aroused.

He pressed his thumbs gently against each vertebra so that she was moaning softly and melting under his touch. He massaged her neck, then her sides, so that her mind went blank and she sighed and squirmed; then the rounded cheeks of her bottom and the length of her glorious legs which parted temptingly, inviting him to go further, but it was an invitation he wasn't going to take up until he was good and ready.

'This is… I never knew…' It was an inaudible sigh.

'Now, shift over. Lie on your back. We can't let an inch of you go unprotected, can we? I would never forgive myself if you were to get sunburned.'

Chase, cynical when it came to interpreting everything he said, wondered if he meant that he would never forgive himself should she be out of action while they were over here. Four days in paradise without the sex he had been anticipating wouldn't do, would it?

She nearly laughed hysterically when she thought that four days in paradise with him without sex would still be four days in paradise for her as opposed to a wasted trip.

'And stop frowning. Just relax. Enjoy.' Her face was first and then his long, supple fingers moved to her shoulders. He did his utmost not to look at her breasts, at the large, pink discs that were responding so enthusiastically to what his hands were doing. He was aware, though, that the tips had tightened into hard peaks as she became more and more turned on.

He watched, fascinated, at the slight flare of her nostrils as he began to lavish his attention on her breasts. 'You can't be too careful in this Italian sun...especially for someone with as little experience of hot weather as you.'

'Don't be silly, Alessandro. London gets hot.' Her eyes were shut tightly and her fists clenched in an effort at self-control as he continued to massage her breasts. It felt so good. 'Are you sure we're on our own here?' This as he bent to take one pouting nipple in his mouth and she moaned weakly as he suckled on it while spanning his hand across her rib cage.

'No one else would have permission to see this body,' he broke off to tell her. 'It's for my eyes only.' Then he returned to the matter at hand, moving to pay the same attention to her other nipple.

How long could he keep this up? Straddling her, he nudged her legs apart. Protection for the full thing, naturally. But he couldn't resist the feel of her moistness against him and he rubbed himself along her wet crease, an insistent, rhythmic movement that made her gasp out loud.

'How does this feel, baby?' he asked, his voice raw and unsteady and she whimpered a response that was answer enough. 'I'm not going to come in you. I just need to do this...'

But he had to stop when he knew that a few more seconds and he would push them both over the edge. The anticipation of having full-blown sex with her was filling his mind and sensitising every inch of his body. When she half-raised herself to take him in her hand, he gently pushed her back down. He had to control this. If he didn't, he would come right here, right now and that was something he didn't want to do. This time, he was going to feel the silky smoothness of being deep inside her.

He smoothed the cream over her inner thighs and breathed her in. The sweet, sexy smell of her filled his nostrils and he half-closed his eyes before dipping his head between her legs. The flat of his hands were on her thighs, pushing them apart, and he felt her tiny convulsion as his tongue made contact with her clitoris.

Chase's fingers tangled in his hair. Here, under the shade of a tree, the sun's heat was pleasantly diluted. The breeze was soft and balmy. Half-opening her eyes, she saw his dark head between her thighs and, framing him, the glory of the Italian scenery with its vista of blue ocean and in the distance the striking cliffs of the peninsula, lush green interspersed with picturesque hamlets, which were tiny dots seen from this far away.

She was living a dream. She was here, with Alessandro, making love to him, having him turn her on in ways that were unimaginable. Why shouldn't she stuff reality behind a door and enjoy what was on offer for its brief duration?

She smiled, moved against his mouth and smiled more when he raised his head and chastised her for moving too fast.

'More doctor's orders?' she teased breathlessly.

'You said it.'

It felt to her as though she had been building up to this moment for years, from the very first time she had had that first latte with him, a sneaky, stolen latte. She had nervously told herself that it would be a one-off, that she was in no position to have lattes with him or with anyone else, but then, as now, what she had told herself had had no bearing on what had actually transpired.

They had had the most sexually charged yet chaste relationship on the planet. Every touch had been accidental and every touch had left her craving more. She had dreamt about him back then and had been terrified that Shaun would somehow climb into her head and see her dreams. And he had continued to steal into her dreams like a silent intruder all through the years, long after she had picked up the pieces of her life and moved on.

So now she was ready.

'Alessandro…' she breathed huskily and he lifted his head to look at her.

'Alessandro what…?' The spoils of the victor. Triumph surged through him. This was what he had wanted: to hear her plead for him to enter her, to know that she could no longer hold out. The grieving widow shedding her black and getting back into mainstream life. With him.

'Tell me how much you want me,' he encouraged thickly. 'I want to hear you say it. No, hold that thought— but don't even begin to think that you can start cooling down.' There were condoms in his wallet. He couldn't fetch one fast enough. His erection was so hard that it was painful.

Cool down? Chase thought that she wouldn't have cooled down if a barrel of ice cubes had been thrown over her. She was on fire, burning for him. She looked at him hungrily, watching as he put on the condom, enjoying the way he was looking right back at her, his dark eyes bold and wicked.

'I'd better just check...' he murmured, straddling her on the super-sized lounger which could have been made for sex and—who knew?—possibly had been because it was as comfortable as a bed. 'Make sure you're still hot for me...' He slid his finger expertly over her throbbing centre and gave a slashing smile of satisfaction. 'Hot and wet.'

'I'm glad you approve.' She wound her arms around his neck and pulled him down to her. Her nipples rubbing against him were doing all sorts of delicious things to her body, adding to the overload of sensation. She sighed and arched up so that she could kiss him and simultaneously opened her legs. 'God, Alessandro, I want you so much right now...'

'Are you sure?'

Their eyes met and she knew that he was asking her if she was ready. Given half a chance, he was always more than prepared to tell her the depth of his bitterness towards her, to inform her that her place in his life was temporary, a passing virus of which he needed to rid his system. Yet, as now, when she could see old-fashioned consideration in his eyes which could flare up almost against his will, he could be just so damned three-dimensional.

'I'm sure.'

Alessandro thrust into her and never had anything felt so exquisite. She wrapped her legs around his waist and he levered her up, his hand on her bottom, so that she could receive him even better as he began moving, fast and hard and rhythmically. Her fingers were digging into his back, driving him on, and her head was thrown back, her eyes closed, her mouth slightly parted.

For a split second, he had a crazy desire to know whether she had ever felt like this with her husband. He certainly had never felt like this with any other woman but, then again, what other woman had he ever had under such extraordinary circumstances? His last girlfriend, a model whose appearance in his life had not outlived the three-month mark, had been a clone of all the other beauties he had dated in the past. Was it any wonder that this one was special? That *this* just felt so damned special?

Chase had died and gone to heaven. On one final thrust, she tipped over the edge as her orgasm ripped through her, sending her body into little convulsions and spontaneously bringing tears to her eyes which she fought to blink back. She felt his groan of fulfilment with every ounce of her being and never had she wanted more to tell him how she felt. Instead, she swept his hair back and smiled drowsily as he opened his eyes to look at her, at first unfocused, and then smiling back.

'That was…good…' she murmured as he slid onto his side to prop himself up on one elbow so that he could look at her.

'"Good" is not an adjective I've ever had much time for. It's along the same lines as "nice"…' He idly circled her nipple with his finger and watched as it responded with enthusiasm. 'How *good* was it?'

'Very, very good…'

'I'll settle for that. In fact, I'll enjoy trying to squeeze more superlatives out of you.' He dipped his head and closed his mouth over her nipple, which was still sensitive and throbbing in the aftermath of their love-making. He was utterly spent and yet he felt himself stir against her leg. 'Let's have a swim,' he suggested. 'And then some food. And then we can play it by ear; see what comes up…'

'Oh, very funny.' But she was laughing as they jumped into the pool. After four lengths, she was happy to take to the side and watch as he continued to slice through the water. She had learned to swim as an adult. Four years ago, she wouldn't have been able to jump into the deep end of this pool, never mind swim four lengths. He, on the other hand, had probably been swimming since he was a toddler, taught by a member of staff in one of the many pools he had probably enjoyed in various locations over the years.

The differences between them were so glaringly obvious, reminding her of the shelf life of what they had and of the shadowy undercurrents lurking just beneath the surface of their sexually charged relationship.

'Tired?'

'Swimming isn't one of my strong points,' she confessed. 'In fact...' what would this one simple admission hurt? '...I only learned to swim a few years ago.'

'You're kidding.'

'No, I'm not,' she said with a shrug.

'That must have been awkward on family holidays. I'm surprised your parents didn't sort that out.' He kissed her again, a little more hungrily this time, and pulled back with a grin of pure satisfaction. 'Besides, don't schools in England have arranged swimming lessons for kids? Something to do with the curriculum?'

'Some of them do,' Chase said vaguely. 'But, you know, I kind of had a phobia of water.'

'A little private tuition would have sorted that out, wouldn't it?' He swung himself neatly out of the pool and held out his hand to help her up. 'Better than Mummy and Daddy panicking every time their precious little darling got within a foot of the hotel pool. Hmm...nice...'

He enjoyed her wet body, running his hands along it, holding her close to him so that their bodies could rub together. 'No matter. Competitive swimming isn't on the agenda while we're here. I couldn't care less if you can only swim four lengths or four hundred.'

Chase opened her mouth, toyed with the idea of revealing a bit more about herself but then kept silent. This fantastic side to Alessandro was only in evidence for a reason.

Further proof of her lying would kill that reason dead because, even for the sake of finishing unfinished business, lust still had its outer limits. And without lust how much greater would be his anger in the cold light of day? She didn't want his anger and she certainly couldn't afford for that anger to be directed at punishing her through her work.

A sudden tidal wave of sheer misery immobilised her and it took almost more effort than she could muster to get herself back on track.

'Tell me what there is around here,' she eventually said, falling easily into step with him as he tossed her a towel and they began walking towards the house. 'All those gorgeous little villages… What do the locals do for a living? Do you know any of them? Personally, I mean?'

Exactly four days later, Chase understood what it must feel like to be in love with someone, living on cloud nine, where everything smelled differently and tasted differently and every single experience was a unique Kodak moment to be committed to memory and brought out at a later date.

She had seen him at his most relaxed. She felt that she could almost be forgiven for thinking that he really liked her and she guessed that, in a way, he did. He appreciated her quick mind; he appreciated her responsive body; he laughed when she tried to tell corny jokes.

Just so long as they both pretended that the past had never happened, everything was good between them. For her, it was so much deeper than anything he could possibly feel, but she refused to think like that. What was the point? She had made her bed and she would lie on it. She had accepted his proposal and only now and again did she think that, whilst she was falling deeper and harder for him, he was gradually working her out of his system.

Wrapped up in his arms at night, lying in a bed that was roughly the size of her spare bedroom, she had let her mind wander, analysed and re-analysed everything he'd said and every gesture he'd made. The one sure thing that sprang to mind was that, the more relaxed he was with her, the more he was putting her behind him.

It was an argument that made sense. When he had seen her again for the first time after eight years, his rage had been raw, out in the open, targeted and deadly. But that had changed. He would never, ever forgive her for what she had done to him, she knew that, but he was in the process of getting over it. Rage was becoming indifference and indifference was allowing him to stop treating her as public enemy number one.

She hated herself for trying to find alternative scenarios but they all led to the same dead end. Very soon, he would completely lose interest in why she had done what she had done eight years ago. He would simply stop giving a damn. He would no longer consider revenge because he would not care less. He would just use her and walk away without a backward glance.

The only consolation was that she had not dropped her guard. She had not let him see just how vulnerable she was, nor would she let him discover how successful he had been at claiming the revenge he had initially considered his due. Without him even realising it, he had indeed wreaked the ultimate revenge, because he would leave her broken and in pieces, whatever show of bravado she employed for his benefit.

And now here they were, last night, sitting across from each other at the kitchen table with an almost empty bottle of Chablis between them.

'So tell me again why you don't come here at least once a month, Alessandro.' Outside, another hot day had gradually morphed into a mild, starry night. They had spent most nights in the kitchen, which was huge, big enough for a ten-seater table at one end, and leading to a conservatory which doubled as an informal sitting area with comfy sofas and a plasma television. From here, they had an uninterrupted view of the sea down below, vast and silent, and the small back garden where they had spent much of their time by the swimming pool.

She felt lazy and replete after another excellent meal which had been prepared in advance by his housekeeper. They could have done their own cooking, and she had suggested it on day one, but he had killed that dead.

'Why waste time cooking?' he had questioned bluntly, 'When there are so many other things we could be occupied doing?' He had pulled her onto his lap and slipped his finger underneath her panties, leaving her in no doubt as to what those other things they could be occupied with were. Enjoying any form of domesticity was off the cards. That was not the reason why he had asked her on this holiday.

'You know why I don't come here once a month,' he replied wryly. 'It's the same reason *you* wouldn't come here once a month. Work wouldn't allow it.'

'But it's different for you. You're the big boss. You can do whatever you want. I can't.'

'Pull the other one, Chase. You're not a bimbo who would be content to while away her time walking barefoot on a beach, no matter how powdery white the sand might be. You're one hundred per cent a career woman. You would be bored stiff in a job that allowed you to take time out every month to enjoy a holiday in the sunshine.'

He stood up, moved to the fridge to replenish the wine and remained there with his back against the counter, carefully looking at her with his head to one side. She had caught the sun. Her skin was the colour of pale honey and from nowhere a smattering of freckles had appeared on the ridge of her nose.

'I recognised that the first time I laid eyes on you,' he continued casually. 'You weren't going to be distracted

by anyone or anything. You barely seemed to notice what
was going on around you.'

Chase fidgeted. Trips down memory lane never turned
out well between them. However, his voice was mild and
speculative, not in the least provocative. More proof that,
whatever fireworks there might be on the physical level,
on the emotional level he was breaking away. The medi-
cine was working. Sex was finishing the unfinished business between them.

'I liked that,' he continued and she looked at him in surprise. 'You once asked me if I'd ever go out with a career
woman and I gave you a negative answer.' He strolled towards her and resumed his seat at the kitchen table, tugging a free chair with his foot so that he could use it as an
impromptu footrest. 'The truth is, you were the anomaly.
Before you and after you, I've only gone out with...'

'Airheads? Bimbos?' Chase dropped into the brief silence. She smiled tightly. 'Women who are never ashamed
to admit that their only ambition is to hunt down a rich
guy and bag him even if it means a lifetime of doing exactly what he wants her to do?' The stuff of nightmares,
she thought bitterly.

'There's absolutely nothing about a woman like that I
can't handle, and you'd be surprised how easily they've
slotted into my lifestyle.'

'Because they make sure to always tell you what you
want to hear and do what you want them to do?'

'Some might say that a compliant woman is preferable
to a liar.' He noted the swift surge of colour that flooded
her cheeks. 'You *have* succeeded in persuading me, however, that there's something to be said for a woman with
a brain.'

'I have?'

'You have,' Alessandro drawled. 'Don't get me wrong,
Chase—agile though your mind is, and challenging though

your conversation can be, you'll never be a contender for the vacancy—just in case your thoughts were heading in that direction.'

'They weren't!' Chase was mortified to think that he might have spotted some weakness in her armour that she hadn't been able to conceal. 'You're not dealing with an idiot, Alessandro. I know the rules of this game as well as you do.'

'I'm glad to hear it.'

'Why would you have thought any differently?' Just like that, his dark eyes had turned cool and assessing, reminding her that the so-called rules of this particular game were different for both of them, despite what she might say to the contrary. Reminding her, too, that his red-hot passion had changed nothing of what he fundamentally felt towards her.

'Look around you and tell me what you see.'

'We're in your kitchen.' Chase frowned, confused and flustered by the softly spoken question that seemed to have sprung from nowhere. 'I can just about make out the little garden at the back, and I can see where the pool is… Look, why are you asking me this?'

'What you see all around you is evidence of my wealth,' Alessandro inserted smoothly. He killed dead the passing twinge of hesitation at the thought that he might offend her. He reminded himself that no matter how good the sex was, and how much he might occasionally enjoy her rapier-sharp mind, she was still a woman whom he had met going by the name of Lyla; who had strung him along and lied to him; who had dumped him unceremoniously and who, certainly, he would never have clapped eyes on again had fate not decided to deliver her to his premises. At the end of the day, whether he offended her or not was immaterial.

'But,' he continued as she stared at him, perplexed, 'I

guess you were aware of the extent of my bank balance the minute you walked into my London place.'

'I don't see what your bank balance has to do with anything,' Chase said tautly.

'No? Let's just say that I wouldn't want you to start getting any misplaced ideas.'

'Misplaced ideas about what?' But she knew what he was talking about now. Well, it didn't take a genius to join the dots, did it? She should be enraged, but instead she was deeply hurt, cut to the quick.

'This is all about the sex—and it's great sex, I'll give you that. But don't think for a second that I've somehow forgotten the person you really are. I think this is a good point at which to remind you that you're a visitor in my life. You won't be getting your hands on any of this...' He gestured broadly to encompass the visible proof of his vast wealth.

He couldn't have thought of a more pointed way of humiliating her but she pinned a stiff smile to her face. She hoped she looked suitably amused and unimpressed. She hoped that whatever expression she was wearing revealed nothing of what she was actually feeling.

'Do you think I would actually *want* to be anything other than a...what did you call it, Alessandro?... *visitor* in your life?' Her heart contracted, squeezed tight with pain. 'You might have all...' she mimicked his gesture '...*this*. You might have the fabulous house on a fabulous coastline in a fabulously beautiful country, and you might have a house in London big enough to fit ten of mine, but I've never pursued money and I certainly would never, ever, set my sights on getting hold of someone else's by...'

'Fair means or foul?' He took his time standing up, flexing his muscles while watching her. Then he leant across to place his hands flat on the arms of her chair. 'I felt it a good idea to make sure we were both still singing off the same song sheet.'

'I could never be serious about someone as arrogant as you, Alessandro.'

'And yet you gave such a misleading impression eight years ago.'

'Will you ever forget that?'

'It's been imprinted on my mind with the force and clarity of a branding iron.'

So much for thinking that he was becoming indifferent, Chase was forced to concede. So much for thinking that revenge was a dish in which he might no longer be interested. 'You weren't arrogant then.' She met his stare levelly. She wasn't prepared for the feel of his mouth against hers as he crushed her lips in a driving, savage kiss that propelled her back into the chair.

Her hands automatically rose to push him away. How the hell could he think that she might be interested in having him touch her when he had just insulted her in the worst way possible? And yet her body responded, went up in flames like dry tinder waiting for the burning match. Reluctant hands softened to cup the nape of his neck.

In one easy movement, he scooped her off the chair and into his arms.

'Alessandro!'

He was heading up the stairs, towards the bedroom with its shuttered windows and thin, cream voile curtains, pale wood and wicker furniture.

'We've talked enough.'

'You called me a gold-digger! Do you...?' She was breathless as he kicked open the bedroom door. 'Do you honestly think that I...I get turned on being insulted?'

'I didn't call you a gold-digger. I warned you of the pitfalls of becoming one. And, no, you don't get turned on by being insulted. You just get turned on by me...' He unceremoniously dumped her on the bed and shot her a wickedly sexy smile as she scrambled into a sitting position to glare at him. 'I'm sick of talking.' He stripped off his black polo shirt and flung it to the floor. 'Get naked for me.'

Chase continued to glare but already her flustered mind was forgetting the hurt inflicted and keening towards the feel of his hands on her body. Still, she didn't rush to obey, but as he led the way, removing his shirt then his jeans, she could feel herself melting.

Their love-making was fast and urgent. She wanted to lose herself in it and forget the things he had told her, the coldness in his voice when he had reminded her of what their relationship really was all about. Did he honestly imagine that she was the type of woman who could look at someone else's possessions and work out how she could get her hands on them? Yes, of course he did. The distance between a liar and a gold-digger was very small.

She wanted to make love until she lost the hurt, and she did. She touched him, kissed him, dominating him in one move before yielding in another. She caught a glimpse of his back at one point and saw the marks of where her fingers had scored into his skin. He ordered her to talk dirty to him and she wondered how she did it so easily when she hadn't a clue what she was supposed to say. It was a complete release of all her inhibitions and it turned her on. It turned her on even more when he talked dirty back to her.

This was what it was all about—having sex. The most amazing, fulfilling sex she could ever imagine. It was all he wanted and, if it wasn't all *she* wanted, then that was something she would just have to live with.

Her orgasm was long and deep and filled every single part of her body. It dispelled all her dark thoughts. It made her feel as though she was soaring through space, out of reach of anything that might hurt her. She longed for it to last for ever. In fact, she closed her eyes and kept them firmly shut even after Alessandro rolled off her. He was breathing as unevenly as she was. She could picture every inch of his face, every line, the sweep of his dark lashes, his gleaming black eyes that could make her body go up in flames with a single glance. She had absorbed all the details and stored them in her head with the efficiency of a state-of-the-art computer housing data.

'Are you going to fall asleep on me?'

'I'm dozing.'

'Should I be flattered that I can send a woman to sleep?'

'Actually...' Chase opened her eyes reluctantly and propped herself on her side so that they were facing one another on the bed, front to front, her breasts brushing his chest. 'I was thinking...'

What would happen if she ever told him the truth about how she felt? Would she find it liberating? 'About work. How much I'll have to get done when I return. I may even go in tomorrow evening after we're back. Have I told you about the work that's due to start on the shelter? Beth keeps asking if I'm sure that the costs will be covered.' She ran her finger lightly along his shoulder blade, tracing muscle and sinew. 'She has a morbid fear of bailiffs banging on the front door because she hasn't been able to pay her creditors.'

Alessandro frowned. As pillow talk went, it left a lot to be desired, yet he realised that he should be feeling relieved. He had laid down his dictates and she hadn't blinked an eye. In fact, he need not have bothered. She had no interest in taking things between them beyond their natural course. Thank God. And, to prove how misguided he had been in imagining that she might get a little too wrapped up in *this,* here she was now, chatting about work. Did it get less romantic?

But who the hell wanted romance? 'I need a shower,' he said abruptly.

'Are you okay? I shouldn't have mentioned the shelter. I wouldn't want you to think that I don't trust you…' She sat up, slightly panicked by his sudden mood swing, and it occurred to her that this was something she would have to get accustomed to if she decided to stick it out. He didn't care about her. Why should it bother him if he was dismissive, if he decided to have a mood swing?

'You clearly have a way to go if you think that I would ever back down on my word, despite my assurances.' Alessandro eased himself off the bed. 'I can bring the flight forward if you have work issues. In fact, might not be a bad idea. I have a couple of major deals about to reach boiling point. I need to be back sooner rather than later. A few hours makes all the difference sometimes.'

Suddenly backed into a corner, Chase nodded brightly. 'I'll begin packing while you're in the shower.' She waited for him to relent, to tell her that they should stick to the original timetable; what did a few hours matter? He didn't.

And what happened with them when they returned? It was a question she was reluctant to ask.

It hovered at the back of her mind for the remainder of the night and through into the following morning. Flights had been rescheduled and still nothing was said and she refused to weaken. His mood had disappeared as fast as it had come. On the surface, everything was bright and breezy. When she looked back at the villa from the back of the limo as they were driving away, she felt a pang of intense sadness that she would never see it again.

He seemed to be lost in his own thoughts and she acknowledged that he was probably projecting ahead, thinking about those deals of his that wouldn't go away unless he was on the scene to sort them out.

The silence between them became oppressive but it was

only when they had touched down at Heathrow that she turned to him and said lightly, 'So, what happens next…?'

Alessandro had had no idea how tense he had been until she asked that question. He had been infuriated with himself for not much liking her air of casual insouciance. Did the woman give a damn one way or another? But now, his keen ears tuning in to a thread of nervousness in her voice, he was satisfied that she did, and that did wonders for his ego.

'I'll call you.' He curved a sure hand on her cheek and bent to place a hungry kiss on her lips.

Chase was ashamed of the enthusiasm with which she returned his kiss. If she could have, she would have dragged him off to the nearest hotel room and picked up where they had left off in Italy. Instead, she pulled away with a sigh. 'I've never had much time for those women who hang around waiting for the phone to ring.'

Alessandro laughed. Her kiss conveyed a thousand messages and all of them were good. 'I haven't had enough of you by a long shot. I'll call you tomorrow. Save you doing too much waiting by the phone…although, if you *do* find yourself waiting by the phone, then give my imagination something to go on. It would work if you waited there in your birthday suit…'

So what if she hadn't said anything? Would he have posed the question himself? Would he have wanted to know what happened next? Was this going to be her destiny for the foreseeable future—a day-to-day existence, only coming alive when Alessandro was around; not daring to breathe a word of how she really felt; living in fear of the phone calls stopping, grateful for whatever crumbs continued to drop her way? Was this what she had spent the past eight years working towards?

She took a taxi back to the house. She couldn't face the vagaries of the underground.

It was a little after two in the afternoon by the time she was paying the taxi driver. A thin, annoying drizzle had started, accompanied by a gusty wind, and as she fumbled in her handbag for her keys there was nothing on her mind other than getting inside the house and out of the rain.

She certainly wasn't expecting the man that stepped out of the shadows at the side of the house. When he spoke, all thoughts of the rain, getting inside and even of Alessandro flew out of her head. She gaped in horror as he smiled and pulled his hoodie down a little lower so that most of his face was in shadow.

'Long time no see, Chase. Been anywhere exciting…?'

CHAPTER EIGHT

CHASE WOKE WITH a start to the sound of her alarm going off. She had a few seconds of intense disorientation and then memories of the afternoon before broke through the barrier of forgetfulness and began pouring through her head. She had no idea how she had managed to get through what remained of the day, how she had managed finally to get to sleep.

She began getting ready for work on autopilot, showering, fetching her smart grey suit from the wardrobe, twinning it with a crisp white shirt. When half an hour later she looked at her reflection in the mirror, on the surface she was the same diligent, nicely dressed professional her colleagues would be expecting back at the office after a few days in the sun, with a companion or companions unknown.

Under the surface, she was barely functioning.

She had not expected to return to her house and find Brian Shepherd on her doorstep. In fact, she had not expected ever to have set eyes on Brian Shepherd again, but then didn't bad things have a habit of bouncing right back? Wasn't it true what they said, that you could run but you couldn't hide?

She had foolishly imagined Brian Shepherd to be nothing but a distant memory from the bad old days. 'Blue Boy' had been his nickname, because of his bright-blue eyes. He had been Shaun's closest friend growing up, the one who, from the age of ten, had shown him all the clever ways they could break and enter houses and all the tricks of the trade for getting their hands on valuable scrap metal. Six years older than Shaun, he had been his mentor until finally she and Shaun had moved to London, leaving behind Blue Boy for good. Fat chance, as it turned out.

And now he was back.

'Heard you were doing well for yourself,' he had said, inviting himself into her house and scanning it with the shrewd eyes of a born petty thief. 'Heard you found yourself a replacement for Shaunie.'

She had flinched every time he had reached out to touch one of her possessions but past experience had taught her that any sign of weakness would be a mistake with Brian Shepherd. She knew all about his temper.

There had been no need to ask him how he had found out about Alessandro. He had volunteered the information with relish: a friend of a friend of a friend had spotted them together on their little love-bird holiday in Italy. At the airport, of all places. Wasn't it a small world?

'Angie—Angie Carson. Remember her? Fat cow. Took a picture of the both of you. On her phone. Bet you never spotted her! Probably wouldn't have recognised her cos it's been a while, hasn't it? Anyone would think you were ashamed of all your old mates...'

He didn't remove his hoodie the entire time he was at the house, prowling through from room to room, touching and picking things up and turning them round in his hands, as though trying to figure out what they were worth.

Chase remained largely silent until, eventually, when she could stand it no longer, she asked him what he wanted, because of course he would want something.

Money. He was in a bit of a tight spot. Just enough to tide him over, and he knew she could lay her hands on some, because they'd driven off in a flash car and the luggage…

He gave a low, long whistle and eyed her up and down in a way that made her stomach lurch. Nice luggage. Expensive. Angie had been impressed. Snapped a few pics of that on her phone and all.

So, just a bit of money, spare change for a bloke who could zoom off in a chauffeur-driven limo with all that nice luggage in the boot. Angie had gone off with her mates but he was betting that, wherever that flash car had driven to, it wasn't going to be a one-star dump with dodgy air-conditioning.

So, what did she say? Did she think that she could spare an old friend a bit of loose change? Maybe, he said, he could persuade her. He knew where she worked…had done a little digging after those photos fat Angie had shown him…

Remember that club, the one that got busted by the coppers….? Course, she'd been underage at the time and she hadn't actually been doing drugs or anything—not like him and Shaunie and the rest of the gang. But those posh people at the law firm, they'd be really keen to know that she used to mix with a crowd who all had police records, wouldn't they? Might even get to thinking that *she* had a police record! Wouldn't that be funny? And, being honest, just the fact that she and he used to be mates would get them wondering, wouldn't it?

He had chuckled. 'You know what they say about the smelly stuff sticking…'

Her mobile rang now just as she was about to enter the office. Alessandro. She switched it off. There was no way that she could talk to him. Not just yet. But talk to him she would have to, because Brian Shepherd wasn't going to go away until he got his wretched money which, as it turned out, was hardly what she would have called 'loose change'.

It was certainly more than she had set aside, which was precious little after her mortgage repayments had been made and the bills paid.

Her life seemed to be unravelling at speed and she had to force herself not to succumb to the meltdown she knew was hovering just around the corner. She had weathered a lot of things and she would weather this as well. It would just take a little working out.

By the time she pushed through the doors to their offices, she had glumly decided what needed to be done.

Her first port of call was her boss's office.

Tony Grey was a short, round man in his fifties who would have been a dead ringer for Father Christmas were it not for the fact that he was almost entirely bald and his dark-grey eyes were way too astute for someone who spent all his time laughing and chuckling. In actual fact, Chase had never seen her boss laugh out loud, but he had always been fair and supportive. She would miss that.

She would have to hand in her notice. She had come to that conclusion as she had left her house. Brian Shepherd wouldn't just do what he threatened; he would go further if she didn't do as he asked. Hadn't he been banged up for nearly killing someone in a bar brawl when he was fourteen? What if he took it into his head to release his explosive temper on *her* if she didn't play ball? If he could nearly kill someone at the age of fourteen because they'd accidentally knocked into him without saying sorry, then he could certainly kill her if he wanted money from her and she refused to pay. She loathed the thought of having to yield in a situation like this but pride was no match for sheer common sense.

Well, on the bright side, she would find a company specialising more in the pro bono work she enjoyed and, even if Brian hunted her down there, he would be able to see for himself that it wasn't a money-making machine.

She still couldn't work out how he had discovered her whereabouts but there was no point wasting time trying to figure that out. With social-networking sites stretching their tentacles into every area of everyone's lives, it wouldn't have been beyond the wit of man for him to ferret her out the second he'd figured he could get money from her.

'My dear,' Tony said when she had explained that she would have to hand in her notice for personal reasons. 'Are you sure this is really what you want to do? You're on course to go far with this firm. Your dedication is second to none.'

But he assured her that, if he couldn't persuade her to change her mind, then of course he would provide her with glowing references. With just that sympathy and fairness which she would miss so much, he also agreed that she could leave as soon as she had tied up loose ends on the cases she was currently working on so that they could be handed over in good order.

She had no idea what he concluded her 'personal reasons' for leaving might be, but she suspected that health issues might be at the heart of it, and he was right in a way. She certainly wasn't feeling very well at the moment. Not when she considered the way her nicely controlled life had been turned upside down.

Alessandro… She thought that this might not be as similarly smooth sailing. She ignored a further two calls from him, only picking up his last just as she was about to leave the office on the dot of five. Clock watching had never been her style, but tying up loose ends was a dismal procedure. Nor was she up to chatting to all and sundry about her decision to leave.

'Where the hell have you been? I've phoned three times!'

'I'm sorry. I was…busy.' Just the sound of his voice

sent little ripples of awareness racing up and down her spine as she took the lift to the ground floor and emerged into yet another cool and overcast day to do battle with public transport.

'Busy doing what?'

'I, well, I've handed in my notice at Fitzsimmons.'

For a few seconds, Alessandro debated whether he had heard her correctly. But there was something in her voice, a tell-tale tremor that she couldn't quite conceal; a nuance which he felt that only he would have been able to pick up. Something was different, *wrong,* a little off-kilter.

He stood up, restlessly moving away from his desk towards the windows and absently looking down. 'You're kidding.'

'No, I'm not. Can we meet? I can…um…come to your office.'

'I can think of a better venue.'

'I'd rather your office, Alessandro.'

'What's going on?' he demanded bluntly. 'And please don't tell me *nothing.* You tell me you've handed in your notice, even though you've expressed nothing but satisfaction at your job there, and now…you want to meet me *in my office?*'

'Please.'

Alessandro sighed heavily and raked his fingers through his hair. He was getting a very bad vibe about whatever the hell was going on but he acquiesced. Whatever was happening, he would be able to get it out of her and things would return to normal. He was nothing if not wholly confident in his ability to take her mind off things.

'I'd rather not parade my personal life in front of my employees,' he drawled. 'And *you* may be scuttling out of the office because you've handed in your notice and lost momentum in your job, but my people are all still at their desks. If you can't wait until later and meet me somewhere private, then I can see you in forty-five minutes at that brasserie round the corner from my office. You know the one?'

She did. She made her way there slowly, forgoing the speed and ease of a black cab in favour of a laborious trip by public transport. It suited her mood.

How had life changed so fast in such a brief moment in time? As she neared the brasserie, she felt a sickening lurch of déjà vu. Eight years ago she had met Alessandro here with one thing and one thing only in her head—the need to get rid of him. She had walked towards a conversation she had known would break her in half and she was doing the same thing now. History was repeating itself. But it was so much worse this time, she would be taking so many more regrets with her when she was finished saying what she had to say.

Sitting at the back of the brasserie, nursing an extremely early glass of red wine, Alessandro had been waiting for ten minutes. He had been unable to get down to work after her phone call. He would never have imagined himself as one of those sensitive, intuitive sorts but something wasn't right and, however much he told himself that he could sort out whatever the hell it was that was eating her up, he was still vaguely uneasy.

And yet, why should he be? They had parted company the day before and everything had been just fine and dandy. There'd been no inconvenient intuition then. So, really, what could have materially changed since then?

He spotted her the second she walked through the door. For the briefest of moments he felt a sharp, inexplicable pang of nostalgia for the carefree girl in shorts and tee-shirts who had been his companion for the past few days. She was in full lawyer mode: prissy grey suit, even prissier white blouse, black pumps. He wondered how long he could wait before he ripped the whole lot off her and bedded her.

On cue, his erection pushed hard against the zip of his trousers and he shifted position uncomfortably to release some of the insistent ache in his groin.

He had not expected this crazy lust to be an ongoing situation after the countless times they had now slept together. He had assumed she would be more than just disposable: he would take what had once been denied him and then discard her without preamble. It wasn't working out quite as he had envisaged, but he shrugged that off. The unexpected could sometimes be a good thing and getting turned on by her on a semi-permanent basis was definitely not to be sneezed at, especially for him, a man whose tastes had become lamentably jaded over time.

He watched with masculine appreciation as she glanced around her. Already he was undressing her in his mind. Slowly. Revealing those generous pale breasts inch by succulent inch; exposing the pink nipples to take them one at a time in his mouth as they pouted temptingly up at him.

He pictured the prissy grey skirt hitting the ground, followed by whatever suitably functional underwear she happened to be wearing… He could almost taste the honeyed sweetness between her legs, hear her broken little whimpers of pleasure as his tongue found her sweet spot and worked it until the broken little whimpers became moans and cries of pleasure. The more horny he became, just sitting and watching her and letting his imagination run wild, the faster he knew he would have to sort out whatever was on her mind just so that he could get her back to his place. They might not even be able to make it to the bedroom.

He grinned as she spotted him and lazily attracted the waitress's attention without taking his eyes off Chase's face. Her looks were really quite startling. There was a sexiness to her, a perfection to her features, that made her naturally guarded expression all the more beguiling. He could see other men surreptitiously following her with their eyes as she weaved her way towards him.

'Alessandro…' Chase said weakly. She could feel her heart thumping like a sledgehammer inside her.

'So you've handed in your notice.' He broke off to order her a cappuccino. 'And you don't look very happy about it.'

'I…I…' She could barely string two words together. This was so much worse than she had envisaged. There was just no way that she could pretend to be cool, calm and collected. Her nerves were all over the place.

'Sit down. Tell me about it. Why?'

'I…I didn't have much of a choice,' she admitted truthfully. 'Personal reasons.'

'What personal reasons?'

'I'd rather not talk about it.'

'Are you ill?' He felt a sudden mixture of fear and irrational panic. 'Is that what this is all about?'

'No,' she said, waving a wistful goodbye to what could have been a fantastic excuse. As if lies hadn't landed her here in the first place. 'No, I'm not ill.'

'Then what? What personal reasons, and why don't you want to discuss them?' Alessandro scowled. Since when had he ever been interested in women's life stories? Mysteries dangling at the end of a line like bait to hook him in had always left him cold.

He eyed her narrowly as a new thought began to take shape in his head. 'If you're not ill,' he said slowly, 'and yet you've reluctantly had to hand in your notice, then there's only one explanation that springs to mind…'

Temporarily diverted, Chase looked at him in bafflement. 'Is there?'

'Someone's made a pass at you. Who is it?' His voice was low and controlled but he clenched his fists. The second he had a name, he would personally make it his business to make sure that the culprit paid.

'Made a pass at me?'

'Even wearing that starchy suit, you're still sexy as hell, Chase. And I won't be the only one who can see that. So, spill the beans. Tell me who it is. Your boss? One of your colleagues? What did he do? Did he touch you inappropriately? Try to feel you up?'

He imagined one of those rich kids thinking that he could have a go at the sexiest woman in the office and he was overwhelmed by an explosive rage. He had met enough twenty-something lawyers in his time to know that the majority of them thought that they were studs.

'No one touched me, Alessandro! And no one tried to *feel me up*! Do you think that I'm so feeble that I would allow anyone to get away with that? Do you think that I'm incapable of taking care of myself?' But his show of possessiveness touched her. She folded her hands on her lap to stop herself from reaching out and covering his hand with her own.

'Then what's going on?' Looking at her, it was clear that she could barely meet his eyes. She was fidgeting nervously with the handle of her coffee cup. Alessandro felt that he could do with the entire bottle of wine, never mind one careful glass. Instead he ordered a black coffee while he tried to sift through some plausible explanation for her behaviour in his mind. 'You're not…pregnant, are you?' It was a thought that only now occurred to him.

Chase glanced up at his face, suddenly ashen, and for a few moments anger replaced gnawing anxiety and dread. It was obvious from his expression that the mere suggestion of pregnancy had knocked him for six. 'And what if I *was*?' she queried boldly. 'What if I told you that there was a mini-Alessandro taking shape right now inside me?'

She fancied she could see the colour drain away from

his face as she allowed him time to absorb the full horror
of that scenario. 'Don't worry, Alessandro. I'm not pregnant. I told you once that I'm not a complete idiot.'

For a few fleeting seconds, Alessandro had found himself ripped out of his comfort zone, staring down the barrel of a gun. She was having his baby. *His baby.* The gun
barrel, strangely, was less of a threat than he might have
imagined.

'Accidents happen,' he said grimly.

'Oh, Alessandro…' She sighed and sat back, head tilted
up, eyes half-closed as the inescapable hurtled towards her
with the deadly force of a bomb. 'I'm healthy, there's no
mini-Alessandro on the way and no one's made a pass at
me at work. And I wish there was some other way of saying this but there isn't…' She straightened and took a deep
breath. 'I need to ask you something.'

'What?'

'I need to…borrow some money from you.'

Deathly silence greeted this request. Chase didn't dare
look at Alessandro. What choice did she have? she wondered helplessly. Brian wasn't going to go away until he
had his money and she simply didn't have it. If she got it,
gave it to him and then convinced him that she had broken
up with Alessandro, then he would go away. If she didn't,
then she was, frankly, scared of what he might do. Scared
of all the old horrors landing on her doorstep once again.

'Tell me I'm not hearing this.'

'I'm sorry and, naturally, I'll pay you back every penny
of what I borrow. With interest.'

Alessandro laughed mirthlessly. 'So finally,' he said in
a lethally soft voice, 'the real face of Chase Evans is revealed. I'm surprised you managed to keep it hidden for
so long.' He felt as though he had been punched in the gut.
This wasn't just anger; this was a level of hurt that he could
barely acknowledge even to himself. He didn't know who

he loathed more—himself for having been conned a second time, or her for having been the one to do the conning.

'What do you need the money for?' He could scarcely credit that he was willing to hear her out, willing to give her an explanation that would allow him to make sense of the situation. That window of willingness died the second she looked at him and said steadily,

'I'm sorry. That's…none of your business.' The harshest of words, yet they would provide the clean break.

'Right. So…when did you decide that you could screw me for money?' he asked in the same ultra-controlled voice that was far more intimidating than if he had stood up and shouted at her. 'Was it when you came to my house? Or was it when we went to Italy and you saw just how much I had? Tell me. I'm curious.'

'You don't understand, Alessandro. I wouldn't be sitting here asking you for money if…if…I didn't have to.'

'And yet you refuse to tell me what you want the money for.' He threw up his hands in rampant frustration as she greeted this with stubborn silence. 'Are you in some sort of debt? Hell, Chase, just be bloody straight with me!'

'I told you, it's none of your business. If you don't want to lend me the money, then just say so.' Her heart was breaking in two.

'And, just for the record, how much money do you fancy you can bleed me for?'

She named the figure and watched as he threw his head back and roared with laughter, except there was no humour there. He was laughing with incredulity and his dark eyes were as hard and cold as the frozen depths of a glacier.

'Well…?' Chase cleared her throat and valiantly met his eyes.

'No explanations, no excuses, not even of the make-believe variety… Sorry, not good enough.' He signalled to the waitress for the bill. 'And consider this conversation over.' Hell, the woman could act. She was as white as a sheet and her hands were shaking—remarkable performance. He felt something painful twist inside him, an iron fist clenching on his intestines, and staunched it down.

'I think we can say that our unfinished business has been concluded. If you ever get it into your head to descend on me, either at my offices or at my house, I assure you I will have you forcibly removed either by the police or by my security personnel. Do you read me?'

Chase nodded. Had she expected him to part with cash just because she'd asked? Because she'd offered to pay him back? Was there some part of her that had hoped he might know her well enough by now to give her the benefit of the doubt? She couldn't tell him the truth. How could she? She was boxed in with no room to manoeuvre.

'I understand,' she said quietly.

'Question.' Alessandro was furious with himself for not walking away without a backward glance. He was even more furious with himself for the unwilling tug of compassion he was feeling for a woman who was nothing more or less than a gold-digger with great acting ability. And, underneath that maelstrom of emotion, he recognised the angry pain of disillusionment. 'If you're so desperate for money, why jack the job in?'

'I can't discuss that either.'

Alessandro stood up abruptly. 'Good luck finding your money,' he told her coldly. 'If anything needs to be discussed about the shelter, you might want another lawyer to handle it.'

'I've already begun tidying up all my ongoing case files. Someone else will be handling all the details with the shelter. I…I've been given permission to leave at the end of the week. I should be working out a month's notice but my boss—'

'Not really interested.'

Chase remained standing, watching his departing back. She told herself, bracingly, that it was always going to end—yet the hollowness filling her felt as destructive as a tsunami. If she wasn't a homeowner, if she had been one of the millions renting, she knew that she would have upped sticks and disappeared. No job, no Alessandro and a threat waiting for her when she returned: it took all her courage to gather herself and head back outside down to the underground.

Brian would be there. He had told her in a chummy voice laced with menace that he would be waiting when she returned, that he didn't mind just hanging out there, although if she wanted to hand her key over to him...

Chase shuddered.

Heading in the opposite direction back to his office, Alessandro angrily realised that the very last thing he was in the mood to do was work. He still had a conference call lined up for later that evening. He got on his mobile, spoke to his secretary and cancelled it.

Hell, could he have been *that* stupid that he had fallen for the walk up the garden path *yet again*? With tremendous effort, he side-lined the fury raging through him and tried to recall the details of their brief conversation in the brasserie.

She hadn't given him an answer when he had asked her why she had handed in her notice if she needed money. That, for one thing, made no sense. Whatever debts she had managed to incur, she wasn't so stupid that she could imagine settling them without a regular salary coming in. So had she been sacked? Had they discovered something? Had she been embezzling? It seemed a ludicrous idea, but hell, how was he to know when she had offered no explanation for her behaviour?

No, this was not going to happen again. He was emphatically *not* going to be left stranded with a bucket load of unanswered questions, as had happened last time round. Whether he ever laid eyes on her again or not was immaterial. He would pay her a little visit and would stay put until she answered all his questions to his satisfaction. Then, and only then, would he leave.

He called his driver to collect him. Rush-hour traffic meant that it took a ridiculously long time before his driver made it to the building, even though his car, parked outside his house, was only a matter of a couple miles away as the crow flew. It took even longer to navigate the stand-still traffic in central London.

His mobile buzzed continuously and he eventually switched it off. He was fully given over to trying to disentangle the conversation he had had with Chase. He felt like a man in possession of just sufficient pieces of a complex puzzle to rouse curiosity and yet lacking the essential ones that would solve the conundrum.

This, he told himself, was why he was sitting in the back of his car, drumming his fingers restlessly on the leather seat and frowning out of the back window. He had been presented with a complex puzzle and it was only human nature to try and figure it out, whatever the cost. Frankly, he would drag answers out of her if he had to.

It was considerably later than he had expected by the time the car swung into her small road. From outside, he could see that lights were on. 'You can leave,' he told his driver. 'I'll get a cab back to my house.' He slammed the door and watched as the Jag slowly disappeared around the corner.

If there was a small voice in his head telling him that his appearance on her doorstep made little sense, given the fact that she had never been destined to be a permanent feature in his life, he chose to ignore it. Finding answers seemed more important than debating the finer points.

He leaned his hand on the doorbell and kept it there for an inordinately long time. Where the hell was she? If the lights were on, then she was home. She had a thing about wasting electricity, just one of her many little quirks to which he had become accustomed. He scowled at the very fact that he was remembering that at this juncture.

Chase heard the insistent buzzing of the doorbell but it took her a second or two before she generated the enthusiasm to get the door. In the lounge, a fuming Brian was filling a bin bag with whatever he fancied he could take from her. There was nothing she could do about it; he was bigger and he had no conscience when it came to violence.

She'd have done anything to get rid of him, to have him out of her house. He told her to get rid of whoever was at the door.

'Too busy here for visitors, darling. Still a lot to get through before I leave!'

Chase pulled open the door and her mouth fell open in shock. Alessandro was the last person she had expected to find on her doorstep.

'You're not getting rid of me until you tell me what the hell is really going on with you!' were his opening words.

'Alessandro, you have to go.'

She was scared stiff; that much he could see. He pushed past her and halted as a man in his thirties sauntered out of the living room. In the space of mere seconds, Alessandro had processed the guy and reached his verdict. This was no smarmy, overpaid young lawyer. This was a thug and, whatever was going on, Chase was afraid.

'And you are…?' If there was going to be a fight, then he was more than up for it.

'Not about to tell you, mate. Hang on…thought you said you'd broken up with lover boy? Lying to me, were you? Don't like lies…'

Alessandro clenched his fists. Chase had backed away

and was stammering out some sort of explanation which he barely registered. No, this wasn't going to do. He had hold of the man's tee-shirt and felt roughly one hundred and forty pounds of packed muscle try to squirm away from him. Escape was never destined to be. He propelled the man back towards the sitting room. Out of the corner of his eye, he could see that the room had been decimated. A black bin bag was stuffed to overflowing on the ground. Another was half-full. Was this the 'spot of bother' she was in?

'You're going to tell me what's going on...' He addressed her but kept his eye on his frantically writhing captive. The man was a bully; Alessandro could spot the signs a mile away. The sort of loser who didn't mind throwing his weight around with anyone weaker than him but would run a mile if faced with stiff competition. Alessandro prided himself on being stiff competition. He listened intently while Chase babbled something about Brian wanting money...taking her stuff...

The missing pieces were beginning to fall into place. So the money had been a legitimate request. She hadn't been trying to con gold out of him. 'Here's what you're going to do, buddy.' His voice was low, soft and razor-sharp. 'You're going to unload that bin bag and return all the nice lady's possessions to her. Then you're going to apologise and, when you've finished apologising, you're going to leave quietly through that front door and never show your face here again. Do you read me loud and clear?

'And just in case...' He tightened his stranglehold so that the man was gasping to catch his breath. 'You get it into your head that you can ignore what I'm telling you, here's what will happen to you if you do. I'll employ someone to dredge up every scrap of dirt on you—and I'm betting that there's a lot—and then I'm going to make sure that you get put behind bars and the key is conveniently thrown away. And don't think I won't do it. I will. And I'll enjoy every second of it.'

He watched in silence, arms folded, as his orders were obeyed. Out of the bin bag came all the bits and pieces which, Alessandro knew, would have taken Chase years to accumulate. Some were worthless, some—such as her computer, her tablet, the plasma-screen television which she had laughingly told him had been an absolute indulgence because she really didn't watch much TV—weren't.

His apology was grudgingly given until Alessandro ordered him to try harder, to say it like he meant it...

He left as quietly as he had been ordered to do. Then there was just the two of them, standing in a room that looked as though a bomb had exploded in it.

'I'm sorry,' Chase mumbled. Yet she was so glad that he had come because now she felt utterly safe. She moved to begin picking up some of her possessions from the ground, stacking them neatly on the sofa, very conscious of Alessandro's eyes on her. 'Why did you come?' she asked.

'You need something stiff to drink.'

'I'm fine.'

'Do you have any brandy?'

'I'm fine.' She finally met his eyes and hesitantly perched on the edge of the chair with her hands on her knees. 'There's half a bottle of wine in the fridge,' she offered when he continued to look at her in silence. 'It's all I can do by way of drink, I'm afraid. I don't keep spirits in the house.' Shock was creeping over her. She didn't want alcohol but she had to admit that she felt a little better after she had swallowed a mouthful from the glass he placed in her shaking hand a minute later.

'I guess you want to know what all that was about,' she said wearily.

'Understatement of the decade, Chase.'

Chase stared down at her fingers. She'd been rescued

by a man who had only returned to the scene to find out what was going on because he was like that—would never have been able to accept a brush off without demanding answers.

She would have to explain how it was that she knew Brian, how he had happened to be in her house. She would have to come clean about her background and know that he would be filled with contempt. Contempt for a woman who had lied about a fundamental aspect of her life and maintained the lie all through the time she had been seeing him. But there still remained a part of her that she refused to reveal, because to reveal it would be to lower herself even more in his estimation.

'You'd better sit down and I'll tell you. And then...' She took a deep breath and exhaled slowly. 'You can leave and it'll finally be over between us.'

CHAPTER NINE

SHE WAS STILL in her work clothes, the same dreary grey suit, except she looked...*rumpled.*

'Did he lay a finger on you?' Alessandro asked suddenly. 'Did he touch you?' This was as far out of his comfort zone as he had ever been. Even with parents intent on squandering their inheritance—parents who had been shining examples of irresponsibility; who had opened the doors of their various houses to artists and poets and playwrights, most of whom had been pleasantly stoned most of the time—through all that, he had never come into contact with the seedier side of life. The side of life that threw up people like the thug who had just been thrown off the premises. Even with diminishing wealth, he had still lived a sheltered, privileged life.

'No. No, he didn't.' Chase could see the incredulity stamped on his beautiful face. He was shocked at what he had found, shocked that the woman he thought came from a solid, middle-class background could know someone like Brian Shepherd. 'Although it's not unheard of for Brian to lay into someone just for the hell of it, never mind if he thinks they've done something to him.'

'How the hell do you know that guy, Chase?' Alessandro frowned. 'When you said that you couldn't tell me why you needed the money, did you mean that you owed that creep money?'

'No, I did *not* owe that creep any money. He just…' She stood up, suddenly restless, but then immediately sat back down because her legs felt like jelly.

'What, then…?'

'If you would just sit down and stop *prowling*.'

Alessandro paused to look at her narrowly. 'If you didn't owe the guy money, then why would he have gathered half of your possessions and stuffed them into a bin bag?' He sat on the chair facing her. Their body language was identical, both sitting forward, arms resting loosely on their thighs although, whilst Alessandro's expression was one of intense curiosity, Chase's was more resigned and reflective.

'Brian and Shaun were friends,' she said quietly, not daring to meet his eyes, fearful of what she would see there. 'They were friends from before I met Shaun, childhood friends, even though Brian was older. They grew up on the same council estate.'

'Which calls into question the type of man you chose to marry.'

'When you're young, it's very easy to get drawn in to the wrong crowd.'

'I'm trying to picture your parents allowing you to get drawn in to the wrong crowd. Or didn't they have any say in the matter? Maybe they were too busy projecting to happy times ahead in Australia…?'

'There *is* no Australia.'

'Sorry, but I'm not following you.'

Chase nervously tucked a strand of hair behind her ears. She wondered what hand of fate it was that had returned Alessandro to her life, only to have her fall in love with him all over again. Instead of getting him out of her system by sleeping with him, by putting that unfulfilled fantasy to rest, she had managed to well and truly cement him into every nook, cranny and corner of her being.

'My parents don't live in Australia. In fact, I have no parents. I was a foster-home kid. I was shuffled from family to family, never staying anywhere for very long. I never knew my father. My mother died when I was very little from a drugs overdose. I pretty much brought myself up. So, you see, everything you think you know about me is a lie.'

Of all the things Alessandro had been prepared for, this was not one of them. 'Lyla...?'

'Was the name I chose when I met you. When I thought that I could create...make myself out to be...'

'You fabricated everything.'

'No. Not everything!'

Alessandro slammed his hand on the side of his chair and vaulted to his feet. He felt tight in his skin. He needed to move. Energy was pouring through him and he was at a loss as to how to contain it. This must be what it felt like to imagine your feet were planted on solid ground only to discover that you were trying to balance on quicksand.

'Everything about you has been a lie from beginning to end. God. Why?'

'I made stuff up. I was young! I met you and I wanted to make a good impression.'

'Not only were you married, not only did you choose to conceal that fact from me eight years ago, but you also chose to conceal everything else. So your husband was... what, exactly? And how did you manage to make it to university? Or maybe you weren't a student at all. Were you? Or was that another lie?'

'Of course I was!' Chase cried, half-rising to her feet in an attempt to halt the flow of his scathing criticism. She sat back down as quickly as she had stood up. What else might she have hoped for? That he might have been understanding? Sympathetic? Why would he be? To him, she was now a confirmed liar and, if she had lied about everything, all those significant details, then what else might she have lied about? Her emotions? Her responses? It felt as though she had built a relationship on a house of cards and, now the cards were all toppling down, she had no idea how to start catching them before they all fell to the floor.

'Really? What strands am I supposed to start believing now?'

'I *was* a student at university,' she said with feverish urgency. 'I never did a lot of studying...' At this she laughed bitterly. Studying, when she was growing up, had not been seen as something worth wasting time doing. They had all known where they were destined to end up: out of work and on the dole, or else in no-hope jobs earning just enough to scrape by with a little moonlighting on the side.

'But I discovered that I barely needed to. I had a good memory. Brilliant, in fact. I would show up at school after a couple of days doing nothing, playing truant, and somehow I'd still be ahead of everyone in the class. I'd skim through a text book and manage to have instant recall of pretty much everything I'd read...'

The handful of teachers who had noticed that remarkable ability had been her salvation. Because of them she hadn't become a quitter, although she had learned to study undercover. There had never been any mileage in standing out.

She looked at him and held his inscrutable gaze. 'I guess you must find all of this completely alien. I don't suppose you've ever known anyone from the wrong side of the tracks...'

The chasm between them had never seemed wider, now that she was revealing the truth about her background. Even if she had been the person she had once claimed to be, the middle-class girl with the normal parents, there would still have been a chasm between them. Of course, he would have been attracted to her because of how she looked. Sadly, physical attributes were not destined to last; she accepted that, in an ideal world, he would have dumped her sooner or later anyway. He had been born into privilege, whatever his disruptive background, and he would always have ended up looking to settle with a woman from a similar background.

Not only had she lied to him, but she had lied to herself for ever thinking otherwise. And she had. When she had met him again and when she had fallen in love with him again. When she had nurtured silly dreams of 'what if?'s…

'Coming from the wrong side of the tracks is one thing,' Alessandro said brusquely. 'Lying about it is quite another. Were you ever going to tell me the truth?' His sense of betrayal overshadowed every other emotion, including anger.

'What would have been the point?' Chase asked defiantly. 'As you pointed out…as *we* agreed…it's not as though we were ever going anywhere with this relationship. Why would I have spoiled things with lots of truths I know you wouldn't have wanted to hear?'

Alessandro's jaw hardened. He took in her beautiful, stubborn face and had a very vivid image of the teenager she must have been: wild, drifting, incredibly bright, incredibly good-looking. 'Shaun…' Just uttering her ex-husband's name left a sour taste in his mouth. 'Must have thought he had won the lottery the day he met you—clever kid who could be his passport out of whatever dead-end life he was looking forward to leading.'

Chase looked up at him with some surprise. 'I never thought about it that way,' she said truthfully. 'I…' Was that how he had seen her, whilst making her believe that it had been the other way around? That *she* had been the lucky one to have been noticed by *him*? 'I met him when I was fifteen. He was the leader of the pack, so to speak. Everyone looked up to him even though he was younger than nearly all the guys in the gang. He was fed up living on the outskirts of Leeds. He said he wanted more. He said that London was the place to be.'

'And of course, he encouraged you to sign up to university life he knew that it was the best way out for him.'

'I don't know how I managed to get through all my exams, and I did them all a year ahead of everyone else,' Chase confessed. 'Maths, further maths, economics, geography...' But she had. Her teachers had seen to it that she'd sat them all. They were the ones who had insisted on university, who had filled in all the applications on her behalf while she had been busy having fun and running wild.

She had landed herself a place at one of the top universities in the country and had been amazed that she had accomplished such a feat. Only in retrospect had she appreciated the energy behind the scenes that had got her there.

'So you went to university and you got married.'

'The other way around, actually. I got married. Yes. And I went to university. I never expected to meet someone like you. Or anyone, for that matter.'

'And yet you did. And, instead of being truthful, you thought that it would be a much better idea to concoct a fairy-tale story about yourself.'

Chase heard the undercurrent of contempt mixed with bewilderment in his voice and inwardly winced. She was not the person she had pretended to be and that mattered to a man like him, a man who occupied a stratosphere of wealth and power that few could even dream about.

She wanted to shout at him that he didn't have a clue, that he couldn't possibly understand, but shouting wasn't going to do. Losing control wasn't going to do. She would offer him the explanation he deserved to hear with detachment and lack of passion. She would demonstrate that she was already breaking away from him, just as he was with her. She would leave with her dignity intact, as much as it could be. She would save her tears for later.

'Yes.' She tilted her chin up and steeled herself to meet his eyes squarely and without apology. 'I was young. I just…gave in to the temptation to turn myself into someone I wasn't. I made up the background I always wanted for myself.'

Alessandro felt another unwelcome, piercing tug of compassion at the thought that a middle-class background could have constituted her dream life. Most girls would have dreamt up stories of money, overseas holidays and parents with fast cars. She, on the other hand, had dreamt of what most other young girls of her age would have grumbled about and considered normal and boring.

He squashed any notion of compassion as fast as it raised its inappropriate head. The bottom line was that she was a compulsive liar, not to be trusted, never to be believed. He had come to get some truths out of her and he was getting them—in shed-loads.

'Which brings us to that piece of rubbish who was filling bin bags with your possessions.'

Getting to the heart of the matter and the reason he had shown up on her doorstep, Chase thought. Because, the faster he could wash his hands of her and clear off, the better.

'When we went to Italy, one of the girls who used to hang out in our gang was at the airport. I didn't see her.' But then, she hadn't had eyes for anyone but the man silently judging her now.

'She took pictures of us on her phone and posted them on a social networking site. Brian saw them, clocked the Louis Vuitton luggage and the chauffeur-driven car and decided that he would turn up on my doorstep and squeeze me for money. I don't know how he got my address, but there are so many ways of finding people; I don't suppose he had much trouble. He may just have gone to the place we were renting before Shaun died, got in touch with the landlord and got the forwarding address I gave him all those years ago. Who knows? He threatened to tell the people at work about my background... It would have spelled the end of my career. And he might have done a lot more besides...'

It seemed ironic now that the life she had built for herself could have been undone by something as crazy as someone taking a picture of her with Alessandro at an airport. There was no point dwelling on what was fair or what was unfair, she thought. The only way was to move forward. She kept her voice as modulated and toneless as she could.

'He was waiting for me when I got back to my house from Italy.'

Alessandro felt rage wash over him, a perfectly normal reaction to the thought of any thug lying in wait for a helpless victim.

'He told me that he wanted money and...that's when I asked you. I didn't want to, and if you *had* lent me the money I would have paid you back every penny.'

'You mean from the proceeds of the job you jacked in? Why did you do that?'

'I thought it best to resign just in case... I've never brought my past to my work. What would happen if Brian decided to show up at Fitzsimmons...?'

'Catastrophe—because they too were victims of your lies. They believed what you told them about your background, just like I did, didn't they?'

'I've never discussed my private life with anyone,' Chase mumbled, feeling even more of a hopeless liar, even though her lies had been through omission of the absolute truth. 'I've kept myself to myself. I fought hard to get where I was.'

'If you had told me the truth, I might have been inclined to give you the money.'

Chase shrugged. 'He would have come back for more. He knew where to find me. It was stupid of me to even… Well, in moments of panic we sometimes do stupid things.'

'He won't be back.'

'I know. And…and I'm very grateful to you for scaring him away. You probably threatened him with the one thing he would have taken notice of.' She wanted to smile, because who would have thought that a billionaire businessman from a cushy background could have had sufficient forcefulness to intimidate someone like Brian Shepherd into running scared? 'Look, I know you probably hate me for all of this…'

'You mean the fact that you were prepared to perpetuate a piece of fiction about yourself?' Alessandro strolled to stand in front of her, legs planted apart, hands at his sides.

Chase looked up at him reluctantly.

'What other pieces of fiction did you perpetuate?' he asked softly. 'No. There's just one more thing I need to get straight in my head.'

'What's—what's that?' she stammered uncertainly. She watched as he slowly leant over her and she half-closed her eyes as she inhaled his familiar scent. It rushed to her head like incense.

'This…' His mouth crushed her in a savage, punishing kiss and Chase helplessly yielded. She arched back in the chair, pulling him towards her, tasting him hungrily. She knew she shouldn't. She knew that it should be impossible to feel this driving, craven lust for a man who felt nothing but scorn towards her, but she couldn't seem to help herself.

There was a refrain playing at the back of her head that was telling her that this was the last time she would feel his lips on hers.

He pulled her to her feet and somehow they found themselves on the sofa, still entwined with one another. She was breathing heavily and she didn't stop him when he began undoing the buttons on her shirt, very soon losing patience. She heard the pop as a couple were ripped off. She wanted him so badly that she was shaking. Pride or no pride, she felt that she *needed* this final joining of their bodies. Her hands scrabbled to open his shirt so that she could feel the breadth of his chest and she moaned when, eventually, her fingers were splayed against it.

Her nipples tingled against her lacy bra. He cupped her breast with his hand and then pushed it underneath the bra, shoving the bra up so that he could suck on her nipple, drawing the stem into his mouth and swirling his tongue against it until she was half-crying for more.

As he suckled, he nudged her legs apart and then his hand was there, not even bothering to pull down her undies but delving underneath them, finding her wetness and exploring every inch of it with his fingers.

He still hadn't taken off a stitch of his own clothes. She had managed to undo a few buttons on his shirt and had yanked it out from the waistband of his trousers. She feverishly tried to complete the task of undressing him but he wasn't helping. She couldn't get to the zip of his trousers, although she could feel the bulge of his erection.

She gave up as he continued driving his fingers against her, pausing in the rhythmic movement only to insert them into her, into that place where she knew she wanted his rock-hard shaft to be instead.

He reared up and yanked down his trousers and, with his hand tangled in her hair, he guided her to his erection and stifled a groan when she took him into her mouth.

Through half-opened eyes, he watched as she sucked and licked him. She knew just how to rouse him down there with her hands and her mouth and he let her.

She might be a liar; he might not be able to trust her as far as he could throw her—because who could ever trust

a woman who made a habit of fabricating her life story?—
but she certainly knew just which buttons to press.

He tugged her away from him and sank onto her. Her
breasts, with the bra pushed up above them, were full and
ripe and irresistible. With a groan of satisfaction, he covered them with his mouth, until the pouting buds were wet
and hard and he continued, giving her no respite, until she
was wriggling like an eel, desperate for more.

Her hair was all over the place and her cheeks were
flushed, her mouth slightly parted, showing her perfect,
pearly-white teeth. She had sunbathed in the nude by the
pool in Italy, and her body was a perfect honey colour.

How well he knew this body. How much of it he had
explored and committed to memory, from the freckle by
her nipple to the tiny mole on her upper arm.

He pulled down her panties, flattened his hand between
her legs and then stroked her down there, harder and faster,
until he could feel her orgasm building beneath his fingers.
He didn't stop and when she came he watched: watched
her eyes flutter; watched her breathing catch in her throat
for a few seconds; watched her whole body arch, stiffen
and finally slacken as the waves of pleasure finally subsided, leaving her limp.

'Alessandro...' She reached for him and he stayed her
hand, circling her wrist before releasing her and standing up.

For a few seconds, Chase was completely bewildered.
When he began to zip up his trousers, she clambered into
a sitting position and looked at him speechlessly.

'What are you doing?'

'What does it look like I'm doing?'

'We were making love.'

'I was proving to myself that the way you responded to
me wasn't yet another lie.'

'How could you say that?' She itched to pull him back

to her but he was already turning away, doing up his buttons and taking his time, as cool as a cucumber. 'I never, *never,* pretended with you. Not about that…'

Alessandro steeled himself. She had made him cry once. The memory of that rose uninvited like poison from the deepest recesses of his mind. He had given a lot to her and her betrayal then had rocked his foundations. Never again.

'So it would seem.' He turned around to look at her. She was utterly dishevelled and utterly bewitching. 'I came here to get answers from you and I got them, Chase. Now the time has come for me to tell you goodbye. It's been… I would say fun, but what I'd really mean is…it's been a learning curve. You can congratulate yourself on teaching me the dangers of taking people at face value.'

'Alessandro!'

'What?' In the process of heading for the door, he half-turned towards her. His eyes were flat, hard and cold. There was a tense silence that stretched between them to breaking point.

Chase found that she didn't know what to say. She just didn't want him to go. Not just yet. Her body was still burning from where he had touched her, where he had deliberately touched her, turning her on, bringing her to a shuddering orgasm just to prove to himself that the attraction she'd claimed to feel for him was real. It was humiliating, yet she still couldn't bear the thought of him walking away. How on earth had she let it go this far? How was it that the control she had spent eight years building, the ability to arrange her life just how she wanted it without reference to anyone else, had been washed away by a man who had always been unsuitable and inappropriate?

'Nothing.'

He looked at her for a few seconds, shrugged and then he was gone. Just like that.

Chase was left staring at the empty doorway. He was

gone and he would never be coming back. She disgusted him. Her awful life, her sleazy ex-friends...

And he'd had the nerve to look contemptuous because once upon a time she had given in to the temptation to make it all go away by pretending to be somebody else! She might not have known about his wealth back then, but she had known with some unerring sixth sense that he would not be the kind of guy who would find any woman who came from her background attractive or in any way suitable.

And of course, she *hadn't* been suitable. She had been married, for starters. But she had seized that window of forbidden, youthful pleasure and now, all this time later, she was paying heavily for it.

She spent two hours returning all the stuff Brian had hauled off shelves and from drawers back to their rightful places. She washed a lot of it. The thought of his hands on her things made her shudder with distaste.

She hoped that by occupying herself she might take her mind off Alessandro but, all the while, he was in her head as she remembered the things they had done together, the conversations they had had.

She shakily told herself that it was a good thing that they were finished. It had been destined to end and the sooner the better. How much worse would she have felt had they ended it in two months' time? Two months during which she would have just continued falling deeper and deeper in love with him! The longer they lasted, the more difficult it would have been to unpick and disentangle her chaotic emotions. She should be thankful!

And yet, thankful was the very last thing she felt. She felt devastated, tearful and...*ashamed.*

More than anything else, she was angry with him for making her feel that way. She was angry with him for being hard line; for not having an ounce of sympathy in him; for not even trying to see her point of view. She had known from the outset that his sole motivation for sleeping with her was to exact some sort of revenge, to have that wheel turn full circle, to take what he thought had been promised to him eight years ago. Yet, hadn't he got to know her *at all* during that period? Had she just been his lover and *nothing more*?

They hadn't been rolling around on a mattress all of the time. There had been so many instances when they had talked, when the past hadn't existed, just the present, just two people getting to know one another. Or so it had felt to her.

She hated him for wiping that all away as though none of it had existed. She hated him for finding it so easy to write her off as though she was worthless.

Over the next week, as she came closer and closer to her final day at Fitzsimmons, the frustration and anger continued to build inside her. If only she could have maintained the anger, she might have felt protected, but there were so many chinks through which she recalled small acts of thoughtfulness, his wonderful wit, his sharp intellect, his lazy, sexy smile. What they had had all those years ago had been unbearably intense and that intensity had given the times they had shared recently a deep level of communication that was almost intuitive. She missed that. She missed him.

She hadn't heard a word from him. He had truly disappeared from her life—although, by all accounts, he had been on the scene far more than anticipated at the shelter, where, from what Beth had blithely told her, he appeared suddenly to have taken a keen interest in all the renovations she had planned.

'He has so many good suggestions for how the money could be spent!' Beth had enthusiastically listed all the suggestions while Chase had listened in resentful silence. 'He's also been kind enough to put us in touch with contacts he has in the contracting business so that we can get the best possible deal!' Chase had muttered something under her breath which she hoped didn't sound like the unladylike oath it most certainly was.

Beth had no idea of the history she and Alessandro had shared. It would have been petty and small-minded not to have responded with a similar level of enthusiasm to the hard-nosed billionaire businessman who had previously threatened a hostile buy-out, only to morph into a saint with a positively never-ending supply of 'brilliant ideas' and 'amazingly useful contacts'.

On the Friday, exactly a week after he had walked out of her house, there was a little leaving drinks party for her at the office, to which far more people turned up than she had expected, bearing in mind she had not been the most sociable of the team out of work.

She would be sorely missed, her boss said in the little speech he gave to the assembled members of staff. Everyone raised their glasses of champagne. These were the people she had kept at arm's length, burying herself in her work and always feeling the unspoken differences between them. And yet, as various of her colleagues came over to talk to her, she could tell that they were genuinely delighted that she intended to pursue her pro bono work in a firm that was solely dedicated to doing that.

Numbers and email addresses were exchanged with various girls whom she had known on a purely superficial basis.

When she tentatively volunteered the information that she would find it tough financially because she had no family to help her out if she started going under, there were no gasps of horror. When she confessed to a couple of the girls that she loved pro bono work because, growing up on a council estate, she had seen misery first-hand and had always wanted to do something about it, they hadn't walked away, smirking. They had been interested.

By the end of the evening, she had drunk more than she had intended but had also made friends in unexpected places.

Had she made a mistake in erecting so many protective defence mechanisms around her that she had failed to let anyone in? Had her cool distance been a liability in the end, rather than an asset? Had her detachment, which had been put in place for all the right reasons, become a habit which had imprisoned her more firmly than the solid steel bars of a prison cell?

Her thoughts were muddled and all over the place when, at a little after nine, she hailed a black cab to take her back to her house. When she closed her eyes and rested her head back on the seat, she could see Alessandro, a vibrant image hovering in the deepest recesses of her mind.

She had told him bits and pieces of the truth. Was that sufficient? An enormous sense of lassitude washed over her when she thought about the rest of what had been left unsaid.

So, nothing would change. He would still despise her. He would still be repelled by the person he thought she had turned out to be, but wouldn't she feel better in herself? Wouldn't coming clean, laying all her cards on the table, leave her with a clear conscience when she walked away? And wouldn't a clear conscience be a far better companion when she lay down in her bed at night and allowed thoughts of him to proliferate in her head?

She had given away more of herself today with her colleagues than she had in all the years she had worked alongside them, and it had felt good.

She leant forward, told the cab driver to turn around and gave him Alessandro's address.

She had no idea whether he would be in or not. It was a Friday night and face it, he was once again a free, single and eligible guy who might very well have jumped back on the sexual merry-go-round.

The alcohol had given her Dutch courage. Even as the taxi pulled up outside his magnificent house, her nerves didn't start going into automatic meltdown. She had reached a point of realising that she had nothing left to lose.

Her hand only shook a little as she reached for the door-bell and pressed hard, the very same way he had pressed *her* doorbell when he had walked in on Brian depleting her house of all its worldly goods.

On his third whisky, Alessandro heard the distant peal of his doorbell and debated whether he should bother getting it or not. A package was due to be delivered by courier. Work related. Could he really be bothered?

His torpor exasperated him but it had dogged his every waking moment ever since he had walked out of her house. Try as he might, he hadn't been able to shake it. The confines of his opulent office had felt restricting. He had found himself avoiding it, not caring what his secretary thought, going to the shelter practically every day.

It was Friday night and, whilst his head told him that it was time to get back on the horse, to find a replacement for the woman with whom he should never have become entangled all over again, his feet had brought him right back to his house and towards the drinks cabinet. A bracing evening diet of whisky and soda had felt eminently more tempting than shallow conversation with the airheads and bimbos who would circle him at the slightest given opportunity.

Of course, there was a limit to how long this crazy state of affairs could continue. Swearing softly under his breath, and with the glass of whisky still in his hand, he strolled to the front door and pulled it open. On his lips were a few select curses for whatever imbecile of a courier had had the temerity to keep his finger on the buzzer when he, Alessandro, was in the process of working his way down to the bottom of his glass, through which he hoped to see the world as an altogether rosier place.

'Alessandro. You're...' Any hint of incipient nerves flew through the window at the sight of an Alessandro who, for the first time ever, did not seem to be completely in control of all his faculties. 'Are you *drunk*?'

Alessandro leaned against the doorframe and swallowed back the remnants of whisky in his glass. 'What are you doing here at this hour? It's after nine. And I'm not drunk.'

The woman he had walked away from. He tried to think of all the pejorative adjectives that had sprung so easily to mind when he had last seen her. Before he had endured the most hellish week of his entire life. Where the hell had his bullish confidence gone about the fact that she was not worth his while? And where had she been anyway? He checked his watch and saw that it was actually a little before ten. Had she been out *partying*? A tidal wave of jealousy left him shaken.

'Living it up, Chase?' His mouth twisted as he focused on the much less prim and proper attire she was wearing, a fitted burgundy dress rather than her uniform of suits which was all he had ever seen her in for work.

'I know you're probably surprised to see me here. Shocked, even.' Although there was a glass in his hand and it was empty. Had he company? A woman? Chase refused to let that thought take shape and gain momentum.

Alessandro noticed that she had neatly avoided answering his question. He shouldn't even care. In fact, hadn't he made his mind up that he wanted nothing further to do with her? That he could never trust a woman who had lied to him? Hadn't he? 'What are you doing here? Thought you might pay a little social call? On your way back from wherever you've been out partying?'

So his mood hadn't changed. He was still hostile and contemptuous, still ready to attack. 'I haven't been *out partying*, Alessandro. I… It was my last day at work today. There was champagne at the office, that's all. I…I've come because there are some things I still need to say to you.'

So she had just been cooped up at the office. He felt some of his dark mood evaporate. She had more to say to him? Well, why not? The choice was either that or the rest of the whisky to keep him company. He turned on his heels, leaving the door open and Chase, after a few seconds' hesitation, followed him into the house.

CHAPTER TEN

SHE FOLLOWED HIM into the sitting room and immediately spotted the bottle of whisky, which was half-empty.

'How much of this stuff have you *drunk*?' she gasped in amazement.

'I think it's safe to say that my drinking habits are none of your business.' The burgundy dress lovingly clung to her body and outlined curves in all the right places. He could feel himself getting turned on and he scowled because the last thing he needed was his wilful body doing its own thing. He subsided on the sofa, legs apart, his body language aggressively, defensively masculine.

'So, what are you here for?' he demanded, following her with a glowering expression as she hesitated by the door. He watched broodingly as she took a deep breath and walked to one of the pale-cream leather chairs by the fireplace, a modern built-into-the-wall affair which she had variously claimed to have both loved and detested.

'I didn't ask,' Chase said in a thin voice. 'But is someone here with you?'

'Is someone here with me? Does it look like I have company?' He gestured to the empty room.

'You're drinking, Alessandro...' She nodded to the whisky bottle which bore witness to her statement. 'And since when do you drink on your own? Especially spirits. Didn't you once tell me that drinking spirits on your own was a sign of an alcoholic in the making? Didn't you tell me that your parents put you off giving in to vices like that in a big way? That they were a bigger warning against drinking, smoking and taking drugs than any lecture anyone could have given you?'

Alessandro's expression darkened. 'And since when are you my guilty conscience?' he demanded belligerently. He couldn't take his eyes off her. It felt as though he hadn't seen her in a hundred years and, whilst he knew that that certainly wasn't a healthy situation given the fact that she had been dispatched from his life, he still couldn't help himself, and that helplessness made him feel even more of a sad loser.

'I'm not.' Chase stared down at her entwined fingers in silence for a couple of seconds. Now that she was here, sitting in front of him, the nerves which had been absent on her trip over were gathering pace inside her. She had come to tell him how she felt but her moment of bravery was in danger of passing. She wasn't his guilty conscience. She was nothing to him. She was surprised that he hadn't slammed the door in her face, and she took some courage from the fact that he hadn't.

'I've…I've…managed to get a couple of leads on some promising jobs,' she heard herself saying, a propos nothing in particular. 'Out of London. One in Manchester. The other in Surrey. I guess I'll sell my place and move sticks. It'll be cheaper, anyway. I would probably be able to afford something bigger.'

'And you've come here to tell me this because…?'

'I haven't come here to tell you that. I just thought… Well…'

'Get to the point, Chase.' When he thought of her leaving London, he felt as though a band of pure ice had wrapped itself around his heart like the tenacious tendrils of creeping ivy.

She sprang to her feet and began walking restively around the room. It was a big room. The colours were pale and muted, from the colour of the walls to the soft leather furniture. It was modern and, when she had first seen it, she hadn't, been able to decide whether she liked it or not. Certainly, right at this very moment, it chilled her to the bone, but then wasn't that just her fear and trepidation taking its toll? The hard contours of his face spoke volumes for his lack of welcome. He might not have slammed the door in her face but he clearly didn't want her in his house. She felt that little thread of courage begin to seep slowly away.

'Do you remember that…that day, Alessandro?'

'Be specific. What day in particular are you talking about? The day you lied about the fact that you were a happily married woman, or the day you lied about the fact that the loving parents in Australia were a work of fiction…?'

Chase fought against the sneering coolness in his voice and sat back down, this time on the sofa with him, but at the furthest end of it.

'We met at that pub. Do you remember? The one by the park?'

He remembered. He could even remember what she had been wearing. It came to him with such vivid clarity that he almost thought that it had been lying in wait for eight years, just at the edges of his memory: a pair of very faded jeans, some plimsolls which had once been white but were scuffed way past their original colour and a light-blue jumper, the sleeves of which were long enough for her to tuck her hands inside them. Which she had done as she had delivered her blow.

'I told you about Shaun.'

'Believe me, I haven't forgotten that special moment in my life.'

'Please don't be sarcastic, Alessandro. This is really

hard for me. I just want you to listen, because you were right when you said that we had unfinished business between us. We did. And, for me at least, we still have until you hear me out. Or, rather, *I* still do....'

The palms of her hands felt sweaty and she smoothed them over the burgundy dress. 'Eight years ago, I fell in love with you.' She braved his silent stare and willed herself to continue. 'I was married and, believe me, I shouldn't have looked at you, far less spoken to you, but I did. You have no idea what you did for me. Being with you was like being free for the first time in my life. I finally understood what all those silly romance novels were all about.'

Alessandro frowned. This was hardly the direction he'd expected the conversation to go in. 'If you're hoping to pull on my heart strings, then you're barking up the wrong tree. I have perfect recall of your little speech to me. It involved you telling me that Shaun was the great love of your life, that it had been fun seeing me, but you were only in it for some help with work...hoped I didn't get the wrong idea. I'm recalling the moment you waved your wedding ring in my face and pulled out a photo of your loved one.'

'Yes.'

'So where are you going with this, exactly? Why have you come here to waste my time?' Another shot of whisky would have gone down a treat but he *did* remember what he had said to her about his parents teaching him the horrors of having no control, by example.

'I was an idiot when I married Shaun...' Chase stared absently into the distance. 'I was incredibly young and it seemed like an exciting thing to do. Or...or maybe not, thinking about it now. *Shaun* told me it would be an exciting thing to do and I went along with it because I had already figured out that it didn't pay to disagree with anything he said.'

'Watch out. You're in danger of wiping some of the shine from your blissfully joyous married life.'

'There was never any shine on it, and I wasn't blissfully married,' Chase told him abruptly. She refocused on his face to find him watching her carefully. When she thought about the horror that had been her married life with Shaun, she wanted to cry for those wasted years, but the self-control she had built up over the years stood her in good stead.

Alessandro found that he was holding his breath. 'Another lie, Chase?' But he wanted to hear what she had to say even though he told himself that he wasn't going to fall for anything she told him. Once bitten, twice shy.

'I haven't come here to try and make you believe me, Alessandro,' Chase said with quiet sincerity. 'I know you probably won't anyway. I know I've lied to you in the past and you'll never forgive me. You've made that crystal-clear. I'm here because I *need* to tell you everything. And, when I'm finished, I'll walk out that door and you'll never see me again.

'When I met you for the first time, I began something that was dangerous, although you weren't to know that. I've thought about what you said, about Shaun hitching his wagon to me because he knew that he would be able to go further with me shackled to his side. I think you were right, although at the time I didn't see it that way. By the time I made it to university, I'd lost the ability to think independently. My studies were the only thing keeping me going. We'd come to London and I had been taken away from my friends, from everything I knew, although I guess you would find "everything I knew" hardly worth knowing anyway. Shaun was in his element. I was married to him and he was in complete control, and he enjoyed making sure he exercised that control.'

'What are you telling me?'

'I'm telling you that I was an abused wife. The sort of pathetic woman you would find contemptible. The sort of woman who can really understand how all those women at Beth's shelter feel. Why do you imagine I have such empathy for them?'

'When you say abused…?'

'Physically, mentally, emotionally. Shaun was never fussy when it came to laying down laws. He used whatever methods suited him at the time.' She tilted her chin defiantly. She had come to say her piece and he could save his contempt for after she'd left. That was what her expression was telling him.

'He was very clever when it came to making sure he hurt me in ways that weren't visible. He let me out of his sight to attend lectures and tutorials but I was under orders to return home immediately, not to hang around and certainly never to cultivate any sort of friendship with any of the other students. I was just glad to be out of his presence. Anything was better than nothing and, besides, I thrived on the academic work. I found it all ridiculously easy.

'One of the first things I'm going to do when I leave London is to find the teachers who encouraged me and tell them how valuable their input was.' She made sure that he got the message that she wasn't looking for anything from him, that she was moving on, that she had her independence, whatever her story was.

'You say you were…in love with me. Why didn't you leave him?' *Because,* Alessandro thought, *I was certainly head over heels in love with you. I would have protected you.*

It was the first time he had ever really and truly given that notion house room and, now that he had, everything seemed to fall neatly into place. The manner in which she had departed from his life had altered his view of women and had, more profoundly, altered the sort of women he went out with. He had developed a healthy mistrust of anything that remotely smelled of commitment and had programmed every single relationship he'd had to fail by systematically dating women in whom he was destined to lose interest after very short periods of time. In the wake of losing his heart to a woman who had deceived him, he had simply pressed the self-destruct button inside him.

And then she had returned to his life under extraordinary circumstances. He had held her to ransom and told himself that he was exacting revenge. In fact, he had told himself a lot of things. The one single thing he had failed to tell himself—because he could see now that he just couldn't have brought himself to even think it—was that he still wanted her because, quite simply, he was still in love with her.

Chase sensed the infinitesimal shift in him. Was it too much to ask that he at least believed her?

'I couldn't,' she said, flushing. 'I've become very independent over the years. It's been so important for me to stand on my own two feet, to give nothing of myself to anyone, to make sure that no one had control over me. But back then there was no way that I had the inner strength to try and escape. He had sapped me of all my confidence. Anyway...'

She stared down at her fingers, drained from the confidences she was giving away. 'I haven't come here to make excuses, just to tell you things as they were. I met you and it was wonderful but Shaun found out. He got hold of my mobile phone; I had been stupid enough to have one of your text messages there. I had forgotten to delete it. It was arranging to meet for lunch. He went crazy. I can't tell you, but I was terrified for my life. He threatened to kill us both if I didn't end it and, to make sure I did what he said, he made me arrange the location we were supposed to meet. He told me exactly what I was to say to you, and he was sitting at the table behind us the whole time I gave you that little speech about being a happily married woman...'

'My God.'

'I could never have told you about how things really were and I still didn't want to when I saw you again because I was...ashamed. I knew how you'd react. I knew all your opinions of me as a strong career woman with a mind of her own would evaporate and I would be just a pathetic, abused woman, like all those women you didn't give a hoot about when you were going to buy the shelter and have them dispossessed.' She took a deep breath and made eye contact with him but what she saw there was far from contempt. The silence stretched between them until it was at breaking point.

'If we had met later...' she said in a low voice, half-talking to herself '...then things might have been different. Even if I'd still been with Shaun, I would have had more self-confidence. I would have had my degree, a good job; I would have had the courage to walk away from him, but at that point in my life it just wasn't there.'

'And then,' Alessandro said heavily, 'we met again and I hardly inspired the trust you needed to open up. I blackmailed you into sleeping with me...'

'I *wanted* to sleep with you,' Chase confirmed in a driven voice. 'I would never have let myself be blackmailed into doing anything. I said so at the time and I meant it. I'd learnt the hard way not to let anyone else have control over me. I *wanted* to sleep with you and I don't regret it.'

'And what happened to the...love?' Alessandro asked so quietly that she had to strain to hear him.

'I still love you, Alessandro,' she said proudly. 'And I don't regret that either. So, there you are.' She stood up and brushed her skirt to distract herself from speculating on what was going on in his head.

'Not so fast!'

Chase looked up at him in surprise. His command was imperious but there was a hesitancy underlying it that wormed its way past her common sense.

'I'm glad you came,' he said, flushing darkly and looking so suddenly vulnerable that she wanted to sidle a little closer to him, just to make sure that her eyes weren't playing tricks on her. She remained where she was, resisting the impulse. 'I'm glad you were honest with me. Yes, when we met again...'

Alessandro raked his fingers through his hair and shook his head with a rueful smile that did even more disastrous things to her common sense. 'It all came rushing back at me. I hadn't realised how much I remembered and I certainly didn't get why it was that I remembered so well. I just knew that I still...wanted you. Somewhere along the line, I figured out that I had never stopped wanting you. I couldn't make sense of it, couldn't understand how I could still want a woman who I felt had betrayed me in the worst possible way. Don't get me wrong; I understand why you wanted to keep your secrets to yourself, why you felt that they would be too dark for me to handle, but if only I had known...'

'Nothing would have changed, Alessandro. Nothing has changed now.'

'No, nothing's changed and everything's changed. You're the same person you always were, Chase, whatever you went through. What you mean to me will always be the same, just as it was all those years ago. You will always be the girl I fell in love with but was too damned stupid to own up to. I let pride rule my behaviour and only now... Well, I'm still in love with you.'

Chase wondered whether she had heard correctly or whether wishful thinking had taken complete control. Was it even possible to hear something you wanted to hear because you wanted it *so badly*? She found that she was holding her breath.

'Um…did you just say… Did you just tell me…?'

'That I'm in love with you? Yes, I did. And I'll tell you again if you'd move a little closer so that I don't have to shout across the width of the sofa.'

'It's not a big sofa,' Chase said faintly.

'Right now, with you sitting at the other end of it, it feels as wide as a canyon.'

She shuffled along and slipped into his arms with a soaring feeling of utter elation. 'What if I hadn't come tonight?'

'I would never have let you go. The past week has been the worst of my life. I've never hated my office more. I lost interest in deals, going to meetings, reading emails… I know more now about that shelter than I would ever have thought possible.'

'Beth said you'd been a frequent visitor.' She curled into him and heard the beating of his heart.

'It made me feel close to you,' he confessed shakily, 'Although I never faced up to that. I love you, Chase. I love you for the person you are now and I loved you for the person you were then. I can't live without you. I want you to be my wife. Will you marry me? Within the next hour?'

Chase lifted her head and laughed, her eyes glowing with happiness. 'Within the next hour might be stretching it,' she said softly. 'But, yes, I'll be your wife.'

'And never leave my side?'

'You're stuck with me for ever…' And never had the thought of being stuck with someone for ever sounded so good.

* * * * *

THE PLAYBOY'S
PROPOSITION

LEANNE BANKS

This book is dedicated to the BBs. Thank you for providing me with never-ending inspiration. Catherine Baker, Peggy Blake, Coco Carruth, Ann Cholewinski, Rose Dunn, Kim Jones, Mina McAllister, Sharon Neblett, Terry Parker, Terri Shea, Sandy Smith, Kathy Venable, Jane Wargo, Kathy Zaremba.

Leanne Banks is a *New York Times* and *USA TODAY* bestselling author who is surprised every time she realises how many books she has written. Leanne loves chocolate, the beach and new adventures. To name a few, Leanne has ridden on an elephant, stood on an ostrich egg (no, it didn't break), gone parasailing and indoor skydiving. Leanne loves writing romance because she believes in the power and magic of love. She lives in Virginia with her family and four-and-a-half-pound Pomeranian named Bijou. Visit her Web site at www.leannebanks.com.

Prologue

Mr. Always-Pays-Cash-And-Tips-Well. Bella St. Clair spotted the hot, sophisticated dark-haired customer in the back corner of the packed Atlanta bar. He'd been there four of the ten nights she'd worked at Monahan's. Always polite, he'd chatted with her a few times, making her feel like a person instead of just a cocktail waitress. Despite the fact that in terms of romance her heart was deader than a doornail, and she was distracted about her aunt's latest problem, Bella felt a fraction of her misery fade at the sight of him.

He gave a slight nod and she moved toward him. "Good evening. How are you tonight?" she asked, setting a paper napkin on the table.

He hesitated a half beat then shrugged. "I've had better," he said.

A shot of empathy twisted through her. She could

identify with him. Her aunt's business had been turned over to the bank one month ago today and Bella knew it was at least partly her fault. "Sorry," she said. "Maybe the atmosphere here will distract you. A jazz artist will be playing in a little while. What can I get for you?"

"Maclellan single malt whiskey," he said.

She lifted her eyebrows at the expensive beverage and nodded. "Excellent choice for either a rough night or a celebration. Can I get you anything to eat with that?"

"No thanks. Rowdy crowd tonight," he said, nodding toward the large table in the center of the room. "Must be the snow."

She glanced toward the curtained windows in dismay. "I've been so busy since I arrived that I didn't notice. I heard the forecast, but it's rare to get the white stuff here. Think it'll be just a dusting?" she asked hopefully.

He shook his head. "We're already past a dusting. The roads should be covered in an hour."

"Great," she muttered. "My little car is gonna love this trip home."

"What do you drive?" he asked, curiosity glinting in his dark eyes.

"Volkswagen Beetle."

He chuckled. "I guess that's better than a motorcycle."

She felt a bubble of gallows amusement. "Thanks for the encouragement. I'll be right back with your whiskey." She got his drink from the bartender and made her way through the crowd, carefully balancing the glass of whiskey on her tray. Heaven knew, she didn't want to spill a drop. The stuff cost fifty bucks a shot.

She wondered what had caused her handsome customer the pain she glimpsed in his dark eyes. He emanated confidence and a kind of dynamic electricity that snapped her out of the twilight zone she'd been in for the last month.

She set the glass in front of him. "There you go," she said, meeting his dark gaze and feeling a surprising sizzle. She blinked. Where had that come from? She'd thought all her opportunities for sizzle had passed her by.

She watched him lift the glass to his lips and take a sip. The movement drew her attention to his mouth, sensual and firm. She felt a burning sensation on her own lips, surprised again at her reaction.

"Thanks," he said.

She nodded, transfixed.

"Hey babe," a voice called from behind her. "We want another round."

The call pulled her out of her temporary daze. "Oops. Gotta go. Do you need anything else?"

"Water when you get a chance," he said. "Thank you very much, Bella," he said in a voice that made her stomach dip.

She turned around, wishing she knew his name. "Wow," she whispered to herself. Based on her reaction to the man, one would almost think she was the one drinking whiskey. *Crazy,* she thought, and returned to the rest of her customers.

Another dead end. Sometimes it seemed his life's curse was to never find his brother. Too restless to suffer the stark silence in his luxury home, Michael Medici settled back in his seat in a corner of the crowded popular bar, one of several he owned in Atlanta.

Michael usually craved quiet at the end of the day, but tonight was different. The din of Atlanta's young crowd buffeted the frustration and pain rolling inside him.

Michael spent the next hour allowing himself the luxury of watching Bella. After the disappointing news from the private investigator, he craved a distraction. He wondered if he would ever find out what had truly happened to his brother all those years ago. Or if he was cursed to stay in limbo for the rest of his life.

Forcing his mind away from his frustration, he watched Bella, enjoying the way she bit her pink mouth when she met his gaze. Feeling the arousal build between them, he toyed with the idea of taking her home with him. Some might consider that arrogant, given he'd just met her recently, but Michael usually got what he wanted from business and the opposite sex.

He slid his gaze over her curvy body. Her uniform, consisting of a white blouse, black skirt and tights, revealed rounded breasts, a narrow waist and inviting hips. Her legs weren't bad, either.

She set another glass of water on his table.

"How are you liking it here?" he asked.

She hesitated and met his gaze. "It's good so far. I've been out of the country for a year. I'm re-acclimating to being an average American again."

"You don't look average to me," he said. "What were you doing out of the country if you don't mind my asking?"

"Disaster relief."

"Ah," he said with a nod. A do-gooder. Perhaps that accounted for her other-worldly aura. "How's the transition going?"

"Bumpy," she said with a smile that made him feel like he'd been kicked in his gut.

He didn't make a habit of picking up cocktail wait-resses, especially those who worked for businesses he owned, but this one intrigued him. He wondered if she was the kind of woman who would be impressed by his wealth. Just for fun, he decided to keep his identity a secret a little longer. He liked the idea of not dealing with dollar signs in a woman's eyes. He'd been featured in the Atlanta magazine often enough that he could rarely meet someone without them knowing way too much about him. Way too much about his business success, anyway.

"I don't see a ring on your finger, Bella," he said.

Her eyes showed a trace of sadness. "That's right. You don't."

"Would you like me to give you a ride home? I think my SUV may be better able to take on a snowy road."

Her eyes widened slightly in surprise and he watched her pause in a millisecond of indecision. "I'm not supposed to fraternize with the customers."

"Once we step outside the door, I won't be one any longer," he said, familiar with the policy.

She looked both tempted and reluctant. "I don't even know your name."

"Michael. I'll hang around awhile longer," he said, amused that she'd almost turned him down. He tried to remember the last time that had happened.

Watching her from his corner, he noticed a man reaching toward her. She backed away and the man stood. Michael narrowed his eyes.

The man reached for her and pulled her against him. "Come on baby, you're so hot. And it's cold outside…" The man slid his hand down toward her bottom.

Already on his feet, Michael walked toward Bella

and pushed the man aside and into a chair. "I think you've had too much." Glancing around the room, he saw the bar manager, Jim, and gave a quick curt nod.

Seconds later, Jim arrived, stumbling over his words. "I'll take care of this Mr.—"

Michael gave another curt nod, cutting the man off mid-sentence. "Thank you. Perhaps your staff needs a break."

Jim nodded. "Take the rest of the night off," the manager said.

Her face pale, Bella hesitated. "I—"

"I'll give you a ride whenever you want to go," Michael said. "I can take you somewhere quieter."

She met his gaze and he saw a glimmer of trust in her eyes as if she felt the same strange sense of connection with him he did with her. She paused a halfbeat, then nodded. "Okay."

An hour and a half later, Bella realized she'd told half her life story to the hot man who'd rescued her at work. She'd told him about how her Aunt Charlotte had raised her. She'd even vaguely mentioned being a failure at her love life. Every time she thought about Stephen, a stab of loss wrenched through her. She knew she would never get over him. Never. The worst though, was her crushing guilt over not being with her aunt while she suffered through the cancer treatment.

Although she hadn't mentioned any names, she was appalled at how much she'd revealed. "I've done all the talking," she said, covering her face. "And I can't even blame it on alcohol because, except for that first mangotini, I've been drinking water. You heard enough about me a long time ago. Your turn. Tell me why this has been a rotten day for you."

"I can't agree about hearing enough about you," he said with a half smile playing over his beautiful mouth. It occurred to Bella that his mouth, his face, should have been carved in marble and exhibited in a museum. She glanced at his broad shoulders and fit body. *Perhaps his body, too,* she thought.

"You're very kind," she said. "But it's still your turn."

He gave a low chuckle, his dark eyes mysterious. "Not many people have described me as kind. But if you insist," he said, lifting his own glass of water to take a drink.

"I do," she said.

"My parents died when I was young, so I wasn't raised by them. You and I share that in common."

"Who did raise you?" she asked.

"I wasn't lucky enough to have an Aunt Charlotte," he said. "No need for sympathy," he said.

"Oh," she said, studying his face. He was an interesting combination of strength and practicality. "That must have been hard, though."

"It was," he nodded and paused a moment. "The accident tore my family apart."

"That's horrible," she said, filled with questions.

"It was," he agreed. "I keep wondering if I could have done something…"

Silence followed, and Bella felt a well of understanding build inside her. The force of the emotion should have surprised her, but she identified with the depth of his misery all too easily. She slid her hand over his. "You feel guilty, don't you?"

He glanced down at her hand on his. "Every day," he said. He broke off. "It's probably just a wish…"

Her heart twisted inside her. "I understand," she whispered.

He rubbed his thumb over her hand. "You're not just beautiful. You're intuitive," he said.

Bella wouldn't have called herself beautiful. In fact, she couldn't remember anyone doing so except Stephen. Her stomach knotted at the memory. He would never call her beautiful again, now that he'd fallen in love with someone else.

"There you go again, being too kind," she said.

"You have that confused. I suspect you're the kind one. I can't believe you don't have to turn away men all the time."

"Now that's flattery," she said. "Unless you're counting the ones who've had too much to drink at the bar." She knew she was unusual looking. The contrast of her dark hair, intense eyes and pale skin sometimes drew second glances, but she suspected they were more due to curiosity than admiration.

"I'd like to spend more time with you," he said, his eyes dark with seduction.

Her heart, which she'd thought was dead, tripped over itself. Bella reminded herself that her heart raced for many reasons, fear, excitement, inexplicable arousal...

"I'm not in the best place emotionally for any sort of relationship."

"I wasn't suggesting anything serious," he said. "The only thing we need to take seriously is each other's pleasure."

Her breath caught at the sensual expression on his face. "A one-night stand?" she said, surprised she wasn't immediately rejecting the offer. Heaven knew, she'd never accepted such a proposition before. That had been before she'd fallen in love and lost her heart. That had been before she'd had her chance and saw it slip away. Michael wasn't suggesting anything like that. She felt a surprising twinge of relief.

"It depends on what we want after the night is over. You and I have some things in common. I could make you forget your problems for awhile. I think you could do the same for me."

The lure was too tempting. He was strong, but she'd glimpsed his humanity and for some reason there was a strange connection between them. A connection that made her feel a little more alive than like the walking dead.

She took a sip to moisten her suddenly dry throat. Was she really going to do this? "I don't even know your last name," she said.

"Michael Medici," he said with a slight smile. "You can run a background check, but you won't find anything on me. We'd also be wasting time. If you need someone to vouch for me, you can call your boss. He knows me."

One

Bella awakened to the sensation of being covered in the softest, finest cotton sheets…and wrapped in the strong, but unfamiliar arms of the man who'd made love to her most of the night.

Her chest tightened into a hard knot at the realization that she'd slept with a near stranger. What had possessed her? Was it because she still hadn't recovered from her breakup with her ex-fiancé? Was it because she needed to escape the guilt she felt for not being there for her aunt when she'd needed her most?

She blinked her bleary eyes several times then closed them again. It had been so easy to accept Michael Medici's offer to drive her home in the rare Atlanta snowstorm with a stop at a cozy bar. Somehow, she'd ended up in his bed instead.

Taking a quick breath, she felt the overwhelming need

to run. This had been a huge mistake. She wasn't that kind of woman. Scooting a millimeter at a time, she got to the side of the bed and gently slid her foot to the ground.

"Where are you going?" Michael asked, causing her to stop midmotion.

She glanced over her shoulder and the sight of him covered by a sheet only from the waist down made her throat tighten. In the soft darkness before dawn, he leaned against one forearm, and his broad shoulders and muscular chest emanated strength. She forced herself to meet his gaze and saw what had attracted her from the beginning—dark eyes that glowed with confidence and attentiveness. She'd pushed her fingers through his dark curly hair. His mouth had taken her with shocking passion.

She cleared her throat and tried to clear her mind. "I realized I have a job interview today. I should get home."

"You don't think the interview will be canceled due to the snowstorm?" he asked.

"Well, I can't be sure," she said a bit too brightly for her own ears. "Always best to be prepared. You don't have to get up. I'll call a cab."

He gave a short laugh and rose from the bed. "Fat chance in this weather. I'll take you."

She looked away. "Oh, no really—"

"I insist," he said in a rock-solid tone.

"But my car," she said.

"I'll have my driver bring it to your place."

One hour later, Michael turned into her apartment complex. Bella let out a tiny breath of relief in antici- pation of escaping such close confines with him. During the silent ride, she'd spent every other minute castigating herself for making such a foolish choice. She needed to step up and be there for her aunt. She refused to be like her mother—irresponsible and careless of others' needs.

"Is this the building?" Michael asked.

"Yes," she said, her hand on the door as he pulled to a stop. "I really appreciate the ride home. It was very kind of you."

"I'd like to see you again," he said, and something in his voice forced her to meet his gaze.

If she were another person, if she had fewer responsibilities, if she weren't still in love with a man she couldn't have…too many ifs.

She shook her head. "It's not a good idea. I shouldn't have—" She broke off and cleared her throat. Lord, this was awkward.

He leaned toward her. "You didn't like being in my bed?" he asked, but it was more of a dare than a question.

She sucked in a quick breath. "I didn't say that. I just have a lot going on right now. I think being with you could be confusing for me."

"It doesn't have to be confusing," he said. "It's simple. I meet your needs and you meet mine."

She couldn't stop a bubble of nervous laughter as she looked into his dark gaze. How could anything with this man ever be simple? She was out of her league and she knew it. "I—uh—I don't think so." She shook her head. "Thank you for bringing me home."

Bella raced inside her apartment and closed the door behind her. She took several deep breaths, still unable to believe that she had spent the night with a man she barely knew.

She checked the time. A little too early for her regular morning call with Aunt Charlotte. She took a shower and let the hot spray rinse away her stress and warm her from the outside in. For a few minutes, she forgot about her worries and focused on the warm water.

After she got out of the shower, she dried off, dressed and checked the time again. She dialed her aunt's number and waited while it rang several times. Bella felt her concern grow the longer it took for Charlotte to answer.

Bella had almost lost her and she still could. Her aunt was recovering from breast cancer and a year of grueling treatment, a year when Bella had been away pursuing her dream. If only Charlotte hadn't kept her illness a secret.

"Hello," her aunt said in a sleepy voice.

"Oh, no, I woke you," Bella said.

"No," Charlotte said and sighed. "Well, actually you did. The shop is closed today."

"So you get a day off," Bella said, excited at the prospect of her aunt getting some extra rest.

"Without pay," Charlotte grumbled.

"Can I bring something over for you? Soup, sandwich, coffee, green tea…"

"Don't you dare," Charlotte said. "I don't want you driving in this messy weather. I have plenty of food here. Maybe I'll do something really decadent and stay in bed and watch the morning shows."

"As long as you promise to eat something," Bella said.

"You sound just like a mom," Charlotte said.

"I want to make up for lost time."

"Oh, sweetie," her aunt said. "You gotta let go of that. I made it through."

"But you lost something important to you," Bella said, speaking of her aunt's spa. It had been her aunt's life-long dream to open several spas in Atlanta and Charlotte had succeeded until the disease and treatment had sucked the energy out of her.

"True, but things could be worse." She laughed. "My hair is growing back. I'm thinking of dying it pink."

Bella smiled. "Or purple?"

"Yeah," Charlotte said. "Speaking of spas, I found out who bought the business from the bank."

"Really? How did you find out?"

"A client who came into the salon works for the bank. She said some local big wheeler and dealer bought them. She said he's known for buying and selling bankrupt businesses."

Bella made a face. The man she described sounded like a vulture. "Not exactly Prince Charming," she muttered.

"I don't know," her aunt said. "The client said if there were a picture in the dictionary beside the word *hot,* this guy would be right there. I haven't heard of him, but apparently he's well known among local businesses. Michael Medici's his name."

Two

Three weeks later, Bella walked into MM Enterprises mustering the fragile hope that Michael Medici would show an ounce of compassion for her Aunt Charlotte. She knew the deck was stacked against her in more ways than one, but she had to try. In an ironic twist of fate, Michael's company had bought her aunt's business before Bella had even met him. Apparently, Michael was known for scooping up the skeletons of failing companies and either breathing new life into them, or partitioning them into smaller pieces and making a profit.

The heels of her boots clicked against the tile floor. Dressed in black from head to toe, she could have been outfitted for a funeral. Instead, she was dressing for success. More than anything, she needed Michael to take her seriously. Stepping into the elevator, her nerves jumped under her skin, and she mentally rehearsed her request for the millionth time. The elevator dinged, signaling its arrival. She walked down the hallway and took a breath just before she opened the door to his office.

A young woman seated behind a desk wearing a Bluetooth glanced up in inquiry. "May I help you?"

"I'm Bella St. Clair. I have an appointment with Mr. Medici," she said.

The receptionist nodded. "Please take a seat. He'll be right with you."

Bella sat on the edge of the upholstered blue chair and unbuttoned her coat as she glanced around the office. Business magazines were fanned out neatly on top of the cherry sofa table. Mirrors and original artwork graced cream-colored walls and a large aquarium filled with colorful fish caught her attention. She wondered if any of those fish were from the shark family. She wondered if Michael would ultimately be ruthless or reasonable.

She resisted the urge to fidget. Barely. This was her chance to make it up to Charlotte for not being there when her aunt had needed her most.

Her heart still wrenched at what Charlotte had suffered. Charlotte had supported Bella while she pursued her dream of taking a year off to work for disaster relief in Europe, and had kept her diagnosis a secret from Bella until she'd arrived back in the States.

"You can go in now," the receptionist said, jolting Bella back from her reverie.

Stiffening her spine, she stood and smiled at the receptionist. "Thank you," she said and hesitated a half beat before she opened the door to Michael Medici's office.

Walking inside, she saw him standing in front of the wall of windows on the opposite wall. The sight of him hit her like a strike to her gut. His dark, commanding frame provided a stark contrast against the blue sky behind him. His eyes seemed colder than the last time she'd seen him.

She bit the inside of her cheek. Why shouldn't he be cold toward her? She'd rejected his suggestion that they continue their affair. She was lucky he was willing to see her at all. That had been her litmus test. If he would talk to her, then maybe she could persuade him to agree to her proposal.

"Bella," he said in the smooth velvety voice she remembered. "What brings you here?"

Step one. Address the past and move on. "I realize that you and I shared a rather unusual experience a few weeks ago," she began.

"On the contrary," he said with a slight mocking glint in his eyes. "I understand it happens every day, all over the world."

Her cheeks burned at the remembered intimacy. "Not quite the way that—" She gave up and cleared her throat. "That night aside, I would like to discuss a business proposition with you."

He lifted an eyebrow in surprise and moved to the front of his desk, sitting on the edge. "A business proposition? Have a seat," he said, waving his hand to one of the leather chairs in front of him.

Moving closer to him to sit down, she caught a whiff of his cologne. A hot visual of him naked in bed with her seared her memory. His proximity jangled her nerves, but she was determined. "There's a lot that you and I don't know about each other, but I did tell you that my

Aunt Charlotte had experienced some health problems and was also having a tough time professionally."

He nodded silently.

She had wished that he would be less handsome than the last time she'd seen him. Her wish had not come true. She took another breath, wanting to clear her head. "What I didn't tell you was that while I was out of the country last year, my aunt was diagnosed with cancer. She hid that from me or I would have come back immediately. She had to undergo treatment that weakened her. She's better now, but she wasn't able to focus on her business during that time. She lost it."

"I'm sorry to hear that," he said.

"Thank you," she said, feeling a sliver of relief at his words of compassion. "This has been so hard on my aunt. She's sinking into a depression over it. I did some research and found out that you bought her business from the bank."

He tilted his head to one side, frowning. "What business?"

"The spas," she said. "Charlotte's Day Spas."

Realization crossed his face. "Right. She had three of them. I'm planning to convert the properties and resell them. One is a perfect location for a pizza franchise."

"Pizza," she echoed, dismayed at the thought. She cleared her throat. "What I would like to propose is to arrange a loan with you for us to buy back the businesses with the agreement that you would get a share of the profit."

He looked at her for a long moment. "Which at the moment is zero," he said.

"It obviously won't stay that way. The only reason the spas crashed was because of my aunt's health problems."

"And what do you plan to use to secure the loan?" he asked.

"We don't have anything tangible, but the important thing is that my aunt and I would be willing to work night and day to make this work."

"Do you really think, with her health, she can work night and day?" he asked.

She bit her lip. "She needs a purpose. She feels as if she's lost everything." She sighed. "No. I wouldn't let her work night and day, but I could work that hard. I'm young. I'm strong. I can do this."

"So, you're asking me to bank on you and your commitment," he said. "Do you have a résumé?"

He was as cool as a swim in the Arctic, only revealing his thoughts when he wanted, Bella thought with a twinge of resentment. No wonder he was known for his business expertise. She thought of all the menial jobs she'd taken to help finance her education and felt a sinking sensation. She gave him the manila folder that contained the business plan and her résumé. "As you can see, I'm a licensed esthetician, and I have a bachelor's degree in communication studies."

He glanced over the paper. "If you're so committed to your aunt's spas, then why did you go to college? You had your esthetician's license."

"My aunt and I agreed that I should get a college education."

He nodded, looking through the papers. He rubbed his jaw thoughtfully with his hand. "I'll get back to you."

Michael watched Bella leave his office. *Damn her,* he whispered after she'd closed the door behind her. He hadn't stopped thinking about her since he'd had her in his bed. Since she'd rejected him after they'd made wild, passionate love.

He chuckled bitterly to himself. *Love* was a misnomer. Amazing sex was much more accurate. He'd sensed a desperation similar to his in her. She'd been so hot, he'd almost felt as if she'd singed his hands, his body....

Scowling at his reaction to her, he wondered why he wanted her so much. He usually took women as lovers then tired of them after a while. After just one night of her, he knew he had to have more. It was more than want. Need.

Not likely, he told himself, releasing the fist he'd just noticed was clenched. He needed to get her out of his system. The fact that she'd rejected him only added fuel to the fire.

He punched the intercom button for his receptionist. "Call my investigator. I want him to run a credit and background check on Charlotte Ambrose and Bella St. Clair. I want it by tomorrow." He didn't know why he was even considering Bella's request. Michael had always kept emotion out of his business decisions. That was part of the reason he was so successful. A frisson of challenge fluttered at the idea of turning Charlotte's business into a success. If success were possible, he would know how to make it happen.

His BlackBerry buzzed. He glanced at the caller ID. Rafe, his brother, a yachting business owner, lived in Miami. His mood lifting, he punched the on button. "Rafe? How are you? You must not be very busy if you're calling me." All the Medici men were work-aholics. Being farmed out to different foster homes after their parents died had left all of them with a nearly unquenchable thirst for success and control.

"On the contrary. I got married a few weeks ago, remember?" Rafe said.

"Yes. Even I was surprised you were able to pull that off. Nicole seemed very reluctant." Michael was still amazed that Rafe had persuaded the beautiful guardian of his brother's child to marry him so quickly.

"I have more news," Rafe said.

"Yes?" Michael asked, hoping Rafe had learned something new about their missing brother Leo.

"You're going to be an uncle again," Rafe told him, joy threaded through his voice. Even though he hadn't seen Leo in twenty years, Michael thought about his brother every day.

Michael felt a twinge of disappointment that the news wasn't about Leo, but he couldn't stop from smiling. "So fast?"

"Some things are meant to be," Rafe said.

"How does Nicole feel about it?"

"Besides being mildly nauseated, she's thrilled," Rafe said.

"And Joel?" Michael asked, thinking of Rafe's son.

"He doesn't know yet. We thought we'd wait until she's showing," Rafe said. "But we want you to come down to visit."

Michael shook his head. "I'm slammed at the moment. Lots of buying and selling action right now."

"Yeah?" Rafe said. "I asked an investigator to look into leads for Aunt Emilia."

"So did I," Michael said, and started to pace. Their aunt Emilia lived in Italy and had sent Rafe photos and some curious letters recently. "Nothing yet. I also had my investigator run another search on Leo."

"Nothing, right?" Rafe said.

"Right," Michael said. "I've decided to try a P.I. who lives in Philly. He's always lived in the state. Maybe a native will spot something that we can't see."

"It might be worth trying," Rafe said, but Michael could hear the skepticism in his brother's voice.

"I have to try," Michael said. "One way or another, I need to do this for Leo."

"You're going to have to give up the guilt someday," Rafe said. "You were a child when Dad and Leo took that trip on the train. You couldn't have possibly known there would be a wreck or that they would die."

"Easy to say," Michael muttered, still feeling the crushing heavy sense of responsibility tighten his chest like a vise. "It was supposed to be me. Leo went in my place. The least I can do, if he really *did* die, is give him a proper burial."

"If anyone can make it happen, you can," Rafe said.

"Thanks." Michael raked his hand through his hair.

"In the meantime, though, Damien is talking about coming for a visit. If he travels all the way from Vegas, then the least you can do is hop down here too. I'm not taking no for an answer," he said forcefully.

"Okay," Michael said. "Keep me posted."

"Will do. Take care of yourself."

Two days later, Michael told his assistant to set up another appointment for Bella. One day after that, she walked through his office door. He noticed she was dressed from head to toe in black again. She might as well have been grieving. He suspected her pride *was* in mourning.

Her eyes—a startling shade of violet—regarded him

with a combination of reticence and hope bordering on desperation.

Michael could assuage that desperation. He could make her wish come true, but Charlotte and Bella would have to do things his way. Michael had learned long ago that one of the primary reasons businesses failed was because the owners were unwilling to give up their ideas in exchange for success.

"Have a seat," he said, and leaned against his desk.

She sank on to the edge of the leather chair and lifted her chin in false bravado. He liked her all the more for that. She might very well hate him by the end of their meeting.

"There might be a way this can work, but it will cost both you and your aunt. We do it my way, or I'm out."

She bit the inside of her upper lip. He resisted the urge to tell her not to do that. Her lips were too beautiful. The pink-purple color of her bee-stung mouth provided a sensual contrast to her ivory skin. Her mouth was pure sex to him, and when she licked her lips…

"What is your way?" she asked.

"We start with one spa and do it right," he said.

"But Charlotte had three—"

"And is still recovering from chemotherapy," he said.

She took a breath and pursed her lips, her gaze sliding away from his. "Go on," she said.

"In this economy, people want luxury at a discount."

"But you have to pay for good service—"

"Yes, but people need to feel as if they aren't spending too much on splurging." He opened the file folder. "I researched the business plans of successful spas. You need to focus on what they call miniservices and discounts for volume purchases. A minifacial. Packages of massages.

A package of ten pedicures at a discount. In turn, you provide a quality service, but limit the time."

"Sounds like fast food," she said, curling her beautiful lip.

"Exactly," he said. "People can justify fast food more easily than lobster and filet mignon. Filet mignon is a commitment."

She paused and threaded her fingers through her dark hair. "I don't know if Charlotte will go for this."

"The deal is nonnegotiable," he said and felt not one qualm. Michael knew how to split the wheat from the chaff. "I'm bending my rules by offering this plan to you."

She blinked in surprise. "How are you bending your rules?"

"If someone loses their business, then they're not a good enough bet for me to give them a second try," he said in a blunt tone.

Bella's eyes widened. "Even though she got sick?"

"For whatever reason," he said. "When you're in trouble or you can't cover your responsibilities, you always make sure you have someone to cover for you. If you're not a superhero, you have to have a backup."

She met his gaze. "What about you? Who's your backup? Or are you a superhero?"

He chuckled at her audacity. "If anything unforeseen should happen to me, my attorney will step in."

"I'm sure you pay him very well," she said.

"I do."

"Not everyone has that luxury," she said.

"It's not a luxury. It's a necessity," he said. "And I'll require it as part of the business plan."

"I'm her backup," she said, lifting her chin again. "That's settled."

"In this case, I will need an additional backup," he said.

"Why?" she asked. "I'm trained and dependable and completely committed."

"I have another job for you," he said, watching her carefully. He thought about Bella far too often. The images of the night they shared together burned through his mind like a red-hot iron. Plus there was something in her eyes that clicked with him. Her effect on him was a mystery. Once he solved that mystery, he would be free.

"What?" she demanded. "I need to help my aunt. There's nothing more important."

"You'll be able to help her. I won't demand all your time," he said. "But as part of the deal, you and I will continue the affair we started a month ago."

Her jaw dropped in shock. "You're joking, aren't you?"

"I told you there would be a cost to both you and your aunt. Can you honestly tell me that you didn't enjoy that night we shared?"

Her cheeks turned pink with the color that damned her protest. She looked away.

"You and I have a lot in common," he said. "And it translates physically. I can give you something you need and you give me something I want." He wouldn't use the word need. He would never be that vulnerable.

"I would feel like a prostitute," she whispered.

"The drama isn't necessary," he said in a dry voice. "I want you. If you'll admit it, you want me, too. I can give you things you need. I can help take care of your aunt, but I want something in return. What's wrong with that?"

She closed her eyes, her dark eyelashes providing a fan of mystery. One. Two. Three seconds later, she opened her eyes and stared at him. "What's wrong with that? Everything."

Three

"Think it over," Bella muttered, repeating Michael's parting words. She was so frustrated she could scream. In fact, she had done just that in the privacy of her Volkswagen Beetle.

Spotting her favorite coffee shop, she squeezed her vehicle into a small space alongside the curb and scooted inside the shop. The scent of fresh coffee and baked goods wafted over her, making her mouth water. A half second later, she was hit with a double shot of nostalgia and pain. She and Stephen, her ex-fiancé, had spent many hours here. She glanced in the direction of their favorite booth in the corner next to the window, perfect for the times they'd spent talking about the future they would share.

The hurt she'd tried to escape slid past her defenses. During her time in Europe, Bella had not only missed out on helping her Aunt Charlotte when she'd needed her most, she'd also lost the only man she'd ever loved.

Pushing past the feeling of loss that never seemed to go away, Bella decided this was a perfect occasion for a cupcake and vanilla latte. She slid into a seat next to the window and took a bite off the top of the cupcake.

Michael had made an impossible offer. Although she had known it would be a longshot for him to give her aunt another chance with the spa business, she'd been certain he wouldn't solicit her again. Reason number one was that she'd turned him down after the night they'd shared. Reason number two was she couldn't believe he would still be that interested in her. A man like Michael could have just about any woman he wanted. So why would he want her?

She would be lying if she said she hadn't thought about the hot night they'd shared. It was branded in her memory, but she'd known it was a mistake the next morning. Her body may have responded to Michael, but she knew her heart still belonged to Stephen. Her heart would always belong to Stephen.

The stress the distance had created had just been too much. Stephen had been unbearably lonely and losing his job had been too much. She remembered the day he'd called her to tell her he hadn't intended to fall in love with someone else. His voice had broken and she could hear his remorse even from all those miles away. He'd fought it, but he'd told her he'd realized he'd needed someone who needed him as much as he needed her.

So, Bella had not only let her aunt down, she'd also let down the love of her life. A bitter taste filled her mouth. Bella had spent her lifetime determined not to be anything like her undependable mother, a woman who'd dumped her on Charlotte. Her mother had been known for disappearing during difficult times. Bella refused to be that person who couldn't be counted on, yet in one year, she'd failed to be there for the people she loved most.

Overwhelmed by the disappointment she felt in herself, she closed her eyes for a long moment and took a deep breath. There had to be a way she could still help Aunt Charlotte. Some other way….

"Bella," a familiar male voice said, and she opened her eyes. Her stomach clenched at the sight of Stephen and a lovely blond woman.

"Stephen," she said, thinking that he and the woman with him looked like a matched pair. Both had blonde hair, blue eyes. And they glowed with love. A knot of loss tightened in her throat. "It's good to see you."

He nodded then glanced at the woman beside him. "Bella, this is Britney Kensington. She is—" He seemed to falter.

The awkwardness seemed to suck the very breath from her lungs, but she was determined not to let it show. "It's nice to meet you, Britney," she said.

Britney smiled brightly, and based on her expression, Bella concluded that the woman hadn't a clue that she and Stephen had been romantically involved. "My pleasure. What Stephen was trying to say was I am his fiancée." She lifted her left hand to flash a diamond ring.

Bella felt the knife twist inside her. She'd known Stephen had fallen in love, but she hadn't known he was officially engaged. Somewhere in her heart, a door shut.

Although she'd mentally accepted that she'd lost Stephen, there must have been some small part of her that had hoped there was still a chance. This was solid proof that there was no chance for her and Stephen. No chance at all.

Bella cleared her throat. "Your ring is beautiful. Congratulations to both of you." She glanced at her watch. "Oh my goodness, I've lost track of the time. I need to run. It was good seeing you," she said and pulled on her coat. Grabbing her latte and scooping up the half-eaten cupcake, she dumped them into the trash. She wouldn't be able to choke down one more bite.

"Bella," Stephen said, his handsome face creased in concern. "How is your aunt?"

"Growing stronger every day," she said. "She's completed her treatment and everything looks good."

"Please tell her I send my best," he said.

"Thank you. I'll do that. Bye now," she said, and forced her lips into a pleasant smile before she walked out of the coffee shop.

Bella spent the afternoon waitressing at the restaurant. Despite the popularity of the place, the lunch crowd had been light, giving her too much of an opportunity to brood over her aunt's situation.

After work, she picked up a take-out meal of chicken soup and a club sandwich to take to Charlotte, in hopes of boosting her aunt's energy level. Walking into the small, cozy home, Bella found Charlotte propped on the sofa with her eyes closed while a game show played on the television.

Charlotte still wore the dark shoes and black clothing from her current job as a stylist at a salon. Her hair, previously her shining glory as she changed styles and colors with each season, now covered her head with a short brown and gray fuzz.

Despite cosmetic concealer, violet smudges of weariness showed beneath her eyes. Her eyelids fluttered and she glanced up at Bella, her lips lifting in a smile. "Look at you. You brought me food again. You're trying to make me fat," she complained as she sat up and patted the sofa for Bella to join her.

"This way you don't have to fix it. You can just eat it. Would you like to eat here or in the kitchen?"

"Here is fine," Charlotte said and Bella pulled out a TV tray.

"What would you like to drink?" Bella asked.

"I can get it myself," Charlotte said and started to rise.

"I'm already up," Bella argued. "Water, soda, tea?"

"Hot tea," Charlotte said and shook her head. "You fuss over me too much."

"Not at all," Bella said as she put the tea kettle on in the adjoining kitchen. "If I'd known what you were going through, I would have come back to help you with your treatments."

"You needed that trip. You'd earned it. I can take care of myself," Charlotte insisted as Bella brought her the cup of tea.

"I would have made it easier for you," Bella said, sitting next to the woman who had raised her. "I could have helped with the business."

Charlotte sighed. "Well, I overestimated my stamina, and losing the spas has been a hard pill to swallow. But I did the best I could. You have to stop taking responsibility for things that you can't control."

"But—"

"Really," Charlotte said sharply then her face

softened. "You can't spend your life trying to be the polar opposite of your mother. You've worked hard, earned your degree in college, did rescue work overseas. Now it's time for you to enjoy your life, do what you want to do. You've got to stop worrying about me."

Bella bit her tongue, but nothing her aunt said made her feel one bit less responsible. How was it fair that Bella had lived her dream when her aunt had lost hers? It just wasn't right. If there was a way to make it up to Charlotte, she should do it.

Unable to sleep, Bella racked her brain for any possibilities. She'd already approached several banks and been turned down flat. Her only hope was Michael Medici.

The mere thought of him gave her shivers. That didn't stop her, however, from calling his assistant to make an appointment to meet him at his office. Luckily, or not, she was told Michael would meet her that afternoon. It would be tight since she was scheduled to work the evening shift at the restaurant, but she knew she needed to do this as soon as possible before she talked herself out of it.

Shoring up her courage, she strode into his office when his assistant gave her the go-ahead. He stood as she entered and with her heart pounding in her ears, she met his gaze. "I'll take the deal."

He raised his eyebrow and nodded.

"With conditions," she added.

His dark gaze turned inscrutable. "What conditions?" he asked in a velvet voice.

"That we set a time limit for our—" She floundered for the right word. "Involvement."

"Agreed. One year," he said. "After that time, you and I can determine if we want to continue."

She gave a quick nod. "And my aunt is never ever to know that I agreed to this in order for her to get her business."

"You have my word," he said.

She wanted more than his word. She wanted a document signed in blood, preferably his.

Her expression must have revealed her doubt because he gave a cynical chuckle. "You'll know you can count on my word soon enough."

"There are other things we need to work out. Is this going to be totally secret? Are we supposed to pretend that we're just acquaintances?"

"We can negotiate that later. I'll expect you to be exclusive."

"And what about you?" she asked.

He lifted his eyebrows again then allowed his gaze to fall over her. "Based on our experience in bed, I think you'll be able to take care of my appetite."

Bella felt a surprising rush of heat race through her. How did the man generate so much excitement without even touching her? She glanced at her watch and cleared her throat. "Okay, I think we've covered the basics. I need to get to work."

"You can quit the restaurant," he said without batting an eye.

"No, I can't. I need the extra money to help my aunt," she said.

"Now, now," he said. "You'll be busy helping her at the spa. Your nights belong to me."

Three days later, Michael was working late as usual when his cell phone rang. *Bella,* he saw from the caller ID and picked up. "This is a surprise."

"I got off a little early. I've worked the last few nights." She hesitated a half beat. "I gave my notice."

"Where are you?" he asked.

"In the parking lot of your office," she said breathlessly.

Michael felt an immediate surge of arousal. During every spare minute he'd thought about Bella, her body, her response, the sound of her voice, her violet eyes filled with passion. "I'll be down in a couple minutes," he said.

Wrapping up his work and turning off his laptop, he strode downstairs, a sense of eagerness running through him like white lightning. He didn't know why this woman affected him so much, but he'd decided not to question it and enjoy her. Every inch of her.

He walked outside and saw the lights from her Volkswagen flicker, guiding him to her vehicle. He opened the door and allowed himself the luxury of looking at her from head to toe. After all, for the next year, she was his.

Still dressed in her white shirt and black skirt from work, she gazed at him with trepidation, her white teeth biting the side of her upper lip. Her hands clasped the steering wheel in a white-knuckle grip.

"Hi," he said.

"Hi," she said and seemed to hold her breath. "I wasn't sure when I was supposed to start."

He couldn't quite swallow a chuckle at her tension. She glanced at him in consternation.

"Why don't we just start with dinner at my place?" he asked.

"Now?"

He nodded. "What do you want?"

She blinked and paused a long moment. "A hot fudge sundae and sparkling wine."

"That can be arranged," he said. "Would you like to ride in my car or follow—"

"Follow," she said, her grip tightening on the steering wheel. "I'll follow you."

On the way home, he called his housekeeper and ordered filet mignon for two, baked potatoes, a hot fudge sundae and a bottle of Cristal champagne. Driving through the guarded entrance to his subdivision, he glanced at his rearview mirror to make sure Bella made it through.

He pulled his Viper into his garage, got out and motioned for her to pull into the space on the other side of his SUV.

He watched her step out of her Volkswagen. Despite the wariness on her face, he remembered how she'd felt in his arms that night. She was a lot more trouble than any of his other lovers had been, but she was worth it. He took her arm and guided her up the stairs into the house.

She glanced around as if she were taking in every detail. Michael was usually so intent on a project or task that he barely noticed his surroundings.

"It's beautiful. Sophisticated, but comfortable," she said as they approached the large den with a cathedral ceiling and gas fireplace already lit. She glanced at him. "Do you have it on a timer?"

He shook his head. "My housekeeper took care of it. You act as if you've never seen my house before."

She bit her lip and gave a half smile. "I guess I was a little distracted the last time I was here."

Her grudging confession sent a sharp twist of challenge through him. She had been honey in his hands and he would seduce her to the same softness again. But she was still tense, so he would need to take it slow. "You mentioned something about a hot fudge sundae. Would you like a steak first?"

Her eyes widened and she sniffed the air. "I thought I smelled something cooking. How did you manage that so quickly?"

He shrugged. "Just like I said: A simple call to my housekeeper. Would you like to dine by the fire?"

"That would be lovely," she said.

He nodded. "Let me take your coat."

She met his gaze and slowly removed her coat, her eyes full of reservation over the loss of even one article of clothing. She glanced away and brushed her hands together as she moved toward the fire.

"I'll change clothes and be back down in a minute. Make yourself comfortable."

Two glasses of champagne, filet and baked potato later, Bella felt herself loosen up slightly. She was still tense, still wondered how their arrangement was going to work.

"So, tell me your life story," he said with a slight upturn of his mouth that was incredibly seductive.

"You know my aunt's situation," she said, taking a sip of water.

"What about your parents?"

"Never knew my father, although I'm told he and my mother were briefly married after a Vegas wedding," she said. "My mother left me with Aunt Charlotte when I was two." Rationally, she knew she was lucky she'd been given to Charlotte. Deep inside though, every once in a while, she wondered why she hadn't been enough for her mother to want to keep her and for her father to at least want to know her.

"So your aunt raised you," he said. "That's why

you're so devoted to her. You glossed over that the night we were together."

She nodded. "It requires an extended explanation. My Aunt Charlotte has always been there for me whenever I needed her. My mother wasn't cut out for mothering. She moved out to California and sent money to Charlotte every now and then. She came to visit me twice—once when I was six and the last time when I was twelve."

"Do you talk to her now?"

"She died a couple years ago."

"We have that in common," he said. "My father was killed when my brothers and I were very young."

"You told me that. I think that was part of what made me feel at ease with you. You mentioned something about one of your brothers dying with him, but you didn't say who had raised the rest of you."

"Foster care for all of us. Separate homes."

She winced. "That had to have been difficult."

"It could have been worse," he said with a shrug. "Each of us turned out successfully. In my case, I spent my teenage years in a group home and was lucky enough to have a mentor."

"Do you see your brothers now?"

"Sometimes. Not on a regular basis. We're all busy."

"Hmm. You need a tradition."

"Why is that?"

"A tradition forces you to get together. My aunt does this with my cousins and relatives at least twice a year. Once at Christmas, then during the summer for barbecue and games weekend."

"Does shooting pool count?"

"It can. Good food helps."

"Oh yeah? Junk food works for us. Buffalo wings, pizza. Maybe with both my brothers married, the women will try to civilize us."

"Maybe so," she said. "I hear marriage can do that sometimes with men."

"I guess I'll always be uncivilized, then because I don't plan to ever get married."

His flat statement comforted her in a bizarre way. After her breakup with Stephen, she couldn't imagine giving another man her heart, if she even had a heart to give. She lifted her glass and met his gaze. "That makes two of us."

Four

Michael held her gaze for a long moment then pulled her toward him. "I've been watching your mouth all night," he said and lowered his lips to hers.

An unexpected sigh eased out of her. His mouth was warm, firm yet soft and addictive. She wanted to taste him, taste all of him. He fascinated her with his confidence, power and intuitiveness.

She lifted her hands to run her fingers through his wavy hair. A half breath later, he pulled her into his lap and devoured her mouth. The chemistry between them was taut and combustible. Every time he slid his tongue over hers, she felt something inside her twist tighter.

He slid his hands to her shoulders then lower to her breasts. Her nipples stood against her shirt, taut and needy. He rubbed them with his thumbs, drawing them into tight orbs. She felt a corresponding twist in her nether regions.

"You feel so good," he muttered against her mouth. "I have to have you again."

His voice rumbled through her, making her heart pound. He slanted his mouth against hers, taking her more fully. She craved the sensation of his mouth and tongue. His need salved a hollow place deep inside her.

She felt his hands move to the center of her white shirt. A tugging sensation followed and cool air flowed over her bare chest. His lips still holding hers, he dipped his thumbs into the cups of her bra, touching her nipples.

She gasped at the sensation.

"Good?" he murmured. "Do you want more? I can give it to you."

She felt herself grow liquid beneath his caresses. Each stroke of his thumb made her more restless. He skimmed one of his hands down the side of her waist then to the front of her skirt.

"It's a damn shame you're wearing tights," he said.

A shiver raced through her at his sexy complaint.

"I think it's time for us to go to my room," he said.

Suddenly, as if the room turned upside down, it hit her that this would be the beginning of the deal. She froze. He stood and pulled her to her feet.

She stared at him, struck with the awful feeling of being at his mercy. Unable to keep herself from breathing hard, she closed her eyes and told herself it would be okay. It was just sex. Since she'd lost the man she really loved, it would only ever be…sex.

"Bella," he said, his hand cupping her chin. "Look at me."

She swallowed hard over her conflicting emotions and opened her eyes, catching his gaze for several heart-twisting beats.

He gave a sigh and a grimace then slid his hand down to capture hers. "You've had a busy day, haven't you?"

"Yes, I have."

He nodded. "You should get some rest," he said and led her out of the den.

"Where—"

"I have a room for you," he said. "Let the house-keeper know if you need anything. Her name is Trena."

"But I thought," she said, confused by the change of plans.

He stopped in front of a door and looked down at her. "I've never had to force a woman. I'm not about to start now."

She bit her upper lip with her bottom teeth. "This is new for me. I haven't done anything like this before."

"Neither have I," he said and lifted his eyebrow in a combination of amusement and irony. "Don't count on me being patient for long. No one has ever accused me of letting the grass grow under my feet. I'll send Trena in to check on you in a few minutes. Good night."

Bella put her face in her hands after he closed the door. Shocked, she shook her head and glanced around the bedroom. Furnished in sea-blues and greens, the soft tones of the room immediately took her anxiety down several notches. Flanked by windows covered with airy curtains, a large comfortable-looking bed beckoned from the opposite wall. A large painting of an ocean scene hung above the bed, making her wonder if Michael enjoyed the sea as much as she did.

The bed stand held a collection of books, a small sea-shell lamp and a tray for a late-night snack. A long cherry bureau with a small padded chair occupied another. The room had clearly been furnished with comfort in mind.

She walked into the connecting bath and almost drooled. Marble double sinks, a large Jacuzzi tub, shower that would easily accommodate two and flowering plants. Much nicer than her one-bedroom apartment.

Don't get used to it, she warned herself.

A knock sounded on the door and Bella opened it to a competent-looking woman dressed in black slacks and a white shirt. "Miss St. Clair. I'm Trena, one of Mr. Medici's staff. Welcome. Please tell me what I can do to make your stay more comfortable."

Bella glanced around. "I can't think of anything. The room is wonderful."

Trena nodded. "Good. There's water, wine, beer and soda in the mini bar along with some snacks. There's a fresh bathrobe hanging in the closet and toiletries in the bathroom."

"Thank you. Oh, I just realized I don't have pajamas," Bella said. She hadn't been sure whether she would be staying the night or not. "Perhaps a T-shirt?"

"No problem."

"Again, thank you. I'll just go get my change of clothing from my car."

"If you'll give me the keys, I can do that for you," Trena offered.

"Oh, no," she protested. "I can do that myself."

Trena looked offended. "Please allow me. Mr. Medici emphasized that he wants you to relax. It's my job and I take pride in doing a good job."

She blinked at the woman's firm tone. "Okay, thank you."

"My pleasure. I'll be back in just a moment."

Wow, Bella thought. The woman brought service to a new level. She shouldn't be surprised. Michael Medici would employ only the best and probably paid very well. Stifling a nervous chuckle, she envisioned Trena shaking her finger at her and saying, *"You must relax."*

Just moments later, Trena returned with Bella's tote bag of clothes she always kept in the back of her car in case she wanted to change before or after work at the restaurant. She also brought her a soft extra-large T-shirt. Staring at a painting of a pink shell on the wall, she wondered about Michael.

What kind of man would make a deal to bail out her aunt in exchange for an affair with her?

Who was she to cast stones? After all, what kind of woman would accept his offer?

She thought it would take forever to fall asleep so she picked up a book on the nightstand, a thriller. Seven hours later, she awakened to the smell of fresh-brewed coffee with the thriller on her chest.

Shaking her head, she quickly realized she wasn't in her own bed. Her sheets weren't this soft, her mattress not so…perfect. Scrambling out of bed, she pulled on her clothes and splashed water on her face and brushed her teeth and hair. And added lip gloss.

Calm, calm, she told herself and walked into the kitchen.

A bald, black man standing next to the coffeemaker looked up at her. "Miss St. Clair?"

She nodded. "Yes."

His mouth stretched into a wide grin of reassur-

ance. "Pleasure to meet you. I'm Sam. Mr. Medici instructed me to fix your breakfast. Would you like a
cappuccino?"

"It's nice to meet you, too, Sam. There's no need for
you to fix my breakfast."

Sam's smile fell. "My instructions are to feed you a
good breakfast. I wish to do as he instructed."

Geez, Michael sure had his staff trained. "I'm not
really hungry…."

"But a cappuccino? Latte?"

She sighed, not entirely comfortable with others
serving her to such a degree. "Latte, thank you. Where
is Mr. Medici?"

Sam chuckled. "Long gone. That man rises before
the sun. Very rarely does he sleep late. He left a note
for you," he said and held out an envelope. "Would you
like oatmeal pancakes? I make very good pancakes."

She smiled at his gentle, persuasive tone. "Sold." She
opened the envelope and read the handwritten three-line
note. *Bring your aunt to my office at 9:00 a.m. for a planning meeting tomorrow morning. Enjoy Sam's pancakes.
Looking forward to our next night together. Michael.*

Her heart rose to her throat. He was sticking to his
part. She would need to meet her end of the deal, too.
Pancakes? How could she possibly?

"I have pure maple syrup, too," Sam said.

Bella took a deep breath and sighed. What the hell.
"Why not."

One day later, she took her aunt to meet Michael. Still
bracing herself for the possibility that Michael would back
out, she just told Charlotte that they were meeting
someone for a special business consultation. Although

Charlotte pounded her with questions, Bella remained vague.

"I wish you would tell me what this is about," Charlotte said, adjusting her vivid pink suit as the elevator climbed to the floor of MM, Inc.

"You'll know soon enough," Bella said, adjusting her own black jacket. The elevator dinged their arrival and Bella led the way to Michael's office.

"How do you know this man?"

"I met him through my job," Bella said.

"At a bar?" Charlotte asked.

"He's the owner," Bella explained then pushed open the door to the office. She lifted her lips into a smile for Michael's assistant. "Hi. Bella St. Clair and Charlotte Ambrose to see Mr. Medici."

His assistant nodded. "He's expecting you." She announced their arrival and waved toward his office door. "Please, go ahead in."

Charlotte cast Bella a suspicious glance. "What have you gotten me into?"

"It's good," Bella promised as they walked toward the door and she pushed it open. "But I think it would be better for Mr. Medici to talk about it."

Michael rose to meet them. "Bella," he said. "Ms. Ambrose. It's good to meet you," he said to Charlotte. "Bella has told me so much about you, but she didn't tell me what a lovely woman you are."

Charlotte accepted his handshake and slid a sideways glance at Bella. "Thank you. I wish I could say the same about her telling me about you."

Michael gave a chuckle. "I'm sure she was just trying to protect you. Let's sit down and talk about the business plan for your spa."

Charlotte stopped cold. "Excuse me? I lost my spa business to the bank."

Michael glanced at Bella and made a tsk-ing sound. "You really did keep her in the dark, didn't you?"

Charlotte frowned. "I would appreciate an explanation."

"The bank took over your business and I bought it. After discussions with Bella, I've made the decision to finance and codirect a relaunch of one Charlotte's Signature Spa."

Charlotte stared at him in amazement. "Codirect?" she echoed. "Relaunch?"

He nodded. "Yes. Let me show you the plan."

Over the next hour, Bella watched her aunt's demeanor change from doubt to hope and excitement. By the end of the meeting, Bella knew she had made the right choice in helping her. The illness and loss of her business had robbed Charlotte of her natural drive and optimism.

"I can't tell you how grateful I am for this opportunity. Your backing means—" Charlotte glanced back and forth between Michael and Bella, her eyes filling with tears. "Oh, no. I'm going to embarrass myself. Please excuse me for a moment," she said, standing. "Could you tell me where the powder room is?"

Concerned, Bella followed her aunt to her feet. "Charlotte?"

Michael also rose and Charlotte waved her hand. "No. You stay here. I just need a moment to compose myself."

"The restroom is in the outer office," Michael said and Charlotte left his office. "Is she okay?" he asked Bella.

Full of her own overwhelming emotion, Bella wrapped her arms around her waist and nodded. "She's stunned. She'd lost all hope of rebuilding her business. I probably should have at least given her a hint, but I didn't want her to be disappointed if—" She paused, meeting his intent gaze. "If things didn't work out."

"Why wouldn't they? I gave you my word, didn't I?"

"Yes, you did," she said, and felt something inside her twist and knot at his expression. He would have her again. She felt it and knew it, just as he did.

"I'll meet you at my house tonight," he said, his voice low.

Awareness and anticipation rippled through Bella. "It will be late," she said. "I have to work."

Michael frowned in impatience. The door to his office burst open and Charlotte strode inside with a smile on her face and a new sparkle in her eye. "When do we start?"

Michael laughed. "Bella told me you were a fireball. She also indicated that you already have a job, so as soon as you give notice we can move ahead."

"I don't need to wait," Charlotte argued. "I can work when my job is done for the day."

He shook his head firmly. "I don't want you to overdo."

"But—"

"It's not just bad for your health. It's bad for business," Michael said. "What we want to create is an environment of success that won't put too much stress on Bella or you. We want to move at a reasonable pace, not lightning."

"He's right," Bella said, admiring Michael's approach with both her aunt and the business. "And since I'll be working with you for at least this first year, I'll be able to tell if you're doing too much."

Charlotte shook her head. "You worry too much

about me. You're young. You should be pursuing your own career goals. I'm fine."

"I'm more than happy to do this with you," Bella said. "It will be an adventure."

"Yes," Michael said. "An excellent way of looking at it. An adventure."

By the expression in his eyes, however, Bella suspected he wasn't talking about the spa.

That night after work, Bella tamped down her feelings of apprehension and got into her car to drive to Michael's house. Using the rhythm of the windshield wipers as a cadence, she talked herself into calm confidence. Succeeding until the coughs and sputters of her ordinarily reliable Volkswagen jarred her out of it. "No, no, no," she murmured. She pressed on the gas and her car stalled.

Flustered, she tried to start it again and the engine coughed to life. Relief washed over her and she made it several more yards before the car shuddered again, refusing to restart. Something was clearly wrong. It revved to feeble life briefly and she managed to pull it on to the side of the road.

She got out of the car to stare at a bunch of hoses, boxes and wires under the hood. It could have been run by squirrels for all she knew. The cold rain poured over her head, drenching her jacket.

Sighing, she got back in the car and reviewed her options. She'd neglected to renew her car service since she'd returned from overseas, so her customer number was now defunct. She refused to call her aunt and bother her at this late hour. Reluctantly, she accepted her last choice and tried to dial Michael's cell number.

Her cell phone, however, gave her the impudent message. No service.

Damn. Maybe someone was trying to tell her something. That she'd best try to find a way out of her arrangement with Michael.

Bella leaned her head against the side window of her car, recalling the joy on her aunt's face when she'd learned she would get a second chance with her business. That was worth everything. A deal was a deal.

The rain appeared to have slowed down, and if she remembered correctly, Michael's gated subdivision was only about a mile from here. Walking alone at night wasn't the best choice for a woman, but she didn't want to stay in her car all night either. Either choice meant danger.

Five

Michael narrowed his eyes as he glanced at his watch. Bella wasn't going to show. He should have known that her wide eyes hid deceit. She'd tricked him into believing she would accept his deal and now she wanted out. Two nights ago, he'd been certain she'd just been nervous. Now, he wasn't sure. A bitter taste filled his mouth. What she didn't understand was that he could still pull the plug on her aunt's spa.

His cell phone rang, distracting him. The number on the caller ID was unfamiliar. "Hello," he said.

"Mr. Medici?" a man said.

"Yes, this is Michael Medici."

"This is Frank Borne, security for the neighborhood. I hate to bother you, but there's a woman here who says she knows you and she needs a ride to your house."

"What?" Michael asked.

He gave a half chuckle. "Poor thing is drenched. I'd drive her to your house myself, but I'm not supposed to leave the gatehouse."

"I'll be right there," he said, wondering what in hell had happened. Although he could have sent one of his staff to collect *the woman* whom he was sure was Bella, he preferred to handle this task himself. He turned on his windshield wipers to fight off the downpour as he drove the short distance to the gatehouse.

As soon as he pulled next to the small building, Bella dashed out. He flipped the locks and she plopped into the passenger seat. Her dark hair was plastered to her scalp, her huge violet eyes a stark contrast against her pale skin, her plum-colored lips pursed into a frown.

"What—"

She lifted her hand and shook her head. "You have no idea what I've been through to get here tonight. If I believed in heebie-jeebie kind of stuff, I would think someone was trying to tell me not to come to your house. My car stalled out on me just after I got off the interstate. My car service is defunct because I forgot to renew it. But it wouldn't have helped anyway because my cell phone said *No Service* every time I tried to make a call. It wasn't raining that much when I first started walking—"

Appalled that she'd been wandering around alone after dark, he cut her off. "Tell me you weren't walking on Travers Road after eleven o'clock at night."

"Well, what else could I do? Flag someone down? That didn't seem like a smart idea."

Michael drove them back, grinding his teeth as she continued.

"I did take my umbrella, but it was useless against this wind. I misjudged the distance a bit."

He pulled to a stop in the garage. "This won't be happening again," he said, surprised at the intensity of his protectiveness for her. He hadn't known her long enough to feel this way.

"Lord, I hope not," she said, rolling her eyes.

The way his gut clenched irritated the hell out of him. He swore. There was only one solution. "I'm getting you a new cell phone and service and new car," he said and got out of the car.

He opened her car door to find her gaping at him. "New car," she echoed. "You're crazy. I love my VW. It's never given me any trouble," she said then corrected herself. "Until tonight."

"Stranding you at night on Travers Road is enough of a reason to replace your car. Do you realize what could have happened to you?" She looked like a drowned little girl. Resisting the urge to pick her up and carry her, he extended his hand to her and led her into the house. "I'll send one of my staff to take care of your car. Do you need anything out of it?"

"I left an overnight bag in the backseat, but about a new car, I can't let you—"

He lifted his hand to cut her off as he pulled his BlackBerry out of his pocket and punched a number. "Jay, I need you to arrange for a tow—a VW on Travers. I'll leave the key on the table in the foyer." He extended his palm for Bella to give him the key. "There should be an overnight bag inside. Just drop it in the foyer. Thanks," he said and turned to her. "Now, I want you to take a hot shower." He glanced at the time on his BlackBerry. "You've got two minutes."

"To shower?" she said, her eyes round with surprise.

"Until I join you," he countered.

He hadn't thought it possible, but her eyes widened even more. "Oh," she managed, her lips forming a tempting circle of invitation. She stood as if her feet were superglued to the floor.

"Bella," he said gently.

"Yes?"

"You're down to one minute forty-five seconds."

She turned and flew down the hall.

Prying off the wet garments that clung to her as she entered the bedroom, Bella snapped her chattering teeth together. She raced to the bathroom to turn on the jets to the shower and wondered what Michael would have done if she'd said she didn't want a shower. It would have been a lie, of course. This wasn't how she'd pictured the consummation of their bargain.

Telling herself to stop thinking, she jumped into the shower and closed her eyes, treasuring the few seconds she would enjoy alone under the spray.

Sure enough, the shower door opened behind her and she felt a shot of cool air before she heard Michael's feet step on to the wet tile. He would be totally naked. The memory of his strong, male body made her pulse race.

"Is the water warm enough?"

She nodded, focusing on the tile wall in front of her.

"Want me to wash your back?"

She opened her mouth to say she could do it herself, but his hands on her bare skin stopped her. He massaged her shoulders and neck, making her relax despite herself. He skimmed his hands down the outside of her arms then back up along the inside. The sensation was both soothing and erotic. The warm water washed away her resistance.

"Not so bad, is it?" he asked.

"No, it's…" She took a deep breath.

He continued to touch her, sliding his hands over the sides of her waist and down over her hips. A slow drag of want pulled through her, starting below her skin and fanning out. Although he hadn't touched them, her breasts grew heavy and her nipples tightened.

Surprise slid through her. How was it so easy for him to turn her nerves into arousal? Must've been the shower, she thought. Not the man. But then he guided her around to face him, pushed her wet hair from her face and brushed his lips over her cheeks. With the water streaming down on them, he took her mouth and her pulse spiked again. Her eyelids fluttering against the shower drops, she caught flashes of his body, his broad shoulders and slick, tanned skin. Another flash, his flat abdomen and hard erection.

She moved closer to him and heard his breath hitch when her naked body slid against his. "I've wanted you since that night we spent together." He slid his tongue past her lips and a primitive yearning beat like a drum inside her.

There were all kinds of reasons she shouldn't want him. This was just supposed to be sex, but for some reason, it felt like more. She felt protected and desired at the same time. She couldn't remember feeling this sensual even with…

Michael lifted his hands to her breasts, short-circuiting her brain. Half a breath later, he lowered his head and took her wet nipples into his mouth. The sight and sensation was so erotic she couldn't look away. He slid lower still and kissed her intimately. Her knees turned to liquid.

"Wrap your legs around me," he said in a low voice. Catching her against him, he picked her up, turned off the water and carried her out of the shower. He grabbed a couple of plush towels folded on a small bathroom table and pulled one around her as he strode into the darkened bedroom.

He put her on the bed and followed her down, his eyes plundering her the way she suspected he planned to plunder her body. A shiver of anticipation raced through her.

"Cold?" he asked.

She nodded, reaching up to stroke a drop of water from his forehead. He captured her hand and lifted it to his mouth. "I can get you warm," he promised and slid his hand down between her legs where he found her swollen.

His fingers sent her in a sudden spiral upward. Unable to contain her response, she arched upward.

He growled at her response and pushed her thighs apart. In one thrust, he filled her to the brim.

Bella gasped, feeling her body shake and tremble around him. She clung to him as he stroked her in her most secret place. Her breath meshed with his and her climax ripped through her like a lightning bolt. A second later, she felt Michael stiffen, groaning in release.

A full moment passed and Bella began to understand why she'd been so hesitant about becoming Michael's lover. He had just taken full possession of her mind and body, and that made him a very dangerous man.

After a full night of lovemaking, Michael awakened refreshed. Still out like a light, Bella sprawled stomach down on his bed. Smiling to himself, he wouldn't bother her this morning. She'd had a rough night in more ways than one.

He left the bed and went to his in-house gym down the hall. He did the elliptical and followed up with weights. Working out was just one more way of staying strong and focused for Michael. Like his brothers, he never wanted to be at the mercy of any person or circumstance. He returned to his suite to take a shower. Bella still slept soundly. After dressing, he went downstairs and read *The Wall Street Journal* as he ate the breakfast his staff prepared for him.

Just as he stood to leave, Bella stumbled into the kitchen, dressed in a bathrobe too large for her and pushed her mussed hair from her face. She tugged at the lapels of the robe and stared at him. "It's not even six o'clock," she said. "How long have you been up?"

"Since just before five," he said with a shrug. "How are you?"

"Four something," she said, aghast. "After the night we—" She paused and lowered her voice. "We had you get up at four in the morning?"

"Well, I didn't walk a mile in the rain," he pointed out, amused by the consternation on her face. "But I don't require a lot of sleep," he said and walked toward her, giving into the urge to slide his fingers over her hair. Soft hair, soft body, mysterious eyes that tugged at something deep inside him.

She met his gaze and pressed her lips together. "Oh, well, heaven help me then. I have to tell you that I'm not accustomed to the degree and amount and—" She shook her head.

"Don't worry. You'll get used to it," he joked. He

glanced at his watch. "I need to go. Make yourself at home. The staff will be happy to prepare anything you want to eat. Here is the key to a new Lexus. I think you'll find it reliable," he said and lifted her hand to press the key into her palm.

"I told you I don't want a new car," she said.

Her resistance amused him. Most women he'd dated would have been thrilled to receive a new car. In fact, a few had hinted that a luxury vehicle would be the perfect gift for any occasion. The only thing better, of course, would have been an engagement ring, and that would never have happened. "I've leased it for you. Since yours is in the shop, you need something to drive. Oh, and I'd like for you to move in."

He turned and walked toward the door.

"I don't think that's a good idea," she said as his hand touched the doorknob.

Surprised by her response, he turned around. "Why not?"

"Because then people might find out that we're involved. I don't want to have to explain our arrangement."

He felt a crackle of impatience. "I make it a policy to never explain myself."

"Yeah, well, I'm not you. Aunt Charlotte will expect an explanation from me. I never know when she'll start with her mother hen routine, even now."

Irritation nicked at him. "We'll see," he said, turning around to look at her. "In the meantime, bring some of your clothes and belongings here for convenience sake."

"Do you order everyone around like this?" she asked, crossing her arms over her chest.

"I'm decisive. I see a logical course of action and take it," he said.

"Part of your charm?" she said, a gently mocking smile playing on her lips. "What's logical about your arrangement with me?"

"I want you, and you might not want to admit it, but you want me, too. I just figured out a way to make it happen," he said, still uncomfortable with the intensity of his desire for her and the way she affected him. He had broken some of his rules to get her out of his system. He knew his response to her wouldn't last. Nothing was forever.

Since Bella was scheduled off from the restaurant, she went to her aunt's house to begin getting ready for the grand reopening. Michael had mapped out an action plan with a target date just weeks away. Inventory needed to be ordered immediately and Charlotte would want to hire staff. Bella also needed to organize customer records so they could send out a mailing. Michael had suggested several customer incentives.

His ability to detach himself emotionally bothered her. Sure, he possessed enormous insight and experience and knew how to make things happen, but she wondered how someone who seemed so cold one moment could be so hot the next.

Her skin grew warm at the memory of how passionate he'd been, how passionate she'd been. She knew his difficult childhood had made him determined not to be vulnerable, but Bella didn't believe such a thing was possible.

Pushing aside her thoughts, she dug into her tasks. Hours later, she heard the sound of the side door opening.

Charlotte looked at Bella in surprise. "It's you. I

wondered whose car that was. A Lexus? Did you win the lottery?"

Bella's cheeks heated. One more reason she should have refused the use of the car. "Lucky break," she said. "My Volkswagen broke down last night. The car I'm using is a rental."

"Lucky break, indeed," Charlotte said. "Enjoy it while you can. What are you working on?"

"I was going to do an inventory order list, but I thought I should check with you first," Bella said.

"Good thinking," Charlotte said. "I made one last night."

Concern rushed through her. She searched Charlotte's face for signs of weariness, but all she saw was a glow of anticipation. "You're still working your other job. I'm afraid you're doing too much."

Charlotte smiled. "I'm too excited to sit still. I thought I'd lost my chance. I can't wait to get everything ready to go."

Bella laughed and shook her head. "Force yourself to sit still every now and then, starting now." She led her aunt to a chair and urged her to take a seat. "Let me get you some water."

"But I don't need—"

"Yes you do," Bella insisted. "Don't try to do everything at once. I'm here to help you. Remember? Speaking of which, I've been working on a customer mailing list."

"Perfect," she said. "And I called a few of my former employees to ask if they could give me some quality employee recommendations and two of them said they wanted to come back to work for me."

"Wow, you're moving right along," Bella said, pleased with her aunt's sunny outlook.

"I am," Charlotte said. "Plus, I have an idea for providing a few men's services. We can give them *Sport* manicures and pedicures and carry sports magazines and *The Wall Street Journal.*"

"That's a great idea."

"And who knows? Maybe you'll end up going out with one of the men who come into the Spa," Charlotte said, throwing Bella a meaningful glance.

Bella immediately shook her head. "Oh, no. I'm not interested in dating right now." Or maybe ever.

"Bella, I know you were terribly hurt when you and Stephen broke up, but you can't stop living."

"I'm still living," Bella said. "I'm just not interested in going down that road. I know I'll never feel the way I did for Stephen about another man."

"You're too young to say that," Charlotte chided.

"You always said I had an old soul," Bella returned.

Charlotte pursed her lips. "I can see I'm going to need to open your eyes to all the other fish in the sea out there."

Bella shook her head again, cringing at the note of determination in her aunt's voice. Bella absolutely didn't want her romantic status on her aunt's radar at all. "Your mission is to stay healthy, be happy and get the spa off the ground."

"We'll see," Charlotte said.

Bella frowned. That was the second time today she'd heard those words.

That night, Bella joined Michael for dinner in the den again. "I really need to get my VW back," she said, pushing the gourmet meal around her plate. She felt nervous around Michael. Hyperaware of his strength and mental prowess, she found being the subject of his undivided attention disturbing.

"Why? The Lexus is much more dependable."

"When my aunt saw it, she asked me if I'd won the lottery."

Irritation crossed his face. "Can't you just tell her you decided to lease it?"

"Not on a waitress's salary," she said.

"I could give her one, too and tell her it's part of her compensation package," he mused.

So they would be even more in his debt? Bella choked. "I don't think that's necessary. I'll be happy to get my VW back."

"I'll get it back for you with the understanding that if it becomes unreliable again, it will be replaced. And if it breaks down, you're to call the emergency number I gave you."

"Okay," she said, because she would make sure the VW didn't break down again. "Now if I can just keep her focused on the spa and not matchmaking for me, then maybe—"

"Matchmaking," he echoed. "Why?"

"When my aunt isn't sick, she's a force to be reckoned with. If she decides I should be dating, then she'll do everything possible to make sure I am."

"Interfering family members. I've never had that. My brothers and I hassle each other every now and then, but we wouldn't interfere." He took a drink from his beer. "Go ahead and tell her you're involved with me."

"Absolutely not. She would freak out if she knew this deal was dependent on you and me…" She cleared her throat. "Besides, you agreed that we would keep it—"

Michael's cell phone rang, interrupting her tirade. He glanced at the caller ID and his expression turned odd. "I need to take this," he said and rose. "Dan, you have some information about Leo?"

She watched as he strode a few steps away with his broad back facing her. Something in his demeanor tripped off her antennae. His stance was tense as if he were braced.

"Damn. Nothing," he said, his voice full of disappointment. "Anything else you can do?"

The taut silence that followed swelled with raw tension. She'd never glimpsed this kind of emotion in Michael.

"Do it, and keep me posted," Michael said then turned around.

She glimpsed a flash of powerful emotion in his eyes, but it was gone before she could identify it. He narrowed his gaze and his nostrils flared as he returned to the table.

Bella vacillated over whether to keep silent, but her curiosity and a strange concern won out. "Who's Leo?"

He met her gaze with eyes that lit like flames of the devil himself. "My brother. He was with my father when he died."

Bella winced at the visual that raced through her head. "I haven't heard you say much about him. Where is he?"

"He could be dead, but we don't know for certain." He took a long draw from his beer. "His body was never found."

"How terrible," she said and gingerly put her hand on his arm. He glanced down at her hand for a long moment, making her wonder if she should pull it away. "Are you trying to find him?"

He sighed and lifted his gaze to hers. "Always. I was the one who was supposed to be travelling with my father that day. Leo was there in my place."

Her heart wrenched at the deep-seated guilt on his face. "Oh, no. You don't really blame yourself. You were just a child. You couldn't have possibly—"

He jerked his arm away. "Enough. This subject is off limits. I'm going to bed." He stood and stalked out of the room, leaving her reeling in his wake.

The depth of the grief and guilt she'd glimpsed in his eyes shook her. Michael might project himself as a self-contained man with little emotion, but she'd just seen something different. He had clearly suffered over the loss of his brother for years. Bella wondered what that must be like, to blame oneself for the loss of a brother. Absolution would be impossible for a man like Michael. She sensed that he would be harder on himself than anyone else. In this case, he didn't have resolution either.

A yawning pain stretched inside Bella. She bit her lip, glancing into the gas fire. She felt a strange instinct to comfort him, to salve the wounds of his losses. He spoke about his upbringing in a matter-of-fact way, as if the losses had been efficiently compartmentalized. But they hadn't.

"Miss St. Clair, I'm Glenda. Can I get anything for you?" a woman said from just a few feet away.

Bella looked at Glenda, still hung up on what she'd just learned about Michael. He was human after all.

"Would you like something else to eat?" Glenda asked. "Dessert?"

Unable to imagine eating another bite, Bella shook her head. "No, but thank you very much. I'll just take my dishes to the kitchen."

"Oh, no," Glenda said. "I'll do that. Are you sure there's nothing else I can do for you?"

Bella picked up her glass of wine and took a sip for fortitude. "Nothing, thank you."

Rising, she glanced in the direction of the hallway that would take her to her room and the stairway that would take her to Michael's.

Six

He heard the door to his bedroom open and the soft pad of her feet against the hardwood floor before she stepped on to the sheepskin rugs surrounding his big bed. He heard a rustle and a softly whispered oath. She must have stumbled a little.

He couldn't suppress a twist of amusement. An illicit thrill rushed through him.

Bella was coming to him.

He heard her soft intake of breath, as if she were bracing herself. Before she'd opened the door, he'd been a turbulent mass of emotion. Now, he was… curious.

She crawled on to his bed slowly. He waited, feeling a spurt of impatience. What was she going to do? When was she—

He felt her body against his. Her bare breasts brushed

his arm. Her thighs slid against his. He felt a blast of need.

She skimmed one of her hands over his shoulder and down his chest. He felt her lips against his throat and his gut clenched at the softness, the tenderness…

Rock hard with arousal, he was more comfortable with sex and passion than tenderness. "Why are you here?" he asked, clenching his hands together, biding his time.

"I—" She made a hmm sound that vibrated against his skin. "I didn't want you to be alone."

He gave a rough chuckle. "I've been alone most of my life."

"Not tonight," she said.

In a swift but smooth motion, he pulled her on top of him. He felt her breathless gasp of surprise and even in the dark, could see her wide eyes. "If this is pity sex, you may get more than you bargained for."

She paused barely a half beat. "Pity a superhero?"

He couldn't withhold another shot of amusement, but the urgency to take her again taunted him. He took her mouth in a long kiss that made her writhe against him. He began to sweat.

"Hold on," he muttered and slid his hands down the silky skin of her back and positioned her so that his aching erection was just at the entrance of her warm femininity.

She moaned and he pushed inside a little further. It took all his control, but he wanted to feel her need, her desperation. She arched against him then lowered her mouth to his; this time, she was the pursuer. Every part of her body seemed to talk to him—her skin, her hands, her hair…

Pulling away from him, she lifted backward and kept her gaze fastened on his. He forced himself to keep his eyes open as she bit her lip and slid down, taking all of him inside her.

His ability to wait shredded, he grabbed her hips and their lovemaking turned—as it had from the beginning—into a storm of passion that sated him at the same time it made him hungry for more.

After that night, the unspoken connection between her and Michael grew stronger. When she was apart from Michael, she sometimes wondered if she imagined the tie, but when she was with him, there was no doubt. It still wasn't love, she told herself. It was passion and power, but it wasn't the sweet, comforting love she'd known with Stephen.

Progress on the spa took place swiftly. It was all Bella could do to keep her aunt from working twenty-four hours a day. Getting a second chance with the spa seemed to have given Aunt Charlotte twice as much energy. Unfortunately, Charlotte wasn't budging from her so-called mission to get Bella back in action.

So far, she'd arranged for four men to stop by to meet Bella. Two of them had asked her out, but she'd demurred.

This morning, she put away inventory that had arrived in the mail and double-checked the postcards advertising the opening. Charlotte bustled around, tinkering with the decor to accommodate the new sports grooming package for men.

A knock sounded on the glass door and Bella glanced up to spot a nice-looking man in his upper twenties. A familiar dread tugged at her. *Not again.*

Charlotte rushed to the door and gave a little squeal.

"Gabriel, it's so good to see you. Come on in. Bella, please fix Gabriel some coffee. His mother is one of my longtime clients."

"It's good to see you," Gabriel said to Charlotte while Bella dutifully poured and served his coffee. "My mother insisted that I stop by."

"Cream or sugar?" Bella asked.

He shook his head. "No, thanks. Black is fine. Is Bella your daughter?"

"In every way that counts," Charlotte said. "Gabriel is a lawyer, Bella. Isn't that impressive? I bet he might want to use some of our new services for men."

"What services?" he asked, his expression wary.

"Sports manicure and pedicure. Massage," Charlotte said. "You look like you work out."

Bella tried not to roll her eyes at her aunt's obvious flattery.

"Some," he said. "I like to run."

Charlotte nodded then frowned. "Bella, I just realized you never took lunch. Maybe you and Gabriel could—"

The door swung open and Michael walked in. Bella felt her gut twist at the sight of him. This could get interesting, she thought.

"Michael, what a nice surprise," Charlotte said. "Michael is our new business partner. If it weren't for him, the spa wouldn't exist. Michael Medici, this is Gabriel Long. He's a lawyer—his office is down the street."

Michael nodded and shook Gabriel's hand. "Gabriel," he said.

"Michael Medici. I've heard your name mentioned often by my business clients."

"I was just saying that maybe Bella and Gabriel could go grab a bite," Charlotte interjected.

Michael paused a second and shot Bella a glance that seemed to say *we did it your way, now we're doing it my way.*

"I hate to interrupt, but I had planned to ask Bella to join *me* for dinner tonight," Michael said in a charming voice that almost concealed the steel underneath.

Charlotte dropped her jaw and stared at Michael then at Bella. "Oh, I didn't know you two were—"

"We're not," Bella quickly said, inwardly wincing at the lie. She glared at Michael. "I'm just as surprised as you are by the invitation."

Cool as ever, he dipped his head. "If you're hungry, then…"

An awkward silence followed where Bella refused to give up her mutinous stance.

"Of course she is," Charlotte rushed to say, then glanced at Gabriel as if she didn't know what to do with him. "I will give you a special coupon for our sports treatments," she added as she walked him to the door. "Now, you be sure and tell your mother I said hello…"

"You agreed," Bella whispered tersely to Michael.

"It was necessary. This is becoming ridiculous. Things will be easier now. Trust me," he said in a low voice.

"You don't under—" She cut herself off as Charlotte returned.

"Michael, I'm so glad to see you," Charlotte said. "I wanted to show you some of my ideas. Bella, would you help me get some things from the inventory closet?"

Upset by the latest turn of events, Bella nodded and followed her aunt to the walk-in supply closet. Charlotte immediately turned to her. "What's your problem? Michael Medici is gorgeous."

"He's not my type," Bella said.

"Gorgeous and wealthy isn't your type, plus, he's been wonderful to us. It won't hurt you to be nice to him in return," Charlotte said firmly.

"It won't?" Bella asked. Charlotte met her eyes and instantly knew what Bella was talking about.

"This is not the same situation as your mother. Get that thought out of your mind. Michael isn't married to a woman."

Bella closed her eyes, struggling with guilt and shame. "He's not Stephen."

"No, he's not," Charlotte said. "Michael Medici is a stronger man than Stephen ever was. I never was quite sure Stephen was the best match for you, anyway."

"Charlotte," Bella said in shock. "You always liked him."

"I like dogs, too. Doesn't mean I want you to marry one. Now go on out with Michael and enjoy yourself. It hurts me knowing that you aren't having any fun in your life right now. Life is short. You need to live it while you can."

Charlotte pulled out some magazines and product catalogs and put them into Bella's hands. "Here, take these."

"What are you going to tell Michael about them?"

"I'll figure out something," Charlotte said.

An hour later, Bella sat silently in Michael's Viper as he drove the luxury car. Drumming her fingers on her denim-clad thigh, she looked out the window, still upset.

"Would you like seafood?" he asked.

"It doesn't matter, but I'm not dressed for a four-star restaurant *since this was a surprise invite.*"

Michael pulled up to the valet desk at one of the more exclusive, popular restaurants he owned in the Atlanta area. "It doesn't matter how you're dressed. You're with me and this is my restaurant," he said and got out of the car.

He escorted her inside the restaurant where the host immediately greeted him. "It's good to see you, Mr. Medici. We have a corner alcove for you."

"That will be fine," he said, touching Bella's arm as they walked to the table. She was so prickly he half expected her to swat him off.

Baffled by her reaction, he shook his head. Many women he'd dated had done everything but taken out a billboard ad announcing their involvement.

"For goodness sake, why are you so cranky? You'd think I murdered one of your relatives," he said after they sat down.

"I told you that I didn't want my aunt to know about our arrangement. You agreed."

"She doesn't know about any arrangement. All she knows is that I wanted you to join me for dinner."

"We were *supposed* to keep this secret."

"That was before she started interfering in order to get you dating. Why did she get so worked up anyway?"

"She knew about my breakup. She knew the guy I was involved with and how much I—" She broke off and shook her head. "It doesn't matter. I just didn't want her to know. And *you agreed.*"

A server appeared, eager to please. He explained the evening specials. Michael ordered a whiskey double for himself and a Hurricane for Bella.

"Hurricane?" she said after the waiter left.

"It seemed to fit with your frame of mind."

Her lips twitched, albeit reluctantly.

"So tell me why you changed your mind about letting your aunt know I want to ask you out for dinner. And I want to know more about this man who you dumped after you got back from your year in Europe."

"First, I didn't dump him. He broke it off with me before I arrived home."

"Really?" he said. "What an idiot."

Her lips twitched again as the server returned with their drinks. "Very flattering. Thank you."

"Lobster or steak?" Michael asked. "Or both?"

"I'm not that hungry."

"Both for the lady," he said, deciding for her. "Make the filet medium. I'll take the same, but make my steak rare."

"Of course, sir," the waiter said.

"I want to know more about this imbecile who dropped you," he said. "I'll bet he's kicking himself up and down the street for his stupidity now."

She gave a reluctant chuckle and shook her head, sighing. "He's engaged to a beautiful blonde."

"Oh," he said and took a sip of his whiskey. "Lucky for me."

"You are the very devil himself," she said, shaking her head again and taking a sip of her potent drink. "End of discussion about my ex."

Not likely, he thought, but shelved the subject for the moment. "Fine. Why are you overreacting about your aunt knowing we're seeing each other?"

"Because we're *not* seeing each other. We have an agreement," she said bitterly and looked away.

He narrowed his eyes, sensing there was more to the story. "What else is going on? There's more. I can see it on your face. This isn't just about you and me."

She frowned, but still didn't meet his gaze. "I didn't tell you everything about my mother. She was living in California when she died, but she wasn't married. She was the mistress of a wealthy, powerful man. A married man. I vowed never to get into that situation."

Michael paused a long moment, searching his mind for the best approach. "So that's why you're uncomfortable about your arrangement with me. This is different."

Her head snapped up. "What do you mean? I may as well be your mistress. I've made an agreement in exchange for your assistance and support."

"For one thing, I'm not married. Never will be for that matter. Secondly, you made that choice for the sake of someone very important to you. I don't get the impression your mother did the same. Besides, I wouldn't have even made the offer if I didn't believe there was a chance of making the business a success."

She stared at him in surprise. "Really?"

"Really," he said. "I broke a few rules of my own for you, but not all of them. So we're on more equal ground than you imagined. You can enjoy your lobster and steak without remorse."

She looked at him, her mesmerizing eyes glowing at him, doing strange things to his insides. "Interesting," she said. "If we're on equal ground, then I'd like to ask you some questions."

Michael's gut clenched. "Such as?"

"Favorite dessert?"

He blinked then chuckled at her curiously. "Tiramisu."

"Your Italian roots are showing."

"I could prepare a lasagna for you that would make you forget every other pasta you've ever eaten."

"True?" she asked.

"True," he said.

"Okay, you're on. I want that lasagna. When is your birthday?"

"Next month, but I don't celebrate it," he said.

"Why not?"

"It's just another day. Why do you ask?"

"Because I want to know more about you. How did you celebrate your birthday when you were young?" she asked. "Before your father died."

"With a favorite meal, small gifts and dessert. That was a long time ago."

"You haven't celebrated it since you reconnected with your brothers?" she asked, a sliver of outrage in her voice.

He shook his head. "We're all too busy. Sometimes they remember to call. That's more than I got when I was in the foster home."

She frowned in disapproval. "Have all of you looked for Leo?"

His sense of humor at her questions faded. "One way or another."

"What do you remember about him?" she asked.

Michael paused, resisting the memories for a moment because he never remembered without subsequent pain and heavy, heavy guilt. "He was a fighter," Michael said. "He was only a year older than I was, and I did my best to keep up with all of them, but Leo was tough. Hell, he would even try to take on Damien. That never lasted long. Damien would just pin him down until he agreed to quit. Then Leo would get up and take another quick swipe before he ran off."

"Sounds like he was a pistol," Bella said with a soft smile.

He nodded. "Yeah, we all were, but he seemed to run full tilt from the minute he woke up until the minute he went to sleep. He was always afraid of missing something...." His chest squeezed tight, making the words difficult. He cleared his throat. "He liked animals. He was always bringing home a stray something and Dad would have to find another home for it because my mother said she had too many two-legged animals to take care of."

"And they never found any sign of him?" she said, more than asked, shaking her head.

"Every body was recovered except his," he said and the old determination rolled through him again. "If it's the last thing I do, I'm going to find him."

Bella leaned forward and slid her hand across the table to touch his. "I believe you will."

Something inside him eased at her confidence in him. He knew it wasn't based on flattery because she'd essentially already gotten what she wanted from him and she was still pissed that he'd pushed her into their affair. Soon enough she'd realize that he'd done what needed to be done for both of them.

He captured her hand with his. "Your turn for questions is over. My turn now. What's your favorite dessert?"

"Double-chocolate brownies with frosting," she said with a guilty expression on her face. "Decadent."

"Just like you," he said.

Her eyes lit with arousal but she looked away as if

she was determined to fight her attraction to him. That irritated the hell out of him. There would be no denial from any part of her when he took her tonight in his bed.

Seven

On Saturday morning, Michael surprised himself by sleeping an entire hour later than usual. He did his usual workout and was surprised even more at the sight of Bella dressed in jeans, T-shirt, and tennis shoes and her head covered by a bandana, walking out of the room where she kept her belongings.

"You're up early," he said.

"I'm painting today," she said.

He frowned. "It didn't look like the spa needed it."

"I'm not painting the spa. I'm volunteering— painting a children's activity center downtown."

"That's nice of you," he said.

"They need help with some repairs if you're interested. If you're handy, I hear they need some help with wiring and the gas heater."

"You sound like Damien," he said, thinking of his

oldest brother. "He started building houses for charity and keeps telling Rafe and me that we should do the same."

"Why don't you?"

"I donate generously to several charities. My money is more valuable than my manpower."

"Do you mentor anyone?"

Her question took him off guard. "No. My schedule is packed. It wouldn't be fair to promise to mentor someone with the limited time I have."

"Hmm," she said.

Her noncommittal sound irritated him and he narrowed his eyes. Most would have heeded his expression as a warning.

"It's a good thing your mentor made the time he did for you, isn't it?"

No one besides his brothers would dare get in his face like she did. "My mentor was retired. I'm not."

"Excuses, excuses," she said, a smile playing around her lips. "But I understand if you're afraid of getting involved."

"*Afraid,*" he echoed, snatching her hand and pulling her against him. "You aren't trying to manipulate me into charity involvement, are you?"

She paused a half beat. "Yes. Is it working?"

He couldn't help chuckling. "Not at all."

"Okay, no goading," she said. "I dare you to come down to the community children's center and help." She met his gaze, her lips lifted in a sultry half smile. She tossed her head and lifted her chin. "See ya if you're brave enough." She turned and walked away, her saucy butt swinging from side to side as she exited his house.

"Witch," he muttered and dismissed her so-called dare. He had real work to do. Walking to his office, he sat down with his laptop and crunched numbers. He worked without pausing for the next hour and a half.

The second he stopped, silence closed around him like a thick cloud. Bella and her dare jabbed at him. Silly, he thought. Stupid. A waste of time. Bella was a misplaced do-gooder. Children didn't need paint. They needed…parents.

The twinge inside him took him by surprise. He frowned at the odd sensation and shrugged, turning back to his number crunching, but his concentration came and went.

Ten minutes later, he sighed, swearing under his breath and leaned back in his leather chair. Raking his hand through his hair, he shook his head. Stupid dare, he thought, remembering the expression in her mesmerizing, nearly purple eyes.

In the long run, how much did a fresh coat of paint really matter? Two more minutes of denial rolled through his brain and he tossed his pen at his desk and turned off his laptop. What a surprise. He toyed with the idea of joining her. He liked the notion of surprising her. He liked the idea of doing something with his hands other than using his laptop or BlackBerry. Even the devil had a conscience. Or perhaps the devil couldn't resist a dare from a woman with black hair and purple eyes.

Bella continued edging the walls of one of the playrooms. She much preferred rolling paint on the walls because that part of the job was easier and more rewarding, but edging was crucial to the finished product. She would take her turn with the roller later on.

"Sandwich? Water?" Rose, a mother of one of the

children who visited the center, offered as she carried a tray.

Bella smiled and lifted her water bottle, having chatted with the young woman earlier that morning. "I'm still good, thank you. How's it going in the other rooms?" she asked as she turned back to edging.

"Very well, except the service man hasn't arrived to fix the heater," Rose said. "It's gas and I'm really concerned about the safety if—" She broke off. "Oh, hello," she said, her voice a bit breathless. "Can I help you?"

"I wondered if you could use two more hands," Michael said.

Surprised, Bella whipped around and kicked over her paint can. "Oh, no." She bent down to right it, but he caught it first. Her face mere inches from his, she felt her heart race.

He gave a half grin that made her stomach dip. "I didn't know you were planning on painting the floor."

She scowled. "It's your fault. You surprised me. I was sure you weren't coming. What made you?" Realization hit her and she answered for him. "The dare."

"I don't accept every dare. It depends on the source and actual dare."

"Well, I feel honored," she said and picked up an extra brush and put it in his hand. "Rose, this is Michael Medici. Rose's son takes part in the center's activities," Bella said.

"Good to meet you," he said.

Rose's eyes were wide with admiration. "Good to meet you, Mr. Medici. I'm so grateful for your help. Excuse me while I check on my son."

"I'm thrilled for you to finish the edging," Bella said, wondering how he would respond to the not-so-desirable task.

He glanced around the room and shrugged. "Should be cake."

Surprised again, she watched him begin and noticed he worked with speed and ease. "When did you get your painting experience?"

"Painted the entire group home twice. Once while I lived there as a teenager and once after I left. Nobody else wanted to edge, so I took that job."

"And became an expert," she said, envying his skill. "You can do it freehand."

"Part of my philosophy. If you're going to do something, be the best at it."

She should have expected that. His competitiveness was born not only from the need to survive, but from his determination to thrive. She still wondered though, why had he accepted her dare? Was there a secret tenderness underneath his hard, cynical exterior? Or was she just dreaming? She felt a hot rush of embarrassment. *Why* was she dreaming?

"Do you want anything to eat or—" A loud explosion rocked the building. "What was that?" She ran toward the door.

Michael snagged her hand. "Whoa, there," he said. "You need to get out of here and dial 911."

"I can't leave. What about the rest of the volunteers?"

"I'll work on that," he said and glanced down the hallway. "Smoke's coming from the back of the building. We don't have time to waste. Get out."

"But—"

He turned and looked her straight in the eye. "Do I need to carry you out? Because I will."

"No, but—"

"No buts," he said. "Get out and make the call."

Frustrated and afraid, Bella saw the rock-hard expression on his face and knew further protests were futile. She ran from the house, checking rooms for volunteers on her way to the door, but it appeared that most people had already left. Punching the numbers for help on her cell phone, she looked at the center and watched in horror as flames shot out of the back of the building.

Less than a moment later, a man pulled Rose out the front door. "My baby," she cried. "My baby. He's still in there."

A knot of dread formed in the back of Bella's throat. "Oh, no," she said, reaching out to Rose and taking the sobbing woman into her arms.

Sirens shrieked in the distance. Bella glanced toward the building. Where was Michael?

"I have to go back," Rose said. "I can't lose him."

"You can't," Bella said, wishing she could go in and look for the boy. "You need to be waiting for him when he comes out."

Rose looked at her with tear-stained eyes. "But what if he doesn't come out? It was so smoky in there. I could hardly breathe."

A slice of fear for Michael's safety cut through her. Why was he still in there? The sirens grew louder as the first red truck pulled in front of the center. Another explosion roared from the back of the house. The volunteers standing outside yelled "No!"

Bella felt her stomach dip to her feet. What if Michael—

Smoke billowed through the front door as the firemen opened it. Michael, coughing hard, stepped outside with a small child in his arms. His T-shirt covered with soot, he quickly stepped away from the building. A medic raced toward him.

"Rose," Bella said, emotion tightening her voice. "Rose, isn't that your son?" she asked, urging the woman to lift her head from her shoulder.

Rose glanced up and looked around. Spotting her son, she lifted her hand to her throat. "My baby. My baby," she said and ran toward him and the medic.

Filled with a range of emotions she couldn't begin to name, Bella watched Michael as he brushed off a medic. He glanced around the area and the second his gaze landed on her, she felt as if she'd been hit by a thunderbolt.

He moved toward her and she automatically did the same. She looked him over, taking in scrapes and burn marks. He covered a cough. "Come on. I don't want you around this."

"Me?" she said. "I've been outside just watching. You're the one who stayed in there too long."

"I heard that boy calling and couldn't figure out where he was. I went in every room. I finally tried the closets. There he was. Everyone accounted for?"

"I hope so," she said and looked around. The crowd around the center was growing. "There's the volunteer coordinator. Looks like she's checking off a list." The woman glanced at her and gave a quick wave.

Michael took her hand. "Let's make sure everyone is accounted for." After Michael double-checked everyone's safety, he answered questions from the police and fire department.

"We can go now," he said.

"Don't you think you should let the medic take a look at you?"

"No," he said. "The press will be here any minute."

"Are you afraid of the press?" she asked.

"No," he said with a scowl. "But I like my privacy."

She studied him for a long moment, taking in his discomfort and realization hit her. "You don't want them to know you were a hero."

He scoffed. "I wasn't a hero. I just heard a screaming kid and dragged him out of the place."

"A burning building," she corrected. "And you really should see a medic."

"Enough," he said, tugging her with him. "Since you're so concerned about my injuries, you can take care of them when we get home."

"What about my car?" she asked as he led her to his SUV.

"I'll send one of my drivers to collect it," he said and stuffed her inside.

An hour later, after Michael had taken a shower, wincing as the water sluiced over his scrapes and burns, he wrapped a towel around his waist and walked into his bedroom to the sight of Bella standing beside his bed. She must have showered also because her hair was damp and she'd changed clothes.

She gestured toward the bed and he noticed she'd placed a sheet on top of his bedspread.

"You have plans for me?" he asked, his body quickening despite his soreness.

She lifted a tube and a small bottle. "Antibiotic ointment for your boo-boos and eucalyptus oil for your massage." She turned on a CD that played soothing sounds of nature and gentle tones.

"Massage," he said in approval.

"I'm not licensed, but I've learned a little on my

own." She waved her hand briskly. "On the bed," she commanded.

"Sounds like an order," he said reclining.

"It was," she said, a smile playing over her lips as she studied his face and began to dab ointment on his scrapes. She slid her hands over his shoulders, arms and hands, making hmm sounds.

Michael was accustomed to having a woman's sexual attention, but Bella's tender touch seemed to reach deeper than his skin. When was the last time someone besides himself had taken care of his scrapes? He couldn't remember. Why did it matter? As she began to rub the fragrant oil into his shoulders, he felt as if a stream of water was trickling through parts of him left dry and abandoned for ages. He wasn't sure he liked the sensation.

He watched her brow furrow as she worked his right shoulder from the front. "Are you always this tense?"

He winced when she hit a sore spot. "I had to pull off the door to the closet. It was stuck."

She pursed her lips in disapproval. "You didn't mention that. Anything else I should know?"

"No. Why are you doing this?" he asked, studying the intent expression on her face.

"Because it needs to be done and you wouldn't take the time for it." He was a complex man, she thought. Far more complicated than she'd suspected. Full of layers that made her curious. She wondered about his secrets as she rubbed his shoulders.

"There's a difference between need and want."

She put her hand over his mouth. "Be quiet. I need to concentrate." She turned back to the massage.

"Are you saying my talking distracts you?"

"Your voice is—" She broke off, sinking her fingers

into his muscles, causing him to moan. She smiled at the sound. "Good spot?"

He nodded. "My voice is?"

"Compelling," she said. "Well, *you* are compelling, but you already knew that."

"How so?" he asked, curious because she clearly wasn't flattering him.

"You're insufferably confident and intelligent. You seem intent on conveying that you only make decisions based on numbers and that you're nearly heartless. But you're not. There's stuff going on beneath the surface. Not exactly sure—" She dug her thumbs into the muscle above his collarbone and he winced. "Oops. Good or bad?"

"I'm okay," he said.

She smiled. "You really need to let me know if I hurt you. If you don't, you're going to need to take something for your muscles later."

He didn't believe her. She was a small woman. He'd suffered more than a massage without needing medication. "I'm okay."

"All righty," she said and slid her hand over his face. "Close your eyes," she said softly. She worked his shoulders, arms, and even his hands. After he turned over, she continued and he wondered how she kept from tiring. Her fingers played him with a soothing rhythm of increasing and decreasing intensity.

Michael relaxed in a way he couldn't recall, feeling himself melt into the mattress. He drifted off....

Later, he awakened to the sound of the CD she'd played while she'd massaged his body. A light sheet covered him. Lifting his head, he glanced around and felt a tug of disappointment that she was gone. A bottle of water caught his eye. Sighing, he rose and grabbed it, spotting a note next to it.

Gone to check on Charlotte. Drink lots of water. Jacuzzi would be a good follow-up to the massage. Be back later.

More orders, he thought, lifting his eyebrows. Few women had tried to give him orders. Those who had hadn't lasted long. At the moment, though, he couldn't help feeling indulgent. Bella had taken him to a new level of relaxation. He would take them both to a new level of sexual pleasure.

He decided to follow her suggestion for a dip in the Jacuzzi. But first he should check his BlackBerry for messages. He picked up his phone from the nightstand, noting that she'd turned it off. Only he controlled his phone. He would warn her later.

Turning it on, he saw a text message from his private investigator and immediately called him.

"Sam Carson," the man said his name. "Is this Mr. Medici?"

"Yes. You have news."

"Yes, but you aren't going to like it."

Michael's gut twisted. "What is it? Did you find his body?"

Carson sighed. "That would have been easier than what I have to tell you."

Eight

Michael's house was dark when Bella let herself in just before nine o'clock. Normally she would have expected one of his staff to greet her, but this time all she heard was silence. Was he still asleep from the massage she'd given him?

Turning on a light, she walked through the hallway to the kitchen and glimpsed a flicker of light coming from the den. The gas fireplace provided the only light in the room. It took a moment for her eyes to adjust. She saw him sitting in a chair holding a squat glass half-full of liquid. Probably some kind of liquor that cost a hundred dollars an ounce.

She met his gaze and glimpsed a turbulence in his gaze. Something had happened since she'd left. "What's wrong?" she asked, moving toward him.

"Nothing I want to discuss," he said and took a sip of his drink. "Do you want anything to drink?"

She lifted her bottle of water. "I'm good."

"Yes, you are," he said, seduction glinting in his eyes.

Uncertain of his mood, she stopped a few steps before him. "Are you okay?"

"I am," he said, but his words belied her instincts.

"You really should still be drinking water," she said. "Did you get into the Jacuzzi?"

"No more orders today, Bella. And no, I didn't get into the hot tub. Come here."

She moved closer, still hesitant. He extended his hand and she accepted it. He pulled her into his lap, his gaze pinning hers. "Don't ever, ever turn off my Blackberry without my permission."

She blinked. "You missed an important call," she said. "I'm sorry," she said. "Kinda," she added. "Kinda not. You needed to relax."

"That's not your decision to make."

"Okay. I don't suppose you want to tell me about the call," she ventured.

"You supposed correctly."

"But I can tell you've got something on your mind. Something is bothering you," she said.

He set his glass on the table beside him and pulled her mouth to his. "Give me something else to think about."

His mouth devoured hers while his hands slid over her, immediately making her hot. She sensed a dark desperation beneath the surface, but she wasn't sure what it was. He distracted her from dwelling on it with the speed and intensity of his lovemaking. Before she knew it, her clothes had been discarded and so had his.

On the floor in front of the fireplace, he took her entire

body with his hands and his mouth. His gaze holding hers with the firelight dancing over his skin, he thrust inside her.

Bella gasped at the feeling of possession. With each stroke, she felt utterly and completely consumed, falling under some kind of spell he cast over her. It couldn't be love, she told herself. Love was gentle and sweet and this was nothing like that. This was compelling and powerful, but complicated. And temporary.

Temporary, she repeated to herself like a mantra. *Temporary.* But it was hard to convince herself of that when she'd never had a man make love to her with such power as Michael. Their arrangement had been about sex, but something else was happening between them.

The next morning, Bella awakened in Michael's bed. As usual, he was gone. Exercising, she guessed and crept out of bed. She pulled on a robe from his closet and walked down the hallway to his small, well-equipped gym. The door was open and she spotted him on the elliptical, moving at a fast pace, his arms gleaming with perspiration. His gaze fixed forward, he looked as if he were racing against the devil. It occurred to her for all Michael's ability to make ruthless business decisions and his tendency to avoid emotional interaction, he had his demons. The strangest, craziest desire to rid him of those demons sprang inside her.

Insane, she thought. As if she had the power to help him. As if he would even want her help.

Bella didn't have time to dwell on her conflicted feelings for Michael. Her aunt's spa opened, and she and her aunt were busy accommodating the surge of customers.

"You have to hire more people," Bella said to Charlotte after the first week. "It's part of your agreement with Michael."

"I know, I know," Charlotte said as she sank into a chair. "I just didn't dream we'd get this kind of response. Michael was right about creating miniservices that give people a taste of luxury without spending too much."

"And we've sold several discount packages for pedicures and massages," Bella added, and gave Charlotte a glass of iced green tea. "So, when are you going to hire new staff?"

"I'll talk to Michael to confirm. I don't want to mess up this time," she said. "I don't want to overhire either."

"But you also don't want to over*tire*," Bella said.

"Hear, hear," a male voice said from the doorway. Fred, a man in his fifties who worked at the computer store down the street, popped in daily for a visit.

Charlotte perked up. "I thought the sign on the door said closed," she teased.

"Not for your best customer," Fred said with a twinkle in his eye.

"Customer," Charlotte said. "You haven't spent a dime on any services here. You just show up after work and drink my coffee and waste my time."

Bella smiled at the dynamics between them. Charlotte might not admit it, but she clearly enjoyed Fred's attention.

"Then how about if I change that?" he asked. "Can I take an overworked owner manager to dinner tonight in Buckhead?"

Charlotte blinked, clearly speechless. "Uh, well." She cleared her throat. "That's very nice of you, but I still have a lot of work to do. Go over the day's book-keeping and supplies."

"I can do that," Bella offered.

Charlotte glared at her. "Don't you have plans with Michael?"

"No. He's actually out of town," she said. Michael had been out of town most of the week. She'd spent her nights feeling alternately full of relief and missing him. The latter had surprised her. After all, wasn't their relationship just supposed to be physical?

"Well, I don't know," Charlotte said, still reluctant.

"I did have a question about a couple of the products we're using. They're in the supply closet," Bella said then glanced at Fred. "Could you excuse us for a moment? We'll be right back."

Bella took her aunt's hand and led her to the walk-in supply closet and closed the door. "Why won't you go to dinner with him? It's obvious that he likes you," she whispered.

"I have too much work to do," Charlotte protested. "Plus, he didn't give me any notice. Just wandered in here and assumed I'd be willing to go." She ran her fingers through her hair nervously. Although her hair was still short, her aunt looked stylish and attractive. "It's probably just a pity request."

"Pity request," Bella said with a snort. "Is that why he stops in here every afternoon and sometimes at lunch?"

"Maybe he just likes the free coffee and cookies," Charlotte said.

"That's why he wants to take you some place really

nice," Bella said, rolling her eyes. "Because he wants to pay you back for coffee and cookies."

"Why are you pushing me?"

"Because I think you like him and maybe he would be good to you. You deserve to have someone who is good to you."

Charlotte sighed. "I just don't know. I'd given up on anything with a man."

"Maybe you gave up too soon," Bella said.

Charlotte tapped her fingernails on a shelf. "You really think I should go?"

"Yes!"

She frowned, studying Bella for a long moment. "How are you and Michael doing? You don't say very much about him."

"There's not much to say. We're getting to know each other."

"Are you starting to get over Stephen?"

Bella felt her stomach clench and turned away. "I don't—" She broke off. "It's a different kind of relationship with Michael."

"In what way?" her aunt said, digging for information.

Bella shrugged. "Michael is just for fun," she said, nearly choking on the words as she said them. "Stephen and I were in love."

"You've been the kettle calling the pot black," her aunt said. "You're telling me to open the door and give Fred a chance. When are you going to give Michael a chance?"

Never, she thought. Instead, she smiled and wagged her finger at her aunt. "We're not going to turn this conversation on me. You need to freshen up and tell that man out there you'll join him for dinner."

* * *

Sitting in a penthouse suite in Chicago, Michael glanced at the invitation for the Valentine wine tasting at the exclusive historical Essex House and debated attending. It was mostly a social event, where Atlanta's elite would try to show each other up. He didn't give a damn about that, but The Essex House had recently courted him. He suspected they wanted him to invest and lend his name because their bottom line was sagging. The trouble was that he wouldn't have complete control, he would only have a vote in the management of the House, and that didn't appeal to him at all.

Still, turning The Essex House into a financial success was seductive, another challenge.

The word *challenge* brought Bella to mind. In fact, she'd been on his mind more often than ever lately. Yes, she knew how to burn up his bed, but she got under his skin in other ways. Those violet eyes of hers seemed to see right through him at times. He knew such a thing wasn't possible, but that didn't stop him from wondering....

He glanced at the invitation again and made a decision. He picked up his cell and dialed Bella.

"Hi. How's the Windy City?" she asked, clearly reading her caller ID.

"Windy and cold," he said. "What are you doing?"

"Some work for my aunt. She's out to dinner with a *man*," she said, the shocked delight in her voice making him smile.

"You sound surprised," he said.

"She's always been such a workaholic. She was married and divorced for a while before she took me in.

She dated every now and then, but nothing serious and nothing in the last few years. A man who works down the street wanted to take her to Buckhead and she almost refused. I had to prod her to go out." Bella laughed. "So she's eating a gourmet meal and I'm eating gourmet jelly beans."

"You could call my chef and have him bring you something," he offered.

"That's okay. I really don't mind. How's your work going?"

"Good," he said. "I'll be back in town tomorrow morning and need to attend an event tomorrow night. I'd like you to join me," he said.

"What is it?"

The wariness in her voice irritated him. "The Valentine wine tasting at The Essex House."

Silence followed.

"Bella," he prompted.

"The Essex House? Isn't the wine tasting one of those events that's featured on television and in the newspaper?"

"Yes, and national magazines. It begins at seven. You can either get ready at my house earlier—"

"Whoa, I didn't say I could go. For one thing, that's making our relationship way too public. I told you I didn't want that."

"Why are you so concerned about that?"

"Because I don't want to have to explain things after we're finished," she said.

His irritation tightened further. "It's not that big a deal."

"Maybe not to you. What am I supposed to say? That you and I had a sexual arrangement and now it's over?"

He narrowed his eyes. "Our arrangement is for an affair. An affair includes other activities. If you're that worried about what to say after we're finished, just tell people you dumped me."

Bella gave a short laugh. "Right," she said. "As if anyone would believe that."

"Why not?"

"Because women don't usually dump handsome, rich bachelors."

"You can be the exception," he said. "If you're not at my house by six, I'll pick you up at your apartment at six-thirty. Enjoy your jelly—"

"Wait!"

"What?"

"I don't have anything to wear," she confessed in a low voice.

"Pick something out tomorrow. I'll pay for it. I'll send my driver over with my credit card."

"I have to work tomorrow. Saturday is our busiest day."

"Make good use of your lunch break then," he said without budging an inch.

She gave a sigh. "You are so bossy. It would serve you right if I maxed out your card."

He laughed. "Sweetheart, give it a try. You couldn't do that in a year, let alone one day."

After a busy morning at the spa, Bella headed straight for the shopping district. She was uncomfortable using Michael's money for her clothing, but there was no way around it. She visited several high-end shops, but nothing felt right. Accepting his money to purchase her clothing just seemed to remind her how much she wished she could help her aunt on her own. On a whim, she went into a vintage shop and found a black, beaded, chiffon flapper-style dress she could pair with black boots and a silk scarf. The style was more funky luxe than strictly luxurious, but it suited her and didn't cost the earth.

If Michael didn't like it, then perhaps he wouldn't take her out in public again, she thought deviously. She worked the rest of the afternoon and scooted out an hour early to get ready. She would never admit to the surge of excitement and anticipation sizzling inside her.

Ridiculous, she thought as she lined her eyes and applied red lipstick. The event would just be a group of stuffy society types. Her doorbell rang and her heart lurched. Michael's driver. Grab scarf, purse and coat, she reminded herself. "Just a minute," she called.

Collecting her things, she opened the door to Michael, drop-dead gorgeous in a tux. Her breath whooshed out of her lungs. "Oh, I didn't expect you."

He lifted his eyebrow. "Who, then?"

"The driver," she said, feeling his gaze travel over her from head to toe.

"You—" He hesitated a second and his mouth lifted in a half grin. "Sparkle."

Pleasure rushed through her. "Thank you. I didn't do too much damage to your card."

"I told you I wasn't worried about it." He glanced beyond her to her apartment. "This is where you live?"

"Yes," she said, trying not to feel self-conscious. Her apartment probably could serve as a closet in the home. "It's small, but cozy."

"It's not the safest neighborhood," he said.

"Neighbors here watch out for each other. I'm okay with it," she said stiffly and stepped into the hallway.

"I wasn't criticizing," he said.

"Your house is much more luxurious, but I'm happy to have a little space of my own."

"You say that as if you think I've always lived like I do now," he chided, closing the space between them. "You know where I came from."

"Looking at you in that tux, it's easy to forget," she said.

"Don't," he said. "One of the things I like about you is that you're not overly impressed by my wealth."

"So you *like* me disagreeable?" she asked. "Does this mean I should tell you I've decided not to attend the wine tasting?"

He took her hand in his. "Not a chance. Besides, I can tell you want to go."

She gave a mock sniff. "I read about it in the newspaper. They are supposed to serve some good desserts, so that should make it worthwhile."

Michael ushered her to his limo and the driver whisked them to The Essex House. The carefully tended mansion buzzed with activity. Crystal chandeliers lit the gleaming marble floors and antique furniture. The sound of a piano playing romantic standards in another room wafted through the house. With her fingers linked in Michael's, she almost felt like this was a real date.

"What do you think?" he asked.

"It's beautiful. It reminds me of a high-class woman from the 1800s. The place seems to have a personality of its own."

"Excellent description," he said. "Maintaining a high-class woman is expensive."

Bella couldn't help wondering if he felt the same

way about his relationship with her. The notion threatened to sour her pleasure, so she quickly brushed it aside. "Good thing they continue to make enough money to do the job."

"We'll see," he said with a sliver of doubt in his voice.

"What do you mean? Are they in trouble?" she asked.

"They've asked me to invest both my money and my expertise, but the collective board votes on final decisions."

She watched him studying the house and staff. "Does that mean you wouldn't get to rule?" she asked and shook her head. "Good luck to them."

He chuckled. "We'll see. At least I'm here."

"I should have known this involved business," she muttered, wondering why she felt let down. Why should she care that Michael was motivated by business for the evening? Sure, it was Valentine's Day and many other couples might view it as a romantic affair, but she shouldn't.

"You sound disappointed," he said, searching her face.

Embarrassed that he'd read her so easily, she shook her head. "There's still dessert," she said, forcing a smile.

A balding man approached Michael at that moment, earning her a reprieve. "Mr. Medici, I'm Clarence Kiddlow. We spoke on the phone. I'm glad you decided to attend. We're the hottest ticket in town tonight," the man said proudly.

Michael nodded. "Mr. Kiddlow, this is my date, Bella St. Clair."

Clarence extended his hand. "My pleasure to meet

you." He waved toward a server. "Have some wine," he said. "We're starting with a white from Virginia of all places. But it's very smooth." He turned to Michael after he'd tasted the wine. "What do you think?"

"Bella is the white-wine drinker. What do you think?"

Surprised he'd deferred to her, she nodded. "Very nice, thank you."

The server then poured her a full glass.

"I'd like to show you around and tell you about some of our plans," Clarence said. "I think you'll find them interesting."

"Thank you," Michael said. "Later, perhaps. Bella and I would like to look around on our own first."

Surprise crossed Clarence's face, but he acquiesced. "Of course. Tell me when you're ready."

Bella felt surprise of her own as Michael ushered her away. "I thought you were here to investigate the possibility of working with The Essex House."

"I didn't come for a sales presentation," he said, impatience flitting across his face. "I'm not an idiot. Given the choice between Clarence's company and yours, which do you think I would choose?"

Bella blinked and fought a rush of pleasure. "I don't know what to say. The mighty Michael Medici just paid me a compliment."

"Don't let it go to your head," he said and led her through a crowded hallway. He nodded in the direction of a room to the left. "I think I've spotted what you're looking for."

"A delicious dessert, but I wonder, Michael, what are you looking for?" she couldn't resist asking.

He turned back to her, giving her a second and

third glance. "I have everything I need and more. If I want something else, I find a way to get it. You should know that."

Her stomach dipped at the expression on his face. "I suppose I should, but I was speaking of dessert."

He smiled. "I'll enjoy watching you have yours. Come on," he said and tugged her into the room. The throng around the serving table made it difficult to get close. "Wait here," he said and positioned her in a corner. "I'll get it for you."

She watched him walk away and wondered how he managed to part the crowd with such ease. It was as if they knew they should defer to him. Bella wondered if his tough upbringing had instilled him with that quality. She couldn't deny that he fascinated her. She wanted to know more about him. She wasn't in love with him and never would be, but she cared about him far more than she'd planned. She wasn't sure how that had happened.

A moment later, Michael appeared, carrying a plateful of the most decadent dessert Bella had even seen in her life. She looked at him and the chocolate and wondered if he had any idea how much he had in common with that treat. Decadent and forbidden, both could cause a woman to pay for indulging.

He approached her and lifted a spoonful to her lips. "Tell me what you think of it," he said.

Nine

Accepting the dare in his gaze, but telling herself it wasn't at all significant, Bella opened her mouth and slowly savored a bite of the decadent dessert. "Now, that is good," she said, reaching for the spoon. "Really good."

Michael playfully pulled the spoon from her reach. "Not so fast."

She met his gaze and scowled at him. "No teasing allowed."

"That's the pot calling the kettle black. You're a walking tease."

She fought his flattery. After all, it wasn't necessary given their arrangement. "Hand over the chocolate and no one will get hurt," she threatened.

He chuckled and lifted the spoon to her mouth again. She took it, but a familiar face shot into view. The chocolate stuck in her throat as she stared into her ex-fiancé's eyes.

"Bella?" Stephen said, clearly shocked to see her at such an event. His new fiancée came into Bella's view and the two wound through the crowd.

Her stomach gave a vicious turn.

"Bella, what are you doing here?" Stephen asked, then looked at Michael and gave a double take. "Michael Medici," he said.

Britney smiled broadly. "Michael, it's great to see you again. We met a couple years ago at the heart disease charity dinner."

Michael nodded and glanced at Stephen. "And this is?"

"Stephen, my fiancé." She giggled. "We've set the date for our wedding in August. We would love for you to come. You know my father thinks so highly of you."

"Send him my best," Michael said. "How do you know Bella?"

"I could ask the same," Stephen said, glancing from the chocolate dessert in Michael's hand to Bella.

Bella felt a rush of self-consciousness. "Stephen and I met in college."

"Ah," Michael said and turned to Steven. "Bella and I met through business."

"Really?" Stephen said. "Bella and business?"

"I've been working with my aunt in her spa."

"Oh, I thought she had some problems…" Stephen said, faltering under Michael's hard gaze.

"She did, but the business is now booming," Michael said. "Best wishes on your marriage. Don't let us keep you from the event." His dismissive tone quickly sent the couple on their way.

"Thank you very much," Britney said.

As soon as they left, Michael turned to Bella. "What's the real story about Stephen?"

She swallowed over the bitterness in the back of her throat. "Water over the bridge, under the dam, whatever. Old news. I wonder what the next kind of wine will be," she said, skirting his gaze. "Let's go—"

Michael caught her hand. "Bella, I have excellent instincts and my instincts tell me you're holding out on me."

"Well, it's not the best kind of story for this venue. Can we please just shelve this and enjoy the rest of the evening?" she asked.

"The question is *can* you shelve it?"

"Since this is probably the only time I'll be at The Essex House, I'm going to give it a damn good try," she said.

A sliver of approval shot through his dark eyes. "Okay. Let's see about that wine."

Michael successfully kept Bella away from Britney and Stephen. It wasn't difficult. The Essex House was packed. He noticed men taking long glances at Bella throughout the evening. He also noticed that Bella didn't notice. She was too busy taking in her surroundings, reading the biographies of the ancestors who'd built and occupied the house.

She sipped wine and sampled little bites of the desserts, but her whole demeanor seemed muted since their interaction with Stephen. Again, he wondered about the two of them. He knew they'd been lovers and the knowledge made him burn with surprising jealousy. Michael had never thought of himself as the possessive type. He couldn't recall any other woman who'd inspired the hot coal of jealousy in his gut.

Why should he care about her romantic history now?

He knew she was attracted to him. She couldn't fake the sensual response she gave him in bed. She was his for now, for as long as he wanted her. That was the bargain.

Suddenly, the way he'd persuaded her to accept her attraction to him made him feel vaguely dissatisfied. Given the choice, she would have denied herself and him. From the beginning, though, he'd known they should be together until the passion between them became less intense, until it burned away.

He watched her cover a yawn. "Ready to go?"

She gave a wry smile. "I guess the day is catching up with me. Maybe you should go see the man who greeted us. He's going to be disappointed if he doesn't get a chance to talk with you further tonight."

"He's a big boy. He'll get over it."

"But you came for business purposes. Don't you want to talk with him?"

"Not tonight. I'll page the chauffeur to pick us up. It won't take but a moment." He ushered her toward the front door and they collected her wrap.

The limo appeared just as they walked down the front steps. Once inside, she leaned her head against the back of the seat, closed her eyes and sighed. He pulled an ice-cold bottle of water from the ice bucket, lifted her hand and wrapped her fingers around the bottle.

She opened her eyes and blinked, then smiled. "Thank you."

"You're welcome. You want to tell me about you and Stephen now?" he asked. "You turned as white as a sheet when he showed up."

"I could remind you that you wouldn't tell me what was bothering you that night you were sitting in the dark by the fire," she said.

"You could, but it wouldn't be wise," he said.

"So, you're allowed to have your touchy subject, but I'm not allowed to have mine?" she countered. "You don't have to discuss yours. I don't have to discuss mine."

Frustration stabbed at him. He wasn't accustomed to being pushed back with such nonchalance. "You could have fainted. I should have had a heads-up so I could take care of you."

"We have an arrangement, remember? You don't need to take care of me. You can't do anything about this anyway. No one can."

The despondence on her face ripped at him. "How do you know I can't do anything about it?"

Her eyes turned shiny with unshed tears. "Stephen and I were going to be married. He fell in love with someone else and now he's going to marry her." Her voice broke. "See? What could anyone do about that."

Michael stared at her, feeling a sick, sinking sensation in his gut. His reaction surprised him. "You're still in love with him, aren't you?"

She closed her eyes and he watched as one telltale tear traveled down her cheek.

It shouldn't bother him. Their relationship was primarily physical. He avoided emotional scenes like the plague. The fact, however, that the woman who'd shared his bed for the last few weeks was in love with another man bothered the hell out of him.

He lifted his hand to her face and rubbed his finger over her wet cheek. He looked into her sad eyes. "He chose unwisely. Britney will drive him up a tree with that shrill voice of hers."

Her lips twitched with a flash of humor then she closed her eyes again releasing another tear. Filled with a crazy combination of emotions, he pulled her into his arms. "If he gave you up, then he's not worthy of you."

She took a shaky breath as if she were trying to compose herself. "Easy to say. My heart says something different."

"What does your heart say?"

She lifted her gaze to his. "He was the one."

He felt as if she'd stabbed him in the gut. His pride quickly rose in defense. "If he was the one, if you were in love with him, why did you agree to an affair with me?"

She looked away. "I'd already messed up my chance for my future, and I'd let down my aunt by not being here when she was so ill. If I agreed to your bargain, I could at least make things right for Charlotte."

"And desire had nothing to do with it," he said in disbelief. "You hated every minute you spent in my bed."

She bit her lip. "I didn't say that." She lifted her gaze reluctantly. "I can't deny there's a strong passion between you and me, but I knew it wasn't love."

He'd gotten exactly what he'd wanted. Her passion with no emotional complications. Why was it suddenly not enough?

Michael didn't sleep with her that night or the next. Bella wondered if he'd changed his mind about her. About them. If he didn't want her anymore. She felt a strange combination of relief and emptiness at his absence.

His passion had been so consuming she found it hard to breathe, let alone think. Without him, she was left with her own thoughts and feelings. Her own loss.

Running from her pain, she worked overtime at the spa to keep herself busy. She went in early and left late wondering if Michael would abandon his support of the spa since his interest in her had waned. He, too, left the house early and didn't return until late. After the fourth night of this routine, she decided to sleep at her apartment instead of his house. Perhaps he wouldn't notice. Perhaps she would be able to sleep better if she wasn't in the same house.

At ten o'clock, a knock sounded at her door. Startled, she muted the basketball game she'd been half watching and ran to her door to look through the peephole. Her heart dipped. Michael stood outside, and even from this microview of him, she could see his impatience.

She opened the door.

"Why are you here?" he asked and strode inside, closing the door behind him.

"Um, well I've been working late at the spa and you've been working late, so I just thought I would sleep here tonight."

His gaze felt like a laser trained on her. "Is that all?"

She cleared her throat, finding his scrutiny nearly unbearable. "Well, we haven't really—" She swallowed.

He lifted an eyebrow. "Really what?"

"Um. Talked."

"You were very upset after the incident at The Essex House. I thought I should give you some time."

Surprised at his consideration, she stared. "Oh. That was thoughtful."

He shot her a wry half smile. "You sound shocked," he said, then waved his hand when she opened her mouth to respond. "No need to defend yourself. Mind if I stay awhile?"

Surprise after surprise. "Uh, no. Would you like something to drink? I don't have much," she quickly added.

"Beer?" he asked as he pulled off his leather jacket and sat down.

"Sorry, no. Water, juice and soda."

"Water's good." He looked at the TV. "You're watching the Hawks. How are they doing?"

Bella pulled two bottles of water from the refrigerator and put a bag of popcorn in the microwave. "You tell me."

"Up by five. Not bad. I didn't know you were a fan."

The microwave dinged and she poured the popcorn into a bowl. "I have a new appreciation for Atlanta sports. I missed them when I was out of the country."

He nodded. "Ever seen them live?"

She shook her head as she joined him on the sofa.

"I'll have to take you sometime," he said.

She almost asked *why,* but managed to stop herself. This was a different side of Michael, one she'd glimpsed before that first night together when the two of them had shared casual conversation and she hadn't known what a workaholic he was. So much had happened since that night that it now seemed ages ago.

They ate popcorn and watched the game. When it was over, Michael turned off the TV and met her gaze.

A familiar, but forbidden ripple of anticipation curled in her belly. She'd seen that look in his eyes often enough to know what happened next. He would take her to bed and for a short time make her forget everything but the passion they shared.

Leaning closer and closer until his mouth took hers, he kissed her with a lover's knowledge of what pleased her. Her body grew warm under his caress. She wanted closer. She wanted more.

He deepened the kiss and she felt herself sinking,

drinking in his taste and scent, feeling the ripple of the muscles of his arms beneath her fingertips. Her body buzzed with want.

He pulled away. She felt the tension inside him. Reluctance and need emanated from him. His eyes glinted with passion. "I had a good time. I'll see you tomorrow," he said and rose.

Bella watched in shock as he pulled on his jacket. Her knees still weak from the promise of his passion, she stiffened them and stood. "Tomorrow?" she echoed.

"Yeah, I'll call you. Lock the door behind me. Okay?"

She mutely nodded and watched him walk away. *What was going on?*

Michael called her the following day, but he didn't ask to see her. More confused than ever, she stayed late again at the Spa.

"You should leave," her aunt said. "You've been working too hard lately."

"No, I haven't," Bella said. "Business is booming and I'm here to make sure *you* don't work too hard."

"Well, you can only do inventory so many times before you wear the labels off the products." Charlotte narrowed her eyes as she studied her. "I haven't seen Michael the last few days."

Determined not to squirm beneath her aunt's scrutiny, Bella wandered to the front desk and unnecessarily tidied it. "He's very busy. You know he's always got a deal going."

"Hmm," Charlotte said and moved closer. "Are you still seeing each other?"

"Sure, I saw him last night. He came over and watched the basketball game," Bella said.

"Hmm," Charlotte said again. "There's something you're not telling me. Something's not right."

"Everything is fine," Bella insisted. "Everything is great. My wonderful aunt is thriving and even dating. The spa is doing great. I couldn't be more pleased."

"And maybe if you keep saying it, you'll believe it yourself," Charlotte said and took Bella's hand. "I'm worried about you. You've sacrificed your professional plans for me."

"What plans?" Bella asked. "Besides, I got to pursue my dreams last year. It's your turn now."

Charlotte's brow furrowed. "I don't want you to be unhappy. Are you still hung up on Stephen?"

Bella tried, but for a flash of a second, she couldn't conceal her feelings. "Stephen has moved on. You know that."

"And you need to do the same," Charlotte urged. "Don't you like Michael?"

Like, Bella thought. As if such a tame emotion could ever apply to the man.

"He's done so much for us," Charlotte continued. "And he's so handsome. Doesn't he treat you well?"

"Of course he does," Bella said. "Michael is just a different kind of man than Stephen."

"Darn right he is," Charlotte said. "He's a leader, not a follower. And if you want him, you're going to have to give him a run for his money."

Bella blinked. "Excuse me?"

"I mean Michael Medici is worth exerting yourself, and I'm not talking about his money. You never had to exert yourself with Stephen. He was always there for you."

"Until I went away," Bella said, feeling a twinge.

"That's just your ego talking," Charlotte said.

Bella dropped her jaw in surprise. "That's not true. Stephen and I were very much in love."

Charlotte waved her hand, dismissing Bella's protest. "You need a man, not a boy. Who knows when Stephen will grow up and stand on his own? Michael Medici is your match. You just need to make sure he knows that."

A knock sounded and Charlotte looked at the door, a smile transforming her face. "Oh, that's Fred. He's taking me to a traveling production of *Wicked*." She walked toward the door. "You need to get out of here and have some fun. You're starting to act like an old lady." She threw Bella a kiss. "Good night, Sweetie."

Go after Michael? Bella shook her head. She wouldn't even know how to begin. Besides, she didn't want him. Not that way. Right? She certainly cared about him as a human being, and she was grateful for his help with her aunt's business. Her cheeks heated as she remembered their lovemaking. Yes, he was passionate, but he was also emotionally remote. That would never work for her. Bella wanted a man who wore his heart on his sleeve. That was not Michael.

Her cell phone rang and she glanced at the caller ID. Despite herself, her heart leapt. Irritated, she answered the phone. "Hi, Michael."

"I got tickets for a Hawks game tomorrow night. Wanna go?" he asked.

She wondered why he was asking. All the other times she'd been with him her presence had been required.

"If you don't, then—"

"No," she said. "I mean yes, I'd love to."

"Good, I'll pick you up at six. We can eat dinner first."

Click. She stared at her phone and chuckled to herself. *Yeah, now that's a guy who wears his heart on his sleeve. Not.* So why was she already planning what to wear?

Ten

The limo whisked Bella and Michael to the restaurant and he led her inside. She noticed that he barely mentioned his name before the host escorted them to a table with a view of the lighted fountain in the center of the restaurant. Seconds later, a waiter appeared and took their wine order.

"I've heard about this place. It's beautiful."

"A bit theatrical," he said. "Not bad, though. I've been trying to hire the chef away for years."

"And the mighty Michael Medici has been unsuccessful?" she teased.

He shot her a mock dark glare. "The chef is married to the owner's daughter."

She laughed. "I guess that could make it a bit more challenging. I'm surprised you didn't just buy the restaurant out from under the owner."

"I tried," Michael admitted. "Anthony is a true restauranteur. He'll be doing this forever."

"And you admire him?"

"Yeah. He came up the hard way. Not the same way I did. But he had it tough."

The waiter appeared and took their food order. Midway through their meal, a portly middle-aged gentleman approached their table. "You are enjoying your dinner?" the man asked.

Michael rose. "Delicious, Anthony. I know where to take someone I want to impress."

Anthony laughed and clasped Michael's hand with both of his. "You are too kind. No matter what you say, I will not sell."

Michael sighed. "I had to try. The lady here is quite impressed. Bella St. Clair, may I present Anthony Garfield."

Anthony turned to her and extended his hand. "*Bella,* Bella. I can see why you would want to bring her to my restaurant. Such a woman doesn't deserve second best."

"You're too kind," Bella said. "Your restaurant is fabulous."

Michael cocked his head to one side. "You're not referring to my restaurants, are you Anthony?" Michael said, sending Bella a knowing glance.

Anthony shrugged and his eyes twinkled with competitive humor. "I would never say that. I've sent several of my customers to you."

"When you were already booked," Michael said.

"As you have done to me," Anthony said. "You're a master competitor, but you need to be kept on your toes."

"And you're just the man to do it. A great dining experience."

"Thank you. High praise from such a man." He turned to Bella. "You keep him in line, okay?"

Me? Bella opened her mouth. "I'm not sure it's possible to keep Michael in line."

Anthony gave a quick nod. "Every man has his Waterloo. Good evening to both of you."

Michael sat down. "We trade top restaurant pick every other year. As much as I hate getting second place to anyone, I don't mind as much to him."

"He seems to respect you, too," she said. "I'm surprised you didn't take me to one of your restaurants."

"Didn't you hear me say that I know where to take someone I want to impress?" he asked.

She met his gaze, feeling lightning race through her. He couldn't possibly want to impress her. She wasn't that important to him. And if she were... Why did the air seem to squeeze out of her lungs?

They left the restaurant and the limo drove them to Phillips Arena. Michael led her to a private box with an unbeatable view of the court.

She looked at him. "I guess I shouldn't ask how you managed this."

"I have standing box seats. I often give them away to VIP clients," he said.

"I don't know what to say."

"How about go Hawks?" he said and she felt another ripple race through her.

Throughout the game, she was super-conscious of every time he touched her. First her shoulder, then her hand. His thigh rubbed against hers, distracting her from the game. Once, he slid his hand behind the nape of her neck, and she could have sworn she felt sparkles down her back.

The game ended far too early, and before she knew it they were in the limo again.

"Do you want a nightcap, or are you ready to go back to your apartment?" he asked.

Frustration twisted through her. He had confused the living daylights out of her. A heavy sigh poured from her.

"Problem?" he asked.

She bit her lip, wondering if she should say anything. Wondering if she could. "Do you not want me anymore?" she blurted out.

He held her gaze for a long moment that made her stomach knot. He took her hand and slid his fingers sensually through hers. "Not want you? What makes you say that?"

In for a penny. In for a pound. "Because we haven't been together in days. And you were ready to leave me at my apartment tonight."

He paused again. "I want you willing. I want you wanting me. Or not at all."

Whoa. Bella's mind reeled with his words. He wasn't going to require her to be with him? What about their deal? What about her debt to him?

She stared into his dark eyes and felt as if her inner core was shifting. This was her chance to turn away and brush her hands of him. She could go back to her apartment and lick her wounds as long as she wanted. She could buy Ben & Jerry's ice cream and eat it every night. By herself.

Or, she could be with the most exciting man she'd ever met in her life. Even though she didn't love him. Suddenly she felt as if she were a runaway train on a track she had to take. At some point, there would be a terrible crash, but for some reason she couldn't miss being with him.

"Are you saying that you would continue to support my aunt's business even if you and I never see each other again?"

"Yes."

Her heart stopped. She took a deep breath. "Take me home," she said. "With you."

Michael did take her, in more ways than one. He didn't give her a chance to change her mind. As soon as they arrived at his house, he led her upstairs to the big bed where she'd been absent too long and made love to her. He relished the scent of her body and devoured every inch of her. He drowned himself in the softness of her skin and the passion that roared beneath.

He didn't want to think about how much he'd missed her, how much he'd wanted her. How had she become such an addiction? Her spirit, her emotions got under his skin. He still felt jealous of Stephen. It was an insane emotion, but he wanted to wipe away every memory of her former fiancé. He wanted her to think only of him. He wanted her to want only him.

Where had these feelings come from? He didn't want to feel this need for her, this deeper-than-his-bones connection with her.

The next morning, he loathed leaving her. The realization bothered him, but he brushed it aside and did his usual workout. After he finished, he noticed a message on his BlackBerry. He listened to it, feeling amused and irritated. Rafe was flying his wife and son, their brother Damien and his wife, to Atlanta this afternoon. Nothing like short notice.

Michael returned to his bedroom to find Bella sleeping in his bed. A fierce possessiveness filled him, but he fought it. This would pass, he told himself. No one had ever belonged to him fully. Bella wouldn't either.

Moving to the side of the bed, he slid his fingers over her tousled dark hair. She made a soft sound and curled her head against his hand. His gut clenched at her unconscious movement.

He swallowed over a strange lump in his throat and stroked her cheek. Her eyes fluttered open, her violet eyes immediately staring at him. She sighed softly. "Hi," she said. "Have you already done your workout, taken over a half dozen companies and started a new country this morning?"

He gave a wry chuckle and tousled her hair. "No. I worked out. I just thought I should give you fair warning. Both my brothers and their families are descending on me this afternoon."

She searched his face. "You want me to leave?"

He hadn't considered any other possibility. "They'll ask you a million questions."

"You didn't answer my question," she said.

"I want you to do what you want to do," he said.

She sat up, bringing the covers with her. "Well, that doesn't help me any. I mean it would be nice to know if you want to keep me hidden or you don't want them to know about me."

"I'm okay with them knowing about you," he said, watching her carefully. "You're the one who wanted to keep this secret."

She bit her lip and met his gaze. "Well, I have to admit this sounds even better than having dinner at Cie la Sea and seeing a Hawks game in a box seat."

Surprise and amusement rippled through him. "Oh, really? How's that?"

"Getting to meet your brothers," she said. "And they're both obscenely successful, right?"

He nodded. "I guess you might say so."

"And their wives?"

"Yes. What's your point?"

"I love it that they pushed themselves on you this way." She clapped her hands. "I can't imagine you allowing yourself to be pushed by anyone."

"You imagine correctly. I wouldn't let anyone but my brothers get away with this. But we missed too many years together to say no."

She took his hand and held it in hers, her gaze holding his with an emotion that made him feel less empty, less hollow. Damn if he knew why. "I'm in."

Michael sent his limo to pick up his family from the airport. Bella paced the den, checked the mirror a few times to make sure she looked okay. She smoothed her hands over her slacks for the third time and paced again.

"Are you sure you want to meet them?" Michael asked as he glanced up from his laptop.

"Sure, I'm sure," she said, fighting her nerves. "I'm just not sure what to expect or what they'll think of me."

"They'll let me know," Michael said and turned back to his laptop.

"That's great," she said. "So they'll talk about me behind my back."

"Relax. They'll like you," he said.

"How can you be sure?"

"Because your presence will give them something to annoy me about."

She put her hands on her hips. "Why is that?"

"I haven't introduced a lot of women to them," he said, still looking at his screen.

"Why not?"

He shrugged. "I don't know. Just haven't felt like it."

The knowledge gave her a start and she crossed her arms over her chest. "I just hope they're not expecting a super wealthy, sophisticated type—"

"They're not expecting anything because I haven't told them about you."

She felt a stinging pinch to her ego and rolled her eyes at herself. Unable to stand her anxiety any longer, she gave a sigh and turned to leave the room.

"Where are you going?" he called after her.

"To bake a cake," she said.

"Why? That's why I have staff," he said.

"It will give me something to do and make the house smell welcoming," she muttered and continued into the kitchen where the cook was preparing lasagna. "Would I be in your way if I baked a cake?" she asked Gary.

He looked at her in surprise. "Not at all, but I can do it for you."

"I know you can and you could probably do a better job, but I'd like to do it if you don't mind."

Gary's face softened. "Of course. Let me know if I can help you. Do you need a cookbook?"

"No. I've got this one memorized," she said and mixed together one of her favorite cakes from childhood.

Minutes after she put the cake in the oven, the doorbell rang. Her stomach twisted. She heard a chorus of voices, male and female, along with that of a child. She considered hiding in the kitchen, but forced herself into the hallway.

At first glance, she almost couldn't believe how similar the brothers looked. All were tall with dark complexions. One of the brothers had a scar on his cheek, his bone structure somewhat angular. If she hadn't seen him smile, she would have thought he looked like a handsome version of Satan. That one must be Damien.

The other brother held a boy in his arms and a glowing woman stood beside him. From what Michael had told her, she concluded this was Rafe, the playboy brother who'd been tamed by his wife.

Suddenly, she felt Damien's gaze on her. Curiosity glinted in his eyes. "Who do we have here?" he asked Michael.

Michael met her gaze and smiled. "This is Bella St. Clair. Bella, this is my brother Damien and his wife Emma. Rafe, his wife Nicole and his son—"

"Joel," she said, smiling at the adorable boy who looked like a miniature of his father with the exception of his blue eyes.

Rafe lifted his eyebrows. "She has an advantage. She knows more about us than we know about her."

"From what I've heard about the Medici brothers, I need every advantage I can find," she said. "Nice to meet you all."

"Nice to meet you, too," Nicole said, stepping forward. "You're a brave woman facing all of them at once." She paused and sniffed the air. "What is that delicious smell?"

"Michael's cook is preparing lasagna," Bella said.

Nicole shook her head. "No. This is a chocolate smell."

Bella smiled. "Oh, I baked a chocolate cake. It's a favorite recipe from childhood. Chocolate applesauce cake."

"You've just gotten a best friend forever," Rafe said. "My wife is having chocolate cravings that grow more intense each day. I'm having a hard time keeping up."

Nicole swatted at him. "He's joking. This isn't related to my pregnancy. I like chocolate anyway."

"So do I," Emma said and extended her hand. "It's nice to meet you. How did you and Michael meet?"

"At one of his restaurants," she said. "I worked there, but I didn't know he was the owner," she quickly added. "Snowy night, lots of conversation, some surprising things in common."

"Sounds romantic," Emma said.

"It was definitely interesting. I haven't met anyone like him," she said, catching him watching her from the small space that separated them.

"I'm so glad Michael has a…um—" Nicole stopped and laughed. "A friend. He's such a workaholic. Of course, Damien was the same. So was Rafe. He just projected another image, so everyone would think he was a playboy."

"Why are you talking about me as if I'm not here?" Rafe asked.

Gary appeared in the foyer. "I can serve dinner anytime you like."

"Now sounds good," Damien said.

"Big brother has spoken," Michael said good-naturedly. "Five or ten minutes okay?" he asked Gary.

"No problem," Gary said. "The table is waiting."

"I need to go to the bathroom," Joel said.

"I can take him," Nicole said.

"I've got it," Rafe said. "Just point me in the direction of the closest bathroom."

"Down the hall to the left," Bella said.

Nicole watched after Rafe as he led his son down the hallway. "It's hard to believe how quickly he has adapted to being a great father."

"You shouldn't be surprised," Damien said. "The Medici men are overachievers in every area."

Emma leaned her head against his shoulder. "So true. I'm sure you've noticed that about Michael," she said to Bella.

"Fishing, fishing," Michael said under his breath as he slid his hand behind Bella's back and led her into the den. "Forgive my lovely sister-in-law. She may look sweet and demure, but she slayed the dragon known as Damien. Does anyone else want to wash up? There are three more bathrooms on this floor."

Moments later, the group took their seats at Michael's beautiful antique dining room table. Gary served the meal while Michael and his brothers caught up on their business activities.

Afterward, Gary served her cake for dessert.

"Delicious," Emma said. "You must give me your recipe."

"Me, too," Nicole said.

"So, you found a woman who can cook," Rafe said.

"It's news to me," Michael said, meeting Bella's gaze. "But I shouldn't be surprised. She's a multi-talented woman."

"She worked for a charitable organization overseas for a year, is a licensed esthetician, and—"

Embarrassed by the attention, Bella stood and interrupted. "Does anyone want anything else?"

"More cake," Joel said, his face covered in chocolate.

Nicole laughed. "Maybe tomorrow. Bedtime, now."

"Mom," he protested.

"May I read him a bedtime story?" Emma asked.

"I'm sure he would love that," Nicole said then glanced at Bella. "Would you like to join us?"

"Sure, thank you," Bella said and watched as Nicole and Emma cuddled Joel. Emma read a story, then Bella read another before the boy fell asleep.

"Only a two-story night. He must have been tired from all the excitement," Nicole whispered as they left the room.

"Between Damien and Rafe playing with him, I'm surprised he didn't fall asleep during the meal," Emma said.

"Joel was very well-behaved during dinner for being so tired," Bella said. "Would the two of you like to go to the den or the keeping room?"

"Keeping room?" Emma echoed. "What's that?"

"A cozy little room off the kitchen with a fireplace. I suspect the men have taken over the den and are watching a game," Nicole said. "I vote for the keeping room. I noticed Damien really seemed to enjoy Joel. Rafe wondered if the two of you are getting interested in having a child of your own."

"He used to say *never,* then he progressed to maybe. Lately he says *later.*" Emma smiled as Bella led the two women toward the kitchen. "I'm perfectly happy taking our time. I'm happier than I ever dreamed possible with Damien." She turned to Bella and sank into an upholstered chair. "What about Michael? How does he feel about children?"

Bella blinked. "Children?" She shook her head. "I wouldn't know. We haven't discussed them, but I know he's happy to be an uncle."

Nicole nodded. "How is Michael doing, really?" she asked. "Rafe has been concerned about him."

"So has Damien," Emma said.

"Really," Bella said, surprise racing through her. "His businesses are doing well and in terms of his health, he works out every morning."

"Yes, but—" Nicole hesitated and sighed. "He's really struggling with the investigation about Leo."

Bella nodded, but she wasn't sure what Nicole was talking about.

"Damien says the latest news from the private investigator really shook him up," Emma said.

What news? Bella wanted to ask, but felt foolish for not knowing. "Michael is a strong man," she said. "I can't imagine anything defeating him."

"I just hate that he continues to torture himself about this. I almost wonder if it would be easier if Leo were pronounced—"

"Don't say that," Nicole said. "Rafe suffers, too. And now knowing that Leo survived the train crash and could have been raised by an abusive man—" Nicole shuddered. "I pray every night that he will be found whole and healthy."

"And ready to reunite with his brothers," Emma said.

"Exactly," Nicole agreed. Silence hovered over the women for a long moment. "I'm glad Michael is doing well. From the way he looks at you, I'm sure you're part of the reason."

Bella wasn't at all sure of that. "Hmm. Would either of you like something to drink? Coffee? Tea?"

"I'd love some hot tea," Emma said.

Bella rose. "Let me get it for you," she murmured and went into the kitchen. Her stomach twisted with agitation as she put the water on and pulled some packets of tea from the cupboard. Why hadn't Michael discussed something so important to him with her? The logical side of her brain immediately came to his defense.

They were having an affair where he dictated the rules. He was completely within his rights to keep the matter about his missing brother private.

After the way he'd insisted that she reveal her painful story about Stephen, though, it didn't seem fair at all. Bella felt like a fool. Why hadn't he told her about the latest developments in the search for Leo? Perhaps because she wasn't truly important.

The knowledge stung. It shouldn't, but it did. She pulled two cups and saucers from the cabinet.

"I can take care of this," Gary said.

She shook her head. "No. I've got it. It's just tea."

"I insist," Gary said, pulling out a tray and cream from the refrigerator. "It is my job."

Stepping back, she smiled although she was still distracted. "Thanks. It's for the two women in the keeping room. I'm going to step out for a breath of fresh air. I'll be back in just a moment."

Bella scooted out the back door and took a deep breath of the chilly winter air. Closing her eyes, she tried to clear her head. She felt hurt and offended. She took another deep breath and wrapped her arms around her waist.

"Too many Medicis for you?" Michael asked, sliding his arm around her back. "Can't say I didn't warn you."

Wondering when he'd joined her, she glanced up at him. "You did warn me."

"Did someone offend you?"

"Hmm," she said and swallowed a wry chuckle. "I guess if anyone offended me, it was me."

His body stiffened. "You? How?"

"It's more about what happened before your family even arrived," she said.

"Is the guessing game necessary or do you want to tell me what this is about?"

"I could say the same about guessing games," she said. "Why didn't you tell me the latest news about Leonardo?"

His face immediately turned dark. "What about Leonardo?"

"The fact that he survived the train crash," she said. "You found that out the night you were sitting in the dark by the fire, didn't you?"

"Yes, I did," he said and moved away from her. "You need to understand that there are some subjects that are off limits."

"To me," she said, angry at herself because this just underscored the fact that she was temporary.

His expression closed up as tight as Fort Knox. "I won't allow this subject to contaminate my time with you. That's my final word."

Eleven

That night was the first time she shared a bed with Michael and they didn't make love. She lay staring up at the ceiling, torn between anger at herself and him. Why should he be the one to call the shots?

Because he was financing her aunt's business.

It seemed, however, that he'd changed the rules when he'd said he wanted her to come to him. Add in the meeting with his family and she didn't know what was going on.

"You're a complicated, difficult man," she said because she knew he was still awake.

"I'm neither," he said. "I'm ordinary."

She laughed. "That's the most ridiculous thing you've ever said."

"I am," he insisted. "I have basic needs. Food, water, sex."

She rolled her eyes. "Along with control, wealth, and a few other things you probably don't realize."

He rolled over and pulled her against him. "Such as?"

She wanted to say *love,* but she wouldn't. "Compassion, affection, understanding."

He shrugged, but slid his fingers through her hair. "Like I said before, there's a difference between need and want."

"So, maybe you want those things," she said, feeling herself sink under the spell of his dark eyes. "There are other things you want, but you'd never admit it."

"Never is a long time," he told her and pulled her on top of him.

Her quarrel with him grew less important with his hard body beneath hers. "Well, it's difficult for me to imagine…"

Sliding his hand behind the nape of her neck, he pulled her mouth against his. "No need to imagine," he said. "I'm here now and so are you."

He seduced her with his sure, magic hands and seductive velvet voice, making her forget her reservations, making her forget that she wanted more than his passion and his body. He took her up and over the top, again and again, and somewhere in that dark night, something changed in her heart….

The next morning, Gary prepared a splendid breakfast and the Medicis enjoyed a rare sunny morning in a private neighborhood park. The three Medici men played ball with Joel, carrying the little boy like a football and making him laugh until he was weak.

Michael lifted his nephew onto his shoulders and carried him around so he could be taller than anyone else.

"That's good father material," Nicole hinted broadly.

The comment made her stomach feel as if she were going up on the down elevator. "I'm sure he'll be a great father when he's ready," Bella said, then tried to change the subject. "When did you say your due date is?"

Soon enough, Rafe checked his watch and announced that it was time to leave. "This has been fun, but some of us have to work tomorrow," he announced.

"And I need a round of pool with Rafe," Damien said. "He's been impossible since I let him beat me."

"Let me?" Rafe said. "You wish."

"We'll see," Damien said.

"Sounds like a challenge to me," Michael said with a secret smile.

"If you came down to South Beach, you could put yourself in the running."

"I'm busy with more important things than billiards at the moment."

"Afraid of getting beat?" Rafe asked.

"You can't goad me," Michael said. "I really do have better things to do."

"Damn." Rafe turned serious. "Are you talking about Leo? You shouldn't let this eat at you so much."

Bella's heart stopped and she stared at Michael.

Michael's gaze turned hard. "I can handle it."

Rafe lifted his brow and shook his head. "Okay." He glanced at Bella. "It was nice meeting you, Bella. Good luck dealing with my brother. He can be ornery as hell, but underneath, way underneath, he's a good guy."

The next day, Michael arrived home at dinnertime. Bella was working late, so he went through the mail. When he saw a package from Italy, his gut clenched.

Curious if this was from his mysterious Aunt Emilia, he quickly opened it. Photographs spilled out.

He held them up and was taken back in time to his childhood. He saw the four wide-eyed faces of him and his brothers dressed in their Sunday best. His gaze wandered to Leo's face and he felt the sting of loss. He wondered how long a person could mourn. Forever, it seemed.

He looked at another photo of a baby held in his father's arms like a football while a toddler craned to see the infant. He turned the photo over and saw a notation scrawled on it. *Baby Michael with brother Leonardo.*

Less than a year younger than Leo, he'd tormented his brother by following him everywhere. He'd been so excited to join his father to ride the train to the baseball game. It would have been his first. He'd even rubbed it in a little to Leo because Leo wanted to go so badly. But Leo had already attended a game with Dad, so it was Michael's turn to go. Until he'd raided the cookie jar before dinner and his parents had decided his discipline would be not going to the game.

To this day, he couldn't eat a cookie without feeling sick to his stomach. His father had died in the train crash and his brother had been missing forever.

His stomach twisting with a guilt that wouldn't pass, he found a short note behind the photos. *Dear Michael, I wanted you to have these photographs your father sent me so many years ago. I am so glad that you and your brothers have found each other and are keeping your family bond alive. Do not ever give up on each other. Love Emilia.*

Michael stared at the note and photos, fighting a

warring combination of sweet memories and nauseating loss. A day didn't pass when he failed to think of Leo, but seeing this underscored his need for resolution.

Unwilling to discuss this with his brothers, Michael called his investigator. "Have you made any progress?" he asked, not bothering to keep the impatience from his voice.

"These things take time," the investigator said.

"You've been saying that for months," Michael said.

"Look, I believe your brother may have survived the crash. I believe he was taken in by a woman who couldn't have children."

"Names, what are their names?"

"She went by a different name than her husband, and apparently her husband went by several different names."

Michael frowned. "Several names. He must've been a criminal."

"Some records indicate he'd been charged with petty theft. When I checked three of the names, I got a bunch of complaints about grifting. Some that involved a boy."

Michael closed his eyes. "What was the boy's name?"

"Depends," Carson said. "John, George, but no Leo. The complaints that included a mention of the boy stopped when your brother would have been about fifteen."

"Do you think he died?" he asked. "Or was killed?"

"Either of those could have happened, but there's another possibility. He could have disappeared and changed his identity."

"I want a written report of everything you've found. Is the woman who kept him still alive?"

"No, and I'm not too sure about the man, either. I'm

still working that end of the lead, but I have to pursue others, too."

"Okay," Michael said with a sigh. "Keep me posted."

The rainy day matched Bella's mood. Since it was slow that morning at the spa, she urged Charlotte to get out and take a break while Bella manned the reception desk. It took some arm-twisting, but Charlotte finally agreed.

With no customers in sight, Bella sipped a latte as she tried to distract herself by reading the paper. She was still angry with herself for expecting Michael to share more of himself with her. When he'd decided to introduce her to his family, she'd let her guard down. She should remember that he viewed her as temporary and she should always, always do the same.

Under the downtown community section, a short article caught her eye. The article reported how a fire had destroyed a community center, the same one where she and Michael had worked that Saturday. An anonymous donor had stepped up to pay for a new center to be built.

Her heart skipped over itself and suspicion raced through her. A warm, lovely kind of suspicion. Anonymous donor. She'd just bet she knew who that was.

Bella sighed. How was she supposed to tell herself that she shouldn't care about Michael when he did these kinds of things? Just when she thought he was too hard and remote, he did something to turn her opinion of him upside down.

Michael heard the side door open. "Hello?" Bella called. "Anybody home? Anybody want a hot dog with mustard and chili and greasy French fries just because it's Monday and it's raining?"

She walked into the den still wearing a yellow slicker and carting a paper bag and what he would guess were two milk shakes.

He chuckled. "Sounds good. Gary may not like it, though. He thinks you're going to put him out of a job."

She shook her head. "Ridiculous. I can make a few things, but he's the professional. Where do you want to eat?"

"In here," he said. "What kind of milk shake did you get me?"

She tossed him a sideways glance. "How do you know I got one for you? I may have gotten both of them for me."

He grinned. "I guess I'll just have to see if I can negotiate one from you."

"It's possible," she said, pulling off her jacket. "I hope you like chocolate."

"I do," he said. She made the room brighter, somehow.

"Okay, then, if you answer this question honestly, I will give you a chocolate shake," she said and unpacked the bags, giving him two hot dogs while she took one.

"Depends on the question," he said, joining her at the table.

She nodded. "During one of my breaks today, I was reading the newspaper." She lifted a French fry to his lips and he ate it.

"And?"

"Well, you remember that community center we were painting, the one that blew up?"

"Yes," he said and took a bite out of one of the hot dogs. "This is really good."

She shot him a conspiratorial smile. "I agree. Back to the newspaper. There was an article about how the community center is going to be torn down and a new one is going to be built in its place."

"That's good," he said, continuing to eat his meal.

"An anonymous donor has made this possible," she said, regarding him with deep suspicion. "You wouldn't happen to know anything about this donor, would you?"

"I suspect if the donor is anonymous then he—" He swallowed another bite. "Or she prefers to remain anonymous."

She slumped. "You're not going to tell me, are you?"

"Tell you what?"

"If you are the anonymous donor," she said.

"Me?" he asked, injecting shock into his voice. "Why would I part with my money to fund a community center that could very well end up doing an inefficient job helping the children who need the services?"

She looked away. "True. You're not the type to have a soft spot for a cause, especially after you've suffered burns from rescuing a child at the community center."

"Right," he said.

"Rescuing a child like that wouldn't have an impact on you. You wouldn't be concerned about that child's future in a community center."

"The old building was a fire hazard," he said.

"A terrible one," she agreed.

"They'd damn well better make sure the new one isn't," he muttered.

Bella looked at him and held his gaze for a moment then slid the milk shake to him.

"I didn't tell you who the anonymous donor was," he said.

"That's okay. I have an idea of my own. Want me to describe him?"

He shrugged. "If you want."

"He's hot," she said.

"Oh, really?" he said, lifting his brow at her.

She nodded. "He's the kind who pretends he doesn't care."

"Pretends?"

She nodded again. "He's all about the bottom line."

"What other line is there?"

She leaned toward him and took his chin in her hand in a surprisingly aggressive move that he liked. "You're such a faker," she whispered and kissed him.

The more time he spent with Bella, the more he wanted her. This wasn't going the way he'd planned. He'd expected to get his fill of her then both of them would move on. The next two evenings, he even came home early so he could spend more time with her.

In the morning, he rose early as he always did and exercised in his gym. When he returned to his bedroom, he found her reading from a folder.

She quickly set the folder down beside her and smiled. "How was the elliptical?"

"You're awake. What were you reading?" he asked, but he already knew. He took a quick, sharp breath to control his anger.

She cleared her throat. "Um, it was on the nightstand. I knocked it off when I went to the bathroom."

"You didn't notice the label said Leo," he said, clenching his teeth.

She seemed to catch on that he was displeased. She

bit her lip and looked away. "I'm sorry. I know this is important to you and you won't discuss it with me. It's hard for me to feel shut out on this. I want to help you."

"You can't," he said. "It's a matter of patient, resilient research by a knowledgeable investigator. I'm going in the shower. If you want to read it while I'm in the shower, go ahead. When I get out, I'll be putting the report away and we won't discuss it."

"But," she began.

"This is nonnegotiable, Bella. Don't push it," he said and went into the bathroom to try to wash the guilt about his brother from his skin, from inside him. He knew, however, that it wouldn't work. He also knew that he couldn't, wouldn't discuss Leo with Bella. Her empathy would be harder to bear than his own self-condemnation.

"You're late," Charlotte said as Bella returned from her lunch on Saturday. "I can't keep up with you. One week you're working overtime. The next week you're spacey and late."

"I'm sorry," Bella said, pulling on the jacket that bore the name of her aunt's business. "I have a lot on my mind."

"Does his name start with M?" Charlotte asked. "What's going on between you two?"

"It's complicated," Bella said. Her heart and mind were still reeling after reading the P.I.'s report. It hit her again that all the Medici brothers had suffered terribly. Knowing how much Michael still grieved brought tears to her eyes. She took a deep breath. "There's more to him than meets the eye."

"That can be good."

"I can't talk about it yet. He would be furious," Bella said. "Just trust me that I want to help him. I need to help him."

Charlotte frowned. "It's nothing illegal, is it?"

Bella shook her head. "Nothing illegal."

Charlotte shrugged. "Okay, just try not to be late. Your client is waiting for you to work your magic. Can you close up tonight? Fred is taking me out for lobster."

"Hmm," Bella said with a smile. "Looks like you and Fred are turning into a regular thing."

Charlotte scowled at her. "Get to work."

Bella worked nonstop until 6:00 p.m., but the entire time she was thinking about Michael and his brother Leo. If Michael was able to answer his questions about Leo, she wondered if Michael would finally be at peace. She wondered what kind of person he would be. She wondered if he would be free to love and be loved.

Despite all his success and hard work, Michael felt unworthy of love. She identified it because she had felt that way after her mother had abandoned her. After all, if her own mother had dumped her, wouldn't everyone else?

Stephen had made her believe in the possibility of love. She thought he'd believed in her. She'd thought he'd been committed. She was the one who'd left to pursue her dream and left her aunt and Stephen behind. Even though Stephen had encouraged her, he'd needed her when he'd lost his job and his confidence. She'd thought Stephen was the sweetest man in the world. Lately, she wasn't as sure about Stephen as she once had been. He just didn't seem as sincere.

She was sure that although Michael was as sincere as the day was long, he also was not the sweetest man in the world. His background had given him rough edges. He didn't love her. He wanted her. The more she was with him, the more she wanted him freed from his demons. Without those demons, he would be so much happier, so much more fulfilled. Free to love and receive the love he deserved, even if she wasn't the one for him.

Twelve

Bella whisked into Michael's home a bit later than she'd planned on Monday. "Hello? Any news?"

Silence followed. "I'm in the den."

Bella felt a sinking sensation in her stomach and rushed to the den. "Is there a problem?"

"No." His gaze was shuttered. "Why do you ask?"

"Because you sound like someone has pushed your mute button," she said.

One side of his lips lifted in amusement. "I'm fine. No hot dogs?"

"No. I was slammed at work then had to run errands. I can fix some if you like," she offered.

"No. Gary can prepare something for us."

"I always feel guilty about that," she said. "We're just two people. We should be able to fix our own."

"I can afford it," he said.

"Still," she said.

"What do you want for dinner?"

"I'll fix a peanut butter and honey sandwich with bananas and potato chips," she said adamantly.

He chuckled. "He's planning shrimp creole for me."

"Oh, that sounds delicious," she said, her mouth watering.

"Wouldn't want to keep you from your peanut butter sandwich."

"You're an evil man," she said.

His face hardened. "You're not the first to know that."

The self-contempt in his gaze took her breath away. "Michael, you have to tell me what happened. Something happened."

"Another dead lead," he said and shrugged. "Nothing new."

"I've been thinking about this," she said eagerly.

"Thinking about what?" he asked, his gaze cold.

"Thinking about Leo," she said. "After I read the investigator's report, I wondered if you should put an ad in some of the Pennsylvania newspapers."

"If that were the best way to proceed, the investigator would suggest it," he said.

"But what if you and your brothers did it?" she asked. "Maybe that would have more impact than it would from the P.I."

Michael's nostrils flared in anger as he looked at her. "Bella, we've already discussed this. It's none of your business."

"But you're suffering," she said, clenching her fists. "I can't stand it."

He lifted his hand. "Enough. I'm spending the night alone. You're on your own."

She felt as if he'd stabbed her by shutting her out. "Michael," she said.

"Good night," he said and turned away.

Frustrated and hurt, Bella wanted to throw something against the floor-to-ceiling windows and make them break. She wanted to break down this barrier between her and Michael. Their relationship had become very different from what it had been when it started. Every now and then she felt as if she were getting past the walls Michael had built around himself, but then she felt as if the walls were forged from concrete.

"Oh," she groaned, pushing her hair from her face. Why should she stay here? She would just become more frustrated and upset. Fine, he said she was on her own. She would leave.

The following day, Bella inwardly fumed, practicing a half dozen speeches designed to set Michael straight, as if such a thing were possible. As if he'd listen to her for more than three seconds. Not on the subject of Leo. After lunch, she was still in flux about her evening plans. If her aunt weren't so busy with her new beau, Bella would have spent the evening with her.

"Bella," Charlotte called in a singsong voice. "You have a visitor."

Bella glanced up to see Michael standing next to the front desk. Surprise washed over her, although she was still peeved with him.

"Don't worry about a thing. I've looked at the book, and Donna and I can take all your appointments. It won't be any trouble at all," Charlotte said.

"Take my appointments," she echoed, confused. "Why?"

Charlotte smiled coyly. "I'll let Michael tell you. But don't worry about your other appointments today. I've got those handled, too."

"What?" she asked as Charlotte walked away. "What is she talking about?"

"I'm considering buying a property in Grand Cayman," Michael said.

"That's nice," she said, looking away from his gaze, wanting to hang on to her anger. Her anger would keep her safe from getting more emotionally intertwined with him.

"I'm flying down there this afternoon and coming back on Saturday morning."

She shrugged. "Have a nice trip."

"I want you to join me," he said.

She blinked and met his gaze. "This afternoon?" She shouldn't go. Who did he think he was telling her to join him with zero notice? *Join him for a trip to a luxurious Caribbean island where it was warm instead of gray and gloomy.* "I can't imagine leaving Charlotte in the lurch like this, especially on Saturday."

"I discussed it with Charlotte and she's all for it."

"I don't want Charlotte overworking," she said, fidgeting as visions of her and Michael walking along a beautiful beach danced in her head.

"Has she been overworking?" he asked.

"Well, no, not yet, but—" She broke off, feeling pinned by his gaze.

"Are you afraid of going with me?"

Her stomach dipped. "Of course not. Why would I be afraid?" Because she was starting to develop feelings for him, strong feelings that could cause problems for her later.

"You tell me," he said.

When she didn't answer, he shrugged his broad shoulders. "I won't force you to go. If you're not interested in stepping into water so clear you can see down fifty feet and—"

"Okay, okay," she said and told him the same thing she had when his brothers had come to town. "I'm in."

"Fine," he said. "We can leave from here. I'll buy everything you'll need down there."

"But can't I pick up just a few things? I don't want to spend my time there shopping."

He gave a wry chuckle. "Not something I would expect to hear from a woman. You don't want to spend your time shopping. Okay. I'll have the driver stop by your apartment. You have one hour."

"Sheesh. "Do you ever give a girl some notice?" she muttered. "Aunt Charlotte, I'm headed out," she called.

Charlotte beamed and walked over to give her a hug. "Take pictures."

"Camera," Bella said, imprinting the item on her list. "Must bring camera."

"And have a good time."

"Are you sure you'll be okay?" Bella asked, suddenly worried again.

"I'll be fine. You shouldn't pass this up." She glanced at Michael. "Treat her right or you'll find a pair of scissors in your head when you least expect it."

"Whoa," he said and gave her a mock salute. "I'll make sure she has a good time."

"You do that," Charlotte said then clapped her hands. "Now get going. Daylight's burning!"

Four hours later, they were sitting at a restaurant on the ocean watching the sunset as they were served a gourmet meal. A parrot squawked in the background and a warm breeze slid over her skin.

"Uncle," she said.

"Uncle what?" Michael asked.

"I can't deny that this is incredible. The food, the sunset, everything."

"It's not bad, is it?" he said. "Grand Cayman is one of the more civilized islands. Rarely gets hit by hurricanes, but it can happen. The rainy season is supposed to be unpleasant. You'll have to tell me what you think after you've spent more time here."

"I can tell you already that it's a wonderful break from winter, if that's what you're looking for," she said.

"That," he said. "And I always consider the investment benefit. This would be more for fun, though."

She smiled at him. "Oh, my. I thought you weren't interested in spending money for fun."

He slid her a sideways glance. "I can do fun things. I just haven't been motivated until recently."

"And why is that?" she asked, lifting her glass of wine to her lips and taking a sip.

"I think you know it's because of you," he said.

"Hard for me to believe I have any influence over you." She stared out at the ocean, drinking in the sight.

"Is that what you want? Influence over me?" he asked.

She met his gaze. "I want you to be happy."

Something flashed in his eyes, something she couldn't identify at first glance because it came and went so quickly. "And you think you know what would make me happy."

"That sounds potentially arrogant, but I think I have an idea of what might help. Not that I'll get a chance to help with that."

"Why do you care about my happiness?" he asked. "You're getting what you want. I've funded your aunt's business. You know I'm not going to renege."

Her stomach twisted and she frowned. "I don't know. Maybe I'm more of a sap than I thought I was." She met his gaze again. "Or maybe there's more to you than I thought there was."

"That last one would be wrong. I'm shallow," he insisted.

"Yes," she said. "That's why you agreed to resuscitate my aunt's business."

"I benefit from that agreement in several ways."

"It was still coloring outside your lines. You're a liar if you disagree," she said.

His eyes lit with amusement, but he said nothing.

"And there's the matter of the community center," she said.

"Anonymous could be anyone."

"Uh-huh," she said. "There's another subject that reveals your tender side, but you get all touchy when I bring it up, so I won't."

"Thank you," he said and nodded toward the horizon. "Don't miss the sunset."

She watched the orange ball sink lower and a green light followed it. "I've never seen that before," she said. "What was it?"

"A green flash," he said. "I'm not much for legends, but legend has it that seeing it means you have the ability to see into another person's heart."

"So, you don't believe it," she said.

He paused. "I didn't say that."

She leaned toward him. "You could have any woman. Why do you want me?"

He shook his head. "Too many reasons. Would you like dessert?"

She also shook her head. "No. I'm ready to go if you are."

Minutes later, the driver drove them down a winding road to a gated driveway which opened after the driver punched in a code. It was a clear night, and the moonlight glowed on the stucco mansion with colored roof tiles as they drove toward it.

Bella sucked in her breath at the beauty of the building and the lush green foliage. She looked at Michael. "I must have misunderstood. I thought you were looking at a condominium."

"The condo's on Seven Mile beach. This one would be for personal use." The driver pulled to a stop and they got out.

Bella looked up at the size of the mansion. "It's lovely from the outside."

"Let's take a look inside," he said and unlocked the front door. Cool marble floors and upscale island decor greeted them.

"Very nice," she said.

He took her hand in his and wandered through the house. All the modern necessities and wants anyone could imagine were included in the home along with several views designed to make a mere mortal drool, even at night.

They stood on a deck for a moment and Bella drank in the gentle sound of the ocean against the sand. "Oh, I think we'd better leave right away," she said.

"Why?"

"Because I don't know how anyone could leave after staying here five minutes," she said.

He laughed and tugged her hand. "Let's go upstairs."

Reluctantly leaving the deck, she climbed the stairs and looked at the hallways of bedrooms, another deck and finally the master suite. She followed him inside, glancing up to see the stars in the skylights which featured blinds for closing. A floor-to-ceiling window which revealed a fantastic view of the sea and the sky sat opposite the large bed. She walked through the sliding-glass door on to yet another deck with an awning, chairs and table and Jacuzzi.

"Ohhhh, this is so good it's bad," she said.

"You like it?" he asked, pulling her against him as he looked out at the ocean.

"Who wouldn't?" she asked, looking up at him.

"Relaxing has never been my forte," he said. "I've received solicitations like this before, but I ignored them. Who has time for trips to the Cayman Islands?"

She saw a lostness in his eyes and her stomach twisted. "Has it ever occurred to you to take a vacation?"

"I've taken vacations. Mountain climbing, scuba diving…"

"No, I mean a real vacation where you actually relax," she said. "Maybe even, heaven forbid, sleep late and ditch your workout for one whole day."

His lips twitched. "Not really."

"Why doesn't that surprise me? I wonder what it would take to get you to sleep late," she said.

His eyes darkened. "Try and find out."

After a night of lovemaking, she felt him stir in the morning. Determined to keep him from getting out of bed, she rolled on top of him, still half-asleep. "Nuh-uh," she said. "You're not going anywhere."

She opened her eyes to find his sleepy eyes staring back at hers. "How are you going to keep me here?"

"One way or another," she said and pressed her mouth against his for a long kiss.

His hands skimmed over her buttocks. "You're cute when you're slee—"

She wiggled lower, sliding on to his hardness, taking the words from his mouth. "Ohhhh," he said.

She began to ride, forcing her eyes to open so she could see the ecstasy on his face. He wrapped his hands about her hips again, guiding her, distracting her. She was supposed to be in control, but he took it from her.

Soon, her pleasure splintered from her and she squeezed him tight within her. His gasps of pleasure fed hers and she climaxed just as the sun peeked through the horizon.

Seconds, minutes, hours later, Michael slid his leg over her. "Lord, woman, what time is it?"

"I don't know and I don't care," she said.

He chuckled, nuzzling her head. He shifted her slightly then swore. "It's eight-thirty. Do you know the last time I slept this late?"

"Not last weekend," she said.

"That's true," he said, rising. "The last time I slept this late, I was thirteen and sick with strep throat."

She waved her hand upward and he caught it. "What do you want?"

"To feel your forehead to make sure you don't have strep throat," she said.

He chuckled and lifted her hand to his mouth instead. "No strep throat. What do you want for breakfast? There's staff downstairs waiting for our order."

She sighed. "Sometimes, I want no staff," she said. "I'm good with a bagel."

"We'll do that next visit. What do you want this time?"

"Scrambled eggs, blueberry pancakes and crisp bacon," she said.

"That's a little more than a bagel," he said.

"Yeah, well if they're dying to fix breakfast…" she said and suddenly felt guilty. "Scratch that," she said. "I'm okay with toast."

"Liar," he said. "Bella wants pancakes. Bella will have pancakes."

Crap, she thought. She'd better not get used to this.

After breakfast, she and Michael explored the house then changed into swimsuits to sun on the private beach. Michael wasn't the type to sit still, so he read for a while then dragged her into the water.

She stared at her feet next to his, marveling at how clear the water was. Tiny fishes swam between their legs. "Omigosh, this is amazing."

"Look farther out," he said, pointing to where the water was deeper.

She spotted larger, multicolored fish and a dolphin jumping. "It's so calm and clear you don't even need to snorkel."

"One of the reasons I like it here," he said.

"How often have you been?" she asked.

"Just a couple times. Always business," he said. He tugged her deeper into the water and dunked her.

She gasped as she returned to the surface. "Why did you do that?" she asked, swatting at his muscular chest. She may as well have been a fly.

"You looked like you needed to get wet all over," he said, grinning as he pulled her against him.

"How about a warning next time?" she demanded, wrapping her legs around his waist because it seemed like the natural thing to do.

He shook his head, his dark eyes glinting in the sun like black diamonds. "Too much fun taking you by surprise," he said and took her mouth before she could protest.

With the water and Michael's arms surrounding her, she felt herself sinking under his spell. What a magical moment to be with him. Away from everything but each other.

Seconds later, she felt her bathing-suit top slip from her body. "What—"

Michael grinned like a demon and moved away from her.

"You," she accused, going after him, but he was faster. "Michael," she called. "Give me back my swimsuit."

"In a while," he said. "Since we have a private beach, you can go topless."

"Some other time," she said, swimming toward him.

"I dare you," he said.

She stopped and groaned. "Oh, don't say that."

"Ah, so you can't turn down a dare, either," he said, reminding her of how she'd challenged him to help paint the community center.

"That was different. You got to keep your clothes on."

"And burn my hands," he said.

"True," she muttered, still reluctant. She met his gaze, for once nearly carefree and she realized she would do just about anything for him to stay that way instead of tortured and mired in guilt.

Taking a deep breath, she closed her eyes. *I can do this,*

she told herself. *I can do this.* She opened her eyes and walked forward, biting her lip as her upper body broke the surface of the water. Even though Michael had seen her naked too many times to count, this just felt different.

She couldn't quite meet his gaze. "Never let it be said—"

He swooped her into his arms, his chest covering hers as he carried her into deeper water. "I really didn't think you'd do it."

She gawked at him. "You dared me. What am I supposed to do?"

"Remind me to never let you around any other men who like to make dares," he said gruffly.

She looked at him. "I'm selective," she said.

"Keep it that way," he said.

Thirteen

They returned to Atlanta on Saturday in time for Bella to attend the wedding of a college friend. The trip to Grand Cayman had been amazing. She'd never seen Michael in a fun mode before. It lifted her heart and made her want to see more of that from him.

As they returned home, however, she saw him pulling into himself more and more. They parted ways at the private airport. He tucked her into his limo and she returned to her apartment.

Dressing for the wedding, Bella couldn't help wondering about her own future. What did Michael want from her? She couldn't believe he wanted marriage, yet she knew he didn't want her to be involved with any other man.

She drove to the church where her old friend CeCe was married then went to a country club for the reception. She smiled as CeCe danced first with her new husband and then her father. A bite of nostalgia prodded her at the memory of her own father, whom she'd never known, and her mother, who had died.

"They look happy," a male voice said from behind her.

She turned at the sound of Stephen's voice and nodded. "They do." She glanced over her shoulder at him, looking for his fiancée. "Where's your fiancée?"

He met her gaze. "Where's your friend? Michael Medici?"

"We just got back from Grand Cayman. He had some work to do," she said.

"You're traveling in different circles these days," Stephen said. "Michael Medici's pretty high on the food chain."

"You're traveling in different circles now, too," she said. "Excuse me—"

"No," he said, blocking her way. "There's no reason for us to be awkward. You and I have known each other too long. Let me get you a drink."

She took a deep breath and looked at his familiar blond hair and blue eyes and relaxed. This was Stephen. She'd known him a long time. He'd been important to her and now he wanted to be her friend. The sting of longing she usually felt for him was absent.

"Okay," she finally said. "White wine," she said.

"I know that," he said with a smile and left to get a drink for her.

Shortly, he returned with a beer for himself and a glass of wine for her. "How did you like Grand Cayman?"

"It was amazing. The water was so clear," she said.

"And Michael, what is he like?"

She tilted her head to the side. "Complex," she said.

"One time I think I've got his personality nailed, then seconds later, I learn more about him."

"Hmm," Stephen said.

"What about your job?" she asked. "Are you liking it?"

"I like being employed," he said and paused. "Britney is a means to an end."

She gasped, shocked at his response. "But you do love her."

He shrugged. "In a way, I guess," he said, lifting his beer and taking a long swallow. "But I've never gotten over you."

Dismayed by his declaration, she shook her head. "I thought you had fallen in love with Britney."

"In a way," he repeated, covering her hand with his. "But you know I've loved you forever, Bella."

"But you broke up with me."

He shrugged again. "I knew Britney could help me get ahead. But you and I had something special. There's no reason we can't continue."

She blinked. "Not if you're engaged, we can't."

"There's no reason you and I can't enjoy each other. After all, you and Michael are enjoying each other."

"What does that have to do with anything?"

"If you and Michael can have an affair, why can't you and I?"

"You are engaged," she said.

"If you're willing to give yourself to Michael, why wouldn't you give yourself to me?" he asked, taking her hand and pressing his mouth against hers.

Bella jerked away, turning her face. She stood, barely holding back the desire to throw her wine in his face. "Again, because you're engaged. Michael is not."

"Bella, you're Michael Medici's mistress," he said. "I can afford you now, too."

"No," she said, nauseated by Stephen's proposal. "Never." She turned around and walked right into Michael's hard chest.

Michael looked at her and Stephen with a scathing glance. Bella opened her mouth to explain, but Michael turned toward Stephen.

"Leave her alone," he said. "You left her behind. She is with me now. If I hear of you bothering her again, your current job could suddenly disappear." He turned to Bella. "Let's go," he said and escorted her from the room to the front door. "How could you let him touch you?"

"I didn't want to. He took me by surprise," she said.

"You must have known he would be here," Michael said, his jaw twitching.

"I didn't," she said. "It's true that Stephen is friends with this couple, too, but I didn't know if he would attend. I was sure his fiancée would be with him if he did." She paused a half beat. "Besides, if I were intent on getting together with Stephen, why would I have invited you to come with me this afternoon?"

"Let's go back to my house," he said and waved for the valet. "I'll take you."

"But my car," she began.

"I'll send a driver for it," he said.

With Stephen's insulting remarks, the event had already been ruined for her, so she was all too happy to leave. The drive was silent, and Michael's brooding disposition made the air in the car so thick she could hardly breathe.

As soon as they arrived at Michael's house, he whisked her up to his bedroom. She hated for him to be upset, but she didn't feel she deserved his wrath. "I realize it may have looked damaging, but you have to believe I didn't invite his advance. You shouldn't be angry at me."

He took a deep breath, his nostrils flaring with emotion. "I'm not angry at you. I'm furious with Stephen. What the hell gave him the idea that he could treat you like that?"

She shook her head, but her stomach sank. "He seemed to have figured out that you and I have an arrangement. This is what I was afraid of, that people would find out that I could be bought."

Michael sliced his hand through the air. "Under the right circumstances, everyone can be bought."

His assessment only made her feel worse. "Actions can be bought, but emotions can't."

"You may have agreed to our affair to help your aunt, but things are different. Can you tell me that the only reason you're with me is because of your aunt?"

The oxygen seemed to disappear from her lungs. "You know I can't," she whispered.

He pulled her against him. "Damn right you can't," he muttered and took her mouth. The passion between them exploded, burning boundaries, excuses and denial. Perhaps a part of her had sensed from the beginning that Michael would change her life. Perhaps the passion they'd shared in the beginning had been a clue and she'd run from it, run from him, because he was a hard, complicated man. How could she ever hope to win his heart? If he even possessed one.

With no holds barred, he stripped off her clothes and his and imprinted his body against hers. He made love to her from head to toe, bringing her to ecstasy again and again. It was as if he wanted to mark her as his woman.

But how could that be possible? He'd always made it clear their relationship was temporary, with no messy emotional ties. She couldn't deny it any longer. She felt a part of him. She craved his happiness, his safety, his well-being in a way she'd never experienced with Stephen.

The knowledge rolled through her like thunder. She loved Michael.

"I want to wipe the thought of every other man from your mind," he muttered against her as his muscular body pumped into her. "I want you to know that you belong to me."

Panting from their wild lovemaking and her own realization, she buried her head against his throat, damp with sweat from his restraint.

"I know," she said. "I know. I love you," she whispered into his ear. "But will you ever belong to me?"

He stiffened and thrust inside her one last time, his climax written on every cell of his body and echoed on his face.

Her heart hammered as they collapsed in each other's arms. Had she really said that? Had she really uttered the three words? Had she asked him if he would be hers? She waited, holding her breath. Maybe he would give her the words she secretly longed to hear. Maybe he would tell her that she had become so important to him that he would never let her go.

Michael stroked her hair. "Go to sleep."

Her chest twisted with disappointment. When had this happened? When had he consumed her? And how was she going to survive knowing he didn't love her?

She fell into a troubled sleep, but awakened when she

felt the absence of his body. He was working out as usual, she thought. Her body craved more sleep, but a part of her craved seeing him more. She glanced at the clock, estimating he was fifteen minutes into his routine.

Dragging herself from the bed, she splashed her face with water and brushed her teeth then wandered down the hall to find him on the elliptical, his back to her. Knowing he still had free weights to go, she waited on the couch in their suite and leaned her head back against the wall.

Michael doubled his workout. He had never felt this way about a woman. He could have easily punched Bella's former lover in the face. Perhaps he should have. Maybe it would have gotten his completely alien possessiveness for Bella out of his system. The woman was having a very odd effect on him. Lord knew, he wasn't the type to take a vacation, let alone *really* enjoy a vacation home, but spending time with Bella without the constant press of work appealed to him. When in hell had that happened?

He didn't know what the solution was. He refused to give her up, but he wasn't sure how to keep her. She was a woman full of passion and heart. He wanted both, but he didn't possess much of the latter, and hadn't for a long time. Giving up his heart had been necessary for survival. If he didn't care, then he wouldn't hurt. If he didn't hope, then he wouldn't be disappointed. Most importantly, if he didn't count on another human being to be with him, then he would know how to stand on his own. Always alone.

He finished his free-weight repetitions and returned to the suite. He spotted Bella asleep, propped on the couch.

His throat tightened with an odd emotion. She looked so sweet and vulnerable.

He bent down beside her and just looked at her for a long moment. Her dark eyelashes fanned out from ivory skin with just a little pink from the Cayman sun left in her cheeks. He felt a stir of pleasure at the memory of how much she'd enjoyed the short trip. He'd already made an offer on the house. He would take her again and other places, too.

"Hey, sleepyhead," he said, touching her soft cheek.

She stirred, looking up at him with sleepy eyes. "Hi," she said in a husky voice.

"Hi to you. What are you doing out of bed? This is no time for angels. This is the time of demons," he said. It had long been the hour he'd chased the demons from his mind.

"I didn't want you to start work without getting to see you," she said, lifting her arms.

Unable to refuse her, he sat on the couch beside her and held her. "I do have work to catch up on, but I won't be in the office all day."

"That's good," she said and looked up at him. "I'm going to visit my aunt today. I feel like I should check up on her to make sure she's okay."

"Any reason to believe otherwise?" he asked.

"No, but she was such a faker when I was overseas, I'm determined to keep tabs on her now."

He chuckled and nodded. "Fool me once, shame on you," he said, quoting the old proverb.

"Fool me twice, shame on me," she finished and sighed as they walked into his bedroom. She looked up at him. "I forgot to thank you for coming to the wedding reception last night."

"I wish I could say it was my pleasure."

"Me, too, but after what Stephen said—"

He pressed his finger to her lips. "Don't think of it again."

She winced. "I can't promise that, but I'll try." Her face turned solemn. "I love you," she said.

His heart stopped. She pronounced it as the sun rose, illuminating the room. Bold and brave, she blew him away. He didn't know how to respond.

She bit her lip. "I thought I knew what love was before. With Stephen."

His stomach twisted and he felt his hands draw into fists, but he held his tongue.

"But I didn't," she said. "I can't remember wanting someone else's happiness more in my life. Ever. I would do anything for you to feel happy and at peace. I love you."

Overwhelmed by her profession, he pulled her against him. Humbled, but unable to offer her the same, he slid his fingers through her lush hair. "You're so sweet," he said. "So precious. I've never met another woman like you." He held her close for several moments where his insides twisted and turned. "You had a rough day and night. You should get more rest," he said. "Go back to bed."

She looked up and met his gaze, and he knew he hadn't given her what she wanted. He knew she wanted more from him. What she didn't realize was that he didn't have it to give.

Bella returned to Michael's bed, but her slumber was filled with strange dreams. When she rose a couple hours later, she was more tired than rejuvenated. She also felt her profession of love sitting between her and

Michael like an undigested Thanksgiving meal. Heavy and uncomfortable.

Well, now she'd gone and done it. She'd blurted out her love to him and he didn't know what to do with it. The awkwardness of that moment hung over her like a guillotine. Why had she done it? Because she couldn't stop herself. A dam had broken open inside her.

With a mixture of humiliation and disappointment, she got herself together and drove to visit her aunt. Bad move. Charlotte's boyfriend, Fred, answered the door.

Charlotte soon followed, wrapped in a long silk robe. "Bella, I didn't know you were planning a visit. Come inside." Her aunt dragged her toward the kitchen.

"That's okay. I don't want to interrupt," Bella said.

"Nonsense, Fred was just going to take a shower." She gave him a quick kiss. "Let me get you some orange juice and blueberry muffins. I want to hear about Grand Cayman," she said, heading for the refrigerator. "Should I go?"

"Yes," Bella said, stunned at the speed of her aunt's developing relationship with Fred. "It's beautiful."

"Even for the not obscenely rich?" Charlotte asked, handing Bella a glass of orange juice and some muffins.

"Yes, even for the middle class. The water is warm and clear and the waves gentle. There's a place that looks like lava where the water spouts. And they have great food. Low crime." She took a sip of orange juice.

"Sounds like heaven. So, has Michael asked you to marry him?"

Bella choked. "No," she managed.

"Why not?" Charlotte demanded.

"What about you and Fred?" she asked, changing the subject.

Charlotte waved her hand. "He has asked, but I'm procrastinating."

"Why?" Bella asked. "Don't you like him?"

"Yes, but marriage… I did that once and it didn't turn out well at all."

"Do you love him?" Bella asked.

Charlotte paused. "I think I might," she admitted. "But if I get sick again?"

Bella covered her aunt's hands with hers. "I hope you won't live your life that way."

Charlotte took a deep breath and shot Bella a sly smile. "And here I thought we were talking about your romance. How did we get off track?"

"We're not," Bella said, forcing a smile. "Michael's not the marrying kind. I'm not sure he even believes in love."

"Oh, sweetie, I'm so sorry," Charlotte said. "And I pushed you into this."

Bella shook her head. "No, you didn't. I went into it on my own. He's from a tough background. I can't really blame him."

Charlotte's eyes filled with tears. "I wanted you to get over Stephen. I knew he wasn't right for you. I had this feeling about Michael. I'm sorry."

Bella shrugged. "Stop it. He's an amazing man. I just don't think he's interested in forever after."

"Are you going to break it off with him?" Charlotte asked.

Bella's mind reeled at the thought. "Oh, wow." She shook her head. "I'm not there yet. We'll see."

Fred returned from the shower. "Any blueberry muffins left for me?"

Bella smiled, but her heart twisted. She couldn't help being happy for her aunt. Charlotte had been through so much, and now she had a man who clearly wanted to be with her regardless of the iffy future.

On the other hand, Michael was a man who didn't believe in love, and Bella feared he never would.

Fourteen

Over the next seven days, Bella waited. She held her breath waiting for a true response from Michael. Something more than him ignoring the love she'd professed to him. But each day and night he said nothing different. He praised her beauty, made love to her, but avoided any real emotional confession.

For Bella, every minute that he ignored her confession she felt her hope grow smaller and smaller. Did her feelings mean so little to him? Did *she* mean so little to him?

On the eighth day, she gave it another shot. They'd made love and he lay sated beside her. She stroked the angles of his face, his hard jaw and sensuous mouth. "I love you," she said, not whispering this time.

He closed his eyes, and she wasn't sure if he was savoring her words or steeling himself against them.

She held her breath, waiting, again.

He tucked her head beneath his chest. "Such an angel," he said.

She felt his heart pound against her ear, but heard no other words, and she quickly realized this was an evasion. He didn't want to tell her that he didn't love her.

Her heart hurt so much she feared it would explode. She had made a huge mistake by being honest with Michael, but she didn't know how she could go back.

After the tenth day of Michael leaving early for work and returning late, Bella could no longer avoid the truth. She had changed things by telling him she loved him. She couldn't go back, and Michael could only pretend so much. She couldn't stand the idea that he wanted to avoid her.

She felt a combination of humiliation and disappointment with a dash of abandonment. *Oh, quit being a baby,* she told herself as she rose from his bed long after he'd left. She stroked the pillow where he'd slept, dipping her nose to breathe in his scent. She'd messed up.

She should have kept her mouth shut. She never should have admitted that she loved him.

Michael didn't know how to handle that. He didn't understand the concept of love. He'd grown up needing and wanting, but not getting. Now it was too late for him to truly receive. He couldn't bear her words or the deep emotion they conveyed. She'd shattered the fragile balance of their relationship.

Accepting the reality was painful. She wandered around his home, sensing this was her last time in his domain. Her stomach clenching so hard she could barely stand it, she wrote a note and left it on his pillow.

Her leaving would provide relief. More than anything, she just wanted his peace.

Michael came home on Tuesday night excited beyond belief. He couldn't wait to share his news with Bella. Possibilities bloomed in his mind. "Bella," he called. "Bella, I have news."

Silence greeted him. Maybe she was working late. Damn, he'd wanted to share this with her. He wandered upstairs to change his clothes. He pulled off his suit and stepped into jeans and a long-sleeve sweater to ward off the chill of the evening. Bella would make him warm later on, he thought, smiling to himself.

His glance strayed to the bed and he caught sight of a piece of paper on his pillow. Curious, he walked to the bed and picked up the folded paper. Unfolding it, he read it.

Dear Michael, I am so very sorry, but I cannot continue our affair. I have fallen in love with you. I know it's not what you want. It's messy and emotional and I don't know how to deal with it. I thought I knew what love was before I met you, but I was wrong. Now I just want you to be happy. If I leave, you won't feel pressured to do anything more than you want. I'll pay you back even if it takes my whole life. I promise. I wish you every good thing. Love, Bella.

Michael sucked in a quick, sharp breath. Bella was gone. He felt as if a knife had stabbed him between his ribs. She loved him and he couldn't love her back. How could he explain that he'd spent his life protecting himself so he wouldn't be hurt again? How could he explain that being self-sufficient was the only thing that had made him survive?

Loving meant being vulnerable, and he couldn't do that. For anyone.

Michael avoided his bed as long as possible and finally faced it without Bella's loving arms. How could he possibly sleep? he thought, tossing and turning. Hours later, he finally fell into a restless sleep where he dreamed of Bella. Her smile, her eyes, her touch. His alarm sounded and his arms were empty. No Bella. No joy.

He rose and worked out anyway.

"Don't ask," Bella said to her aunt as Charlotte looked at her with concern.

"How can I not?" Charlotte asked. "You have circles under your eyes. Your smile is a grimace."

"I just have to soldier through," Bella said. "It's one day at a time right now. Okay," she amended. "One hour at a time. It will get better. It will just take time."

"What happened?" Charlotte asked.

"I don't want to talk about it," Bella said.

Charlotte sighed. "Well, I realize this is horrible timing, but Fred and I have decided to get married."

Bella blinked in amazement. "You're going through with it?"

"Yeah," Charlotte said. "He says he can deal with anything that happens, even a recurrence of my cancer."

Bella smiled despite her own pain. "What a man."

"Yeah," Charlotte agreed. "What a man. We're going to do it in two weeks."

"So soon?" Bella said.

"When you get to be our age you don't want to waste time. We're going to go to the justice of the peace then have a party at my house. Would you be a witness?"

"Of course," Bella said, and hugged her aunt. "I'm so happy for you. You deserve this."

"Thank you, sweetie. Your time will come. I know it will," Charlotte said, but Bella had given up on Michael.

Bella had finally realized that to be willing to surrender to love was to be strong. She deserved to be loved.

Michael's cell phone vibrated as he reviewed the balance sheet for one of his restaurants. He glanced at the caller ID and picked up. "Hey, Rafe, what's up?"

"I'm in town," his brother said. "Feed me an early dinner."

Michael glanced at his watch. "It's three o'clock now. Are you going back tonight?"

"Yeah," Rafe said. "Now that I have Nicole and Joel, I don't like being away overnight if I can help it."

"Big switch for you," Michael said.

"Yes and a good one," he said. "So where do you want me to meet you?"

Michael was tempted to get a rain check. He hadn't been in a social mood since Bella had left. But Rafe *was* his brother, and after all they'd been through, he couldn't brush him aside.

"What are you in the mood for? Steak, Asian, seafood?"

"I'd like a good greasy burger and fries," he said.

"You got it. Meet me at Benson's downtown. See you in a few," he said, and hung up.

A half hour later, he and his brother sat in the bar of one of Michael's popular downtown restaurants. The server took their order as soon as they sat down.

Rafe grinned in approval. "One of the things I like

about eating with you is how great the service is. There's never a wait."

"I doubt you do much waiting wherever you go," Michael said.

Rafe shrugged and studied Michael. "Hey, are you okay? You look a little rough around the edges."

"Thanks, bro," Michael said wryly. "I've been working a lot lately."

"Yeah, well take a break every now and then. Even us Medicis have to do that."

"When I get a chance," Michael said and changed the subject. "How is Nicole?"

"Morning sickness appears to have hit except for her the nausea is worse in the evening. She can't stand the smell or sight of any kind of meat."

Michael nodded. "That's why you wanted a greasy burger."

"Yeah, this may be my only chance for a while. But I'm not complaining. She's worth it," Rafe said. "And this time, I'll be with her and the baby from the beginning."

Michael knew that Rafe still suffered from not knowing he'd had a child for the first three years of Joel's life. "It looks like you and Joel are getting along pretty well."

"Oh, yeah. He's a great kid. Nicole has done an amazing job with him. She sends her best, by the way, and still wants the recipe for that cake Bella made. You don't mind passing that on for me, do you?" Rafe asked as the waiter served their meal.

Michael had suspected the subject of Bella might come up, but he'd hoped it would happen nearer the end of the meal. His appetite suddenly disappeared. "That might be tough. Bella and I aren't seeing each other anymore."

Rafe blinked in surprise. "Really? I thought she must be important if you were introducing her to us. But I guess it's easy come, easy go."

"I wouldn't go that far," Michael muttered and took a drink of water.

Rafe frowned as he bit into his burger. "I don't understand. Are you saying she dumped you?"

"I didn't say that," Michael said. "She just wanted something I couldn't give her."

"Hmm," Rafe said and continued to eat his meal. "This is a great burger, by the way. I haven't had one in a week. So what did Bella want? A house in the South of France?"

Michael shook his head. "No. It wasn't anything like that. Nothing material. She just wanted me to have feelings for her that I'm not capable of."

"Oh," Rafe said. "You mean love."

Michael felt as if his brother had pointed a gun at his heart. "Yeah. I told her at the beginning, but things changed."

"You don't look too happy about it," Rafe said.

"I'm not, but there's nothing I can do about it."

"Do you love her?"

"I don't believe in love for myself. For other people, it's fine. It's not for me."

"Chicken," Rafe said in a matter-of-fact voice and lifted his hand before Michael could reply. "Hey, I was there, too. You think Damien wasn't? With our background, we keep our hearts under lock and key. Too much damage already done. Don't want to lose anymore. Trouble is, if you don't let the right one into the vault, you lose even more."

Michael couldn't listen to his brother's advice right now. He was still miserable about losing Bella. "Okay, thanks for the lecture. Can we change the subject?"

"Sure," Rafe said. "But it won't change that wretched feeling of loss in your gut."

"Thanks again," Michael said. "How's the yacht business?"

He listened to the news of Rafe's latest business ventures and shared some of his.

"Have you gotten any more news from your P.I. about Leo?"

"Just what I told you last week. What a roller-coaster ride. Last week, the PI tells me maybe he's alive but it will take longer to find him." He shook his head. "I don't know what to make of it."

"Me, either," Rafe said.

"I'm not giving up," Michael said.

"I wouldn't expect you to give up," Rafe said. "I need to go," Rafe said, rising. "Thanks for the meal. That burger was better than gourmet food for me."

"Glad I could do it," Michael said, joining his brother as he made his way to the door. "Tell Nicole to hang in there and give Joel a hug."

"Will do," Rafe said, then paused. "If you're this unhappy over Bella being gone, you might want to rethink your anti-love theory."

Michael shook his head. "No."

"Well, it looks to me like that ship has sailed. Maybe you've already fallen in love." Rafe lifted his hand and squeezed his shoulder. "Call me if you need me."

Two weeks later, Bella drove to the courthouse for Charlotte's wedding. Her aunt—dressed in an ivory and red silk suit and top—paced just outside the office of the justice of the peace.

"Are you okay?" Bella asked.

"Yeah, just a little edgy," Charlotte said. "Do you think I'm making a big mistake?"

"Do you love him?" Bella asked.

"Yes."

"Does he make you happy?" Bella asked.

Charlotte's expression softened. "Oh, yeah."

"I think you've answered your own question," Bella said, still devastated from her breakup with Michael.

"Okay," Charlotte said, glancing at her watch. "I think it's time."

Bella walked inside the office with her aunt. She looked up to find Michael standing beside Fred. She flashed a look of desperation at her aunt.

Charlotte mouthed the word *sorry* and turned her attention to her groom. Bella took a deep breath and focused on Charlotte. She absolutely couldn't think about Michael.

After Charlotte and her groom made their vows, the justice of the peace pronounced them husband and wife. Bella couldn't keep tears from her eyes.

"We'll see you at the house," Charlotte said then lowered her voice and kissed Bella. "Don't be too mad at me."

Charlotte and her new husband swept out of the courthouse, leaving Bella to face Michael.

"They look happy," Michael said.

"Yes, they do," she said, not wanting to meet his gaze. "I hope they will always be happy." She bit her lip. "I should leave. They're having a reception at Charlotte's house."

"Bella," he said, his voice causing her to stop in her tracks. "Charlotte called and told me you would be here."

She bit her lip again, not knowing what to say.

"You told me you loved me," he said.

She cringed because he hadn't been able to return her love.

"I don't know much about love," he said. "I gave up on it at an early age in order to survive."

She took a deep breath. "I can understand that."

"You've taught me something different," he said. "You've taught me that I'm capable of more than I thought I was. I don't know much about love, Bella, but I know I want you with me forever." He lifted her chin so that she would look at him. "I want you to teach me about your way of love."

Bella felt as if her heart would burst with happiness. "Oh, Michael. You already know how to love. You've already shown me so much love."

"Maybe we need each other to find the way," he said.

"Maybe," she said hopefully.

"I love you," he said. "And I'm determined to love you more."

Her eyes filled with tears. "You are an amazing man, Michael Medici. I want to help make you happy."

"You already have, Bella. You already have."

Epilogue

Ten days later, after her Aunt Charlotte and new husband had returned from Michael's new house in Grand Cayman, Bella caught her first break in days. She'd been in charge of the shop during her aunt's honeymoon and was looking forward to a quiet night with Michael.

How things had changed during the last week. Michael had completely opened up to her about his brother Leo, and she, too was on the edge of her seat waiting to find out more from the P.I.

Michael had arranged for all her belongings to be moved to his house. She was ready to soak in the Jacuzzi. She just hoped she could talk him into joining her. He was picking her up from work. She saw his vehicle pull alongside the curb and hopped in.

"Finally, a break," she said and kissed him. "I have plans for you."

"Oh, really," he said, his lips lifting in a slight grin. "What kind of plans?"

"Wet, bubbly plans," she said.

"Hmm. Not a bubble bath," he said.

"Not the kind you're thinking of," he said. "I thought I'd take you to one of my restaurants."

She would have preferred to be alone with him, but she was with him. That was good enough. "Okay. How was your day?"

"Busy. Rafe called. I keep forgetting to tell you that Nicole wants that recipe."

"Give me her e-mail and consider it done," she said as he pulled into the nearly empty parking lot of his restaurant. "Wow, I wonder what's going on. I've never seen the parking lot this empty at this time of night."

"I'll have to talk to the manager about that," he said and helped her from the car.

They walked to the door where a sign was posted. Private Event. Please return tomorrow.

"What's this?" she asked, confused.

He pushed open the door, and seemed much more calm than she would have expected. "We'll find out."

The lights were low and Michael led her to the bar where a bottle of champagne and two glasses sat on a table with two chairs.

She shot him a curious glance. "You knew about this. What's going on?"

"Have a seat. Let me pour your champagne," he said with a mysterious smile on his face.

He poured the bubbly and sat beside her. "Do you know what I like about this place?"

"Besides the fact that it's profitable?" she asked.

He chuckled. "Besides that."

"The good food. The atmosphere. The staff?" she asked, trying to gauge his mood. She'd never seen him like this before.

"I like this place because this is where I first saw you."

Her heart turned over and a lump formed in her throat. "I don't think you could touch me more deeply."

"I'm a high achiever. I'm not done yet," he said.

"What do you mean?"

"I mean that meeting you has changed me in ways I didn't dare dream. You were a wish I didn't even know I was making. I never believed in love until you."

Tears burned Bella's eyes. "Oh, Michael, you mean the same to me. I so want you to be happy."

"Then wear this," he said, pulling a black box from his pocket and opening it to reveal a sparkling diamond. "Wear this and marry me," he said. "I love you."

Bella shook her head in amazement. "Are you sure? Are you really sure?"

"I've spent my life figuring out the odds of winning and losing. I've never been more sure of something or someone in my life. There's no losing for me as long as I have you."

"I love you," she said. "I love you today, tomorrow and forever."

* * * * *

Join Britain's BIGGEST Romance Book Club

50% OFF your first parcel

- **EXCLUSIVE** offers every month
- **FREE** delivery direct to your door
- **NEVER MISS** a title
- **EARN** Bonus Book points

Call Customer Services
0844 844 1358*

or visit
iillsandboon.co.uk/subscriptions

MILLS & BOON®

Why shop at millsandboon.co.uk?

Each year, thousands of romance readers find their perfect read at millsandboon.co.uk. That's because we're passionate about bringing you the very best romantic fiction. Here are some of the advantages of shopping at www.millsandboon.co.uk:

* **Get new books first**—you'll be able to buy your favourite books one month before they hit the shops

* **Get exclusive discounts**—you'll also be able to buy our specially created monthly collections, with up to 50% off the RRP

* **Find your favourite authors**—latest news, interviews and new releases for all your favourite authors and series on our website, plus ideas for what to try next

* **Join in**—once you've bought your favourite books, don't forget to register with us to rate, review and join in the discussions

Visit **www.millsandboon.co.uk** for all this and more today!